THE HALLOWEEN BALL

Focusing on novels with contemporary concerns, Bantam New Fiction introduces some of the most exciting voices at work today. Look for these titles wherever Bantam New Fiction is sold:

BANTAM NEW FICTION

THE HALLOWEEN BALL

JAMES HOWARD KUNSTLER

BANTAM BOOKS
TORONTO • NEW YORK • LONDON • SYDNEY • AUCKLAND

THE HALLOWEEN BALL
A Bantam Book / November 1987

Grateful acknowledgment is made for permission to reprint the following: "Dark Eyes" by Bob Dylan, copyright © 1985 by Special Rider Music. "I'm Going Down" by Bruce Springsteen, copyright © Bruce Springsteen. "The Weakness in Me," lyrics and music by Joan Armatrading. Copyright © 1981 by Rondor Music (London) Ltd. Press. All rights administered in the U.S. and Canada by Irving Music Inc. (BMI). All rights reserved. International rights secured.

Library of Congress Cataloging-in-Publication Data

Kunstler, James Howard.
    The Halloween ball.

(Bantam new fiction)
    I. Title.
PS3561.U55H35   1987   813'.54   87-47569
ISBN 0-553-34443-9

Published simultaneously in the United States and Canada

PRINTED IN THE UNITED STATES OF AMERICA

FG   0 9 8 7 6 5 4 3 2 1

This book is for Jim McElhinney

But I can hear another drum
Beating for the dead that rise,
Whom nature's beast fears as they come
And all I see are dark eyes.

—Dylan

ONE

S andy Stern woke up to the faraway honking of wild geese, but dimly sensed that they were not the cause of his awakening. The cause, he soon perceived, was a dull ache deep in a back tooth on the right side of his jaw. The ache pulsated with the beating of his heart until it was indistinguishable from the heartbeat itself. Then, in rapid succession it came to him that he didn't have any money to pay the rent; that his landlord, Roy Greenleaf, had sworn to evict him the next time Sandy fell so much as a day in arrears; that he had said terrible things the night before, while drunk, to the girl he loved; and that it was Halloween morning, his thirtieth birthday.

In a little while, the cries of the geese faded down the Atlantic flyway and were replaced by a series of muffled hammerblows. Sandy imagined Roy Greenleaf, armed with writs of eviction, pounding on the door three stories below. But even hungover, his brain skewed, Sandy realized that the rent was not yet overdue. No, the noise below

1

was coming from men at work. This signaled fresh concern to Sandy, for the lower two floors of the Victorian house had been vacant for six months since a quartet of college kids moved out after practically trashing the place. Sandy knew that Roy Greenleaf wanted to chop up the house into smaller apartment units, including the third floor garret that was Sandy's studio. His lease ran six more months, through next April, but all Roy Greenleaf needed was an excuse to declare it broken. Sandy lived in terror of losing his studio.

A glinting yellow blur on the wooden floor caught his eye. Sandy reached for it and, lacking his eyeglasses, held it very close for inspection. The object turned out to be a gold earring in the design of a seashell. He did not recognize it as belonging to his girlfriend, Robin Holmes. It was possible, he tried to reason, that he was less than completely familiar with her entire earring collection or she had recently bought a new pair. But Robin had not slept over in more than a week. Moreover, Sandy was a very tidy person, and he doubted that an object so golden-bright on the floor would have escaped his attention that long. What really worried him was the thought that he had drunkenly brought another girl home with him the night before.

With considerable effort, physical and mental, he rolled over a quarter turn onto his back affirming that he was the sole occupant of his mattress on the floor. If there had been any girl—and he simply could not remember—then she was gone now. He groped beside a wine-jug lamp for his eyeglasses and put them on, carefully tucking the wire cables around each ear. The objects in the large room surged into focus with a sharpness that frightened him. His head pounded, accentuating the ache in his tooth.

The large room comprised the entire third floor of the

Victorian house: a classic garret. Big dormers on three sides each held an arched window ten feet tall that filled the garret with light. In the hundred years since the house was built, the garret had never been finished in the carpentry sense. It was still all rough. There was no ceiling, for instance, and on stormy nights the rain resounded on the slate roof like bird shot.

At the near end of the garret was a kitchen area with a salvaged sink, refrigerator that noisily hummed, and an ancient electric stove. A battered Formica-topped table held a red telephone, a green glass jar full of pens and pencils, sketchpads, and a paint-splattered backpack.

To the left of the kitchen area, cordoned off only by a folding wooden screen upon which Sandy had painted an arcadian idyll, lay a bathroom area that was not the last word in privacy. In the beginning Sandy had ideas about framing it in with two-by-fours and sheetrock, like a real bathroom, but he had lacked the funds for such a building project.

"Please don't listen," Robin Holmes said the first time he'd made supper for her at his place and she had to use the toilet. It bothered Sandy, too, and at first he couldn't pee with her around unless he turned the shower on.

The far half of the room was Sandy's painting studio. At this time of year and hour of the day a great glowing blade of amber October light slanted in from the east dormer window. In the path of this swordstroke of sunlight stood a heavy-duty wooden easel, upon which was Sandy's latest painting.

Like the room, the painting also was large in scale, eight feet by five. It depicted a recognizable scene in nature, a boisterous stream of water veering off into woodland and sky. The woods were dark and hinted of mystery, the sky troubled. It was in many ways not a thing of this century. Sandy now gazed across the room at it in dismay, worrying about his future and marveling at how difficult it was to capture the soul of living water in oil paint.

He also wondered, as he gazed, how on earth he was going to raise $250 in twenty-four hours to pay the rent. Behind him he heard a familiar thump followed by many quick, light footsteps. Clementine, his gray and black tiger-striped cat, crept up the dark blue unzipped sleeping bag that served as a quilt and settled on Sandy's chest. She tucked her paws beneath herself and, enjoying the warmth from his body, began to purr. Sandy drew his right arm out from under the covers and rubbed her head. She nuzzled his hand with a cold pink nose outlined in black. He knew this visit meant that she wanted her breakfast.

" 'Oh, my darling, oh, my darling, oh, my darling Clementine . . .' " He began singing to her softly but then stopped. "Whatever are we going to do?"

The cat only purred in reply. Sandy noticed that the persistent ache in his tooth was not going away. He was extremely thirsty and wanted to take some aspirin, which required setting himself in motion upward. To do so, he lifted the cat off his chest as he prepared to get out of bed. "God Almighty but you're getting heavy," he observed, and before the words even left his mouth, he realized that Clementine was pregnant.

Joel Harlowe, twenty-eight, born Joel Horowitz in Brooklyn to Fred (retired dry-cleaning store owner) and Sophie (d. 1978) Horowitz, changed his name to Harlowe the day that he graduated from the Ventura Institute, a California school which trained professional auto racers. Like other self-made men, he'd been in the process of inventing himself and the name-change was part of the process. His racing career ended almost as soon as it had begun, when the raffish young heir to a cosmetics fortune (later decapitated in a wreck at Monte Carlo) put Joel's Marchand-Ayers modified Ford into the wall at Sebring in an early qualifying heat. He was two months mending in a Florida hospital with multiple fractures, ruptured spleen, and a punctured lung. It was a year before all the stainless steel pins were removed from the bones in his left leg. Thanks to the helmet and safety harness, his face hardly received a scratch. But racing automobiles had lost its plausibility as a vocation. One thing led to another, and Joel became involved in the retailing end of the illicit drug industry. A combination of circumstances had brought him to Excelsior Springs.

Chief amongst these was a bungled cocaine deal in Santa Barbara that sent Joel scurrying eastward for his life with both the coke *and* the $250,000—mostly other people's money—earmarked to pay for it. Several of the principals at either end of the deal had acted very churlish toward him, prompting Joel to take revenge and seize opportunity at one stroke by ripping off both the toot and the loot. Years later, he would view this lapse in his professional comportment with some regret, for Joel grew to regard himself as a model of rectitude in "business," as he termed his occupation.

In the meantime, on the lam with all this coke and money, Joel sought refuge at the opposite end of North America in far upstate New York near where, one summer that lived in his memory as golden, his struggling parents had managed to send him to Camp Pine Knot. He rented an unostentatious chalet six miles outside the village of Lake Placid and for a mighty long while lived in terror that hirelings of the West Coast drug goons he had ripped off would find him and feed him to a log pulper. He didn't like to think about it.

To take his mind off waiting for the knock on the

door that never came, Joel read voraciously, and not just junk, but real literature, everything from Chaucer to Garcia Marquez. Naturally Kafka became a great personal favorite. He truly educated himself. And if this solitary two-year immersion in the classics didn't set him on a new career path, at least he became the best-read temporarily retired dope dealer in the Adirondacks.

He kept a very low profile in his mountain hideaway. He carefully laundered his money, transferring sums to accounts in Europe and the Caribbean, and then back to America. He steered clear of serious amorous entanglements, though there were a few girls during that period. He skied a lot, often alone, sometimes way back into the wilderness below Mt. Marcy, where he could breathe freely like nowhere else. Most important, he buried the California toot in a waterproof military ammo box and managed to keep his own nose out of it.

In time, Joel warily ventured out from his hermetic seclusion. The Olympics came to Lake Placid. The six months leading up to it was one big party. He began dealing again. The TV network executives and their guests snarfed up quantities of blow that even Joel considered indecent, but he kept them supplied through the Games and made another small fortune. Then, suddenly, the great winter carnival ended. All the glamorous strangers vanished overnight. Joel thought he would die of ennui. He couldn't take any more of that lonely life of the mind.

He had visited Excelsior Springs several times during these outlaw years. Joel would go down to see the horses run on what was reputed to be the most beautiful racetrack in America. He grew to like the town itself, its wealth of high Victorian architecture, its funky elegance, its gambler's insouciance, its high-society gloss, its abundance of pretty girls, its numerous restaurants, cafes, and saloons, its bohemian subculture. It was cosmopolitan in flavor, yet small and manageable, with many of a big city's amenities and none of its horrors.

So, in May, when the blackflies were making spring miserable as usual in Lake Placid and with loneliness dogging him like a chronic illness, Joel came down and bought an old house in Excelsior Springs. It proved to be a highly satisfactory move. There was a vacant niche in the Springs for an honest and dependable broker of drugs, the established dealers being by and large a bunch of chiseling petty hoods. But most of all Joel found himself becoming a part of something practically extinct elsewhere in the republic, that network of human souls known as a community. He found it in Excelsior Springs, and he took his place.

This morning, in his little jewel box of a restored 1820s Doric revival house two blocks east of Sandy Stern's garret on Serpentine Street, Joel Harlowe stirred under a vast goosedown-filled comforter and rose swiftly to consciousness. Heavy draperies blocked the morning sun, but a digital clock beside the bed said 7:48 A.M., 10-31 in blue numerals. Joel instantly apprehended that it was Halloween, a red-letter day for him in two outstanding respects.

First, it was the day that his father would move into the brand-new condominium in Clearwater, Florida that Joel had bought for him. His heart raced just thinking about it: the old fellow natty as always (but slightly shrunken with age) in his checked trousers and crisply pressed, hundred-percent cotton, short-sleeved shirt, standing at the threshold with the key, three or four of his retiree buddies looking on, joshing—"Let's go already, Fred."; "We could all be dead before he opens the door."; "Hey, make with the key!"—and his father, eyes misted, thinking, *my son, my good son, Joel did this for me.*

A good son. That's what it boiled down to. And how

Joel would have loved to be there to see it all. Unfortunately, there was the problem of his being wanted by the Florida authorities on an old conspiracy-to-distribute-marijuana rap, nothing to worry about, really, nothing extraditable, a penny-ante deal. But the charge made it somewhat hazardous for him to set foot in the Sunshine State. So he had to be content imagining the scene.

What thrilled him equally this morning was the prospect of tonight's Halloween Ball he had arranged for all his friends in Excelsior Springs, a grand affair of the type not seen in town since the heady days of the gilded age. He'd been thinking about such a soiree for a year and actively planning it for months. He'd rented the dilapidated old casino in Union Park for the night and brought in painters, at his own expense, to brighten up the ballroom. He'd hired a crew to shampoo the antique horsehair sofas in the anteroom, beat the rugs, and clean the grit of the ages off the chandeliers. He'd sent out engraved invitations to everyone he knew even slightly in the Springs—friends he'd made in his four years there, friends of friends, customers, over three hundred people in all. He'd made arrangements for a string quartet to greet the costumed revelers when they arrived and a rock and roll band to play all night long. He'd hired a caterer and purchased (at wholesale) crates of liquor and case upon case of decent domestic champagne. He hoped that his Halloween Ball would be remembered as an affair of legend, at least by upstate New York standards.

This was the only part that bothered him. When all was said and done, Joel was afraid that there was something terribly small-pondish about his party. Something was missing. There must be *something* he could add, some ingredient he could dream up in these final hours to elevate his Halloween Ball into the annals of the truly legendary grand gestures—if he could only figure out what it was.

Next to Joel in bed this Halloween morning was a young woman, apparently still asleep. It distressed him that he had forgotten her name. Stacy? Heather? Dawn? It was one of those suburban names, he was sure, but which one? She was a sophomore up at Greer, the horsey little college on the north side of town—he remembered that. And like Joel, she was interested in the arts. Or was it only her major?

He gazed now in the dimness of the room at her sleek bare shoulder and tawny nimbus of hair and remembered in jumbled detail how sweet her lovemaking had been: the creaminess of her skin, silky breasts as large as Cranshaw melons, slender legs twined hungrily around him, perfumed breath and the little yawps of pleasure as she threw back her head on the pillow. Her father was a broadcasting executive and she grew up in Connecticut, he now recalled her telling him. He imagined the house itself: a huge two-hundred-year-old authentic colonial half-hidden amid the blossoming dogwoods and azaleas. With a paternal lurch of his heart he imagined her girlhood. No doubt it had included a horse and maybe a sailboat, too. If only he could remember her name. Courtney? Jody? Brooke?

He would have liked to make love with her again but he had a million and one things to do. To get the day's activities under way, therefore, Joel reached for the remote control unit of his television and switched on *Good Morning America*. He appreciated the show's unrelenting cheerfulness, and it was a good way to find out whether any world leaders had been assassinated overnight.

The set came on at the foot of the bed, and the room swelled with blue light like an aquarium. The girl stirred, but did not awaken. The show's host was smiling toothily so Joel surmised that the leaders of the "A" countries had made it safely through the night. It was possible that the prime minister of some "B" country like Greece had been blown up en route to his office or that *el presidente* of some "C" country like Honduras had been shotgunned in the company of twenty-nine whores, but Joel frankly didn't give a damn as long as the leaders of the major powers remained healthy and alert.

He turned up the sound a click. The girl stirred again and mumbled something incomprehensible into her pillow.

"What?" Joel asked.

At last, she turned completely over on her back, eyes still closed, and tucked the warm comforter under her chin. "Put on Daddy's show," she said. "Channel six."

"Sure," Joel said and aimed the remote control at the TV set. On the *Today* show, a stunning newswoman was grilling a cabinet secretary who was about to be indicted for taking bribes from union racketeers. The newswoman looked as though she would like nothing better than to personally drive a wooden stake through the secretary's heart. Joel gazed again at the drowsing girl beside him, marveling at her effortless beauty. Then he turned and reached for a green malachite box on his night table. In it was a walnut-sized rock of pure Colombian cocaine and a razor blade. The box's lid contained a small mirror. Working with the expertise of the true connoisseur, Joel used the razor to chop the crystal into a snortable powder. He formed four lines of it on the mirror and blew two of them up his nose with a short gold straw.

As the drug ignited in the pathways of his brain like fireworks, a brilliant idea took shape there. What was missing in his plan for the Halloween Ball, he suddenly saw, was a whole lot of free drugs. In the same illuminative instant, Joel understood exactly what was required of him: he had more than twelve hours to arrange a buy, drive down to the city and back—two and a half hours each way—and show up heroically at his own party with enough coke to keep everyone zonked out of their skulls all night long. The idea wasn't merely brilliant, Joel mused ecstatically. In it glittered the stuff of legend.

All that he needed to pull this off was someone, some reliable person, to be left in charge of a few details while he was away on his knightly errand, someone to make sure that the liquor was delivered, that the caterer showed up, and so on, someone like his friend George Wells or Sandy Stern.

On the TV screen, a woman was demonstrating various things that could be done with bananas to amuse children on a rainy day. Joel leaned to his left and kissed the girl beside him on her forehead. Her eyes opened like a fairy princess's. Joel proffered to her the mirror with its two remaining rails of cocaine and the gold straw.

"Good morning, Heather," he said, sounding radiant.

"Heather?" she replied, squinting at him. "It's Kelly."

In a small, weathered farmhouse at the northernmost fringe of Excelsior Springs, near the site of the old defunct Columbia Mud Baths, George Wells suddenly awoke terrified, as one who might have sensed an intruder in the house through the dissolving grip of a nightmare. His powerful body tensed, his breathing became shallow and rapid, and his eyelids rolled up like sprung window shades. He knew at once that he was terribly hungover and that he was in for a scary day.

He got drunk only once in a blue moon precisely because he couldn't stand the hangovers, couldn't stand the nerves stripped raw and the intimations of doom that always came with it. Another man—Joel Harlowe, for example—might have just gotten up and tossed back a couple of Bloody Marys to take the edge off. But George's father (who liked his whiskey) had always said that this was the sure way to become a drunk, and George never forgot it. This Halloween morning George's father was doomed, but George couldn't bear to think about it just now.

He pulled the blankets up around his chin and listened to the crows bickering over grains of corn in the stubble field across the road from his house. Each caw seemed to pierce the soft tissues of his brain, as though the crows were fighting inside his head. Details of the previous evening returned to him slowly in painful little fragments.

It started after George got off work at the Feedlot, the popular steak house downtown where he waited on tables. He had run into Joel Harlowe in the Black Rose on Catherine Street, where many of the bars were, and Joel had made a remark about George being the world's oldest hippie, or something like that.

"Never was a hippie," George, who at thirty-four was growing increasingly sensitive about his age, had replied, knocking back a double brandy.

Joel, meanwhile, sensing the depressing effect of his wisecrack and trying to salvage the situation, put an arm (with some difficulty) around George's much taller, broad shoulders and said, "Do those jerks at the Feedlot know that they have a PhD waiting their crummy tables?"

"I've told you a hundred times, Joel, I don't have any PhD," George had corrected him, his mood plummeting by the second.

"But you were in the program, right?"

"Yeah," George had agreed. "And I didn't do the dissertation. I'm no more of a PhD than you are."

"But you have the master's, right?" Joel had persisted relentlessly.

"What is it with you, Joel?"

What it was with Joel was nothing more than an intense desire to be liked, which sometimes expressed itself in egregious attempts to flatter, and which sometimes backfired when lavished on those unsusceptible to flattery like George.

"Aw, for God's sake, relax and let me buy you a drink," George had finally said, trying to smooth over Joel's embarrassment, but then Joel had insisted on buying George a drink instead, and the whole thing escalated stupidly all over again. Suddenly George saw Sandy come into the bar and elbow his way through the crowd.

"I'm drunk and getting drunker," Sandy had announced. "Want to get drunk with me, George?"

"I'm not a person anymore?" Joel had said.

"Oh, hello, Joel."

"What's the occasion?"

"Tomorrow's my thirtieth birthday," Sandy told him.

Joel had immediately called for champagne. On top of the brandy, it made George's head swim. He remembered that the three of them left the Black Rose shortly after that for Ubu Roi, a student hangout with an arty crowd around the corner on Burgoyne Street. At some point Sandy's girlfriend, Robin Holmes, had materialized, carrying a canvas tote bag and looking very fierce. Though he would be ashamed to admit it to himself, the prospect of trouble between Sandy and Robin thrilled George because he was crazy about Robin too, had been in love with her for six years since she arrived in town as a Greer freshman. But somehow Robin became Sandy's girl, and every time George was around her, he sensed that he had been unworthy of her through a failure of aspiration.

"Do you just fade out of the picture now?" Robin had asked Sandy, shouting over the loud music. "Is that how it goes?"

"Nobody's fading anywhere," Sandy had protested lamely, no longer very steady on his feet.

"You haven't called me for three days. You don't answer the notes I leave."

"Yes, Mother—"

"I'm not your goddam mother!" she had screamed back. Then, tears in her eyes, she extracted something lumpily gift-wrapped from the tote bag and more or less shoved it into Sandy's midsection. "Happy birthday, anyway," she had sobbed, leaving Sandy holding the lumpy package with its paper wrapping of little mauve hearts as she elbowed her way out of the crowded bar.

"Might as well open it," George had said, and Sandy did. It was a dark green sweater with a pattern of red reindeer at the shoulders, and it looked hand-knit. Seeing it, George had for a moment envisioned a future in which he might treat Robin better than Sandy did, but the thought sunk him in guilt, so he bought another round of drinks.

After that, things got blurry. Sandy went off somewhere. He remembered Joel working on some leggy Greer girl off in a corner. Edmund Black had come in ripped on Lord-knows-what, throwing money around and going through such rapid personality changes that it wore George out just standing next to him. Then, he was weaving home in his battered, blue Chevy pickup truck, the kind of vehicle you could safely bounce off trees in.

Now, the morning light flooded his bachelor bedroom as pure and ineluctable as death itself. His breathing quickened again as he recalled the doctor's words over the phone the day before.

". . . with this kind of cancer he could go any time. I'd come down tomorrow if I were you. . . ."

The doctor was a young man, a man George's age that is, while the patient was George's father, who lay dying in a hospital room thirty-eight miles away in the old

14

Mohawk River mill city of Delft, the town he had virtually owned, as mayor, for over thirty years.

Now it was tomorrow. The crows screamed blackly outside, filling George's mind with darkness and pain. A chill shook him. In this condition, he didn't know how he could face the old man. Even on his deathbed the old man would be the strong one, the winner. It was as though life was a contest and death the finish line. If perhaps he joined his father in death or beat him to it somehow, George thought, he might finally prevail. The crows seemed to shout encouragement of this notion. This Halloween morning, George longed for a reason to keep on living the way that a man without a country yearns for a place to call home.

The house next door to Sandy Stern's—a Victorian monstrosity of twenty-three rooms, combining elements of the Moorish, Italianate, Gothic, and chateau styles all in a jumble of turrets, spires, dormers, balconies, bays, parapets, chimneys, and wooden gingerbread, the whole of it verging on tumbledown condition, its front porch sagging and almost concealed behind wild growths of wisteria, trumpet vine, and Virginia creeper, its green exterior paint peeling off in scabrous patches, its mansard roof missing slates, the rain gutters hanging askew in places, its yard rank with wild asters, thistles, and the spiky seed heads of mulleins, its spear-point cast-iron fence rusting in the weeds, in short, a regular haunted house—belonged to Edmund Black.

At the heart of this house was a windowless six-by-six-foot room, formerly a second-floor linen closet. The walls of the little chamber were hung with heavy red velvet drapes, threadbare in spots, affording strong funereal overtones, like the inside of a casket. The back wall looked like a kind of altar, and indeed it was one. Here the draperies were parted, and glued to the bare plaster was a hodgepodge of old sepia photographs, lithographs, yellowed newspaper clippings, diplomas, award certificates, tickets, declarations of honorary citizenship from various foreign countries, and entries from several encyclopedias. This was Edmund Black's shrine to his paternal grandfather.

Tyrone Washington Black (1859–1942), great Negro educator, scientist, orator, was born in slavery in Bulloch County, Georgia. In the confusion that followed the Civil War, the boy T.W. Black was taken to Philadelphia where his mother, a beautiful, intelligent, and ambitious laundress named Hecuba, found employment in the household of Francis Haliburton, plutocrat and kingpin of the pork trust. She was reputed to have been his mistress.

A freethinking Quaker despite his brigandages in the world of commerce, Haliburton saw to the child's education, more or less to prove that it could be done. At sixteen, T.W. was sent to Harvard. Branded a pariah by his Brahmin classmates, the young man's sheer dogged genius eventually earned him their quiet respect, if not their friendship. As a junior he won the Russell Award for oratory with an address titled, "The Utopia of Brotherhood." He graduated at the pinnacle of his class.

By 1884, T.W. Black became the first member of his race in America to hold simultaneously doctorates in law, medicine, and divinity. He also acquired a great mission: to lift up his people from the intellectual darkness of their long night in bondage. With a $50,000 inheritance from the millionaire Haliburton (d. 1887), T.W. Black removed to the southland of his birth and founded the Talapoosa Institute and its associated Talapoosa laboratories. By 1896, Black had devised one hundred three uses for the soybean (including the pod fiber as an insulation medium in Edison's electrical transformers). He made a million dollars off his patents alone—and this in the days before the income tax. The Institute turned out fifty, then one hundred, and finally five hundred graduates a year, all Negroes, trained both in the classics and in the nascent technologies. His success was an inspiration to generations of his people. He dined alone with Theodore Roosevelt at the White House. Warren G. Harding called him "the lantern of his race."

T.W. Black married late in life at 61 and in 1922 begot a son, the unfortunate Abraham Lincoln Black, poet, dreamer, and ultimately, in 1959, a suicide. There was so much for him to live up to; finally, too much. Before his untimely death, A.L. had married one Gladys Jones of New York City and sired three offspring, a daughter, Sappho (b. 1952), and two sons, William Shakespeare (b. 1950, d. 1975 in an automobile wreck on Memorial Drive, Cambridge, Massachusetts), and Edmund Spenser (b. 1956).

Now, while Sandy Stern, Joel Harlowe, and George Wells woke in their respective beds on Halloween morning, Edmund Black knelt groggily on a worn rug in that small windowless room and gazed up at the votive candle that burned on a table before the hodgepodge wall of T.W. Black memorabilia. On each side of the candle stood a framed photograph. To the right, Steichen's famous shot of T.W., taken at the very apex of his career in 1911, the subject seen in three-quarter profile, a face of monumental dignity and gravity, lips downturned, stern, almost cruel, the eyes incandescent with purpose. To the left, a photo of his son, Edmund's father, A.L., a studio shot taken after World War II, superficially similar to the Steichen pose, but on close inspection utterly lacking that aura of conviction, of importance. The eyes that look out to the edge of the frame are glazed in bewilderment. He had already begun the heavy drinking.

Like his father, Edmund was apt to abuse intoxicants,

and he had been on a cocaine jag for days, not to mention the vodka he'd consumed between the rails of coke or the pot he'd smoked almost continually.

Kneeling on the floor of the little windowless room lighted by that single votive candle, he clutched in his left hand a child's stuffed rag doll. The doll was not the sort of thing sold in toy stores these days. Edmund had found it in an antique shop. Its face was black with big rolling eyes made of felt, wide pink felt nostrils, and pink felt minstrel lips. Its hair, some kind of black wool, was plaited in a dozen antic braids that stuck out. Scrawled in jagged script in marking ink across the doll's pale blue frock was the name Gladys.

In his right hand Edmund held a silver bodkin. Slowly and methodically, he pierced the doll with the bodkin, first through the holes in its laughing eyes, then through its felt ears, its nostrils, armpits, stomach, genital region, and so forth, concluding with multiple penetrations of its hypothetical rectum.

If it had not been a good night for Edmund, it had not been an especially good year either, and all in all an uneven decade.

There was the case of his career at Andover—in a word, dismal. No question as to his natural intelligence, just a lack of interest. He prefered reading tabloids to Ovid. Harvard, alma mater to both T.W. and A.L., would not have him with his D average, nor would any of the other Ivies. So he ended up in Excelsior Springs at Greer, a small liberal arts college which was renowned—if snickeringly—for offering majors in such relatively recent fields of study as public relations and consumer sciences (i.e., shopping).

He was admitted among the first handful of male students in its history when the school went coed in '75. His mother donated a new gym, though Edmund never set foot inside it. The sight of a basketball, for example, would set his teeth on edge. He majored in art history, played the leading roles in several drama club extravaganzas, drove around town in a reconditioned pink-and-gray Cadillac convertible in order to attract attention (he did), slept with ninety-three different girls in four years, graduated (rather miraculously) with a C average, and had remained in Excelsior Springs ever since, out of both a lack of any notion where next to turn and a desire to lead his version of a Gatsby life upstate. (Though he had never actually read *The Great Gatsby*, he had a rough idea of what that life was supposed to be about.) New York City scared him so he stayed away. For one thing, Gladys lived there.

He remained in the monstrosity of a tumbledown Victorian house on Serpentine Street that he had bought on a lark in his junior year to use as a sort of colossal party shack. He remained, waiting, waiting, waiting for that glorious day when he would turn thirty, when a gigantic trust fund running to millions—that portion of the T.W. Black fortune neither tied up in Talapoosa nor in the clutches of his mother—would devolve upon him and set him free at last. He had a little less than a year to wait now, and in the meantime Gladys tormented him, even from the distance of New York City, never losing an opportunity to belittle or disparage him for his lack of purpose in life. She called him "a pissant," "probably a fairy," and "Jim Crow."

TWO

General George Washington visited Excelsior Springs in 1787 when the village was little more than a clearing in the endless woods north of Albany. For centuries the Indians had refreshed themselves in the curious, carbonated waters that fizzed through the reddish rocks at the spot they called Manitou Quashpah Wuk Tee or Place of the Gods' Broken Wind Water, the springs being sulfurously redolent of eggs gone bad.

In 1815 there came one Israel Babcock and with him arrived Excelsior Springs' first era as a resort. He erected the Federal Hotel, a huge structure for its day, fully four stories with porches all around and rooms for one hundred guests. Soon some of the best families in the east began to sojourn there in July and August. In 1851, horse racing was added to the Springs' attractions when the first stakes race, the Juggernaut, was held at a course carved out of the pines and bracken.

No sooner had the ink dried on the Peace of Appomattox than the Springs entered its grandest era, its classic period. The grandson of Israel Babcock added two stories and a gigantic cupola to the renamed Great Federal, making it, at the time, the largest hotel in the world. Patrick "Paddy" McCumber, the former bare-knuckles champion and later congressman, opened his glittering casino in Union Park. The sports and millionaires, beauties and fortune hunters, flocked to Excelsior Springs every "season" as the summer was called. Fantastic cottages (meaning mansions) sprang up along the broad avenues lined by the beautiful wine glass elms. Diamond Jim Brady and his companion, the actress Lillian Russell, made gluttony fashionable.

A new century turned. The gentleman sportsmen of yesteryear like McCumber were replaced by a new breed of gambler, swarthy, sebaceous men with names that ended in vowels, who wore massive pinky rings—in a word, hoodlums. But no one seemed to mind as long as the gambling dens were run well with plenty of Canadian booze and showgirls straight off the Great White Way. In the Springs, society swells rubbed elbows with some of the F.B.I.'s ten most wanted men, and Cole Porter wrote a song about it.

All this came to an end in 1952 when a United States senator from Tennessee (a teetotaler no less who'd never even been to the Springs) opened a congressional inquiry into the nature and scope of organized crime in America. An amazing number of criminal pathways were found to lead out of the quaint spa in the pines. The embarrassing revelations prompted a newly elected governor of the Empire State to finally go in and clean the town up. The gambling dens were closed for good, the shutters nailed tight. Only horse racing remained. Anyway, by this time the action had shifted far west to Nevada, a state practically created by gangsters for gangsters, where gambling was perfectly legal.

Ah, the splendor of yesteryear! Gone, gone, gone. Mostly all gone. The Great Federal Hotel, built in an era when labor was cheap, went through dizzying ownership changes during its final years, but none could arrest its decay. And in 1955, its cupola filled with pigeons and their by-product, its roof leaking everywhere and the threadbare carpets stinking with mold, its vast porticos sagging with dry rot, the clapboard colossus was declared a fire hazard by the city council and razed. Today a Great Federal supermarket occupies the site where railroad tycoons and robber barons once passed the August evenings in rocking chairs, dreaming up new swindles and enjoying their cigars. The Republic Hotel, second only to the Great Federal in their day, fell to the wrecker's ball in '58, making way for a five-and-dime, an auto parts store, a franchise pizzeria, and a cinder-block tavern patronized by motorcycle thugs.

Then, just when things looked bleakest, along came the era of peace and love and with it an influx of fresh blood in the form of vagabond youth seeking a community to call its own, kids who took one look at Excelsior Springs and fell in love with its down-at-the-heels former elegance, which they termed "funky." George Wells, for example, turned up in '73, a long-haired grad-school dropout with a banjo and a collie named Sarah. Sandy Stern had come along somewhat later in '79.

Now Excelsior Springs was entering yet another era. A new boom was under way. A shopping mall had recently been built on—and obliterated—a perfectly good dairy farm two miles north of town. Condo clusters and tract homes were creeping out into the countryside like cancer cells. The over-thirty crowd, former members of the Woodstock generation, suddenly had more money in their pockets than they knew what to do with. In some fundamental way the old spa's spiritual center was no longer holding. It was Halloween, and the ghosts were restless.

As soon as he got out of bed, Sandy Stern saw the green and red reindeer sweater thrown carelessly on the floor with the rest of his clothing from the night before. The sight of the sweater made his stomach tighten. Still clutching the gold earring in one hand, he plodded into the kitchen area, swallowed three aspirin, lit a flame under the teakettle, lurched behind the hand-painted folding screen into the bathroom area, and turned on the shower.

His bathing apparatus was comprised of an old claw-footed cast-iron tub (that he had lugged upstairs with George Wells's help some years ago) around which he had jury-rigged a shower curtain. He thought how wonderful it would feel to stand under the stream of hot water while the aspirin took effect. Unfortunately, the water was not getting any warmer. If anything, it actually seemed to be getting colder. It finally occurred to him that Roy Greenleaf or one of his minions had turned off the water heater downstairs. He could still hear someone banging away down below.

So, Greenleaf intended to freeze him out. Well, the sonofabitch wouldn't get away with it, Sandy seethed. He'd report it to the authorities! He'd drag the bastard into city court and show the whole town what a scoundrel he was! He'd notify the newspapers! But first, he would brave the frigid water and have his shower, by God!

Setting the gold seashell earring and his eyeglasses on the shelf above the sink, Sandy stepped into the tub. He stood hunched under the icy torrent hyperventilating while the predictable shock effects set in, and when he could not endure another moment of it, he spastically flung open the shower curtain—popping several plastic curtain rings—and practically fell out of the tub, gasping and shivering like a North Atlantic shipwreck victim.

The teakettle began to whistle. He stumbled into the kitchen, made a cup of tea, and admiring his own resourcefulness, poured the rest of the steaming water into the stoppered bathroom sink so that at least he could enjoy a hot shave.

No sooner had he brushed warm lather over his cheeks and chin than Sandy discovered a gray hair among the brown ones on his chest. At first, he thought it was some trick of light from the bare bulb above the mirror. But he looked at it from a variety of angles, finally plucked it between his thumb and forefinger, held it close to his eyeglasses, and saw that it was indeed in every salient respect a gray hair. His heart sank, and for a time he just stood numbly staring into the mirror. Then he peered closer into the mirror and searched the longish light brown hair on his head for other gray strands. Though he did not find any others, he felt about as relieved as a prisoner on death row granted a temporary stay of execution.

Above all, the gray hair served to remind Sandy that both of his parents had died fairly young. His father Daniel, a Washington architect full of humor and fire, had dropped dead of a heart attack in the DuPont Circle station of the brand new D.C. subway in 1978 at the age of fifty-two. His mother, Jane, a stately and intelligent woman who loved both art and nature and imparted those loves to her only child, was swept off the planet by leukemia barely a year later, also at the age of fifty-two, and in only a couple of months time. At Thanksgiving she'd been perfectly all right—in fact, Sandy had marveled at how young and pretty she looked, considering the grief of her recent loss. But by Washington's Birthday she was a husk in a hospital bed, and then she slipped away and he was all alone in the world.

He carefully placed the gray hair on the shelf beside the gold earring and resumed shaving. The water in the sink was now merely lukewarm, and the razor dragged against his skin. He noted with some satisfaction that the pain in his tooth had gone away.

When he had toweled off the last flecks of lather, Sandy gazed again into the mirror and rehearsed asking Edmund Black for a loan of $250. Each variation of the request seemed hopelessly abject. He decided that the problem lay in his prefacing remarks, such as, "You know, Edmund, I've never asked you for a favor like this before. . . ." or "How long have we been friends, Edmund? . . ." or "I don't suppose you'd like to buy a painting. . . ." In the end, Sandy finally settled on this simple sentence: "Edmund, please lend me $250." It was plain and to the point, and if it still sounded pathetic, then there was no way around it.

He left the bathroom, snatching up the waiting mug of tea on his way through the kitchen. Standing before his oak dresser, he took a swallow of the strong brew, and though it too had cooled off somewhat, the remaining warmth inflamed the nerve in his back tooth to a degree that almost lifted him off his feet. He clutched the edge of the dresser and squeezed his eyes closed, hoping that the pain would pass. Slowly, it did, though there remained a pulsing sensation of pressure when the pain itself had gone. He perceived in this small but intense event how a day of horrors possibly lay in store for him and then tried to shut the idea out of his mind. Finally, he put on his jeans, a pale blue football jersey with the yellow number fourteen on it, a beat-up pair of running shoes, and a tan windbreaker, and headed downstairs.

Joel Harlowe threw open the louvered doors to his walk-in clothing closet and gazed inside with the vast satisfaction one might have imagined on the face of an eighteenth-century English squire looking lovingly upon his meadows, flocks, and orchards of an October morn. Since he often changed outfits several times a day, Joel required an impressive wardrobe. He purchased his clothes with the utmost care at only the best shops in New York, Boston, or Montreal, and maintained them in rigorous order. The lessons of Fred Horowitz, dry cleaner, had not been lost on his only son.

There were, for instance, an even dozen business suits of various weights and weaves—which he wore mainly in restaurants or on his visits to clothing shops and car dealers—stored in individual semitransparent garment bags. They gave the uncanny impression of cadavers hung up in a medical school cold-locker. Once while experimenting with a combination of drugs, Joel hallucinated and saw his own face floating waxily among the suits. Such was the practical side of his nature that he kept the garment bags and never again took cocaine with Dilaudid and sensimilla.

Joel's collection of sweaters was arrayed in neat rows on an overhead shelf, a veritable Technicolor fantasy of Shetland knits ranging from boysenberry to tangerine. His thirty pairs of shoes were lodged in a custom-built teakwood wall unit with individual cubbyholes, each with a little spring-loaded, clear Lucite door. There were a baker's dozen of Italian loafers in black, brown, and cordovan, English brogans, oxfords, and bluchers, even a pair of patent leather formal evening shoes with satin bows, which Joel had worn once at a black-tie bash thrown by one of his clients, the son of an inconceivably rich thoroughbred owner on a two-year coke jag (who had since committed suicide by flying his four-seater Cessna into one of the expert ski slopes at Aspen, Colorado). Each shoe was treed against warpage and contained a little packet of a chemical which absorbed excess humidity.

On the closet floor was footwear too large or casual to put in the cubbyholes: Joel's knee-high snakeproof expeditionary boots, his orthopedically-fitted hiking boots, his après-ski moon boots, his Tony Lama gecko- and hyrax-skin cowboy boots, his shearling-lined mukluks, and the numerous pairs of athletic shoes that he wore while jogging, biking, playing raquetball, tennis, and squash.

Hanging from a pipe opposite the bagged business suits was Joel's incomparable collection of blue jeans. They were mostly Levi's, with a few designer labels thrown in on an experimental basis. Joel had personally engineered the fading process, going about it with the skill and zeal of a true artisan, babying each pair through untold wash and rinse cycles using a secret formula of detergents, bleaches, and fabric softeners until they reached perfection. Under the ultraviolet lights of the local discos, Joel's jeans glowed with supernatural luminescence. Topped off by a $100 blue oxford shirt, he blazed like a demigod.

Joel now plunged into the depths of his closet and emerged shortly with a pair of jeans, a pink-on-white pin-striped button-down shirt (J. Press), a gray herringbone tweed sport jacket (Wilkes Bashford), and a pair of oxblood loafers (Gucci). As he laid the garments out on a reproduction bow-back Windsor chair, the sight of the girl in his bed watching him caught his attention. She was indeed more beautiful than she had seemed the night before in the noisy barroom.

"Does this mean I have to get up, too?" she asked.

"I've got an unbelievably busy schedule," Joel replied, faintly embarrassed by his nakedness.

"I thought you worked for yourself."

"I do, I do," he assured her. "But there's this big party—"

"That's right, your party. You told me all about it."

"—and I've got a million things to do."

The girl studied him with slitted eyes, as though he was an extremely complex machine and she was trying to figure out how he worked. She reached for the TV remote control unit on the night table and switched off the set.

"Well, I'm not finished with you yet," she said.

"Not finished?" The willful edge to her words thrilled him, intimidated him in a pleasurably exciting way, but he still felt driven by myriad tasks that the day was also demanding of him. "Really, I'd love to, but I can't."

"Look at yourself," she said with a giggle.

He looked down, and indeed his physiognomy indicated a state of readiness that contradicted his claim.

"Come here," she said and threw aside the covers. Joel dropped his loafers and went to the bed. Then he was upon her, his own hungers lost in her formidable and more mysterious hungers. "You're a good lover," she said when they were finished.

"Do you mind if I take a shower," he replied, flustered.

"No," she said, as though his question were preposterous.

He would have invited her to join him except that he felt the urgent need to move his bowels first and couldn't have managed it with her across the room looming in the shower stall. So he left her in bed, used the toilet with the water running to conceal the embarrassing sound effects, and then stepped into the shower. Afterward, while shaving and searching his dark-eyed face in the steamy mirror, Joel wondered how many other lovers the girl had, whether they were college boys, whether they came from rich families, whether any of them were Jewish.

28

When he reentered the bedroom, she was still under the covers.

"Really," he said, "I have to take you home now."

"You *are* strange," she said, as though it amused her, and got out of bed with the poise of an actress taking stage. Joel paused putting on his jeans to marvel again at her physical beauty, the long slender legs still tan from her summer at the Vineyard, her large, slightly pendulous breasts with the spreading brown nipples, the long, fine muscles all over, and the spatter of freckles beneath her collarbone that underlined her healthy athleticism. Even the way she reached for her wraparound print skirt suggested, to Joel, the word thoroughbred.

"The bathroom's right over there," he told her, gesturing.

"That's all right," she said.

"I mean, in case you want to wash or anything."

"Are you afraid I'll leave a spot on your car seat?"

Joel mouthed the word no and failed in his attempt to produce a convincing smile.

"Good," she said, pulling on a baggy, pastel purple, V-necked sweater and a pair of espadrilles. "I'm ready if you are."

All the way across town in his burgundy-colored 1956 Austin-Healy convertible, Joel kept stealing glances at the silent, haughty, self-possessed girl. The idea that a female could also be a person held a certain theoretical charm for him, but this embodiment of the idea left him rather unnerved. Soon they pulled into the driveway of the Hildebrand dormitory, a modern, four-story, red brick structure with a slanted copper roof and a vaguely Aztec look about it. Joel imagined hearts being cut out inside its mysterious chambers.

"Well, here we are," he said.

The girl climbed out of the sporty little car and leaned

on the door, her large breasts practically spilling out of the baggy sweater. She pushed her sunglasses up.

"Aren't you going to invite me to your party?"

"Of course, you're invited," Joel assured her. "I thought it was understood."

"What time are you going to pick me up?"

"I can't pick you up," he said regretfully, thinking of his cocaine-buying mission to New York City. "But you're invited. Please come."

She nodded her head in an enigmatic way, her tongue in cheek.

"Really, I'd love you to come." Joel tried to reassure her. "I insist."

"But not as your date."

"I can't. I have some very important business to take care of before I arrive," he said, adding, "It's out of town."

"All right," she said with a shrug. "Hey, I bet you don't even remember my name."

"Sure I do."

"Okay, what is it?"

Joel felt a cold spot spread through his bowels. "Ju . . . Kelly?" he ventured.

She nodded again and said, "You remind me of someone," sucking in her cheeks in a way that Joel found both forbidding and provocative.

"Who?" he asked breathlessly.

"My eleven-year-old brother."

Henri Rousseau, the French painter, it is said, used to venture forth from his house every day into the world that was Paris, saying gratefully, "All this is mine!" Sandy Stern's feelings about Excelsior Springs were a lot like that. Everywhere he turned his eye he saw another possible painting, and his heart filled with gratitude.

What a glorious day it was in the north country this Halloween morning, the trees brilliant in different hues of scarlet, orange, and gold, the sky a faultless azure behind the spires, cupolas, and gables of the town's decomposing Victorian roofline, the sun strong and warm, yet the air crisp and full of that sweet-acrid smell of burning leaves so evocative of school days and childhood and yesteryear.

Sandy stood on tiptoe in a bed of yellowing ostrich ferns and peered into a first-floor bay window on the north side of his house. The room within was empty. He moved around to the front and ascended the porch. The windowshades were all drawn. The door itself contained a stained-glass window; looking into it was like trying to see through a rack of soda-pop bottles. The hammering resounded deep inside somewhere, but he gave up trying to locate it.

Once back on the sidewalk, he saw a familiar, large, doddering, and remarkably ugly dog limp across Serpentine Street toward him. The dog was named Champion and belonged to the Nethersoles, a childless couple in their seventies. Champion was reputed by his owners to be eighteen years old, placing him at the human age equivalent of 125. A mix of Alsatian and collie, he must have been a handsome creature in his day. Now, however, he looked like a starved, piebald hyena. One eye was blind and as white as a hard-boiled egg.

In recent years, Champion had acquired the habit of crossing the street in order to be petted by Sandy. Lately, it had become a very hazardous enterprise for the old dog. His gait was lame and every few steps he paused to catch his breath. Unfortunately, there seemed no way of dissuading him now from these perilous crossings, and Sandy didn't have the heart to be mean to him. Since the summer, Sandy had even found it necessary to escort the dog back across the street to prevent him from being run over.

Today, a jack-o'-lantern sat on the Nethersoles' tidy porch. Sandy pictured the two of them seated at their kitchen table the night before dutifully carving their pumpkin, as if each were the child that the other had dreamed of across all the barren decades. He hurried back across Serpentine, telling Champion to "Stay! Stay!," mounted the steps up Edmund Black's decrepitating porch and rang the doorbell.

These days, there was no telling when Edmund was apt to be asleep—he kept such erratic hours—so it wasn't necessarily too early. Sandy pressed the button again and waited, rehearsing his request. He was about to give up when a thumping could be heard within. Then Edmund became visible through the fenestrations of the massive oak door. His tall, slender frame was wrapped in a crimson antique silk smoking jacket. His face, long and horsey, looked gray-brown from lack of sleep, and it wore a smile that appeared a little demented.

"Why, hello, you dear, dear fellow," he said, throwing open the door. Sandy wondered if Edmund was doing Noel Coward today. The Mayfair accent was not, after all, Edmund's native dialect. As Sandy well knew, these personality shifts in Edmund often prefigured an emotional crisis, so he was especially wary. Edmund was a good actor and an even better mimic, and he could transform himself from Count Dracula to Maurice Chevalier to Aunt Jemima as suddenly as the light and shadow of passing clouds transform a landscape.

"Edmund," Sandy began, and then cleared his throat, "please lend me two hundred and fifty dollars."

"Get a job, motherfucker!"

The door slammed with a fearful rattle of the glass

panes. Sandy had already turned back down the stairs when the door reopened.

"Where are you going, Dickie?" Edmund asked, being British again.

Sandy stopped one step short of the sidewalk. "Dickie?" he said.

"Play along, huh?" Edmund coached him, with a trace of a whine. "Things have gotten so dreary around here."

"You know, Edmund, I've never asked you for a favor like this before—aw, shit. . . ."

"Oh! You really are in need! Poor thing," Edmund trilled. "Come in. Come into Mother Theresa's shelter for the dispossessed, the unwell, the unfit, the uncertain, the undead. I was about to put on some coffee. Or would you prefer vodka? Valium? A few 'ludes? Come, come. Don't stand down there like a department store dummy."

Sandy cautiously retraced his steps and followed Edmund inside the gloomy house, thinking there was a chance that Edmund might tire of the game and lend him the money. The drapes were drawn throughout the first floor, and when Sandy's eyes adjusted to the meager light, he noticed that the living room was in more than its usual state of disorder. Magazines (*People, Vogue, Interview, Hustler, Architectural Digest*) and tabloids (the *National Enquirer*, the *New York Post*, and *Screw*) were strewn everywhere. Pizza boxes, beer bottles, Chinese take-out cartons, and Styrofoam hamburger caskets occupied every square inch of tabletop. The room stank of stale cigarettes and uncirculated air.

"Shut your eyes, Dickie, we are in a pigsty. Carmelita did not show this week, the slut."

Carmelita was another of Edmund's figments. He was forever hiring cleaning women and then not letting them in the house when they showed up to tackle the job. He was afraid they'd meddle in his things, or so he said. There was a period about twice a year when Edmund would go on a Methedrine binge, buy a carload of cleaning products, wrap a "do-rag" on his head, and see to the job himself. But he gave that up the day a candidate for the state assembly rang the doorbell and asked Edmund if he could speak to "the lady of the house."

"I *am* the lady of the house, you unctuous asswipe," Edmund informed him, and the simultaneous realization that he was beginning to assume multiple *female* personalities put him temporarily in such fear for his sanity that he stopped cleaning the place altogether for a while.

"This way, Dickie," Edmund yodeled, and passing down a corridor hung with Edmund's collages, they eventually reached the kitchen, a horror. Crusted plates, scraps of food, and bags of garbage were everywhere. The counters overflowed with more beer bottles and empty aluminum TV dinner trays. The kitchen table was awash with papers, a mountain of unpaid bills, bank statements, overdraft slips, cancelled checks, threatening letters, and termination of service notices. Edmund filled a grimy saucepan with water, set it on the electric range, and sat down at the table. He gestured at another empty chair, and Sandy took a seat.

"Ah, here we go," Edmund said, rummaging through the papers and locating his checkbook. A feeling of immense relief flooded Sandy. "Pen, pen, pen," Edmund muttered, rooting around some more. "Aha!" He held up a ballpoint pen and winked at Sandy, then opened the checkbook, filled in the blanks, carefully tore the check out of the book, and presented it with a flourish and an off-center smile. "Here you go, dear boy."

"I won't forget this, Edmund," Sandy told him gratefully.

"Of course, you won't. Cup of coffee?"

"Sure," Sandy said and looked down at the check in his hand. Edmund had crossed out the word "dollars" on the middle line and written "kisses" over it. He had made the check out to Dickie Doodoo and signed it Princess Lala of Lala Land.

Trying to pretend that it was an ordinary day like any other, George Wells brought a cup of coffee out to the small back porch of his cottage and looked over the garden he had tended so carefully all summer. But everywhere he looked, he saw death: in the browning rows of peas and squashes and the tomato plants black with frost; in the apple trees behind them, the fruits already rotting on the ground; in the woodlot of maples and beeches that occupied the rear of his ten-acre property, the leaves fiery and dying.

Death was no stranger to this cottage. The old woman who sold George the run-down property told him a curious story about death and the house. It had belonged during the 1930s, she said, to a bachelor farmer named Jenks who committed suicide in a macabre manner. He was about forty years old, beetle-browed, with a nose like a pruning knife, and a stutter so incapacitating that he carried a notepad and pencil stub to write out his requests to shopkeepers, as though he were a deaf-mute. A neighbor's twenty-year-old daughter, a plump, plain, religious girl, used to take in his laundry. Jenks wanted the girl to marry him. He asked, and she politely declined his offer.

One Sunday morning when she and her family were in town at the Lutheran church, Jenks left a note at the girl's house saying that he was determined to end his life unless she came to see him. Meanwhile, he went home and, using a length of baling wire and a pulley, rigged up a 12-gauge shotgun so that it would fire when someone opened the front door. Then he sat down to wait in the parlor, looking straight into both barrels. The girl later told the authorities that she was so relieved when she knocked on the door and heard his voice that she rushed right inside. Only after the tragedy did she realize it was the one instance in all the time she had known him that Jenks managed to utter two words in a clear, direct, unstuttering voice: "Come in."

Gazing into the fiery trees, George remembered his mother's funeral. She had died giving birth to his younger brother, Davey. He was five when it happened. He remembered little about her except the timbre of her voice and the warm feel of her sweater. But he recalled the burial in the graveyard on a hill overlooking Delft and the Mohawk River ribboning off to the hazy west, then afterward his father's rage that went on for weeks in the big house that seemed so empty now without her.

Lewis "Boss" Wells never married again, even with two young boys to raise. "The City of Delft is my wife now," the mayor would tell a reporter from the *Daily Patroon* some years later. "I'm wedded to the people." It was such horseshit. George always seemed to know that. Yet to George, the old man was still larger than life, certainly larger physically and in personality than the "pipsqueaks" (Lewis Wells's own term for them) who surrounded him, who worked for him, who ran his errands, who did his dirty work, who curried his favors, who brought him bundles of small banknotes from the wards, who dared every four years to run against him in the election (and invariably failed in their bids to unseat him). Pipsqueaks: in short, the rest of the world.

THREE

"**D**o you mind if I use your phone? Edmund.

"Huh . . . ?" Edmund said. He had been staring off into the near space of his own fatigue and confusion. "Oh, of course. Certainly. By all means. Please, help yourself," he finally answered.

Sandy got up, the useless check dangling from his fingers, and glumly crossed the kitchen to the wall phone beside the door. Among the few remaining possibilities on his list of last resorts was asking Joel Harlowe for a loan. He supposed that Joel would not simply turn down his request, but that he would preface the refusal with a patronizing and sententious lecture on (1) the nature of pure friendship, and (2) the need for a fellow to stand on his own feet financially and earn a living. He could try to sell Joel another painting, but Joel already owned five of Sandy's canvasses and had joked about his house turning into The Alexander Stern Museum, so Sandy knew the

37

prospect was dim. Still, Joel was his best shot. So, with a sigh of resignation, he lifted the receiver to his ear to place the call—but he could not get a dial tone.

"Edmund, your phone doesn't seem to be working."

"I know. They turned the motherfucker off on me yesterday."

"Why didn't you say so?"

"It's the thought that counts, isn't it?"

Sensing that an angry retort here would be both futile and unkind, Sandy took leave of Edmund by way of the back door, crossed the driveway to his own house, climbed three flights up to his garret, and dialed Joel's number on his own phone. There was no answer. He had barely hung up when his phone rang.

"Hello?" he said, rather surprised at the dry and desperate sound of his own voice.

"Mr. Stern?"

"Speaking."

"This is Mrs. Breen at the telephone company? Mr. Stern, you have a bill outstanding of one hundred thirty-one dollars and fifty-four cents?" She made these statements in the interrogatory tone of voice, and when Sandy failed to reply, she said, "Hello? Mr. Stern? Are you there?"

"I think so," he said, scaring himself a little.

"Mr. Stern, we have a termination order ready to take effect at four o'clock this afternoon if this bill is not paid."

"You're going to kill my service?"

"We're going to terminate it, Mr. Stern. We have to do something?"

"We both know what you mean by 'terminate.' You're going to kill it. Do you think those extra syllables make it sound more hygienic?"

"That is the word they tell us to use, Mr. Stern—"

"Well, I don't like it."

"I'm sorry, but if you'll just come down and pay your—"

"And I don't like you either, Mrs. Breen. You and all your little people are terminating the whole goddam neighborhood."

"Four o'clock, Mr. Stern."

Click.

He stood there holding the handset, alert once again to the renewed pain in his tooth, and probed the tooth cautiously with his tongue until the phone began emitting an earsplitting shriek like the cries produced by giant radioactive ants in a horror movie of the 1950s, and he reeled into the bathroom area for more aspirin. The mirror over the sink reminded him of the gray hair he had found earlier and of his thirtieth birthday, and he envisioned all the components of his life poised at the funnellike opening of a great tube, down which it would all soon go. This led to a consideration of last resorts beyond last resorts, for example, robbing a bank. There was a lonely little branch office of the North Country Trust up Route 50 in Shrewsbury, Excelsior Springs' agricultural neighbor to the northeast. Farmers are busy milking their cows at this hour, Sandy reasoned with the logic of a desperate character like Duke Mantee in *The Petrified Forest*. The bank would be nice and empty. Of course, they didn't have drive-in windows in Duke's day. But then Sandy remembered that he didn't have a gun either, and he did not subscribe to the theory that a bank job could be pulled off with a cap pistol, contrary to popular belief. He wished for a moment—perhaps the millionth time in five years—that his parents were still alive. Finally, he saw that there was nothing left to do but go see Roy Greenleaf and try to cut some kind of deal.

Clementine was batting a Ping-Pong ball around the garret. He hoped that this meant she was not really pregnant after all. The mysterious hammer blows downstairs had temporarily ceased. Sandy grabbed an orange motorcycle helmet—one of two—that hung along with various coats and raingear from a series of pegs near the door and hurried back downstairs.

The motorcycle down in the driveway was both an emblem of the bohemian lifestyle he had deliberately adopted and a practical compromise with the facts of economic reality. He had bought the Suzuki 500 cc "Titan" for $499 the month he arrived in Excelsior Springs. It was May and upstate New York was at its loveliest, everything blooming and the air full of lilacs. He had brought $11,520 with him from Washington, all that remained after the hospital presented its bill of $114,765 for treatment of his mother's leukemia (her insurance had lapsed). This grubstake was supposed to buy him a year's time in which to do nothing but paint. Frugality was therefore the order of the day. Yet he needed a way to get around, something cheaper than a car but sturdier than a bicycle, something to haul his easel and paintbox out into the countryside. He'd never owned a motorcycle before, never even driven one, barely given a moment's thought to the idea in his adult life. But once the idea presented itself—he met a fellow in the Black Rose, George Wells, who owned a Triumph 750—it acquired a certain logical charm that was ineluctable. For one thing, the insurance was only fifty dollars a year.

"How come it's so low?" he'd asked George that first day.

"Most bikers don't survive their accidents."

"So?"

"No courts, no lawyers," George had explained with a wicked smile.

Sandy now mounted the cycle, switched on the ignition, closed the choke, and dropped his weight on the kick starter. The old two-stroke twin-cylinder paint-can engine roared to life on the first kick. Since it was a chilly morning, he let the engine warm up so the spark plugs wouldn't foul with oil when he gave it some throttle. Just then, Robin Holmes appeared at the end of the driveway.

She was wearing office clothes under the Burberry trenchcoat that was one of her trademark articles of apparel, and she carried rather awkwardly in both arms a plastic laundry basket heaped with an odd assortment of objects. Sandy saw that the objects were things he had given her over the years: a Navajo blanket, a brown English teapot, various records (Bach, Gluck, Telemann, Ry Cooder), some books, a leather bombardier's jacket that had been his father's in Korea and which Robin loved to wear, and a stuffed pine marten posed upon a fragment of log which Sandy had found at a barn sale and given to Robin on her twenty-fourth birthday in June. She marched down the driveway now and more or less dropped the laundry basket beside the motorcycle. He felt suddenly as foolish sitting astride the clattering machine as if he had been naked, sitting on a chair with an erection pointing up at his own head. He switched off the ignition key.

"I don't get it," he said unconvincingly.

"Sure you do. I'm ending it."

Much as he ached to contradict her, the words just wouldn't come. He felt paralyzed, as in a bad dream when a scream won't come.

"There might be a few more things," she said. "I'll have to check."

"This really isn't necessary," Sandy mumbled into the gravel.

"Oh, yes it is," Robin said with a laugh that was

41

intended to sound plucky, but which came out more like a sob instead. "I don't want to see you anymore."

"I won't set up housekeeping with you, so you want to end the whole thing—is that how it works?"

"You are so conceited it's . . . it's nauseating!"

"Isn't that it, though?"

"Everything boils down to logistics for you," Robin said furiously. "This is mine, that's yours. No feelings. Just things."

"That shrink I used to go to back in college was really big on projection, you know, how we see in others what's really going on in ourselves."

"What's *that* supposed to mean?"

"Look who's marching over here with a basket-load of *things*."

Sandy watched her face grow livid, regretting what he'd said, not because he believed it was untrue, but because he hated the idea of using it to score debating points.

"Did you open your birthday present?" She surprised him by swiftly changing the subject and her tone of voice. He had worn the sweater home from Ubu Roi, if that was indeed the last bar he had visited—he wasn't sure. And who's earring had that been on the floor next to his bed this morning if not one of hers?

"It's a beautiful sweater," Sandy told her.

"Then how come you're not wearing it today, you sonofabitch!" Robin shouted and lunged down into the laundry basket. Next thing Sandy knew, and much to his astonishment, she was beating him about the head with the stuffed pine marten. A blizzard of sawdust flew around him as the blows landed, finally driving him off his seat on the bike so that he toppled over and landed on the ground. His eyeglasses hung askew from one ear, and he struggled to put them back on. When he did, Robin was at the end of the driveway between the two Victorian houses, her face scarlet, her mouth an angry dark hole, and the tendons straining against the flesh of her neck like webbing, giving her the look of something frighteningly nonhuman.

"I may be hung up on a thing or two," she screamed, "but you're hung up on your goddamned independence. Well, *be* by yourself!" And with that, she ran up Serpentine to Catherine Street, where her aged Volvo was parked in front of her apartment.

"I won't let you take care of me like some kind of pet!" Sandy hollered after her, still seated in the dust, his jaw throbbing where she had struck his inflamed tooth. His eyes filled with tears, as much from the drumbeats of pain as from the thought of losing Robin for good. Eventually, the pain subsided again to that neutral feeling of throbbing pressure. He stood up, brushed off his jeans, shook the sawdust out of his hair, picked up the broken upper half of the pine marten, put it in the basket full of things on the steps to his garret entrance, and climbed back aboard his motorcycle. He had just flicked the ignition back on when Edmund's voice called down mellifluously from somewhere above.

"Alexander . . . Alexander . . . ?" he said, calling Sandy by his full given name.

"What?" Sandy replied irritably, reaching down for the choke tab.

"You should be ashamed of yourself, treating that sweet thing like trash."

"Mind your own business," Sandy told him without even looking up. He dropped down on the kick start, and the engine came to life again. "I'm an artist, not somebody's puppy dog," Sandy added emphatically, as though to inform himself as well as Edmund of what lay at the bottom of it all. Only then did he look up at Edmund, who was leaning over the balustrade of the second-floor balcony that adjoined his bedroom in the great ramshackle house. He was buck naked, but his face was covered with white makeup, the lips and eye sockets highlighted in purple, so that he looked rather like a minstrel out of somebody's nightmare.

"Tell me about your art," he said venomously.

"You know about it," Sandy replied, suddenly wary.

"Ah sho 'nuff does!" Edmund said and hooted in mock hilarity. "You know what, boy? You livin' in a dream world. Every other artist worthy ob de name be doin' somethin' revolutionary! Wrappin' up de Empire State Buildin' in tinfoil! Stackin' up a hundred TV sets! Puttin' up brand new ancient Indian mounds out in de Mojave Desert! Shootin' dey fingers off in some art gallery! Dat's art! Dat's commitment! And what de fuck you be doin'? Lan'scapes? Shee-it! Man, you be too lame fo' words! Get yo' act together, motherfucker! Dis be de twentieth century!"

"I guess I'm an old-fashioned guy," Sandy said, his voice full of weariness and despair, "just trying to capture the sublime with dumb old paint."

"Man, seems like de least you could do is glue a few dinner plates on yo' canvas. Just make a li'l gesture to yo' own times."

"Maybe I'll take your advice, Edmund. By the way, what do you call what you're doing?"

"Me? A conceptual piece," Edmund said, switching back to Noel Coward all of a sudden. "I call it *Nigger Gone Crazy*." He hooted again and vanished inside the house. Sandy prepared to drive off. He pulled in the clutch lever on the left handlebar and punched the gearshift into first gear with his foot. The bike lurched forward a few yards and died. The clutch lever went limp in his hand. Sandy knew without even looking at it that he had snapped the clutch cable.

George was trembling as he gazed into the trees when the phone rang. He shook his head as though waking from a bad dream and moved, with surprising quickness and grace for such a large man, inside to the galleylike kitchen where the phone was.

"George, can you possibly lend me two hundred and fifty dollars?"

"Sandy?"

"Yeah. It's me."

"I can lend you a hundred."

"That'd be a great help."

"It's really all I can manage."

"I understand."

"Why don't you hit up Harlowe?"

"I can't get a hold of him. Besides, you know Harlowe. Uh, there's another problem: my clutch cable snapped this morning. I can't come over to your place. Could you possibly meet me downtown?"

"Sure," George agreed, trying to sound cheerful. "Where?"

"The luncheonette?"

"Okay. Quarter of an hour?"

"Great. I really appreciate it," Sandy said. "How do you feel this morning?"

"Not so hot," George admitted, hastening to explain, "Wicked hangover."

"Your voice sounds all shaky."

"I was outside on the porch for a while."

"Doing what?"

"I don't know. Breathing."

"Oh. It's getting so cold mornings. Did you stay out late?"

"Yeah. Edmund was buying everybody drinks. I don't remember driving back here, to tell you the truth."

"Me either," Sandy said. "Coming home, that is. Only I think Edmund's really losing it, George. He's been doing *The Three Faces of Eve* next door all morning."

"Tell him to get a grip," George said. It was an old joke between them. Years ago he and Sandy had worked as orderlies in the psychiatric ward at the local hospital. They used to say that to the patients. For a moment now, George felt as though he might pass out, standing there with the phone in his hand. He reached for the counter to steady himself.

"Right-o," Sandy said. "Well, I'll see you downtown in a little while I guess. And thanks."

"Sure thing."

Joel Harlowe watched Kelly Seagraves sashay up the brick walkway to the entrance to the Hildebrand dormitory, thinking what a fine-looking creature she was. Might she have spent the night with him for the sheer sexual thrill? Impossible, he thought. Girls were not like that. Girls were always shopping for a mate, one way or the other. Their biology demanded it. Since romance always connotated the hazard of motherhood, then the question of whether a fellow might make a suitable husband was always on their minds.

Would Joel make a suitable husband, he wondered? He had always assumed so—when the time came to take that step. He'd certainly had an excellent role model in his father, Fred Horowitz, the devoted husband of Sophie. It occurred to Joel that his father might just this very moment be stepping into the brand new condominium apartment in Florida, purchased by his loving son. Of course he'd make a good husband, Joel thought. Could there be any question? But would Kelly make a good wife? My God, Joel thought, just look at her! Heads would swivel wherever they went. Other men would turn green with envy. And only he would know that she was every bit as delicious in bed as she looked. Would she make a good mother to their children? Why, look at the job her parents had done. Joel Harlowe's wife would want for nothing. He already had more money than he knew what to do with. Their life would be like a fairy tale. Their children would go to the best schools. They would grow up to be great figures in the professions. Perhaps one would become the first Jewish president of the United States! It wasn't so outlandish. Look at Joseph P. Kennedy, the shanty Irish bootlegger, and his kids.

He knew what his father would think of Kelly—his eyes would pop out of his head when he saw her—but what would Kelly's parents make of him, Joel wondered. He tried to imagine a weekend at her parents' place in Connecticut, the awesome discomfort of it all, the little stroll around the property with her dad, the TV executive, drinks in their hands, the ice clinking during the silences, then her father zeroing in with his former newsman's instinct for the jugular: "You seem like a successful guy, Joel, just what is it you *do*, anyway?"

As Kelly vanished inside the dormitory, Joel reached into his car's glove compartment and took out a small clear Lucite vial. It contained several grams of cocaine. At one end of it was a sort of valve. By turning this valve ninety degrees, one could load up a little snorting chamber with the drug. A plastic nipplelike terminus provided delivery to the sinus cavities. Joel snorted a chamber-load into each nostril, and the world around him lit up like Rockefeller Center at Christmas time when the mayor throws the switch that lights the tree.

Suddenly, the Greer College campus seemed to be the most enchanting spot on earth. The incredible architecture! The golden leaf-filled quadrangles! The life of the mind! A trio of girls in skintight jeans and various neon-colored tops debouched from the door of the Hildebrand dormitory with armfuls of books. They were laughing. My God, Joel thought, the splendid creatures were everywhere! Perhaps he could enroll in some kind of accelerated program for especially brilliant people, get a quick degree, and aim himself toward one of the professions. Medicine was the obvious choice. Surgery! He'd always enjoyed taking things apart and putting them back together. Then when Kelly's father asked, "Just what is it you *do*?" Joel could say, "I'm a heart surgeon, sir."

And here was the beauty part, he thought: while breezing through his premed courses, he could easily take care of all his regular "business" *and continue to earn the income to which he was accustomed*! After all, how many hours a week did he actually devote to the buying and selling of his specialized products? Maybe three hours altogether? He would have a chat with someone in the admissions office on Monday, Joel decided, as soon as his Halloween Ball was out of the way. The thought of the ball suddenly jolted him to remember that there were still a million things to do, including in particular lining up a reliable person to help with some of the details, since Joel would be out of town on his heroic mission for several crucial hours this day. And because George Wells's cottage was a quarter of a mile up the road from the Greer athletic fields, he put his Austin-Healy back into gear and motored off in that direction.

48

George's cottage always depressed Joel. It had first been built in the 1850s; Joel could easily tell from some of the surviving early Gothic revival details. If George had paid sufficient attention to these details and restored them properly, the place could have been a goddam gem, Joel thought. If he'd painted it white, for instance, instead of the revolting robin's egg blue he'd found on sale, no doubt at Montgomery Ward. If he'd gotten rid of the stupid-looking evergreen shrubs in front and put in some authentic nineteenth century plantings instead, some lilacs, roses, and hollyhocks, things like that. If he'd replaced the ridiculous cast-iron porch supports thoughtlessly tacked on by the previous owners with the kind of honest wood pillars the structure demanded. Then there was the inside of the place, Joel thought, ugh . . . !

He parked in the dirt driveway behind George's battered pickup truck and stepped jauntily up to the porch. George answered the knocks, appearing with a towel wrapped around his waist, his hair wet, and some flecks of shaving lather around his square jawline. George was almost a head taller than Joel with the physique of a linebacker. It occurred to Joel that his friends were generally all good-looking people, and he realized that he'd never become chummy with anyone really ugly or obese. He considered, for a moment, whether this revealed latent homosexual tendencies, but decided that noticing another person's looks, male or female, was simply a matter of aesthetics and didn't mean you were queer any more than noticing an interesting piece of furniture meant you were queer. To be queer meant sticking your dick in places where it did not belong, Joel thought further, and he had no intention of doing that with George Wells or anybody else, so merely observing that George was a big handsome guy was perfectly okay.

"What a handsome guy," he remarked as George opened the door.

"You make me blush," George said, indulging Joel's penchant for flattery.

"Aren't you going to invite me in?" Joel asked.

"Please come in," George said.

"I'm not interrupting anything, I hope."

"There's some coffee on the stove. Help yourself. I'll be out in a minute."

George left Joel alone in the living room and went off to get dressed. Joel got himself a cup of black coffee from the adjoining galley and sat down on a dull brown sofa to study the furnishings. First of all, he decided, the stuffed fish and animal heads had to go. It was a disgusting and barbaric practice to slaughter unarmed creatures and hang their mummified body parts on the inside of your dwelling. What were we here in America? A bunch of goddam savages? On one wall directly beneath a stuffed speckled trout hung one of Sandy Stern's paintings. The canvas was three feet by two. It depicted a meadow bright with wildflowers running down to a stream. The bright flowers predominated, but the woods behind the stream were dark and full of mystery. Joel admired the painting very much. It possessed both the dreamy vagueness of a George Inness with the raw exactitude of Winslow Homer in his late Adirondack phase.

Just then George returned tucking the tails of a green and red plaid shirt into his buff corduroy pants.

"When did you get the painting?" Joel asked.

"This summer."

"How much did you pay for it?"

"It was a birthday present."

"He gave it to you?"

"Well, it was a present, Joel. See the guy fishing in it?"

"No."

"That dark splotch under the wavy fly line."

"Oh. Okay."

"That's me, standing in the stream. We were over on the Battenkill."

"He always makes me buy them."

"You're his patron."

"He didn't give me one on my birthday."

"If he started giving them to you, he wouldn't have a patron anymore."

"I'm not his patron," Joel said. "I'm his goddam curator."

George went to the galley and poured himself a mug of the steaming coffee. Joel took out his cocaine vial and held it up for George to see.

"Care for a hit?" Joel asked.

"No thanks. I'm kind of hungover this morning."

"It'll make you feel better."

"For maybe a half an hour. Then I'll feel worse."

Joel shrugged his shoulders and replaced the vial in his pocket.

"The thing is," Joel said, clearing his nasal passages, "I was wondering if you might be able to help me out with something."

"With what?"

"You know about this huge party I'm throwing tonight, of course."

"Joel, I don't think there's a single person in town who doesn't know about your party."

"Really? Well, there's a chance I might have to disappear for a while late this afternoon. There's this . . . this business matter I have to take care of. And there are a bunch of little details that someone simply has to be in charge of while I'm away. The caterers, the liquor delivery, the—"

"I'm sorry, I can't help you, Joel. I have to go visit my old man in the hospital this afternoon." The thought practically made George swoon again.

"He's in the hospital, your father?"

"He's very, very sick."

"Why, that's terrible. What's he . . . what's his problem?"

"Cancer."

"Oh, of course. What else? The whole goddam world's being slowly poisoned, isn't it? Gee, I'm sorry. Where is he? Down in Albany?"

"No, over in Delft."

"He should be in Albany Med, George, not some two-bit meat shop."

"He wants to be there."

"You can't let sentimentality rule in a matter of life and death. You should have him moved, George. There comes a time in life when we have to become our parents' parents, you follow me?"

For a moment George vividly recalled with all his senses his childhood home in Delft: the big dark house on Genesee Street. He could see the yellow light in the parlor and the shadows in the hallway, hear the gruff voices of politicians, smell the smoke of their cigarettes, feel the warmth of his little brother pressed beside him as they watched from the top of the stairs in their pajamas. Every year after their mother vanished from the world, the house seemed to grow darker inside.

"You should just take charge of the situation and move him, whether he likes it or not," Joel said.

George flinched as though coming out of a trance. "The move would probably kill him," he said.

"Oh. Well then," Joel said, thinking for a moment of his own father reverently inspecting the rooms of his new

seaside condominium. What if he got ill? Became too sick
to move? Why, Joel would fly specialists in. He'd set up a
goddam field hospital in the bedroom, if necessary.

"There's Cecil Wonton?" George suggested.

"Huh?" Joel slowly came out of the reverie of illness.

"Ask Cecil Wonton to help with your party."

"I don't think he can handle it." Joel shook his head.
"Cecil's strictly a one-task kind of guy. Give him more
than one thing to do, and he's way over his head. Totally
lost. Believe me, I know. I've employed the poor bastard
before."

"There's Sandy."

"Oh, of course. And do you suppose Alexander the
Great would lower himself to do me this one little favor. I
doubt it."

"He would if you paid him. I know he's hard up. In
fact, I'm supposed to meet him downtown in a little while
and lend him some money myself. I'm sure he'll help you
out if you help him out."

"That's just it, George. I don't like the idea that I
always have to pay the guy. Once in a blue moon he
should do something out of friendship, you know? I have
feelings too."

"Maybe. But then you're still stuck with the problem.
Why don't you just consider it strictly a business transac-
tion—paying someone to do a job like you'd pay the
plumber to fix your sink? Of all people, I'd think you
would understand that."

"It's the principle of the thing, George." Joel was
adamant.

"Look, I've got to leave now or else I'll be late,"
George said, pulling on a blue crewneck. "We're going to
grab some breakfast at Larch's. Meet us there and ask him
yourself."

"If I do that, he'll just ask me for a loan, and I'll have to say no, and it'll be even more demoralizing. Or else he'll try to sell me another goddam painting."

"Come on, I know you like his stuff."

"I couldn't think more highly of it," Joel admitted, glancing enviously at the one that depicted the meadow full of wildflowers and George fishing. "But he could have at least given me one for my birthday. Nothing monumental. A small one. A gesture of friendship. He could've at least done that."

FOUR

In the late nineteenth century Excelsior Springs was renowned for its resident millionaires. In the late twentieth century, the town might be noted more for its extraordinary number of resident madmen and village idiots. Many came to town in the 1980s when the government of New York State decided to all but empty its public mental institutions under the theory that the patients were an oppressed minority group and that sheltering them constituted a political injustice. The Springs attracted them largely because it lay midway between two of upper New York's largest facilities: the state psychiatric hospital at Sardis and the state school for the retarded at Winterville.

This plan to release the patients "back into the community" was something of a fiasco, for there was really nowhere for them to live except in cheap rooming houses where they enjoyed little to no supervision and where they often stopped taking the medication which made it possible for them to live outside an institution in the first

55

place. All in all, the situation was irksome enough to make some of the older town residents look back nostalgically on the invasion of the hippies.

Sandy Stern had gotten to know quite a few of these unfortunate characters during the year he spent working on the psychiatric ward at the local hospital, where almost all of them were brought at one time or another to be put back on their medication and cooled out. And as he proceeded down Serpentine to Catherine Street, he now encountered the first of the neighborhood regulars.

This was Joe Sloat, who stationed himself on the corner in front of the Excelsior Springs Bible Baptist Church. Joe was in his fifties and had been an inmate at Winterville since the days of Governor Dewey. Whatever the season of the year, be it raging blizzard or broiling sun or something in between, he wore an Arctic expeditionary parka and galoshes and whiled away the hours dancing a weird little slow-motion hornpipe while holding a transistor radio to his ear. Sometimes the radio was on, sometimes it wasn't. This didn't seem to matter to Joe, whose chief delight was greeting passers-by with antic utterances.

"Think the rain'll hurt the rhubarb?" he called as Sandy turned his corner.

"Not if it's in cans," Sandy replied, familiar with the routine.

"What, the rain?" Joe asked.

"No, the rhubarb." Sandy supplied the punch line, sending Joe into a paroxysm of hilarity.

"That's my boy," Joe said and resumed his stiff, shuffling dance.

From the corner of Serpentine Street, which followed a wavy natural ridge, lower Catherine Street dipped into a two-block-long valley that George Wells had dubbed the Slough of Despair. Here, on the stoop of the rattletrap rooming house where he lived, sat Glen Toole, exhibitionist. Another Winterville release, Glen's specialty was showing up at public events like fires and church picnics in order to expose his genitals. The police would throw him in jail overnight, and then Judge Prescott would remand him over to the psych ward to be put back on Thorazine. Glen was twenty-five (with an IQ about triple that), five foot four, wore his hair in a ducktail pompadour, and carried a large folding knife with which he was cleaning his nails this morning. As Sandy passed his stoop, Glen cast a fishy glance his way.

"How are you doing today, Glen?" Sandy inquired.

"Cocksucker," Glen muttered.

"What was that?" Sandy stopped for moment. It was like being back on the old psych ward again.

"Nuthin'," Glen mumbled, folding up his knife.

Glen hated Sandy because on several occasions when Glen was brought into the hospital raving, it had been Sandy's duty to hold him down for his Thorazine shots. Sandy was reasonably certain that Glen Toole would someday commit a heinous crime. He said no more and walked on.

At the very nadir of the Slough of Despair, at the corner of Catherine and Burgoyne, in the near ruin of a former "horse room" (as the betting parlors were known in the old days), stood the Springs' meanest drinking establishment, a bar called the No-Name. To the No-Name flocked the town's lowliest dipsomaniacs, and here, pacing back and forth on the sidewalk waiting for the bar to open its doors at ten o'clock, was the wino Willie Teal, a native son and graduate of Sardis State.

"Hello, chief," he saluted Sandy.

"How are you, Willie?"

"Say, you ever have the goddam d.t.'s?"

"Never have, Willie."

"Lot's of flying critters today. Say, would you happen to have a spare buck on you?"

"I'm pretty near flat busted myself, Willie."

"I'll pose for you. Five dollars the hour. Remember that time I posed? You said I was real good."

"You were unconscious."

"Buy me a bottle of Wild Irish Rose, and I'll get stiff as a board again."

Sandy dug into the pocket of his jeans, drew out a few coins amounting to fifty-three cents, and handed them to Teal. Now he was literally flat broke.

"You're the tits, chief," Willie said with a big smile, and then flinched at something overhead. "Say, did you see what I just saw?"

"What did you see?"

"Looked like a giant flying cock-a-roach with Lana Turner's face on it. Holy shit! There goes another one."

"Those are pigeons."

"Yeah? The town ought to do something about 'em. They could hurt somebody. Gonna be winter soon, huh, chief? Brrrr. Say, would you have a spare buck on you?"

Catherine Street had nowhere to go but up, and across Burgoyne it began its steep ascent to Broadway in a block of bars and bistros that had been named the Street of Dreams by the counterculture folk back in the 70s. Here, on the sidewalk in front of the Black Rose Cafe, stood Elmer McClusky, sixty-seven, passing the time of day with his legal guardian, Tom Dugan, thirty-five, owner of the Black Rose. That Elmer's legal guardian was a man nearly half his age was a great curiosity of circumstances.

Elmer had spent more than half his life at Winterville (his skull still bore the indentations of the doctor's forceps) when he was suddenly released in 1981. A hale man over six feet tall, friendly and garrulous if somewhat incoherent, Elmer soon made himself known as the dean of the town's misbegotten. He was their goodwill ambassador. The shopkeepers and bar owners called him Mr. Mayor, and Elmer himself believed that he ran the town. He had not been in the Springs two years when he became a three-million-dollar winner in the New York State lottery.

Tom Dugan, who had already made a small fortune selling liquor to college kids, immediately stepped in to protect Elmer. He had his attorney set up a trust for Elmer. He successfully petitioned the court to become Elmer's guardian. He purchased a cottage on Marion Place, close to downtown, for Elmer and installed him in it with a cook/housekeeper whom Elmer called Mom. Elmer's life in the Springs, where he was much beloved and harmless, otherwise remained as it had been. His career consisted of a daily and systematic walking tour of the business district, chatting semicoherently in his trademark raspy klaxon voice with shopkeepers, stopping Greer girls on the sidewalk to ask them for dates, beating checks at the pastry shop (a monthly bill was sent to his attorney-trustee), and delivering copies of the Excelsior *Banner* to the saloonkeepers, who made him his favorite cocktail (Coca-Cola and grenadine syrup) in reward.

"Morning, gentlemen," Sandy said as he approached them.

"You get your costume yet?" Dugan asked.

"What costume?"

"For Harlowe's party."

"I didn't know it was a costume party," Sandy said.

"It says so right on the invitation," Dugan said. "I'm going as Elmer."

Elmer grinned.

"Who's Elmer going to go as?"

"He can go as Harlowe," Dugan said, and Elmer laughed loudest.

The lame, the halt, the weak of mind, and the sick of

heart were everywhere on sunny Broadway this Halloween morning. Here, as on most clement days, on an ornate cast-iron bench, facing traffic, sat white-haired Helen Grimes, once a gifted violinist, who was beaten viciously by a man in Greenwich Village forty years earlier, committed to Sardis by her family, and who never picked up her instrument again. There, leaning against the standing clock on the sidewalk before the Grecian temple facade of the North Country Trust, was Hans Fetka, an obese wreck of a man with a sour look on his face, who stank like a dead carp. There, exiting the photo shop, was Terry Batey, six foot four and dressed in women's clothes, practicing for the sex-change operation that he was saving his pennies for. From his stint on the psych ward, Sandy knew them all.

He entered Larch's Luncheonette in the heart of the business district and was lucky to find an empty booth beside the front window. Millie, the waitress, soon appeared and cleared away a clutter of egg-smeared plates.

"Cup of tea, please," Sandy said.

"That all?"

"I'm waiting for someone," he tried to explain with a weak smile.

Shortly, his tea arrived. He emptied a sugar packet and a shot of cream into it. As soon as he took the first sip, however, he knew that he had made a horrible mistake, for when the sweet, hot liquid washed over his ailing tooth, the resultant pain almost put him through the ceiling.

Robin Holmes sat hunched before her video display screen in the newsroom of the Excelsior *Banner*, afraid to turn her head to the left or right lest the other reporters see her tears. Gazing into the green glow of the screen, she wondered whether she had made a terrible mistake casting Sandy out of her life—for she was sure that she had lost him forever. Her breasts ached, and she felt sick to her stomach. Painful memories surged through her mind on a flood tide of regret.

She thought of the very first time they met four years ago. She was a sophomore at Greer, waiting tables at the pastry shop on Grove Street, when Sandy came in one May afternoon for tea and a wedge of chocolate-whiskey cake, the specialty of the house. He said he was celebrating his first-ever sale of a painting (to Joel Harlowe). Robin had noticed him around town for a year. He was conspicuous on his motorcycle, rather dashing, and appeared to be an educated person of good background. But he was not a student, and she could not figure out what he was doing here in Excelsior Springs. She had seen him down on Catherine Street, hanging out with an older crowd, and she had made a few unsuccessful attempts to get him to notice her—like standing beside him at the bar of the Black Rose. Suddenly, this thing about the painting explained it all. Sandy put it even more succinctly later that evening when she got off work and, at his insistence, joined him for dinner at Ogden's Restaurant on Catherine. "I'm a starving artist," he told her over a plate of Jeff Ogden's excellent lamb with rosemary sauce, and she replied by saying, "Well, you're not starving anymore, are you?" which she feared was perhaps an insensitive remark, maybe even snooty. But Sandy had agreed and laughed, putting her at ease. They talked for hours over glasses of the house burgundy. Later, they strolled a few blocks to Union Park (designed by Olmstead) and stood in the little marble gazebo beside the duck pond in the moonlight, listening to the frogs peep, and Sandy drew her in his arms, saying, "I have a notion that you're everything I've been looking for in a girl." She wondered if that was a line, but she let him kiss her anyway. It thrilled her that he wasn't a college boy. Though he was still very much a mystery, she felt quite safe with him. Then it grew chilly in the park, and she surprised herself by asking to see his studio. It looked almost churchy with the peaked roof visible above the bare ceiling joists and moonlight streaming in through the big dormer window, so naturally it reminded her of her father, an Episcopal minister at Wappingers Falls on the Hudson. The paintings took her breath away, even while she could see immediately why he had such a hard time selling them. They depicted recognizable things. The two of them huddled with their clothes on under the sleeping bag on his mattress on the floor for a while, and then she let him undress her in the moonlight. The hours with him had filled her with a strange and sumptuous feeling akin to dread, the certainty that she had formed a momentous link in her life.

Now that link was broken, and Robin was afraid that she might come apart as a result. The tears slipped down her cheek and pooled on the metal desktop in front of her keyboard. Though she stared right into the video display screen, she did not comprehend the green words, a paragraph about a ham supper to be held at the grange hall in Shrewsbury. Suddenly, the phone at her elbow rang, jolting her as though her seat were electrically wired. She blew her nose hastily in a tissue and reached for the handset.

"Holmes?" a voice barked. It was her boss, the editor Fred Garrity, a gruff, rotund man in his forties who ran the newsroom like a drill sergeant and called all his reporters by their last names, regardless of age or gender. Robin had started at the paper as a gofer right out of Greer. Now, after a year, she was a general assignment reporter. She could see him talking to her on his phone from his desk at the opposite end of the newsroom. "Holmes, you're on a ten o'clock deadline. Where the hell's that Shrewsbury Town Topics column."

"I'll have it for you in a few minutes, Mr. Garrity."

"Hey, Holmes, you know anything about some big Halloween party this hotshot is supposedly throwing over at the old casino tonight?"

"Yes," she answered, without elaborating.

"Well, how'd you like to go over and cover it?"

Robin suddenly drew the phone away from her ear and stared at it as though it were a diabolic instrument of torture.

"I wouldn't be caught dead at that goddam stupid party!" she shouted at Garrity across the newsroom, and all the other keyboards stopped clicking at once as a deathly silence filled the big office.

Rupert Van Der Wie, otherwise known as Cecil B. Wonton—a name conferred upon him by some forgotten Catherine Street wag years earlier, a name that stuck with a vengeance, to its owner's dismay—rang the front doorbell at Edmund Black's house and waited nervously on the porch for someone to answer. The only son of the only great-great-great-great-great-grandson of Colonel Miles Van Der Wie, the Revolutionary War hero of Schenectady, Cecil had graduated from a Rhode Island art college and drifted to Excelsior Springs during the Age of Aquarius hoping to find a rich Greer girl to marry. His fortunes in this respect had come to naught, and recent years had seen his prospects dwindle sharply. Now, at age thirty-seven, he scraped together a meager living doing odd jobs—often for Edmund Black. He stood just under six feet tall, was well formed with patrician features, parted his still thick brown hair almost in the middle like the man in the Arrow shirt advertisements of the 1920s, and wore horn-rimmed eyeglasses that lent him a studious air. In wardrobe he affected a casual Brooks Brothers look—khaki pants, polo shirts, Topsiders—as though he were a vacationing stockbroker. A self-confessed "beeraholic" who drank nine bottles of Molson's ale every day, no less, no more, his original aspirations in life as Rupert Van Der Wie were lost or at least so obscured that, to his melancholy chagrin, he had all but become Cecil B. Wonton.

The heavy front door flew open, and Edmund appeared in his silk smoking jacket, still wearing the white makeup on his face.

"What the fuck do you want?" he asked Cecil, fluttering his eyelids.

"Y-y-you told me to come over at ten o'clock," Cecil replied defensively.

"I told you that? When did I tell you that?"

"Last night. In the bar."

"Well, I must have had a reason. Don't stand there like a dummy. Tell me, what was it?"

"S-s-something about your phone?"

"Ah, yes! My phone! The motherfucker is out of order. Come in. Don't stand out there like a potted palm. Follow me."

Cecil followed Edmund into the kitchen. Edmund signed a check, tore it out of his checkbook, and presented it to Cecil.

"Here. Make the problem go away," Edmund said.

"You want me to go pay your phone bill?"

"It begins to seem that way, doesn't it, dear boy." He put his arm around Cecil's shoulder and began walking him slowly back down the hall toward the front door. "This happened once before, you see. I personally went over to their smelly little office and paid the bill myself. Hundreds of dollars. You'd think they'd be beside themselves at such a windfall. And you do know what? It took them three days to turn the motherfucker back on. Three days. Do you know why?''

"No."

"Come on, guess."

"I can't."

"Take a wild stab at it. Go ahead."

"They forgot."

"No. They didn't forget. They left it off for three days on purpose. Because I am a Negro. How do you like that?''

"It's awful."

"Come on, you can do better, dear boy. Show some real sympathy."

"I'm sorry you're a Negro."

"I'm so glad you understand. It truly warms my heart. Tell me, by the by, Cecil, have you got a date for Harlowe's Halloween Ball?''

"No. But I wasn't invited."

"Not invited! Poor thing. There must be some mistake."

"No, I think he did it on purpose."

"But it doesn't make any sense, dear boy. Why, to exclude such a sparkling, worldly, charming, amusing fellow as yourself—it simply confounds me. Is there any bad blood?''

"I haven't had a physical in a while. But I feel all right.''

"No, no, no. Is there any bad blood *between* you and Harlowe? For instance, did you fuck up some job he paid you to do?''

"Not that I know of."

"Did you trample his hollyhocks?"

"No."

"Pee-pee on his toilet seat?"

"No."

"Make any remarks in passing about his mother, the old slut."

"No."

"Well then, obviously some mistake has been made. Therefore, you must come as my date. To preclude any chance of embarrassment."

"That's very nice of you, Edmund, but—"

"No, I insist. Let's hear no more about it. You will pick me up at this very spot at eight-thirty and whisk me off to the ball."

A look of more than the usual discomfort came over Cecil. He shifted his weight back and forth repeatedly from one leg to the other, made faces, and stared energetically into the doorsill.

"Maybe I'll just crash it," he finally said.

"I shall pay you fifty Yankee dollars to escort me."

Cecil glanced sharply back up.

"You suddenly appear more pliable," Edmund observed, "more reasonable, more open to persuasion."

"What time did you say to pick you up?"

George Wells found Sandy in Larch's Luncheonette in one of the booths beside the front window. Sandy's eyes were squeezed tightly shut, and he was holding his head between both hands as if it were a basketball.

"Are you all right?" George touched Sandy's shoulder. Sandy looked up, startled, and drew in a deep, shuddery breath.

"I've got a terrible toothache," he said. "It kind of flares up when I drink something hot or touch it. I'll be okay in a minute."

In fact, Sandy already felt better just seeing George there, George who was always dependable, unflappable, the constant friend. If anyone could help him find a way through a rough situation, it was George.

Millie, the waitress, reappeared and took George's order—large grapefruit juice, cheese omelette, home fries, double order of wheat toast, and coffee.

"How about you?" She turned to Sandy.

"Nothing for me, thank you."

"Nothing?" she said, with a note of surprised indignation.

"I can't eat anything," Sandy said.

"Have a milk shake," George suggested.

"No, I'd better not."

"He's got a toothache," George explained.

Millie shrugged her shoulders and marched away.

Sandy glanced out the window and flinched when he saw something on the sidewalk that looked like the dog-faced dwarf he once came across in a book about human freaks. It took him another moment to realize that it was only a child in a *Star Wars* mask.

"Did you happen to notice if I left Ubu with some other girl last night?" he asked George carefully.

"A girl other than Robin?"

"Yes."

George shook his head. "Actually, I don't remember seeing you leave, period. I was pretty wasted myself. Why?"

"I don't remember how I got home. What time, or who with. But I found a piece of jewelry next to my bed this morning."

"Oh?"

"No girl. Just this earring. Then Robin came over with everything I ever gave her—presents, records, my father's flight jacket—and dumped it all on my doorstep. I was wondering if maybe she saw me with another girl late last night—unless she's just decided to kick me out of her life because I won't set up housekeeping with her."

"Why *not* move in with her?" George said, even

though the idea sent a pain through his sternum. "It would solve a lot of your problems."

"She wants to take care of me."

"What's wrong with that?"

"I'm not somebody's poodle."

"Who says you have to act like a poodle?"

"I'd *feel* like one. I can barely meet my own basic needs right now. And I won't have Robin picking up the slack for me financially. I couldn't stand that. It'd be humiliating."

"But if you moved in with her, you wouldn't have to pay so much rent."

"I can't move into her apartment. There's nowhere for me to paint, and the light's no good. I'd just have to rent another studio space somewhere else. And she couldn't move into my place. It's too primitive. There's no privacy. We'd drive each other crazy in a week. Aw, you know there's a million things wrong with it. It just wouldn't work. Besides, I'm afraid Greenleaf's going to freeze me out before too long anyway. He's turned the hot water off on me already. And there were people working downstairs this morning. Hammering or something."

"Sooner or later you're going to have to find another place, one way or the other."

"Maybe. But the bastard's not going to force me out. I've lived in that place a hell of a lot longer than he's owned it."

"Sandy, I hate to disillusion you, but legally that doesn't mean a damn thing. You're still just a tenant."

"It's not legal to freeze a tenant out."

"Don't pay him any rent unless he turns the hot water back on."

"If I don't pay the rent, he'll have a perfect excuse to evict me. Look, I know I'm not going to be there forever.

It's just that this couldn't be a worse time to have to move."

"If I were you, though, I'd start looking for another place."

Millie arrived with George's breakfast. Sandy gazed longingly at the fluffy omelette with cheese oozing out of the folded edge, its side order of crispy brown home-fried potatoes, and the tall stack of wheat toast with butter melting on the top slice. He also noticed that George's hand was shaking when he picked up his fork.

"What's wrong with your hand?" Sandy asked.

"Hangover," George said.

"Me, too."

"I have to go down and see my dad today."

"How's he doing with the radiation and all?"

"Pretty bad," George said, and Sandy observed what looked like a cloud passing over his friend's face, a dark, frightened, faraway look that he'd never seen on George before. Sandy remembered his mother's last weeks, how death had become a kind of constant companion for him while he waited for the inevitable end. He sensed that George now knew this silent companion.

"It's a lousy deal, cancer. Toward the very end, though, my mom seemed grateful, like in Thomas Cole's final painting of the 'Voyage of Life' when the river leads to the tranquil sea and the angel reappears. Let me know if I can help with anything."

"Okay," George said, and it took another long moment for the fearful, rapt look to leave his face. Eventually he jabbed his fork into the mound of steaming home fries. "Harlowe stopped by my house this morning. You know about this Halloween Ball he's throwing tonight?"

"You'd have to live on another planet not to know about it."

"Well, he said he needed help with a bunch of

last-minute details. He's got to leave town for a while late this afternoon when the liquor and stuff is being delivered to the casino, and I think he needs someone he can rely on to be there when it arrives. I told him to speak to you."

"As a matter of fact, I was going to ask him for a loan," Sandy said, marveling at the growing irony of his situation. "I figured he'd turn me down, but maybe I could swing some sort of deal with him after all."

"Uh, I think you've touched on the sticking point right there." George tried to couch it diplomatically. "You see, Joel feels that you should help him out as a gesture of friendship, not to get something from him."

"Namely money."

"Exactly. To him it's a matter of principle."

"To me it's a matter of being desperate to cover the rent."

"The poor guy doesn't think anybody likes him for himself."

"You wonder if there's any real self there to like. What I see is mostly a big act."

"Still, I think you ought to volunteer to help him out," George said. "If you do, he'll probably turn around and lend you some dough. He might even offer to buy another painting from you."

"Is that what he told you?"

"Not in so many words. But that was the impression he left."

"So, as long as I don't ask him for money, he'll give me some money."

"Something like that," George agreed.

"That's crazy."

"Deep down, you know, Harlowe's a very sentimental guy."

"So was Hitler."

"Are you sure you don't want a milk shake?"

Sandy sighed and shook his head. "I'm really afraid to put anything in my mouth."

George finished the last of his eggs, tucked a final triangle of toast in after them, and washed it all down with coffee. Then he took two new fifty dollar bills out of his wallet and handed them to Sandy. "Don't spend it all in one place," he said.

"On one person, you mean: Roy Greenleaf. But thanks. You're a real pal," Sandy said as he put the money in his empty red nylon billfold. "I sure wish it was June again and we were going up to the Ausable to catch some trout."

"We had some great fishing this year, didn't we?" George said wistfully.

"Remember all those brookies we got up on the West Branch?"

"That big gorge below Whiteface."

"Yeah. I suppose we can always go back next year."

"I suppose," George said, the dark look returning as he spoke.

"Only I don't know if I can make it through another winter here," Sandy said, his face suddenly contorting while tears pooled in his eyes. "I'm thirty years old now," he said in a breaking voice, "and I can't even pay the rent."

"You'll pay the rent, don't worry," George said.

"I'm such a flop in life."

"You're not a flop," George said.

"I even found a gray hair this morning. On my chest."

"I stopped counting a while ago." George smiled ruefully.

"It scares me."

"You'll make it through the winter all right," George said to reassure him. "If anyone does, it'll be you."

Edmund Black was removing his white minstrel makeup in a first-floor bathroom when the doorbell rang.

"Jesus H. Christ!" he muttered to himself, toweling off his face and then stalking down the hall as the bell rang again. "This place is like Grand Central Station today!" he said, as he threw open the door. Outside on the porch stood a fat woman flanked by two hideously deformed midgets. One of the midgets had an eye in the middle of its forehead. The other looked as though half its head had melted away in an atomic blast.

"Trick or treat!" they cried, as Edmund gaped at them.

The fat woman attempted a game smile, but could not disguise her nervousness at the sight of Edmund, bare-chested in his smoking jacket and with smudges of white greasepaint here and there on his face.

"What have we here? Why, what a loathsome sight," Edmund remarked with delight.

"We can come back later," the woman said.

"And deprive these little mutants of their hard-earned treats? I won't hear of it."

The trick-or-treaters giggled, thrilled that their masks had made such a effective impression.

Edmund knelt to their level.

"What's your name, little one-eye?"

"Dawn," the child piped back in reply.

"What kind of treat would you like, Dawn?"

"Snickers bar!" she told him.

"I'm afraid I don't have a Snickers, Dawn. How about twenty hours of free plastic surgery at the Mayo Clinic instead?"

She shook her head.

"And you, little pizza face?" He turned to the other, a boy.

72

"Reese's Pieces!"

"Sorry, we're fresh out. Life hardly seems worth living without them, does it?"

"Kids, I think we should be leaving now—"

"Madam, don't be rash. Halloween comes but once a year. I implore you. Wait here with your horrifying offspring while I search my pantry for some delectables."

"Please, Mommy! Please!"

"Well, all right."

Edmund hurried into the kitchen and returned shortly with several bulky objects behind his back. The children clamored for their treats.

"Hush now, little beasties. Hold out your hands, and close your eyes, and you will get a big surprise."

The children held out their hands. Edmund brought forward two flat cardboard boxes which he placed upon their outstretched hands.

"Is this your idea of a joke?" the mother asked, one hand cocked aggressively on her ample hip.

"I beg your pardon, madam."

"Giving stuff like that to kids on Halloween." She reproved him more specifically. "You should be ashamed of yourself."

"Oook," the little boy cried.

"Yuk," his sister exclaimed.

The two frozen TV dinners clattered to the worn planks of the front porch.

"Why, these are my own personal favorites," Edmund informed her, bending to retrieve them. "Salisbury steak with mashed potatoes and roast tom turkey with dressing. Perfectly delicious, and packed with vitamins and minerals."

"Take Mommy's hand, kids," the woman said, as she dragged the boy and girl, who were now crying, down the front steps to the sidewalk. "I'm going to report you," she told Edmund over her shoulder, her eyes narrowed to vengeful slits, "to the police!"

"You appear at my doorstep begging nutriment for your little ones, and this is the thanks I get when a veritable banquet is offered," he railed at her in reply and shook his fist as the trio waddled up Serpentine Street. "Why, it's no wonder your children are deformed!"

FIVE

George gave Sandy a ride to the cycle shop a mile across town, through the Springs' little ethnic enclaves on the west side—down Pine Street, the Italian street with its one dark tavern and a small bakery that sold cookies which tasted like sweetened sawdust; around Lafayette Square, the black neighborhood with its crumbling Greek revival cottages that included the original Israel Babcock homestead; past a desolate "urban renewal" block known until the 60s as Cathouse Row; and finally onto a smarmy strip of modern cinder-block retail establishments, among which stood Spa Cycle City, the motorcycle shop. There, in the parts department, among a mixed clientele of rustic teenagers shopping for dirt bikes and leather-clad chopper thugs, Sandy got a new clutch cable.

George paid the nine dollars for it, gave Sandy a lift back to his house on Serpentine, and stuck around briefly to make sure Sandy hooked it up right. They were routing the cable under the gas tank when a sibilant voice called

out over their heads "Ooooo! Boys working on motorcycles! Nothing gets me so hot. Yoo-hoo, boys!"

George and Sandy looked up. Edmund hung over the
rail of the small balcony that fronted his bedroom, smoking a joint the size of a cheroot.

"Get a grip, Edmund," Sandy said.

"Get a grip?" Edmund rejoined. "Why don't *you* get
a grip, white boy. Bend over and pick up that . . . that
. . . whatever it is," he hissed, pointing to a cylindrical
tool that lay on the ground beside the cycle.

"Impact driver," George informed him.

"Impact driver! I love it! It sounds so . . . I dunno
. . . so Spanish Inquisition. Does it vibrate, by any chance?"

"Did you have a bad night, Edmund?"

"Honey pie, a bad night? It's this thing called my life
that ain't workin' out too good," Edmund replied with a
snort. He then took a long drag on his reefer, vamping
with the belt of his smoking jacket.

"Why don't you just relax and enjoy your advantages?" Sandy said, unscrewing the clutch cover.

"Advantages! I don't suppose you noticed my face,
white boy."

"What's the matter with it?"

"It's a little on the dusky side."

"It never seemed to bother you before."

"I've suffered in secret all these years," Edmund said.
"Deep down, I feel accursed. Say, would you fellows
care for some of this ganja? It's really wicked stuff. And,
God knows, if I smoke anymore I'll float clean away. I
can toss down the rest of this spliff and watch you two
white boys fight for it in the dust. That *would* be a thrill.
Shall I do it?"

"He's being Noel Coward now," Sandy told George,
trying to keep him apprised of Edmund's rapid personality

76

shifts like a sportscaster explicating the sudden turns in a football game.

"I say, Dickie, why don't you and him fight," Edmund proposed.

"I'm Dickie, you see," Sandy explained, routing the cable between the bike's twin carburetors.

"Who am I?" George asked Edmund.

"How the fuck should I know if you don't?" he retorted.

"Are you having a nervous breakdown up there, Edmund?" Sandy asked. "You can tell us. We used to be mental health professionals."

"Far from it. Ha! Nervous breakdown! The idea. My dear fellow, if anything I am getting my shit together, every second, even as we palaver. As a matter of fact, I am—how shall I say—I *feel myself* on the verge of . . . of truly becoming something."

"Becoming what?" Sandy asked.

"Oh, it is a deep, dark secret. Notice, I said dark, not dusky."

"This is all very mysterious, Edmund," George observed.

"It's Halloween, Lionel, a day of mysterious transformations—may I call you Lionel?"

"If it makes you feel better."

"Don't patronize me, motherfucker. Do you like the name or not?"

"I already have a name. And you know what it is."

"Well, if you ask me, it's a bore. I mean, *George*? Come on. It reeks of the classroom. Father of our country and all that happy horseshit. If our first president had been named Lionel Washington, they would have named you Lionel."

"And if you were born in Southhampton, I suppose

they would have named you Lionel Hampton," Sandy replied jauntily.

"That's hitting below the belt, my good man."

"Sorry. But you asked for it."

"I asked for *this?*" Edmund protested, pointing once again at his face. "I assure you I did not. I put in for something rather different. I remember the occasion as though it were yesterday: a long counter in a place vaguely like Bloomingdales, but with a lot of puffy clouds everywhere for ambience. The sales clerks all had wings and halos. It seems to me there was a crush, like at holiday time. My turn came after a moderate wait. 'Can you show me something in a Swede or a Teuton?' I asked. 'Sorry,' this apple-cheeked angel of a girl said, 'no Swedes or Teutons left in stock.' 'I see,' said I. 'Have you anything in a Dane or a Celt?' 'Sorry, we're fresh out of Danes and Celts.' 'Hmmm, you don't say,' I remarked, beginning to stew just a bit, you understand. 'Have you perhaps a Saxon? A Norman? A Magyar? Good heavens, even a Slovak?' 'Sorry,' she said. 'The last of those went just this morning before lunch.' 'Well, what in hell have you got?' I put it to her, need I say, in desperation. 'Just a few of these Hottentots,' she answered, holding up this dark little mockery of a human being, naked but for a loincloth, and bedizened with barbaric little ornaments, including—ye Gods!—a very bone through its nose! 'Thank you, Miss, but I'll come back tomorrow,' I said. 'I'm afraid that will be impossible,' said her supervisor, an old gentleman in a flowing white beard who materialized all of a sudden as though from thin air. 'You must take what we give you, Sambo,' he added in a stentorian voice not unlike that of Charlton Heston, the impersonator of dieties. And that, dear friends, is the story of how I came to my estate in life, such as you find me. A sad tale, don't you agree?"

"I can't help thinking that you exaggerate," George said.

"You would think that, you heartless honkie fuckface. Any comment from the Hebrew community, Alexander?"

"I think you ought to go to Hollywood, Edmund," Sandy said. "You're wasting a tremendous talent goofing on us from your balcony when you could be making millions of people laugh all across America."

"I am not Sammy Davis," Edmund said. "I do not entertain." And with that, he spun on his heels, disappeared inside, and shut the French windows to his room.

"See what I mean?" Sandy whispered to George when Edmund was gone.

"I don't know," George hedged. "For him that's pretty normal."

"I think he's flipping his wig."

George glanced up again at the now empty balcony.

Sandy finally hooked up the cable to the clutch assembly and, with George helping, worked the adjustment screw so that the hand lever operated properly once more.

"Thanks for everything, the money, the help and all," Sandy said, walking George back to his truck parked on the street. "I'll pay you back as soon as I—"

"There's no hurry," George assured him. "I know you're good for it. But do yourself a favor, huh, and call Harlowe. I really think he'll help you out if you play your cards right."

"Okay, I'll call Harlowe," Sandy promised and watched George drive away up Serpentine, thinking how lucky he was to have a friend he could really depend on. Across the street, old Champion made a slight move, as though he were about to start another arduous journey over, but in a commanding voice Sandy yelled, "Stay!" and the dog sank back on his bony haunches.

Yelling made his tooth hurt again. He went back

upstairs to his garret to call Joel, but Joel did not answer his phone. While he stood there listening to it ring and ring, another possible source of funds came to mind. This too was a long shot, because her finances were sometimes as precarious as his. But even if she couldn't lend him any money, on this difficult morning Sandy felt gravitationally drawn to his mentor and former lover, Annie Gaines.

Joel Harlowe appreciated the finer things in life, and he believed that indulging in luxuries denoted a healthy self-respect. Therefore, after dropping off Kelly Seagraves at her dorm and paying his unsatisfying call on George Wells, Joel treated himself to a restorative session at the Excelsior Baths on South Broadway.

At one time, a dozen baths flourished all over town, indeed were its very *raison d'être*. The Excelsior Baths, now run by the state of New York, was the only such establishment left. In 1968, it was discovered that the famous waters contained traces of radium, but the state played the hazard down for the sake of tourism, and pamphlets issued by the town's chamber of commerce omitted mentioning it altogether. Joel Harlowe himself was a true afficionado of the baths, especially as a hangover cure, and scoffed at his friends' qualms.

"In a few years, you're going to glow in the dark like a Timex watch," Sandy would say when Joel tried to coax him along.

Built in 1927, the Excelsior Baths comprised a rambling one-story building about the size of an elementary school, but with a facade designed to resemble the Egyptian temple at Karnak, set in an incongruous grove of white pines. Nowadays, the ochre and blue paint was peeling everywhere and one whole wing was closed, its plumbing shot. The baths were staffed by a rather surly crew of state employees who could not be fired except for the grossest malfeasances, and who therefore ran the baths with a sort of Soviet-style apathy. This didn't detract from Joel's enjoyment in the slightest. In fact, he loved seeing the sleepy-eyed attendants hop to life when he proffered them five dollar tips for trivial services rendered. He quickly became known among them as a big spender and was treated like a royal dignitary.

Joel pulled his Austin-Healy right up to the front entrance and met his masseur, Art Schwenk, in the lobby. Schwenk, fifty-four, clothed in white like a hospital orderly, was an ex-army mess sergeant who wore his steel-gray hair in a brushcut and had a belly like a bay window. He preferred reading wrestling magazines to doing his job, except when Joel Harlowe appeared on the premises. Joel liked Schwenk because he was the farthest thing from a homosexual that Joel could imagine, for Joel could not bear the thought of having his flesh kneaded by a person of the homosexual persuasion.

"Beauteeful day today, huh, Mistah Hahlowe."

"You said it, Art."

They proceeded down a long dreary corridor lighted by bare bulbs. Along each side were small rooms with louvered doors. Schwenk opened one of them and followed Joel inside. Within was a tub about twice the size of an ordinary home bathtub. Above the faucets were several needle meters. While Joel undressed, Schwenk filled the tub with water, keeping an eye on the dials. He also dropped a thermometer on a beaded metal chain over the rim.

Joel hung his tweed jacket and jeans on the wooden valet provided and carefully put his socks inside his loafers.

"It's ready, Mistah Hahlowe," Schwenk announced in a bright voice that failed to conceal his essential weariness with existence and all the indignities it had heaped upon him, such as having to call this rich, idle, young twerp Mistah Hahlowe.

"Thanks, Art."

"Enjoy ya bath."

Art left the little room. Joel inhaled a couple of chambers of cocaine from his snorter and lowered himself into the tub as his flagging brain came back to life again. The water was exactly body temperature, sulfurous and fizzy. The tiny bubbles were indeed the most thrilling part of it. (The state's promotional pamphlets, which themselves exuded a strong odor of quackery, claimed that these bubbles had amazing curative powers.) They coalesced on the hairs of Joel's chest, and he loved the fizzy feeling of sweeping them off and then watching a new batch grow there. He sank lower now in the tepid bath so that his ears filled with water and all he could hear were the inner workings of his own body. His heart sounded as strong as a sump pump, and his brain gave off what he interpreted as a high-energy hum, like the sound a powerful dynamo might make in a hydroelectric plant.

Life was wonderful, he mused. The most inordinate happiness was his. Once again he pictured his father stepping into the Florida condo. He had done it! He had paid his father back for the gift of life. His accounts were clear. Tonight he was throwing a party that would knock the town's socks off. An awful lot of details remained to be ironed out, but Joel felt perfectly in control, perfectly calm. Here in this warm tub was the space he had made for himself, a space to relax and feel the happiness that was his, the happiness he had earned from making so many smart moves and from sticking to his principles in business as well as in life. This contemplation of the perfect wholeness and rightness of his life prompted in him a delicious feeling akin to sexual pleasure. It originated (he guessed) in one of the ganglia of the lower

thorax and spread sweetly down his legs. And this delicious sensation reminded him of Kelly and her fine lanky
body, the long tawny legs that seemed to start somewhere
around her neck, those slender suntanned arms and skill-
ful, long-fingered hands, her large breasts so pale and
creamy next to the darker butterscotch of her suntanned
belly—like a certain kind of candy he remembered from
his Brooklyn childhood: a marshmallow encased in silky
golden caramel—and the little yelps of pleasure she produced in the throes of their love act. Perhaps he should
have invited her to the party as his date. After all, she was
fated to be his wife, Mrs. Joel Harlowe. Kelly Harlowe.
Had not the crystal clear vision come to him only moments after she disappeared into that dormitory building?
He would call her up and apologize. He would be incredibly gallant. She would forgive him and call him *darling*.
Yes, yes, she would be his girl at the party. She would be
his girl and be so beautiful that the other men would
quake and swoon. The other men would want to make
love to her so badly that their loins would ache to be
deprived of her. Yet, she'd wear a look on her beautiful
face that would say *he alone, Joel Harlowe, is privileged
to know my body, which I give freely unto him for his
pleasure alone*. And after the ball she would indeed give
herself fully to him. And they would live happily ever—

"Mistah Hahlowe?"

"Huh . . . ?"

"I'm ready faw ya."

"Sure thing, Art," Joel replied, as Schwenk reentered
the little room with a warm terry-cloth bath sheet fresh
from the electric brisker.

The thermometer outside the north dormer window
in Sandy's garret registered fifty-nine degrees. Knowing
how bitterly cold it was riding a motorcycle any distance,

even at that seemingly mild temperature, Sandy retrieved his father's leather flight jacket from the basket of assorted treasures Robin had given back. The leather was soft and pliable from a recent application of mink oil preservative, and it pleased Sandy to think how well Robin had taken care of the precious jacket even while his heart ached to imagine what his life would be like in the future without her. He had loved her for her thoughtfulness, her competence, her fundamental intelligence as much as he had loved her smile, the smell of her hair, the feel of her warm and slender body next to his. But then hadn't that very quality of competence caused him to feel in comparison like a floundering twit? He knew it was irrational, but it galled him that she could pay her bills and he couldn't pay his. It hurt to feel incompetent. It hurt to not be able to buy a clutch cable or pay the goddam rent. His tooth hurt.

He grabbed his cycling gloves, went downstairs, started up the bike, and finally rolled out of the driveway onto Serpentine Street without any more annoying delays. Ordinarily, he'd be painting at this hour, eleven o'clock in the morning. Afternoons when the weather was good, he liked to ramble the countryside with his sketchbook or flyrod or both, and sometimes with George. In the winter they would bushwhack the logging trails on skis in the vast tract of timber owned by the Phelps-Longley paper company north of Locust Grove, where the Adirondacks began in earnest with surprising suddenness.

Accelerating on the cycle, he was braced by the chilly wind against his clean-shaven face. He noticed that the coldness caused his tooth to stop hurting, especially when he opened his mouth and the cool air rushed in with force. The sky was deep deep blue and especially luminous as a background to the golden crowns of the trees that interrupted the skyline of oddly shaped rooftops.

Turning from Serpentine onto High Street, he saw little groups of masked goblins accompanied by their mothers. The children carried shopping bags and plastic jack-o'-lanterns. Sandy remembered when he was a boy, trick-or-treating in the Foxhall Road neighborhood of Washington, the fun they used to have soaping up the car windows of a certain congressman from Nebraska, widely regarded as a right-wing blowhard. He recalled with a real thrill the bonanza of miniature Mounds bars and Baby Ruth bars and Butterfingers and Sugar Daddys and malted milk balls and Hershey's Kisses and pounds of candy corn, and how he kept this treasury of sugar in his closet for weeks, feasting from it until he was sick of the stuff, until he could barely stand the sight of a chocolate bar or another kernel of candy corn.

Traversing the small ethnic enclaves on the west side, Sandy soon came to Prospect Avenue, which officially marked the town limits. The avenue was lined with five car dealerships, their asphalt lagoons crammed with goods, their plastic pennants flapping in the breeze. Here, Sandy thought, was the heart and soul of twentieth-century America. Perhaps, he mused, he should give up nature and paint cars: portraits of cars, landscapes of cars, panoramas of cars, convocations of exalted cars. It made sense from the economic angle, though he hated cars.

Of course, the fact was that he himself owned a driving machine, a motorcycle, and would have gladly owned some kind of four-wheeled vehicle had he been able to afford one. The problem, then, was not so much that driving machines existed, but that so many people had them. It was democracy gone amuck. He remembered one day years ago being with his father stuck in a traffic jam on the Capital Beltway, an eight-lane road circling Washington, D.C. He must have been fourteen or so, capable of understanding, because his father's remark left a bold and lasting impression. "If Thomas Jefferson ever saw this," his dad had said, "he'd puke."

Beyond Prospect Avenue, High Street became a two-lane county highway. Sandy felt good to be leaving the Springs behind him. He wished that he was heading up into the Adirondacks on a long trip. The mountains were their most beautiful at this time of the year. All the deerflies, blackflies, and mosquitos would be gone. Soon it would be winter. Real soon, he thought with a shiver. Up in the Adirondacks, there's snow on the ground before Thanksgiving. It would be something to spend a whole winter in a remote part of the Adirondacks.

Sandy knew that Harlowe had done it for several years in a row and Harlowe always said it had turned his life around. Had it taught Harlowe something about making money? Sandy wondered. Because for all Harlowe's flaws, there was no denying that the guy could at least take care of himself, and very nicely, too. In fact, it awed Sandy. Deep down, didn't he envy Harlowe a little? Envy all the beautiful and expensive things? Envy Harlowe's fine house and antique English sports car and German motorcycle and elegant clothes, the trips to Bermuda, the restaurant dinners, the ski trips to Vermont, the simple freedom from financial worry of any kind?

It seemed to Sandy now that perhaps he did envy Harlowe, and that perhaps this was at the bottom of his resentful attitude toward him. For wasn't it true that the guy had never asked Sandy for anything except to be his friend, and that he had bought five of Sandy's paintings because he really appreciated them? Sandy was suddenly ashamed of himself for knocking Harlowe to George. He would indeed get a hold of him later, he thought, and volunteer to help Joel with whatever he needed in connection with this big Halloween party of his, and he would do it because Joel had helped him so many times

before, and most of all because Joel understood and re-
spected the heart of his life, which was his painting, and if
there was no money in it for Sandy, then so be it. In the
meantime, he'd try to solve his financial problems some
other way.

Three miles north of town, Sandy swung left onto
Locust Grove Road. It had been a month now since he
came out this way because trout season ended September
30th and Sandy had gone fishing on Mill Creek the last
day. It was a great day, too, one of the best he ever had.
The big brown trout had come upstream from Excelsior
Lake to spawn early this year, and he'd hooked onto a
nineteen-inch monster in a riffle not much deeper than his
ankles. He'd taken it to Annie Gaines's place nearby and
she'd pan-fried it for the two of them on her woodstove.
He doubted that he would ever again take a better fish
than that nineteen-inch brownie out of Mill Creek.

Here on the road to Locust Grove in the Adirondack
foothills, many trees had already been stripped of most of
their leaves by the wind, and the branches stood bare
against the sky. Five miles out, he passed a row of suburban-
style dwellings that some enterprising developer had thrown
up the year before. They had alarmed him then, and they
alarmed him now. The four houses, it seemed to Sandy,
had been designed with a special brand of ugliness so
profound that it approached the sublime.

There seemed to be a competition going on as to
which family could fill its lawn with the most plastic junk.
One was decorated with three dozen plastic whirligigs. A
squad of plastic fairy-tale dwarfs marched across another.
A third held an array of birdbaths, various religious figures, and a silver-painted tractor tire planted with plastic
geraniums. The last house actually had a yard sale in
progress, the lawn littered with items too useless and ugly
to suit even the inhabitants.

Locust Grove itself, once a farming hamlet with a store, a post office, and three churches, now owed its existence primarily to the two trailer parks that occupied former cornfields on either side of the cinder-block town garage, where the snowplows were kept. Each trailer park contained about fifty of the boxcarlike dwellings. The store still operated, specializing in beer, cigarettes, and snack foods on which the trailer denizens subsisted. Of the churches, one (the Presbyterian) was a vacant ruin with no roof, one (the Quaker meeting house) had been turned into a perpetual flea market, and one (formerly Unitarian) was used as a Soul Saving Station by born-again fundamentalists.

Here, Sandy took a right on Lake Lamentation Road. Not far up the road, he came to Mill Creek and stopped briefly on the bridge that crossed it. He was shivering from the windchill, and it felt good to get off the bike. He left it running in neutral on its kickstand and hung over the bridge's railing with a hand shading his eyes. Below, several good trout finned with their noses in the current. Every now and then one of the trout would dart a few feet from its lie to devour some morsel of food that floated in the current and then return to its place. Sandy watched them for a while and then studied the surface of the water, seeing it as a composition of swirling dark and light colors. Before long, it would be too cold to come out and do any painting here, too cold and icy to ride the motorcycle, and of course the trout season was over until next year. His tooth resumed aching now that he had stopped moving with the cool air in his face. He climbed back aboard the cycle and had not gone a quarter mile around a bend in the road when he came upon a sight that left him dumbfounded.

It appeared at first to be a strange, bright slash in the dark forest, like a painting someone had taken a razor to.

But as Sandy braked to a stop, he saw that it was a new clearing in the woods, that the yellow slash was a strip of bare soil plowed two hundred yards into the woods, and that there were other yellow swatches, clearings, deeper in. As soon as he switched off his motorcycle engine, he could hear the mechanical grunt and roar of the bulldozer and see it way down the newly carved road. Then he saw the sign, a four-by-eight painted plywood sheet nailed between two trees. In neat professional lettering it said:

MILL CREEK SOLAR ESTATES
Luxury Homesites Now Available
Select From More Than Twelve Home Plans
Roy M. Greenleaf, Developer

This couldn't be, was Sandy's initial reaction. A month ago there had been no hint of this, not so much as a surveyor's orange ribbon tied to a tree. There must be some mistake. But he looked at the sign and back at the huge scar in the woods and back at the sign again, and soon he perceived that it wasn't a mistake. Greenleaf really was putting up a housing development on top of the best trout stream in Excelsior County.

S I X

It was bird season. Now, when the days were still warm, with the leaves falling so that the bare branches showed against the sky, now would be the time to go out for woodcock and grouse, George Wells thought, as he drove back to his cottage from Sandy's place. He had never felt more alive than when he was hunting birds in the October light. And yet today, with his large hands cold on the steering wheel, and a cold feeling spreading down his throat, he felt himself moving helplessly, inexorably toward permanent darkness.

He had loved hunting woodcock especially. Their taste was strong, vaguely like liver, and George, who had worked in quite a few restaurants and knew some tricks of the trade, made a piquant mustard sauce to go with them. Unfortunately the woodcocks—and ducks, too—were now full of industrial poisons, lead, mercury, PCBs, and it was no longer safe to eat them.

There was always grouse, George thought, as he

parked the battered blue pickup truck in his dirt driveway. Grouse didn't migrate or live near major waterways where pollutants were dumped. Mostly, they stuck around so-called "edge habitat," such as abandoned farmland that was slowly going back to woods. George had just such a favorite spot for hunting grouse: an abandoned dairy farm on the west side of Indian Hill, twelve miles north of the Springs.

It had been tied up in an estate dispute ever since George came to town. He knew because once he inquired of a realtor about buying the place. It contained over fifty acres of woods and old pasture covered with poplar scrub—just what birds loved. The land was posted against hunters, but George had also learned that the quarreling owners lived in Illinois, and that virtually nobody kept an eye on the place. And it was simply lousy with grouse. You couldn't take twenty steps without flushing a bird. And boy oh boy, George thought, when a grouse flushed out of a thicket, that was a thrill. It was like a boobytrap going off in your face. They exploded out of their cover with a rush of wingbeats that made your heart stop.

Inside his cottage, George went directly to the hall closet and got down his shotgun. It was a fifty-year-old, 16-gauge, double-barreled, side-by-side Savage. He'd picked it up secondhand for ninety dollars at a gun shop in Saranac Lake. It was a bastard gauge, the sixteen, supposedly a compromise between a duck gun and an upland bird piece, and not all that great for either, but George was sentimentally attached to it.

With trembling hands, he broke it open at the breech and peered down both barrels into the light of a window. Rust had grown like mold in a few spots since the previous fall. Aware that it was a way of keeping the inexorable darkness at bay, George got his cleaning kit from the same closet, screwed together the aluminum cleaning rod, dribbled some solvent on a gun patch, and ran it through both barrels. The gun cleaning solvent had a tangy, sweet, exciting smell like no other aroma on earth.

There was a handful of loose shells in the shoebox along with the cleaning supplies. They were game loads: number 7½ shot. He picked up two of the shells with their purple jackets and brass powder casings and rolled them around in the palm of his hand. Their weight and solidity was oddly pleasurable. There was hidden beauty in the potential power of a loaded shell. It was like charm in certain highly charged personalities. Edmund Black, for example. Harlowe had it, too, almost in spite of himself, George thought. The old man, Boss Wells, might have appreciated Harlowe's relentless drive.

What Harlowe said the night before about George being "practically a PhD" stung because it had been such a long time since George even thought about all those years in graduate school. It was as though Harlowe was talking about somebody else, a stranger. Somewhere in the house George actually had a sheepskin from Cornell University awarding him a master's degree in history, and also fifty-odd pages of a doctoral dissertation. Why hadn't he finished it? It was hard to remember why, he thought with the cold feeling spreading to his stomach. The old man had thought it was stupid in the first place.

"Doctor of history?" His father guffawed. "There's no cure for what's past."

Someone like Harlowe might have hung in and finished it despite anything his father thought. But George dropped out, packed his collie Sarah, since deceased, in a VW microbus, and came to Excelsior Springs, a town he had known from his teens, when he used to drive up from Delft on Saturday nights to try to pick up Greer girls on Catherine Street.

92

Sitting in the quiet of his cottage on this Halloween morning that could not have been more beautiful, George felt nearly overwhelmed with regret. The darkness was so close he could feel its oceanic presence, like nearing the shore and hearing the surf pound. Gazing all the while into his hand, George finally refocused on the two shotgun shells there. Their weight was still oddly comforting. The shotgun lay across his lap. Slowly and carefully he slipped each shell into the breech. They felt good in the gun, so well-fitted, so solid. The brass primer bases looked handsome against the blued steel of the barrels. With a knowing motion, as though he were in the field, he jerked the barrels sharply upward, closing the breech. It felt good to hold a loaded gun. The potential of it, the charm of it, was reassuring.

Annie Gaines and her husband Kenneth were a Greer faculty couple (Art and English) who had owned the house on Serpentine Street when Sandy Stern first moved into the garret studio there. Their marriage had been on the rocks a long time and soon foundered altogether. Sandy observed the couple's final months with the embarrassment of an involuntary voyeur. There were often sharp words, which he heard through the floor at night when he tried to read.

Then one day Kenneth was suddenly gone for good, and Annie—whom Sandy had known until then only to chat with when he handed over the rent check—appeared at his garret door in tears asking if he wouldn't mind sharing a cup of coffee with her. She needed someone to talk to, she said, and couldn't trust her friends, who happened to all be Greer faculty members and their spouses. In the weeks that followed, he was at first just a shoulder to cry on. Then she began to notice who he was and talk to him about his painting. Then they became friends. And finally, one August afternoon when her teen-aged daughter Jodie was away working at her summer job as a riding counselor, Sandy and Annie became lovers.

The divorce had nasty repercussions in Annie's professional life. Kenneth had tenure and Annie didn't. The year after they split up, Annie's contract was not renewed. It was simple dirty faculty politics. Kenneth was pals with the college provost, and Kenneth didn't want his ex-wife around anymore. The provost saw to it.

She bore this humiliation with courage and dignity. But she loved the area and had no intention of being drummed into exile by an ex-husband whose faggotry and alcoholism were open secrets. Alternatives presented themselves. She hung around the fabled racetrack sketching that summer and was soon painting commissioned portraits of horses owned by the high-society crowd. The competition was brisk, but she made a fair living at it—more than her Greer salary, in fact—and as a self-employed artist, she enjoyed more tax write-offs.

When the house on Serpentine Street was sold, Annie bought an abandoned one-room schoolhouse on Yake Road in the hills between Locust Grove and Lake Lamentation. It was a near ruin. She muddled through the first winter like a prospector in the Yukon. There was no running water. She had to melt snow on the woodstove. And yet she loved it and appeared to thrive. While her hair went increasingly gray, her face took on a ruddy girlish glow, her blue eyes seemed to deepen (or was it just the Adirondack light?), and to Sandy she had never looked more beautiful. He helped her fix the plumbing in the spring when the ground thawed. She hired a professional to jack up the building and repair the foundation. The following fall, Sandy helped her insulate and put up sheetrock. He even proposed the idea of moving in with her.

That was what changed things between them. The idea set off a kind of alarm bell in Annie. For she now had a firm sense of entering a more solitary, reflective phase of her life. And while she loved him, she could not see taking him on that way. She told him in so many words that it was time to go out and find a girlfriend closer to his own age.

At first, Sandy was desolate, for she filled such a large void in his life, and so uniquely, that he could not quite conceive of replacing her. But she encouraged him to look for another, and some weeks after he had found Robin Holmes, he brought her out on his motorcycle to meet Annie, who approved at once of the slender, shy girl with chestnut hair and the mordant wit that took you by surprise.

Late this Halloween morning now, Sandy arrived at Annie Gaines's house north of Locust Grove in a state of great agitation and found her painting in the front yard. Down Yake Road a bit further and across from Annie's place, stood a rusty turquoise mobile home of superlative ugliness and squalor. It belonged to the Tooles, a family of congenital morons and criminals, of whom Glen Toole, the exhibitionist and released mental patient, was the youngest offspring. Its dusty front yard was strewn with all sorts of broken appliances in heaps by category: water heaters, broken clothes washers, and so on, plus a lot of miscellaneous trash. A late model black Chevy Camaro stood gleaming with menace in the midst of it all. Sandy pulled into Annie's yard, took off his helmet, and went over to where Annie stood at her easel.

"Hello there, stranger." She greeted him warmly.

"Can you tell me why it is these woodchucks take such wonderful care of their cars and live like goddam pigs?" Sandy asked, marveling at the neighbors' place.

"Well, someone's in a foul humor this beautiful morning," Annie replied cheerfully, looking up now after a brushstroke, a radiant smile on her face, her eyes squinched in the sunlight like an oriental's. She wore her silver hair in a single, thick braid that reached nearly to her waist, and she was dressed in faded jeans with a dark green shawl-necked sweater that emphasized the shape of her somewhat fallen and walleyed breasts.

"No, it really baffles me," Sandy went on. "I think if we could figure this out, it would be a giant stride in sociology."

"Sociology is a humbug," Annie said. "Take it from one who has consorted with sociologists."

"All the same, I'd really like to know."

"Come give me a squeeze, and I'll tell you," she said.

He dropped his helmet in the grass and stepped forward to embrace her. His tooth began to ache again, yet he could not help but notice the feeling of her breasts, warm against his diaphragm, and memory fragments of their former love life flashed through his brain. "Tell me?" Sandy breathed into her ear.

"Because they know it drives snobs like you crazy," she murmured back. He did not want to let go of her, but soon she extracted herself and, slapping him playfully on the behind, said, "It's been at least a month. How are you, my dear one?"

"I've got a whale of a toothache," he told her. "And I cannot believe what I just saw two miles down the road."

Annie looked at him blankly for a moment.

"Mill Creek Solar Estates," he reminded her. "You must have noticed it by now."

Annie sighed, nodded her head, shrugged her shoulders and resumed painting.

"That goddam Roy Greenleaf is single-handedly destroying this whole county," Sandy added.

"He's got plenty of help. Don't worry."

"He's going to pave over my trout stream."

"I hope not."

"Someone's got to stop these bastards."

"You sound like a character in a science fiction movie."

"Well, you sound mighty goddam complacent about it."

"And what do you propose I do?" She turned back to him sharply, her mouth set in a grim line that made her look suddenly older and indeed quite upset. "Should I go lie down in front of the bulldozers? Huh?"

"No."

"Shoot the workers?"

"Obviously not."

"Well, what then?"

"I don't know," Sandy yielded sheepishly. "You're a property owner out here. Don't you have anything to say about who builds what?"

"No," Annie said. "Not a blessed thing."

"Well, that's depressing. Where'll I go fishing?"

"I don't know, dear heart."

"This tooth is going to drive me crazy."

"You ought to go to see a dentist in that case."

"I know," Sandy agreed dolefully, thinking of how much it would cost, and wishing the pain would magically go away, like a fever breaking, so he could avoid the dentist. Instead of dwelling on it further, which only made it hurt more, he turned his attention to Annie's easel. "Well, what have we here? How nice. A turquoise trailer. You make it look romantic. A pastoral for our times."

"You are in a bitter mood today."

"You know what the trouble with this goddam country of ours is?"

"I'd love to know. Tell me."

"Too much democracy."

"Really," she glanced at him, genuinely surprised. "I always thought it was just the opposite. Not enough."

"Do you know what Thomas Jefferson would do if he saw that dump across the road?"

"I can't imagine. No, wait. He was an intensely curious man, wasn't he? He'd want to know how all those things worked."

"No," Sandy disagreed. "First, he would have puked."

Annie winced. "What has gotten into you today?" she asked.

Sandy was about to explain his desperate need for an additional $150 to pay the rent he owned Roy Greenleaf, but he suddenly saw it as only one component of something much larger that was afflicting him, something as yet unclear, and therefore very ominous. And at the same time, he realized that he could not bring himself to ask Annie for a loan for fear that it might further and fundamentally alter things between them. Finally, he just stared into the grass and mumbled, "I don't know. Things have sort of got me down."

Annie looked at him with concern, dipped her brush in a jar of mineral spirits, and then wiped the bristles clean with a rag. "Come inside," she said, taking him gently by the elbow. "I'll put on some tea for us."

Joel Harlowe sat at a small, round, marble-topped table in the Grove Street Bakery, enjoying his breakfast and perusing a couple of newspapers. The bakery was renowned as far away as New York City and Boston for its exquisite French pastries, cakes, and breads. It was very popular with the tourists who flocked to the racetrack in August, and a favorite haunt of Greer girls, who didn't bat an eyelash at its high prices—$2.50 for a plain croissant, for example; $5.00 for a slice of chocolate-whiskey cake and a cup of coffee. Joel breakfasted at the bakery two or three times a week. It was another one of life's luxuries, the indulgence of which he viewed as the sign of a healthy, self-respecting ego.

He finished the last morsel of a buttery almond-filled croissant and turned to the stock quotation pages of *The New York Times*. He did not own any stocks, but he envisioned a future when most certainly he would get into a new line of business, something involving investments. He was growing very dissatisfied with the sort of business associates his current work required him to deal with at the wholesale end: ill-mannered louts, many of them from south of the border, south of the equator even. The big problem in changing businesses would be the Internal Revenue Service. They always wanted to know where your money came from, the nosy bastards. And Joel hadn't yet figured out an angle that would permit him to take the considerable profits amassed from his present business and shift it into stocks and bonds—without having to account for its origins.

One idea he dreamed up was to go out and quietly buy a lot of old gold, old coins, old jewelry, et cetera, and conveniently plant it all near the site of some known old wreck offshore, say off Key West, and take a few friends he could trust down there for a month, say July when the weather was perfect, but before the hurricane season, and make a bunch of dives and bring the stuff up, pretending it was treasure. What queered the scheme, though, was all the attention it would undoubtedly attract. Someone like the goddam *National Geographic* would want to photograph all the stuff, and none of it would be encrusted with that undersea crap that grows on everything, and sooner or later the affair would be exposed for the fraud it was. And even if it miraculously succeeded, the IRS would swoop in before the salt water dried and haul away fifty percent of the booty. It just wouldn't do.

In fact, none of the schemes he had dreamed up so far seemed workable. Perhaps medical school was the answer, after all. As a heart surgeon, he could fabricate all sorts of consultation fees and slowly integrate his business fortune into what would certainly prove to be a lucrative surgical practice. And then, of course, there would be Kelly. He could set her up in some sort of dummy corporation—buying art or something—and sift the rest of the money through that. Wasn't she an art major?

"More coffee, sir?" a pert blond girl, in the bakery uniform of a pink skirt and lacy white blouse, asked him. Joel looked up at her slowly as though he were surfacing from that imaginary fake treasure ship five fathoms down in the briny deep. My God, he thought—taking in her sweet Protestant features, her upturned nose, rosy cheeks, perfect teeth, and pearl ear studs—the creatures are everywhere!

"Did you want some more coffee, sir?" she repeated.

"No, thank you," he told her with a quick smile. "I'll take the check."

When she returned five minutes later with his check, Joel asked her name.

"Jennifer," she said, blushing.

"I'm having a little party at the old casino tonight, Jennifer," he began. "Actually, it's kind of a big party. A moderately large party—"

"I know," she said. "I've heard about it."

"You have?" He reacted brightly, delighted that the affair had already gained renown. "Well, I was wondering if you would like to come to it."

"I'd love to," she said.

"It's a costume party," he told her. "Wear something that you think truly expresses your inner nature."

"Okay," she agreed, as though he had simply asked her to dress in something sporty or green.

"I'll see you at the casino, then, around nine o'clock. Oh, here," he said, proffering the check along with a twenty dollar bill. "Keep the change." The tab had come to $6.45 altogether. The girl just goggled at him as he got up from the little marble table and walked out the door. He loved blowing young girls' minds about as much as he enjoyed anything in the whole wide world.

Joel hopped into his Austin-Healy, motored two blocks up Grove Street to Serpentine, and pulled in the driveway between Edmund Black's house and Sandy's place. Much as it depressed him, he could think of no other friends besides George or Sandy on whom he could rely to help him out with this party. For one thing, the person left in charge would have to be trusted with a substantial amount of money. The liquor people had to be paid on delivery, the beer guy, the florist, et cetera. George was simply unavailable, so that left Sandy. It would be a fateful test of their friendship, Joel decided. He had to know whether Sandy truly regarded him as a friend, or just sucked up to him as a patron. If Sandy only agreed to do it for money, then Joel would pay him some trifling sum to get the job done, and henceforward would consign him to the ranks of underlings with whom he merely did business, and that would be the end of it. But if Sandy came through as a true-blue friend, well, then there might be a considerable reward in it for him after all.

Joel's mind was churning at such a rate that he failed to even notice that Sandy's bike was not in the driveway. He climbed the five steps to Sandy's side entrance and rang the bell. There was no response. He rang again and tried the doorknob. It was locked. He gave up, descended the steps, and was about to hop back into his car when a voice called out overhead.

"Yum yum yum! Kosher salami!" the voice remarked musically.

Joel glanced upward and flinched slightly at the sight of Edmund leaning over the balcony rail, wearing his silk smoking jacket and what looked like an orange fright wig. "Oh, it's you," Joel eventually said, and with some nervousness.

"It's not who you think, Hymie."

"Isn't that you, Edmund."

"No. I'm his cousin Gladys from Philadelphia."

"Ha ha ha!" Joel feigned a laugh, knowing Edmund to be quite a card, but this particular routine left him rather cold. He didn't think that boys dressing like girls was all that funny. "Have you seen Sandy around this morning?"

"Sandy who?"

"Come on, Edmund."

"It's Gladys."

"Okay, Gladys." Joel unhappily played along. "Have you seen the guy who lives over here in this house."

"That white boy with the motorcycle?"

"That's right."

"He told me his name was Dickie."

"Then you have seen him?" Joel asked.

"No."

"If you haven't seen him, then how could he have told you his name was Dickie?" Joel shot back with the zest of an attorney tripping up a hostile witness. Perhaps law school was the answer, he stopped to muse. What a thrill it would be to outfox the opposition, and for fat fees, too. It might even pay better than medicine, and one could certainly learn all the angles on beating the IRS. Besides, it was less messy than surgery—none of that blood and other gook to get all over you.

"We communicate by brain waves," Edmund said. "Artists are like that, you know. We feel things that normal folks don't."

"Seriously, Edmund, what's with you and this getup?"

"You, of all people, should know. It's Halloween. I'm readying myself for the gala."

"Don't you think it's a little early."

"Honey pie, it took what's-her-name, you know, that Hollywood slut, it took her seven *hours* to get ready for the Academy Awards. I read it in the *Enquirer*. And I haven't even started my nails yet!"

"Well, if you see Sandy, ask him to get in touch with me, huh? Tell him it's important," Joel said, opening his car door.

"Oh, one moment, Binky. Don't leave just yet."

"Binky?"

"Do you mind if I call you Binky?"

"What's wrong with just being ourselves?" Joel asked sincerely.

"I can't stand it anymore," Edmund declared in a suddenly quiet, but firm voice that, for the first time all morning, contained no trace of a put-on dialect. "Wait there. I'll be right down."

He vanished momentarily from the balcony while Joel waited below, uncomfortable with these shenanigans but also somewhat concerned about Edmund's state of mind. In the roughly five years he'd known him, Joel had never seen him act quite so peculiar. A minute later, Edmund appeared in the side door that led into the rear of his house.

"Psssst. Binky," he called in a stage whisper, and gestured at Joel to come. Reluctantly, Joel went over. "Have you any pharmaceuticals on your person, by any chance?" Edmund asked.

"I have a little something," Joel affirmed.

103

"Frankly, what I could use is a stimulant. I must be a victim of tired blood. Iron deficiency anemia, I think they call it on TV. Some rectified essence of the coca tree would go a long way toward relieving the symptoms, I'm sure."

"I can help you out."

"Then do come in."

Joel entered Edmund's kitchen. The incredible chaos of it deeply offended his sense of order, but he didn't say anything about it for fear that Edmund would take it the wrong way and not like him. Few people were as tidy and well organized as he was, Joel realized, and it was unfair to hold the rest of the world to his standards. Besides, in his twisted way, Edmund was a sort of genius—he was certifiably the grandson of a well-known American genius— and persons of that caliber were notoriously sloppy in their personal habits. Of course, the real problem with Edmund, from Joel's point of view, was that he wasn't doing a goddam thing with his God-given genius. It was pathetic. Worse even than George Wells, who at least held a job and took care of his property and had a few healthy outside interests—though unquestionably he was wasting a tremendous education waiting on tables. Sooner or later a person had to take charge of his own life! And what was Edmund doing here in the Springs year after year but pissing away a trust fund? Maybe it was finally getting to Edmund. Perhaps that was what this crazy play-acting was all about. Joel wished he could sit down with Edmund and have a heart-to-heart talk, but if he presumed to advise him, and thereby pass judgment on the way he conducted his life, wouldn't Edmund hate him for it?

Edmund sat down wearily at the kitchen table piled high with papers and indicated that Joel take the other seat.

"You seem a little on edge today, Edmund," Joel observed, reaching into the pocket of his sport jacket for the snorter.

"I always get this way on Halloween," Edmund said, bracing his chin on one hand and fluttering his eyelids.

"There's something bothering you, though, isn't there?"

"Don't play amateur psychiatrist with me, Harlowe. You're a dope dealer, not a headshrinker."

Joel fairly recoiled at this remark, momentarily speechless.

"The happy powder, please," Edmund said. But Joel remained more or less frozen, so Edmund reached for his checkbook and held it up. "Lots of Yankee dollars in here. I'll pay for what you got, if necessary. Come on, Harlowe. I'm a hurtin' buckaroo."

"I hope you don't think I was being presumptuous a moment ago."

"Forget it. The medicine, please."

"I didn't mean to hurt your feelings."

"My feelings, such as they are, were already atatter, and I assure you it has nothing to do with you. But, for God's sake man, give me some of that cocaine before I go completely to pieces."

Joel handed over the snorter.

"God bless you, Binky," Edmund said, fumbling with the device as his hands shook and he attempted to load the outer chamber. Eventually he succeeded, inserted the nipple in one nostril, and inhaled a quarter gram of the drug. His eyes dilated almost at once, and a most serene smile spread across his face. He repeated the operation with the other nostril. "I say!" he exclaimed when he was finished. "It feels just like the old days in the nursery. I'm a newborn babe. Not a care in the world, and everything is beautiful. I'm beautiful. You're beautiful. It's a beautiful day. I don't suppose there's more where this came from?"

"I'll be getting some more this evening," Joel confided, and then with a coy smile added, "a whole lot more."

"This evening," Edmund said, a look of concern clouding the sunny expression he had only just a moment ago acquired. "Why, that's hours and hours away. Good heavens! What will I do in the meantime?"

"Maybe these will tide you over," Joel said, reaching into another pocket and producing a small red plastic pillbox with a screw cap. Within were a dozen black capsules.

"Oh, speed! You dear boy. Something to keep a fellow going when his Wheaties wear off. Gimme, gimme!"

"Why don't you take these four," Joel suggested, carefully picking that number out of the pillbox. Edmund snatched them up and cupped them in his palm. He was about to toss them into his mouth when Joel reached for his forearm. "No! I don't mean take them all at once. These are black beauties, Edmund, for Chrissake."

"Oh, of course."

"Take one when you come down from the coke, and another before you come to the party. And save the others for a rainy day."

"Okay," Edmund said. "You're the doctor."

Joel winced again.

"Say, Edmund, is it all right if I use your phone for a minute."

"Sure. Go ahead," Edmund said, standing up. "I have to go wee-wee anyway." And so saying, he bustled out of the kitchen, leaving Joel alone there.

As soon as Edmund was gone, Joel went over to the phone and direct-dialed a number in New York City, the borough of Queens to be specific. The person he contacted, whom Joel called Roberto, was not entirely comfortable with the English language, while Joel's command of Spanish was tenuous to say the least. Joel had done business with Roberto only twice before, since his previous supplier was shot to death in a multiple slaying that made page one of the *New York Post* back in July. He wanted to buy rather a large quantity, he told Roberto. A half kilo, actually. And on kind of short notice. Late this afternoon or this evening, in fact. Could something like that possibly be arranged? Yes, he could come up with the money. *No problemo*. Where? How about the same place as last time: the long-term parking lot at LaGuardia Airport. *Bueno*? Okay. The same gray van. You bet. Six o'clock. See you then.

Joel hung up, and was startled to see Edmund standing framed in the doorway an arm's length from him.

"It works!" Edmund said.

"The phone?" Joel asked, unsure what Edmund meant.

"Yes. The phone."

"Why? Was there something wrong with it?"

"The motherfucker's been off since yesterday."

"Seems to be working fine now."

"They must have turned it back on," Edmund agreed, looming now above Joel as though using his superior height to make some kind of point, and in a way that made Joel extremely uncomfortable. "Only do me a favor in the future, huh, Harlowe?"

"Sure. What?"

"Don't be making any more motherfucking dope deals on my phone, okay? Use your own phone for that. I've got enough problems without having to spend the next thirty years of my life in some motherfucking Attica prison."

SEVEN

"Edmund says I should glue broken dinner plates to my paintings," Sandy said as Annie took the kettle off the stove and filled a dark brown English teapot with boiling water.

"I had Edmund in Intro to Painting, you know, ten years ago."

"No, I didn't know that."

"I don't think I ever had a brighter student. Or one less willing to commit himself to a single brushstroke. It was like that fear some people have of heights, or of being in a cave. He would literally shake. I suggested cutting images out of magazines and using them instead. I hate to bandy around this overused word, but his collages were brilliant. In the end, though, I had to give him a C because he never picked up a paintbrush."

"Well, he says if I glued plates onto my paintings, my stuff would sell."

"Do you believe that?" Annie asked.

"No."

"I think your instincts are correct."

Annie took two mugs off their hooks above the sink and began filling the first, using a strainer to catch the tea leaves. "None for me, thank you," Sandy told her, and then he had to explain the problem with his tooth again.

"You really ought to see your dentist," she said.

"I know," he agreed sadly. He knew.

The layout inside Annie's renovated schoolhouse was something like Sandy's studio, and the similarity was not a coincidence, for much of what he knew about organizing his own life, he had learned from her in the past five years.

The kitchen at the old schoolhouse's far end was elevated on what had been a platform for the teacher's desk. There was a massive ninety-year-old cast-iron wood-burning cookstove with ornate chromium facings that Annie kept brightly polished, and a small salvaged 1940s refrigerator with the motor outside on top of the box. For dining she had the same beautiful oak table that used to be in the house on Serpentine.

A step down from the kitchen was a sitting area containing more of the antique furniture from the old house: a beautiful horsehair sofa covered in worn, flowery cotton chintz that had belonged to her mother; an old mahogany English butler's table; a Queen Anne wing chair. Library books of all sizes and subjects were piled on the butler's table and on one end of the sofa. Another woodstove, this one with a front-loading hearth, squatted comfortably on a fireproof brick pad in the big room's center. Everything on the other side of this stove to the bedroom wall was Annie's painting studio.

The deep windowsills on each side contained all sorts of curious objects Annie had collected around the property: a horse's skull, birds' nests, a huge gray papery hornet's nest the size of a rugby ball, a collection of songbirds' eggs, miscellaneous feathers, insect galls, a stoneware vase filled with the seed heads of dried wild-flowers, old medicine bottles gone rosy-pink from expo-sure to sunlight. Between two windows on the white wall hung a plaster life mask of her daughter, Jodie, now a junior at Brown.

While Annie put milk and sugar in her tea, Sandy ambled across the studio to the easel. On it was the portrait of a young man, gaunt, with greasy longish hair, a wispy mustache, gold hoop earring, stoned-looking blue eyes, and a purple bandana wrapped around his head—in short, the epitome of a hood. The face emerged from a very dark background in the nineteenth-century manner. The subject wore that look of haughty defiance seen in so many portraits of American Indians by George Catlin, the frontier artist—everywhere, that is, but in the eyes, which looked glazed and bewildered. Still, there was something disturbingly familiar about the face that Sandy couldn't put his finger on.

"Who's this handsome swain?" he inquired, studying the canvas.

"Hurley Toole, the oldest son," Annie said.

An alarm bell went off in Sandy's mind. "I hope you don't let him come here and sit for this."

"Of course I do."

"His younger brother Glen was a regular customer in the wacky ward, you know. He's become the town flasher lately."

"Hurley's not like that." Annie scoffed at the sugges-tion that antisocial behavior runs in families.

"I don't like you being here alone with him."

Annie laughed with some incredulity. "Are you trying to frighten me?"

"You ought to take realistic precautions. This guy's brother is a whacko."

"Well, they do live across the road, dear heart, and if Hurley were to, I dunno, *assault* me, he'd have ample opportunity whether I do his portrait or not, don't you think?"

"I suppose so," Sandy agreed sullenly. "I just don't think you should give him an excuse."

"Hurley's been very nice and helpful to me. He jump-started my car more than once last winter. And they're an extremely interesting clan," she said, bringing her tea and a plate of sweet Italian biscuits down to the sitting area. "Very backwoods."

"Really? You'd think they were a bunch of Manhattan socialites gone native or something."

"Your outlook seems extremely sour this morning."

"I hate that dump across the road and the lowlifes in it," Sandy declared with sudden vehemence that surprised him as much as Annie. "And I wish you did too."

"They may be more primitive than the people you're used to, but they're still human beings."

"Now you sound like a sociologist."

"Oh, come on, Sandy. The truth is you can't stand them because they're poor like you are. So you throw up this wall of contempt in order to feel superior."

The accusation stung him; it was right on the money. "Excuse me," he shot back without much conviction, "you're a psychoanalyst, not a sociologist."

"And you are a pain in the ass today. If you came all the way out here to revile the rest of the human race, then I wish you'd go back to town and come again on a better day."

"Today's my thirtieth birthday," he mumbled with his face to the easel, but Annie heard him clearly nonetheless. He'd meant her to. She put down her teacup and crossed the room to him, placing a hand on his shoulder.

"That's an important day in a person's life," she said gently. "Come, sit with me a while." She took him by the elbow and guided him over to the sofa, Sandy feeling awkward and foolish but also grateful. "I'm sorry, but I forgot all about it."

"I certainly didn't expect you to remember, Annie. It's no big deal."

"I remember the birthday dinner you made last year at the old house, the pumpkin soup and the turkey, and that funny orange cake with the licorice on it, and all your friends, and the splendid time we had," she said, smoothing the hair on his forehead with an index finger. "Forgive me?"

"Nothing to forgive," Sandy told her. She put her arms around him and he clung to her, feeling her warm against him and inhaling the scent of the powder she always used that reminded him of their many nights together.

"Did Robin forget too this year?" she asked.

"No, Robin remembered," he assured her, thinking of Robin pummeling him with the stuffed pine martin and then the frightening way she had looked at the end of his driveway, screaming at him, and all the tendons standing out in her neck.

"How is Robin these days?"

"She's fine," Sandy lied.

"It's been what, two years now?"

"Three," he said.

"That's a long time to be together. Ever think of getting married?"

"Oh, sure. Someday."

"There's a lot to be said for marriage," Annie murmured in his ear. Then he felt her lips on his bare neck, under his ear, and one of her hands gently moving up his thigh. "I've been lonely a long time," she said.

Sandy's heart began to pound, and the desire he felt for her was a longing much deeper than he remembered from the years when they were lovers. But as his heart pounded, the pain in his tooth throbbed with an intensity that nearly brought tears to his eyes, and he forcefully extracted himself from her embrace.

"I'm sorry, Annie," was all he could say.

She brushed a loose lock of gray hair from her eye. "I lost my head," she said with a breathless little laugh that could not fail but seem cheerless.

"This tooth is killing me."

"Of course, your tooth. Do you have a regular dentist?" she asked, reaching again for her teacup. Sandy could see that her hand was shaking. "I can send you to mine."

"I have one," he said. "I'd better go now."

He stood, and then she did likewise a moment later.

"Don't think that I'm a hypocrite," she said, taking one of his hands and holding it between two of hers like a sandwich.

"I know you're not, and I'll always love you, Annie," he said, kissing her chastely on both cheeks, and then she followed him out the door. She stood aside watching him zip up his father's flight jacket, pull on the helmet and then the heavy cycling gloves. She had her arms wrapped around her torso as though she were chilly, and she wore a grimace from looking into the strong sunlight.

"Come back soon?" she said, really a question.

"There's a huge party at the casino tonight," Sandy told her, mounting his motorcycle, exhilarated that he had managed, at least, not to ask her for money after all. "A big Halloween ball."

"I'm too old for parties."

"You are not!" he told her in an almost scolding tone of voice, "and I expect to see you there tonight. The whole goddam town's going to be there. You come!" He let his weight fall on the kick start, and the engine roared back to life. "You gonna be there?"

"Sure," she said, brushing more hair out of her face. "What time?"

"Nine or ten o'clock," he said and turned down Yake Road, leaving her in the quiet yard hugging herself.

One winter, George recalled, a bird flew inside his cottage in the midst of a blizzard. He was carrying in an armload of stovewood on a snowy February evening when something odd and terrifying flew past his shoulder through the door he had just thrown open. He thought it was the very rustle of death itself, because in his childhood one of the nannies his father employed told him and his brother Davey a folktale from her native land about death stalking a man in the guise of a big bird. Its shadow followed the man for weeks, and when death finally overtook him, it descended from the sky like a raptor and carried him away.

The bird loose in his house had only been a wayward partridge crazily seeking shelter from the storm. He'd chased it around the living room, caught it, wrung its neck, and roasted it for his supper. Later he was sorry that he had killed it in such a brutal fashion.

With all these thoughts of birds, George felt himself very much in the presence of death's shadow. He remembered the day his father took him into the library of the family house in Delft and broke the news that his mother was "gone forever." When George asked *where* his mother had gone forever, his father had told him "heaven" with so little conviction that even the five-year-old George was left skeptical. The old man made it sound like the links at the nearby Spirit Lake Country Club, except that the people played harps instead of golf. And yet, he continued to wonder all his life long: where had she gone?

The question beguiled him so much that, sitting in his house late this beautiful Halloween morning, holding the shotgun in his lap, he neared his decision to seek the ultimate answer to it. And so George slowly let the butt of the weapon down until it rested on the floor between his legs. The two barrels appeared, at first, to be twin wells of mystery, a special pair of binoculars, the gazing into which would reveal momentous truths and dazzling new worlds. He took off his right shoe and wiggled his big toe. No problem pulling one of the triggers with it, but could he pull both? He wouldn't know until he tried it, and then he might never know. And what would the moment of impact be like? He imagined it as a sort of blinding blow. Bright light, and then . . .

He heard the sound of a car pulling up his dirt driveway followed by the solid thunk of a door shutting. George looked up from the muzzle of his shotgun like someone awakening from a trance. A shudder ran through him as light footsteps resounded on the front porch and then two timid knocks at the door. He stood up, broke open the breech of the gun, pulled out the shells, and said, "Come in."

Robin Holmes opened the door and stopped short in front of it as her eyes registered the shotgun.

"Bird season," George explained feebly, as though it was something to be ashamed of.

"Are you going hunting?"

"I was thinking of going out. Yes."

"I didn't mean to—"

"You're not."

George now saw that Robin's eyes were red-rimmed

and bloodshot. Her nose too was somewhat red, and she sniffled.

"Really," she said, "If you're—"

"No. Please come in."

She stepped into the living room. George leaned the shotgun beside a bookshelf, but when he straightened up, Robin was groping awkwardly toward him, her face red and distorted, and her arms reaching, all of this resembling the way kids imitate Frankenstein's monster. It unnerved him, and then a moment later she had her arms around him and her face buried in his sweater, sobbing. He could think of nothing else to do just then, except to pet her brown hair and repeat the words, "It's all right, it's all right." As the moments accumulated, he became aware of his longing to embrace her in return, and also of his fear. He wanted to hold her tight, to kiss her weeping eyes and moist cheeks, her small quivering mouth, but he felt that to do so would transgress decency. So, he put one arm around her shoulder and in a brotherly way guided her to the sofa where they both sat down.

"I'm sorry," Robin said between sobs, fishing in her brown leather shoulder bag for the pack of tissues among the reporter's notebooks, pens, aspirin bottles, lip balm tubes, and dozens of other necessaries. "I didn't mean to come here and slobber all over you. I just had to talk to somebody, and you're his best friend."

"It's all right," George assured her, understanding now that the trouble was all about Sandy.

"I don't want to let go of him," she said, and her face became a mask again as the tears resumed and a thin, high-pitched wail came out of her, though she tried to stifle it.

"It's all right," George repeated.

"Tell me," she blurted out, "does he hate me or something?"

"I'm sure he doesn't hate you."

"Then why is he fading out on me like this?"

"He's having a hard time lately," George said, almost choking on emotion as his own despair was overcome by an upsurge of tenderness. Had Sandy simply stopped loving her? George wondered. I would never stop loving you, he thought.

"He must talk to you about it. You're his best friend."

"I saw him this morning," George confessed, and Robin gazed at him very attentively over her tissue while she blew her nose.

"Please tell me what he said."

"Something about being somebody's poodle." George tried to recall Sandy's exact words, without being too specific, without betraying his confidence, and wondering at the same time why he should play dumb when Sandy's actions could speak for themselves, and the truth was that he, George, loved this girl with all his heart and had for years, never letting on.

"It's in his head," she said helplessly. "I just want to help him whatever way I can."

"I guess it only reminds him what a hard time he's having," George said. Her closeness intoxicated him, made his head swim, like the way it was after a grouse flushed in his face and he watched the bird wing away without even lifting his gun to his shoulder.

"Maybe you're right. I've pushed too hard," she said.

"I know he still loves you," George said. "You can tell by the way he talks about you. I could tell."

"You're a sweet, wonderful man," she said, reaching for his hand and squeezing it damply. "I really shouldn't have come here just to dump all this on you."

"It's all right," he said, paralyzed with longing for her.

"I'm embarrassed."

"Don't be."

"May I ask you a personal question, George?"

"Sure."

She hesitated as though composing it in her head, and then, in a tone that was rather journalistic, asked: "How come you don't have a steady girl?"

"The right one hasn't come along," he lied, still unwilling to take advantage.

"One will."

"I guess so."

"Sure, she will." Robin nodded her head, sniffling. "You're such a sweet man," she said, the tears starting all over again, and she bowed her head, leaning toward his chest as though seeking to bury her face against it again. But somehow she collected herself and stood up instead, saying, "I'd better go now."

He stood too, barely able to speak. "All right."

Blowing her nose, she made her way to the door, a little wobbly on her feet.

"I don't know if you can tell, but you've made me feel a lot better," she said from the doorway.

"I'm glad you feel better, Robin."

"I guess I'll just back off for a while and let him work out whatever it is he has to work out—huh?"

"That's right," he said.

"Well, thanks, George. Hey, if you ever want to come over and slobber on my shoulder, go ahead," she said with a plucky laugh.

"Okay," he said, trying to smile back.

Then she was gone, the door shut, her engine starting and fading back up Marcy Street toward town. A feeling of tremendous emptiness welled within him while the crows cawed in the cornfield across the way. His eyes, arcing in woe as he turned back into the room, fastened once again on the shotgun propped beside the bookshelf.

The birds outside seemed to be shrieking inside his own head. Just then he heard another car roll in his driveway. Thinking it was Robin returning for one reason or another—because he had made her feel so good?—he rushed to the door and threw it open, only to see a tall, slightly paunchy, but good-looking man in a beige corduroy suit climb out of a burgundy-colored German automobile.

The man's modishly long, dark hair tousled in the breeze, and he wore his paisley foulard necktie loose at the throat, the top button undone, affording him the casual, slightly rumpled look of someone too successful to bother about his appearance after donning the correct attire. He carried a battered, overstuffed, leather folio case with no handle clamped under his left arm. George recognized him at once because the man was a regular customer at the Feedlot where George worked. He ate dinner there at least once a week, usually a party of four—him, his wife and another couple—and he always picked up the tab. His name was Roy Greenleaf.

"Hi," he said, approaching the porch with a hand outstretched as though to shake, then forthrightly mounting two of the four steps to the porch where George stood. Greenleaf wore a smile with the same casual confidence as his apparel. "You're George Wells," he said, shaking George's hand vigorously.

"That's right."

The visitor formally introduced himself, then said, "I've seen you at the steak place downtown."

"I work there," George said, and all of a sudden it pained him to admit that he worked there, as though it had only begun to dawn on him that it was an ignominious position.

"Seems to me you've been our waiter a few times over the years."'

"Guess I have."

119

"Nice little spread you've got here," Greenleaf said, indicating the cottage, barn, and garden with one economical sweep of his arm.

"Thanks."

"You own it, huh."

"Yes, I do. How do you know that?"

"I inquired at the county clerk's office," Greenleaf said, refurbishing his confident smile. "I'm in the real estate business. Public records are one of the tools available to us."

George nodded his head in a provisional way and hooked his hands behind his belt in the back of his pants.

"I'd like to buy your place," Greenleaf said, just like that.

"It's not for sale," George told him, marveling at the visitor's audacity.

"Maybe you just haven't thought about it in those terms," Greenleaf slyly suggested with another smile, this one more boyish, meant to disarm.

"I haven't thought about selling it in any terms," George said.

"That's exactly what I'm here to talk about: terms," Greenleaf said with a salesman's ebullience, and quickly extracted from his leather folio case a green vinyl-covered loose-leaf binder, his corporate checkbook. "I'll pay you sixty thousand for the whole spread."

George's mouth opened several centimeters, though he did not reply.

"Okay, seventy thousand," Greenleaf said. "You've done some nice things with the property. I remember when this place was a dump. I wish I'd had the foresight to buy it then."

"Why didn't you?"

"At the time it didn't figure into my plans. We grow. We change. We develop new plans."

"How does it fit into your plans now?"

"Well, I've purchased thirty-four acres around your place. It's a horseshoe-shaped parcel, actually. Literally surrounds you."

George glanced over at the neighbor's cornfield in the distance to his left.

"What are you planning to do with it?" he asked.

"Build solar homes here."

"I like it the way it is."

"I can understand that. But it's going to change. Seventy-five thousand."

"You've got a lot of gall."

The wattage of Greenleaf's smile increased again, evidently construing George's charge as a compliment.

"Eighty. That's as high as I go," he said, extracting a gold Cross pen from his shirt pocket and opening the loose-leaf binder to a page of fresh checks. "You can take this right down to the North Country Trust this afternoon and cash it if you like."

George recoiled slightly.

"I'm not going to sell you this property so you can throw up a bunch of crummy tract houses on it," he said.

"They're not crummy, George," Greenleaf said, as though the remark hurt his pride. "These are very well built homes, designed by a top architectural firm, aesthetically beautiful, with the latest in passive solar technology, and environmentally correct down to the composting toilets. This is not Levittown we're talking about. These will be expensive homes. Nice people will live here—high income professionals. Ninety thousand, George."

"Forget it."

"You drive a hard bargain, my friend."

"I'm not your friend."

"A hundred thousand," Greenleaf said, still smiling.

"One tenth of a million dollars. That's my final offer, George."

"It's guys like you who are fucking over this country."

"That's a very unfair charge, George," Greenleaf said, his smile finally vanishing, replaced by a look of high-minded earnestness. "Excelsior Springs is growing, like the rest of the United States. You can't wish away this kind of growth. Every day there are more people. People have to live somewhere. I'm doing my level best to provide them with first-rate housing that goes easy on the environment and looks terrific. It's guys like me who are saving this country from guys who are much worse. Believe me, George. If you think what I'm doing is so bad, why don't you just take the hundred thou and buy yourself a much bigger hunk of acreage further out. Buffer yourself. That way you'll be happy, I'll be happy, and the nice people who buy these homes will be happy."

"Sorry," George said, crossing his arms and shaking his head, even as he thought about the abandoned farm up at Indian Hill and wondered whether $100,000 might cover the price of renovating it. "No deal."

"Tell you what I'm going to do, George. I'm going to make out a check for a hundred thousand and leave it here with you. If you decide to change your mind, give me a call."

Greenleaf finished writing the check and proffered it to George. But since George wouldn't take it, Greenleaf rolled it up and inserted it in an iron curlicue of a porch support. Then he briskly saluted George and strode purposefully back to his elegant car. George could only marvel at Greenleaf as he departed, as though he had just been visited by a shrewd and fascinating incarnation of the devil, like some character out of an American folktale.

Edmund Black, feeling about as chipper as he had all day, put on a pair of baggy chino pants and fished around in a plastic laundry basket for a shirt that was tolerably clean. He found a pink oxford in passable condition, donned a cream-colored cardigan sweater, and went back downstairs. In the kitchen, he swallowed one of the four amphetamine capsules that Joel had given him, stuck his checkbook in his back pocket, and finally left the house via the rear door.

In the small backyard, Edmund's pink and gray 1956 Cadillac sat rusting in the weeds on four flat tires. He hadn't driven it in over a year, since his driver's license was revoked on a third DWI conviction. Being outside his house made him feel vaguely uneasy, but nevertheless he forged ahead toward downtown on foot. At the corner of Serpentine and Catherine, Joe Sloat asked him if he thought the rain would hurt the rhubarb and Edmund answered by saying, in a sort of Bengali accent, "I am very happy to be in your country too. Merry Christmas."

He passed Glen Toole, still enjoying the October sunshine on the stoop of his rooming house, and with growing unease walked through the Slough of Despair. Crossing Burgoyne Street and then ascending the Street of Dreams to Broadway, his mouth grew dry and his palms began to sweat. By the time he turned the corner onto the town's main drag, he was experiencing some very peculiar thoughts and feelings indeed. He began to think that the gravitational force which held everything and everybody else to the surface of the earth was about to fail him, and that his body might somehow leave the earth and fly out into space. Other moments he got the equally strange idea that it might be possible for him to sink through the sidewalk, as though it were made of marshmallow, and be swallowed up by the earth. He crossed the busy main street, Broadway, too preoccupied with his snowballing fear to even watch where he was going, and almost walked right into the front of a pickup truck loaded with cordwood. The driver's angry horn blast reawakened him briefly, but then, on the other side of the street, he felt the strange sensation that the sidewalk was undulating like the floor of a fun house. It made him feel seasick, walking on land. His mind was rushing so fast and in so many directions that he was afraid he was going to lose control of it forever, that he was on the brink of some terrible mental catastrophe, the sudden onset of insanity. The oddest thing about this many-faceted terror was that he had gone through it at least a hundred times before.

In a panic now, Edmund hurried along the sidewalk past Larch's Luncheonette and the Working Man's Clothing Shop toward the white limestone Corinthian-columned entrance to the North Country Trust building on the corner. He was oblivious to the passing pedestrians, including many Greer girls enjoying the noon sunshine, and here and there a child in a goblin getup. He made it through the door to the bank, but in the vestibule between it and an inner set of doors another wave of panic overtook him, and he conceived a sudden horror of proceeding another step. Equally afraid of going back outside, he pressed himself against the inner marble wall and hyperventilated while his heart raced, and he stammered some lines of a prayer from the Bible over and over to himself: *"My God, my God, why hast thou forsaken me? Why art thou so far from helping me, and from the words of my roaring . . . ?"* He had come across the 22nd Psalm his freshman year at Greer, in the awful hours after his big brother Billy was killed in a car crash in Massachusetts, when it was all Edmund could do to keep his world from flying to pieces. It perfectly summarized all the terrors and confusions of his days on earth, and it served ever since as his personal, secret prayer.

At that very moment, Robin Holmes, on her way back to the office from George Wells's house, stopped in the bank in order to deposit her weekly paycheck. She was naturally concerned to find Edmund huddled against the wall of the vestibule, and in such an apparently abnormal state, trembling and waxy-looking.

"Are you okay?" she asked cautiously, wondering if he had seen her coming and was about to spring some kind of Halloween gag on her—for he was acting a little bit like a character in a horror movie undergoing one of those momentous transformations from man to beast.

"I'm scared, I'm scared," was all he said.

"Did you take some kind of drug, Edmund?" she asked.

"Yes. No. I don't know," he said quickly, and as he spoke, a greasy young man in garage mechanics togs entered the bank and passed through the vestibule, but not before casting a fishy, hateful glance Edmund's way. "I've got to get out of here," he said, looking positively stricken.

"Here. Take my hand and follow me."

Before he could protest, she led him inside the bank, across the teller's floor to a side door, and out onto High Street, around the corner from Broadway. Behind the bank was a parking lot. At the edge of the lot, separating it from the sidewalk, was a raised concrete planting bed that held several small ornamental mountain ash trees with their clusters of bright red berries and some lesser shrubs.

"Sit here," Robin said, guiding Edmund down onto the concrete lip, which was just about the same height as a park bench. Edmund sat beside Robin, continuing to hold her hand. "Take long, even breaths through your nose and breathe out through your mouth," she told him.

He did as she said. In a little while Edmund's heartbeat returned to normal and the feeling of panic receded like physical pain, which is either felt or not felt, and ceases to terrify once it is gone.

"Feeling better?"

Edmund nodded his head, then said, "Yes, thank you," in a voice somewhat raspy with dryness.

"What'd you take?"

"Nothing really. A little speed," he said, omitting the cocaine that he was coming down from, not to mention the marijuana he had been smoking all morning. "I'll be okay now. Just a little anxiety attack. I have them all the time."

"For how long?"

"A few minutes. It's nothing really—"

"No, I mean since when?"

"Oh. Well, honey pie, for years. Centuries, it seems like." His long brown face drooped from the effort of trying to appear blithe. "Ever since my brother got killed ten years ago," he admitted with a shuddery sigh.

"Why, Edmund, I had no idea."

"I cover it up nicely, don't I?"

Robin couldn't bring herself to agree. "What happened to him?"

"Car crash in Cambridge. Some drunken honkie crushed his Volkswagen. The honkie lived."

"I didn't even know you had a brother."

"He was the serious one, like our exalted grandpa. A senior at Harvard."

"I'm sorry, Edmund."

"Well, it was ages ago, after all."

"Isn't there something you can do about these anxiety attacks?"

"Keep you by my side to hold your hand and listen to your gentle voice."

"No, really."

"It helped a lot today. I assure you."

"I'm glad it helped. But Edmund, maybe taking speed isn't such a good idea for someone with this kind of problem."

"I confess, it does seem to boost the unpleasantness of your basic anxiety attack. But to tell you the truth, I wasn't exactly planning to have one. It always comes on like a big surprise."

To Robin, Edmund's spirit wasn't rebounding so much as going back into hiding.

"There you are," he gestured actorishly, slipping into the Noel Coward mannerisms, "walking merrily down the street on a fine fall day like any poor slob when some vagrant little thought intrudes, leading to a slightly more horrible thought, and before you know it, the adrenal glands are running amuck. A nasty business. Staying stoned helps, but you're right about the speed. I shouldn't have et it. Harlowe practically forced the shit down my throat. Speaking of Miss Harlowitz, have you got your gown for tonight's gala?"

"I'm not going."

"What! Why not? Because that white boy you go with talked trash to you?"

"And I don't 'go with' that white boy anymore, either."

"A shocking development. But then every cloud has its silver lining. For example, I happen to still be available. Come to the ball with me."

"That's very sweet of you, Edmund, but I think I'll just stay home tonight."

"And sulk? While the rest of the world waltzes the night away?"

"I'll read or watch TV."

"I won't hear of it. You must come on my arm."

"Thanks, Edmund, but I really just want to be by myself tonight."

"It's not because of this, is it?" he said, pointing to his face.

"Because of what?" She didn't get it.

"You don't know what I'm referring to?"

"No."

"Well then, never mind."

"Are you going to be okay now?" she said, standing up.

"Oh yes. Just sitting here with you has worked wonders."

"I have to get back to the office."

"If you change your mind about the gala, remember I'm available."

"I will," she said, and bent down to kiss him on the cheek.

"I'd blush," he said as she left him among the plantings, "if it were possible."

Sandy returned to his house on Serpentine from Locust Grove, shivering as he got off the motorcycle, and mounted the steps to find a note from Joel stuck in the door jamb. "Call me. Urgent. Harlowe," the note said. He grabbed a handful of mail out of the nearby box, and without bothering to look through it, hurried upstairs and dialed Joel's number, but once again there was no answer.

His tooth was anesthetized from the cold ride, but he was afraid that it would start aching again at any moment. So he quickly crossed the big room to the oak flat file and took out a loose-leaf binder of several clear vinyl pages with pockets that contained the slides of all his paintings. The paintings themselves were stored on an overhead rack he had made by laying a plywood sheet across three ceiling joists. He selected five slides of paintings that he

would be willing to trade with Roy Greenleaf for a month's
rent, put them in a small yellow cardboard Kodak box,
and was about to depart for Greenleaf's office at the mall,
when he stopped to call George.

"You won't believe what I saw a little while ago out
in Locust Grove," he said when George picked up the
phone at his end after three rings.

"What did you see?"

"They're building a goddam housing development
right on top of Mill Creek."

"You're kidding."

"No. I couldn't believe it. They've already bulldozed
about ten acres of woods in there."

"This is terrible," George said.

"And you know who's doing it?"

"Who?"

"My goddam landlord—Greenleaf. His development
company—"

At that moment, a loud squeal of tires cut through the
quiet noon air somewhere outside on Serpentine Street. It
was followed directly by an elongated and baleful human
scream. Even George heard it over the phone.

"What the hell was that?" he asked.

"I don't know," Sandy said, his fear rapidly mounting, along with the pain in his tooth. "I hope it wasn't my
cat, though. I better get off. I'll call you back later." The
scream resounded a second time.

He hung up. Grabbing his gloves and helmet, he
rushed downstairs and out of the house. In the middle of
Serpentine Street, Mrs. Nethersole knelt over the body of
Champion, who lay beside the left front wheel of a telephone company service van. The dog lay inert, and as
Sandy slowly approached, he could see a small stream of
bright red blood flow from its dark, leathery nose. The
driver of the truck, a thin young man in his twenties

wearing a company shirt, took off his yellow plastic hard hat and appealed to the members of the small crowd that was now gathering—including Sandy, Joe Sloat, motorists from both lanes who had left their cars to see what happened, and several passing pedestrians—as though they were a jury.

"It just walked right into the truck," the telephone man tried to explain to the crowd of horrified strangers.

"Murderer!" Mrs. Nethersole screamed at him. "Murderer!"

EIGHT

K elly Seagraves couldn't wait for her eleven o'clock Color and Composition class to end. Of all the boring, dippy courses, she thought, as she looked with dismay at her current assignment, which was to divide a canvas into small squares using only one color, plus white and black, in gradations of tone. Her canvas—like the canvases of her fourteen classmates—looked like a kind of checkerboard. She had chosen the color green, and the checks she had painted ranged in tint from greenish-black at the lower left to swimming-pool-green toward the upper right. In the hour and fifteen minutes that had elapsed so far, she had filled in 103 of the 144 squares her canvas was divided up into, and as she wiped off her brushes, she hated the idea that she would have to finish the stupid project on Monday. She knew she'd have to finish it because the prof, Charles Brickley, was a punctilious asshole who graded you for *everything*. Brickley was forty-four years old, bald, myopic, and sluglike from a lifetime of physical inactivity. To sleep with the man even once would be totally out of the question, Kelly thought with a shudder, though she enjoyed teasing him by wearing baggy V-necked sweaters he could peer down the front of—and he always did.

She wanted to paint big wild messy pictures like Julian Schnabel, the famous young art superstar whose incredible New York City loft was featured in *House & Garden*. She had an idea for a monumental work of her own, something that would involve getting a lot of the crap from her home in Greenwich, Connecticut, and gluing it or screwing it onto the painting surface. She envisioned the entire contents of her room back home—all her old stuffed toy animals and outmoded playthings, a lot of records by dumb bands she could no longer listen to, her ant farm, her ice skates, her horseback riding ribbons, her sailing trophy from the club—all fastened onto a giant painting that she would title "Kelly's Passage." In the meantime, dumb assignments like this were driving her crazy.

Brickley kept the class to the last possible moment, as usual, after they'd all cleaned up, rambling on about the need to *really understand* color, how crucial it was, and how nothing they ever did would "amount to beans" unless they grasped these fundamental principles. He became so emotional about it that his face turned a curious shade of grayish red, and Kelly imagined one of these pedantic tirades someday bringing on a heart attack. She knew it was a wicked thought, but she couldn't help wishing it would strike him sooner rather than later, because the course was required for the degree, and she wasn't sure she could last the semester with Brickley teaching it.

At half past twelve, the class mercifully came to an end, and like a prisoner sprung from some miserable house of detention, Kelly fled McAuliffe Hall, the fine arts building, and wended her way across the sunstruck campus to Griggs Hall, the student union and snack bar. There she went to get lunch and meet three of her friends whose fall class schedules permitted a regular Friday get-together. From the cashier's counter—where she paid for an order of french fries, a diet Coke, and a brownie—Kelly spied them at their usual table near the jukebox.

The other three were Molly Kinlock, Betsy Rowe, and Liz Coffin. Molly, pale-skinned with short black hair, vaguely Eurasian features, and clay-splotched hands, was a fellow art major. Betsy, Kelly's suitemate in the Hildebrand dormitory, was a freckled blonde, an American Studies major who had gone to Colorado for the U.S. Ski Team tryouts the year before and had blown out her left knee on the first slalom run. Now she swam a lot. Liz, nicknamed "Lizard," was brown-haired, tall, with prominent teeth, a figure like a boy, majored in English (Creative Writing), and had a grandfather who controlled the largest bank in the state of New Hampshire.

"All right, who's going where with who this weekend?" Liz began in a world-weary tone of voice, as though she were calling to order a meeting of the world's oldest and most exclusive club—and then noisily slurped the icy remnants of her chocolate shake through a straw.

Betsy: "I was thinking of going up to Burlington."

Kelly: "What's happening up there?"

Betsy: "Fall Sprawl at UVM. They've got football and everything."

Molly: "I wish we had football. It's so . . . I don't know . . . normal."

Betsy: "Greer's got dick."

Liz: "Not enough of it, if you ask me. And what little there is has got one hell of an attitude problem."

Molly: "I love the way the players touch each other on the fanny after one of them does something fabulous."

Kelly: "I see that around here all the time."

Betsy: "This place is pathetic."

Liz: "No doubt about it, we have *the* absolute worst, the scuz, the bottom-of-the-barrel men of any school in the northeast. Name a place that's worse."

Kelly: "Sarah Lawrence."

Molly: "I think they only have like a hundred guys."

Kelly: "And all twinkies. I mean, to a man."

Molly: "You'd think a school that cost like fifteen thousand a year could at least have football."

Liz: "They should *hire* a fucking team."

Betsy: "That's what we need here, all right: a fucking team."

(Giggles all around.)

Liz: "No, I mean it. What do you need? Some helmets and shoulder pads, right? I'd pay for the goddam equipment myself."

Kelly: "They'd need a few balls, of course."

Liz: "More than a few, dearie."

Molly: "Don't forget those tight pants. Honestly, I'd like to know how they get into those pants."

Kelly: "Go up to UVM with Betts and maybe you'll discover the secret."

Liz: "I think they use this thing that looks like a giant shoehorn."

Molly: "Jeff VonWaggoner and his roommates are supposedly having some kind of Halloween open house thing tonight."

Liz: "Speaking of the bottom of the barrel, I wouldn't sit in the same class with Jeff VonWaggoner in it, let alone go to his domicile. Ycchhh. A sleaze."

Molly: "At least he's straight."

Liz: "He's like our Labrador retriever, Pancho. He'll stick his little thingie anywhere."

Molly: "How do you know it's so little."

Liz: "It must be, the way he acts."

Betsy: "A total slime."

Liz: "And those roommates of his. Please! Dopey, Mopey, and Shithead."

Kelly: "There's this huge party tonight at the casino in town."

Betsy: "I heard something about it at the Black Rose. It sounded like a townie kind of thing."

Kelly: "Well, sort of. I met this guy who's actually throwing it—"

Betsy: "He's a dealer, I heard."

Liz: "What? A car dealer?"

Betsy: "No, a dope dealer."

Molly: "So, who is this mystery man?"

Kelly: "His name is Joel Something-or-other. I'm sure you've seen him in the bars. I know I have before. Kinda short, dark hair, preppy-looking, Jewishy. Anyway, last night I met him. He had some really super coke, and he acted kind of like someone who, you know, would deal the stuff."

Liz: "Like how?"

Kelly: "Sort of intense, nervous, an insecure kind of slightly paranoid way about him, but real eager to please. Charming, almost, but like a little boy. Very much into material things. I don't know. But nice. It sounds like a huge party. And he invited me to it."

Molly: "As his date?"

Kelly: "No, just to come. Hey, you guys could come as my dates."

Liz: "Do you have to wear a costume for it or what?"

Kelly: "I don't know. We could just go as a bunch of

Greer sluts. I have this incredibly slinky Karl Lagerfeld my mom gave me that I haven't had a chance to wear once."

Molly: "But, God, Kel, *townies!*"

Kelly: "He was pretty okay. They'll probably be the better sort of townies, anyway. It'll be amusing, getting all dressed up. I bet we could really fuck their minds."

Liz: "Why stop there?"

The police cruiser arrived at the scene minutes after Champion was struck down, but there was really nothing to do about it except take some names for the record. The driver of the telephone truck was not charged with anything, and the policeman thought it wise to send him on his way since Mrs. Nethersole would not stop shrieking "Murderer!" at him. Then, it was simply the officer's duty to get traffic moving again on Serpentine Street, and it was Sandy who volunteered to carry the body away, that is, into the Nethersole's house.

Mr. Nethersole, a small, pear-shaped man wearing his retiree's outfit of wool pants, red plaid flannel shirt, and green suspenders, and moving with frail deliberation, placed a wad of paper towels under Champion's bloody muzzle where the dog lay on the Formica kitchen table, and then stroked its inert, piebald flank as though consoling it for the terrible indignity that it had suffered. Mrs. Nethersole, pale and gaunt, stood further off in a corner by the sink, dabbing her eyes and nose with a tissue held in one hand and clutching herself with the other.

"Well, I guess I better find a box," Mr. Nethersole said. He went down to the basement and returned shortly with a blue pasteboard storage box about three feet by two by two deep. It smelled of mothballs. "Help me put him in here."

Sandy helped the old man place the dog in the box. Then Mr. Nethersole went into the front parlor and returned with a handful of oddments: a rawhide bone, an ancient gray tennis ball, and a dirty yellow object that Sandy took a few moments to recognize as a rubber rabbit. "His things," Mr. Nethersole explained, placing them alongside Champion, and then manipulated the body so that Champion appeared to be sleeping peacefully.

Each taking an end, Sandy and the old man slowly carried the box outside into the back yard. Mrs. Nethersole followed, but not until some minutes later. By that time, her husband had gotten a long-handled shovel from the detached garage. He started digging a hole in the grass under a lilac bush. Sandy said he would do it, since the job was obviously a great strain on Mr. Nethersole, but the old man insisted on breaking the sod and turning over a few shovelfuls of earth. Then he handed the tool to Sandy, who took off his father's flight jacket and commenced to dig Champion's grave.

It took him nearly half an hour to dig a hole large enough to accommodate the box. After they lowered it down, both Mr. and Mrs. Nethersole picked up a handful of earth and cast it onto the blue lid. Finally, Sandy filled in the hole and heaped the excess dirt in a mound on top. For another few moments all three of them stood silently before the mound, and Sandy was surprised to feel Mrs. Nethersole squeeze his hand and say, "He loved you very much, too."

"Is it all right if I wash up in your kitchen?" Sandy asked.

Both Nethersoles nodded and said to go ahead. While washing his hands and cleaning Champion's blood off his father's jacket, Sandy became aware of how much his tooth hurt again. There was a plastic bottle of extra-strength aspirin over the kitchen sink, and he swallowed four of the pills.

Edmund Black, his anxiety attack behind him and his nerve clusters tintinabulating to the twenty milligrams of biphetamine now fully absorbed into his system, decided to forego another visit to the bank. Instead he proceeded to the nearby Top Shopper Supermarket where, thinking of all the goblins who would visit his house as the day wore on, he purchased eleven bags of various candy treats and paid by check. From there he set out for several retail establishments on Broadway, buying lipstick, mascara, eyeliner, and nail polish at Phelps Pharmacy, acquiring two Wynton Marsalis albums and Bach's Mass in B Minor at the Sound-O-Rama record outlet, picking up copies of the new *Interview, Vanity Fair, Rolling Stone, Life,* and *People* magazines at Bookworks, and stopping off at the Black Rose Cafe for a vodka and tonic (tall, in a shaker glass, with a side of ice-water—he was *so* thirsty!), paying for everything along the way with personal checks.

His thirst slacked, Edmund departed the Black Rose for The Little Match Girl shop two doors down Catherine Street. The Little Match Girl was a secondhand clothing store operated by Gwen Chapman, who had come to Excelsior Springs with her boyfriend and baby as part of the great hippie invasion of the sixties, and who now, at thirty-eight, was a grandmother, though she looked and acted much like the leggy, red-haired macrobiotic cutie she had been the year of Woodstock. The boyfriend (and father) was long gone, of course, and her eighteen-year-old married daughter, Starr, was a born-again Christian. Gwen made a precarious living from the shop, where she sold a lot of funky antique dresses, accessories, and rhinestone baubles to the Greer girls and took in sewing jobs on the side, for she was a talented seamstress and liked the work. Among the jobs she had taken in lately was an assignment from Joel Harlowe to construct his Halloween costume.

The costume he had ordered was an old-fashioned military uniform in the style of an officer in Napoleon Bonaparte's hussars. What he wanted, generally speaking, was something ineffably dashing. He had shown Gwen a book of heroic historical paintings by Delacroix and Gericault, and asked her to whip up something like the brave cavalrymen wore in those scenes of glorious battle. Price was no object, he said. So, for $500, not including the cost of materials (a bargain, Joel thought), she made him an officer's tunic in forest green wool with gilt-frogged buttonholes and epaulets and a scarlet satin lining to go with a pair of snow-white knee breeches and a dueling shirt. Joel would supply the riding boots and other accessories—sword, gorget, antique pistol. Gwen even suggested adding a tall, fur-covered hat for another $100, but Joel didn't like hats. They were hot and messed up his hair.

Post-noontide this day of the Halloween ball, however, and in direct connection with his soon-to-be-legendary last-minute errand to New York City, Joel had decided to scrap the hussar's uniform and had come down to Gwen's shop to persuade her to make him another, simpler costume, something that would fit underneath his motorcycle leathers: the emblematic uniform of Robin Hood. At first Gwen was crestfallen, thinking of the twenty-three hours she had already put in, and wondering what she had done wrong—for the uniform came out splendidly, she thought—and worrying whether he'd pay what he'd promised. But Joel allayed her worries. He convinced her that the whole thing represented merely a sudden and radical change of plans. To make the point, he took ten one hundred dollar bills out of his billfold and stuck them in the jar on the counter where she kept odd antique rhinestone buckles, and Gwen immediately took up her tape measure.

"What should I do with the other outfit?" she asked, remeasuring his shoulders, and he said to just hold it for him in the shop, when Edmund Black walked in the door.

"Binky! What a surprise!" Edmund cried, putting down his many packages on the counter.

"Hello, Edmund," Joel replied guardedly.

"Gwen, my blushing peach, I am in need of something to wear to you-know-who's little soiree tonight. Have you any glad rags I might try on?"

"How about a French cavalry general's uniform? Never been worn," she said.

"I think not. Some kind of airy confection is more what I'm in the market for. You know, like a prom dress."

"A dress? For Chrissake, Edmund," Joel said, appalled.

"Sweetheart, it's Halloween after all. And the invitation did say to wear something that reflects your inner nature."

"Is that what you want people to think about you?" Joel shot back, unable to conceal his disapproval.

"Honey pie, I don't give a flying fuck what people think. That's their problem. Besides, they already think I'm a jungle bunny. Oh look!" he cried, moving among the racks and pulling out a 1962 vintage gown in cantaloupe-colored taffeta with great sprays of tulle along the neckline and an asteroid belt of sequins corkscrewing up the bodice. "This is too much!" He first held the garment out at arm's length so as to examine it in full, and then held it up to his shoulders. "May I try it on?"

"Go ahead," Gwen said. She was used to this kind of thing. For instance, Terry Batey, who was saving up for his sex-change operation, was one of her regular customers.

"I can't believe he's doing this," Joel muttered as Edmund vanished into the changing room at the rear of the shop. His cocaine buzz was wearing off, and he was rapidly descending into a foul humor. The snorter was empty, and he was anxious to go home and replenish his supply. "You promise you can have this outfit ready for me by three-thirty?" he asked Gwen.

"Oh, sure," she said. "The jerkin itself is a piece of cake, and the pants are just green tights."

"Green tights?" Joel said with renewed dismay.

"The same thing that Errol Flynn wore in the movie." Gwen tried to reassure him, picking up on his extreme sensitivity to anything that cast doubt on a person's virility—Joel's or anyone else's.

"All right," Joel said glumly. "What'll I do for shoes?"

"What's your size?"

"Eight medium."

"I'll find something for you," Gwen said.

"Okay, then, I'll come back later this afternoon," Joel mumbled. He turned to depart the shop just as Edmund burst out of the changing room at the rear, wearing the prom dress.

"Is it me, or what?" he asked ebulliently, vamping in the outfit, touching himself under the empty built-in bra cups and twirling like a $150-per-hour model on a Seventh Avenue runway.

Joel stood beside the door, his mouth screwed into a scowl of reproach, his head starting to pound from the lack of cocaine. "If you want my honest opinion, Edmund"—he spoke with pained abandon—"I think you're going to make a fucking spectacle of yourself."

"Oh, goodie," Edmund exclaimed, clapping his hands.

"Really, if I were you, I'd think twice about it."

"All right," Edmund said, bringing the knuckle of his index finger to his mouth in the manner of a quiz show contestant searching his mind for the answer to a question with an immense sum of money at stake. After a few

141

seconds, he turned back to Joel, an incandescent look in his eyes.

"Well . . . ?" Joel asked, hopefully.

"I'll take it!" Edmund said.

Had the dog seen him return from Annie's? Sandy wondered, as he climbed back on his motorcycle to go see Roy Greenleaf up at North Country Mall. Was Champion crossing the street to visit him when the truck ran him down? Sandy felt sick to his stomach. Maybe I shouldn't have petted him all those times he came over, he reproached himself. For what was it but a simple case of operant conditioning? He had reinforced the animal's behavior to keep crossing a dangerously busy street, long after the animal was capable of it. He had killed the dog as surely as if he had been behind the wheel of the telephone company truck. But the dog had loved him, Mrs. Nethersole herself had said. Obviously she didn't blame him. And wasn't Champion awfully old? Ancient! And don't we all have to go sooner or later? Still, Sandy couldn't help feeling directly responsible for the dog's death.

With the box of slides in the pocket of his father's flight jacket, Sandy rode across town for the third time that day. To the west, beyond the pigeon-filled cupola of the town hall, puffy clouds boiled off the horizon like a sky out of a painting by Constable. He swung right onto Broadway. Two blocks north of High Street, the town's main intersection, Broadway came to a V.

The left fork, called North Broadway, was the town's most exclusive neighborhood, a wide, tree-lined street of enormous old mansions in every conceivable nineteenth-century style, which ultimately led to the front entrance of the Greer campus. The right fork was Mall Road, a new, two-mile-long auto corridor built over a defunct Delaware and Hudson Railroad right-of-way, dotted by fast-food franchises, a muffler shop, a car wash, a drive-in bank, a footwear factory outlet, and a Mini-mart grocery store—all of it thrown up in the five years since Sandy came to the Springs—at the end of which lay North Country Mall.

The thing of the utmost importance to keep in mind, Sandy told himself, was not to lose his temper. No matter how much he hated the sonofabitch, he couldn't afford to blow up at Greenleaf because then the bastard would just evict him from his studio and that would be the end of it, right there. Somehow, he had to keep his cool. He had serious doubts as to whether this would be possible, because he could just as easily—and much more thrillingly—picture himself going berserk in Greenleaf's office if the bastard wouldn't accept a painting in exchange for a month's rent. He saw himself absolutely trashing the place while Greenleaf looked on in horror and astonishment from behind his desk. But to indulge in such a tantrum was simply out of the question, Sandy told himself. And besides, it could very well land him in jail under some fairly serious charges, especially if he happened to hit the sonofabitch in the process, even if only by accident.

A gigantic freestanding sign loomed fifty feet high above the outermost corner of the vast mall parking lot. The sign proclaimed the titles of the three movies playing at the mall's triple cinema. Below it, in a slightly smaller message box, were the words Art Show Today. A tremor of foreboding ran down Sandy's spine as he pulled past the sign and turned in the parking lot entrance.

The mall was positively aswarm with its natural denizens at this hour on a Friday afternoon. The atmosphere inside was much like the busy main street of a make-believe town, but imbued as well with the ambience of a train station, the lassitude of massed strangers killing time. The fact that none of them were bound for any special destination made it seem all the more dreary, and the pumped-in Muzak—an incongruous, upbeat arrangement of Bob Dylan's "Blowin' in the Wind"—lent the whole gaudy consumer panorama an added dimension of falseness and desolation.

Sandy hurried through the corridor of shops. Up ahead he could see the art show in progress along the mall's main corridor and proceeded warily. The show consisted of twenty-four artists accompanied by a manager/publicist; they traveled the United States in a formal caravan of motor campers, appearing as an attraction at one mall after another. The artists were all carefully handpicked by the manager. Each had a distinctive style and subject matter. They sat at their easels, politely conversing with the gawking shoppers, surrounded by portable divider walls hung with their work. All of them worked from the imagination, so to speak, and their subject matter varied from canvas to canvas, mainly in size, number, or color, like so many ashtrays in a discount store.

One of them specialized in paintings of circus clowns. His allotment of wall space was hung with seventeen paintings of clowns. Each clown wore a slightly different type of makeup, but essentially they were all the same clown. Another artist specialized in paintings of ghost sailing ships. Each ship was a sort of generic brigantine rendered in tones of grayish-white against a dreamy cloudscape that was not quite either sky or water. Some of his ships sailed to the east, some to the west, and some aggressively straight at the viewer, but all of them gave the final impression of heading nowhere, filled with nothing. Another specialized in the ubiquitous black velvet technique, and his subjects were those demigods from the pantheon of black velvet heroes: Ronald Reagan, the Kennedys, Elvis, Martin Luther King, Sylvester Stallone as "Rambo." Yet another was the creator of what a sign on his wall called "sofa-sized landscapes." These were all three- by two-foot depictions of a mountain lake at the same time of day, dusk, or possibly dawn. He was busy painting a new version even as Sandy stood there. He painted with amazing rapidity, daubing in half a forest of tree trunks in the three minutes that Sandy watched.

"I think I know that place," Sandy remarked.

The artist, an older man puffing on a meerschaum pipe, looked up with proprietary pride.

"Isn't it in the same country where all those little plastic dwarves live?" Sandy asked.

"What are you? A wise guy?" the artist asked.

"No, I'm a painter. What are you?"

The artist, looking hurt, gave no further reply and Sandy was suddenly ashamed of himself for losing his cool and making such a cruel remark to someone who, whatever his artistic shortcomings, was probably doing his best and might well have been a kind and considerate human being to boot. He hurried away from the art show as though from a personal humiliation and soon stood before the entrance to Greenleaf Realty. A receptionist's desk lay at a slant near the office's entrance, with a plump young woman in a flowered shirtwaist dress behind it.

"Can I help you?" She stood up at once and addressed Sandy with an air of extreme friendliness which suggested that from the looks of him he couldn't possibly be in the market for a piece of property, and this being the case, then perhaps he better not walk in any further.

"Yes," he said nervously. "I'm Sandy Stern, one of Mr. Greenleaf's tenants, and I'd like to see him, please."

Smiling energetically, she reached for a phone at her desk, punched a single button with an extraordinarily long, cherry red fingernail and announced Sandy to the unseen Greenleaf. Then, her smile transformed to something like a grimace, as though she had been defeated in a game, she gestured broadly to a closed door beyond the rows of desks and said, "Mr. Greenleaf will see you now."

The developer was eating lunch at his desk. The ten-by-ten-foot cubicle office was crammed full of stuff without being disorderly. There was a large philodendron plant thriving beneath an ultraviolet grow-light in one corner of the windowless room. The walls were adorned with blueprints, architect's renderings, and, Sandy was surprised to see, a Metropolitan Museum of Art poster featuring John Kensett's familiar painting of Lake George. Seeing the poster, his hopes shot up.

"Hey, Sandy, great to see you," Greenleaf said, pointing to one of two aluminum and Naugahyde armchairs opposing his desk. In the other hand he wielded a moon-shaped pita bread stuffed with egg salad. "Mind if I eat while we talk?"

"Not at all," Sandy said, and a moment later he realized that Greenleaf meant he would eat and listen while Sandy talked. Being suddenly put on the spot like this completely unnerved him. He'd expected a little chit-chat first. So, instead of getting straight to the point, Sandy asked, "Are you having some work done downstairs in the house?"

"Yes," Greenleaf said, nodding, and his failure to elaborate clearly signaled danger to Sandy.

"There was no hot water this morning, and the heat's not on."

"I'm sorry. I forgot to notify you about it."

"Well, is it coming back on, or what?"

"Of course, it's coming back on."

"When, exactly? I'd like to take a shower one of these days," Sandy said, instantly regretting his sarcasm, and hoping it hadn't set Greenleaf hopelessly against him.

"It should be back on tonight," the developer said,

inserting a corner of the sandwich in his mouth and taking a huge bite.

"It was kind of brisk in the old shower this morning, you know." Sandy tried to salvage the situation with a show of humor, while also pointing up his personal hardship. "Like one of those schools they send you to when you've been a bad boy."

Greenleaf nodded his head, closed his eyes, and smiled while he chewed, making it all the more painfully obvious that he considered the problem trivial and the matter closed, and was waiting to hear what else was on Sandy's mind. As the seconds extended to an awkward interval, Sandy became aware of his tooth throbbing again. He reached into the pocket of his father's flight jacket and fumbled with the box of slides, hesitating to take it out. Finally he did, placing it at the very edge of the desk, as though the little yellow box might be subject to a charge of trespassing.

"I don't suppose you'd accept one of my paintings in lieu of next month's rent," Sandy said, surprised to hear himself finally state the simple proposition.

"I'm afraid I can't do that," Greenleaf said, wiping his hands on a napkin and reaching for the box as Sandy's heart sank. "Is that what you've got here?"

"Yes. Slides of my work."

"Mind if I take a look?"

"No, please go ahead," Sandy said, brightening with hope again, glancing at the museum poster, thinking that Greenleaf might see something he liked and change his mind.

The realtor held up the slides one by one to the fluorescent panel overhead, taking care only to handle them by their cardboard edges.

"Hmmm. Very nice. What's this of?" he asked, handing the slide to Sandy.

"Upper Ausable Lake from Saddleback Mountain. Twilight."

"How big?"

"Thirty-six by sixty inches."

"Sofa-size?"

"I don't know. Sure. I guess."

"You're quite an artist," Greenleaf eventually remarked, and glancing at Sandy, added, "not like these bozos here in the mall, huh?"

"I think the difference in quality is pretty obvious," Sandy agreed, trying to be modest.

Greenleaf finished looking at the slides, carefully put them back in the yellow box, and resumed eating his sandwich. Sandy's heart pounded as he waited for the realtor to express a change of mind, and with every heartbeat, a stab of deep pain pulsed in his tooth.

"Will you reconsider my proposition?" Sandy forced the issue.

"No," Greenleaf said, pausing to sip from a can of sugar-free root beer through a straw. "Don't get me wrong. I think they're really good, but this is strictly business."

"So is my proposition."

"I wouldn't want to establish some kind of precedent."

"It's not a precedent. It's value for value."

"The answer is still no," Greenleaf said, placing the box of slides back on the front edge of the desk, as if for emphasis. Sandy reached for them at once and put them back in the pocket of his father's flight jacket, as though he couldn't bear to look at the yellow box another moment.

"What's the deal, Roy, really?" he asked after another short but oppressive interval of silence. "Are you trying to force me out of the place?"

"No one's trying to force anybody."

"Sure you are. I heard someone banging away downstairs today. You're renovating the place, right?"

"I'm having some work done."

"Why don't you just come out and say it: you're renovating the place."

"Because I'm not." Greenleaf denied it coolly, with a smile. "I'm having some work done so I can rent the units. It's an old house. It requires a lot of maintenance."

"How about my unit?"

"You're welcome to stay up there as long as you pay the rent," Greenleaf said, and resumed sucking on his soda.

"And if I can't?"

"Then you're out."

"I see."

"Any landlord would tell you the same thing, Sandy."

"And what do you call that little bulldozing job you're doing out at Mill Creek? Forest maintenance?"

For the first time, Greenleaf appeared to be caught off guard. "No, I'm building a solar home community out there," he said.

"You're fucking up a perfectly good trout stream."

"I'm not fucking it up. It's the centerpiece of the development."

"And you think bringing in houses and people and goddam cars isn't going to destroy it?"

"For your information, Sandy, I've had several ecological impact studies done—more than what was required by law—and these houses are not going to adversely affect the habitat in any way."

"Not with fifty toilets flushing into the ground five times a day?"

"We're putting self-composting toilets in every unit," Greenleaf countered.

"What about all the soapy waste water from their washing machines and bathtubs and goddam Jacuzzis."

"We're putting in all the appropriate dry wells and leach fields." Greenleaf remained staunchly confident.

"Sooner or later all that stuff is going to leach down into the stream bed."

"Hey, sooner or later the sun's going to expand into a red dwarf star and the whole earth is going to be reduced to a little cinder. Everything changes, Sandy. The universe is in a constant state of flux. Someday I'm going to die. Someday you're going to die. You think what I'm doing out at Mill Creek is bad? Let me tell you something: I happened to outbid a guy who does nothing but put up trailer courts all over upstate New York. I'm building upscale, environmentally correct homes for nice people who are going to respect the land and that creek that runs through it. Guys like you should give guys like me a little credit once in a while because, believe me, there are a hell of a lot of guys like this other guy with the trailers out there, and they're the real enemy."

Sandy thought of the Tooles' trailer across the road from Annie Gaines's place, and all the junk surrounding it, and he found himself in the uncomfortable position of being unable to disagree with Greenleaf on that particular point.

"I still think that what you're doing out there is wrong," he said anyway. "I've been fishing that creek for five years, and seeing those bulldozers out there today just made me sick."

"They'll be gone by the springtime. And I want you to feel free to keep fishing the creek. Really, you have my blanket permission. Did I mention that we're going to stock it with fish?"

"No."

"Well, we are."

"Great," Sandy said without enthusiasm. He knew that the developer wasn't going to keep stocking it year after year in perpetuity. It would be inconsistent with his philosophy, as stated. Everything changes, and sooner or later the creek would be devoid of trout, Sandy thought. How soon this would occur before the whole world turned into a cinder, he couldn't hazard to guess. But he imagined himself at twilight on a June evening, casting in one of the pools he loved so well, with several new solar homes in the background. Smoke from their barbecues wafts through the air, as the families gather on their upscale decks to eat weenies and watch the picturesque fly-fisherman. His tooth was killing him.

"How old are you?" he found himself asking Greenleaf, almost idly, as his mind veered between bleak visions of the future and the increasing pain in his head.

"Twenty-nine," Greenleaf replied, tilting back in his chair. "Why do you ask?"

"No reason," Sandy said, though it was obvious to both of them that Sandy was measuring himself against Greenleaf. And the knowledge that the developer was younger than him, even if only by a few months, underscored Sandy's feelings of failure and futility to a degree that made him momentarily dizzy.

"How old are you?" Greenleaf asked.

"Twenty-nine," Sandy replied weakly.

"Hey, you too! What a coincidence," Greenleaf said. "When's your birthday?"

"Today."

"Well," Greenleaf said, extending a hand across his desk, "a happy twenty-ninth birthday to you."

"Actually, that's not quite correct," Sandy replied, humped in despair. "Today I'm thirty."

NINE

Joel Harlowe returned to his immaculately restored Greek revival house on upper Catherine Street in foul and turbulent spirits. What was it with people like Edmund? Were they determined to throw away their lives? To make a mockery of the precious opportunity that life afforded . . . to . . . to make something of it? *Especially* in Edmund's case, with all that sheer intelligence, not to mention the trust funds! It made Joel sick and a little angry to think of how he'd had to claw his way up in the world—a kid from Brooklyn, and not a very nice part of it at that, whose father ran a small dry-cleaning store, for Chrissake! —while Edmund Black just frittered away all that inherited wealth. And now, carrying on like a . . . like a goddam *fairy*! Joel's head hurt.

He knew he'd feel better after a toot, so he went directly to the bedroom to get the green malachite box with the rock of cocaine in it. The chunk was now about as big as the tip of his thumb, enough to see him through the ride to New York City. At times like this, when he felt out of sorts, a little strung out actually, Joel reproved himself for starting up with the drug again in the first place, for dipping into his own supply, the most fundamental no-no of the profession. The amount he was using was mild, of course, compared to some other people, to some of his customers, for example, but that was no excuse. Every week, since late summer, he had been blowing maybe $1,000 in profits up his nose. Not that he couldn't afford it. But what a waste! Stupid, stupid!

He brought the malachite box into the dining room and sat down at the inlaid mahogany Duncan Phyfe dining room table with acanthus-carved legs that he had paid $11,750 for at a Sotheby's auction. His hand trembled as he chopped a pea-sized fragment of the crystal into powder using a razor blade on the built-in mirror of the box's lid. Without bothering to sweep it up into a line, he inserted the solid gold straw first in one nostril, then the other, and vacuumed up all the loose powder on the mirror.

He tipped his head back in the Slover & Taylor dining chair with the acanthus-carved uprights that almost, but not quite, matched the table and rapidly began to feel normal again. Better than normal. He felt very, very good. He didn't approve of all this promiscuous drug use, but he would get off the stuff next week, when the party was over with, when he could get away. He'd take himself somewhere very pleasant—Bermuda or Eleuthera—with Kelly! That's right! With the sweet, beautiful Kelly! And she'd rub his temples on the pink sand beach until he no longer felt any desire for the drug. Only for her. And after that, he'd keep his nose clean. No more dipping into the company assets. Never again! It could be a lot worse, he knew. A hell of a lot worse. He could be freebasing, like that guy over in Burlington, Vermont, Buddy Talbot, who smoked up three quarters of a million dollars in the year before they found him on his sailboat in Mallet's Bay with the neat little spot on his temple and the Ruger Single Six in his stiffened fingers. But he, Joel Harlowe, was no Buddy Talbot, and there was not a chance in the world that he was going to end up that way. He'd get off the stuff next week, starting Monday.

This settled, and feeling very much better, Joel decided to go for his daily run. He ran 3.6 miles every weekday, always the same distance, the same route, in fact. Longer distances made his knees ache. It was a moderate aerobic workout, which took under a half hour and, coupled with his three sessions per week at the Nautilus weight-training center, kept him fit and trim, and allowed him to indulge in a lot of eating out without worrying about his waistline. Lately, he'd been losing weight, as a matter of fact, but anyhow the run was still spiritually important to him. He usually ran with a Sony Walkman tape player clutched in one hand, and the music had the remarkable effect of deadening the physical pain of exertion, while it stimulated the production of those hormones which gave the runner such a nice buzz.

He changed into his running gear—black nylon shorts, aqua tank top, and Nike air-cell shoes—and loaded the tape player with a cassette he had recorded of tunes culled from various albums. He had selected the songs for their high energy and spirituality. They made him feel fifty pounds lighter.

In a Chinese bowl on a table in the entrance hall he found the nylon wrist-wallet in which he always kept a house key and a five dollar bill (in case it rained and became necessary to take a cab home). He walked out the front door and locked it behind him. The cool air felt a little raw on his bare shoulders, but he knew it was perfect weather for running, that he'd feel fine after the first quarter mile. He put on the lightweight headphones and pushed the play button on the Walkman. A song called "Little Red Corvette" by Prince came on with its snakey synthesizers and inspiring handclaps as Joel set out up Catherine Street eastward toward the edge of town.

The music immediately helped bring his leg muscles to life—for Joel was not the type to waste time doing some wimpy warm-up routine. He soon fell into a jogging rhythm that was not quite the same as the song's tempo. The street, with its handsome well kept Victorian homes, was lined with magnificent old trees. Their arching branches full of yellow leaves overhung the street like the golden groined vaults of a Byzantine temple. Jack-o'-lanterns grinned from many a porch in anticipation of the evening's ghoulish goings-on, and Joel could not help but dote on the magnificent party that was now seven hours away. He made a mental note to call Sandy again after his run. Then "Little Red Corvette" faded and a new song came on, Stevie Nicks singing "Landslide," not a fast number, but a song that never failed to stir Joel's heart and uplift his spirit.

The last big party he had been to was Tom Dugan's Fourth of July bash at Dugan's "ranch" up in Shrewsbury. It was also the fifteenth anniversary of the Black Rose Cafe. There had been a big striped tent on the lawn, a professional barbecue pit crew brought all the way up from New York City for the occasion, and a pretty good band. But it had been a day of stultifying tropical heat, with the mercury hovering above ninety degrees, and few of the two hundred or so people present had thought to bring their swimsuits to dip in Dugan's pool—most everyone had come dressed rather formally, as for a "grown-up" lawn party—and before the party even picked up any momentum, people began to wilt from the heat and liquor. To make matters worse, the flies from Dugan's nearby stables were merciless. They were that particular species of deerfly which goes into orbit around a victim's head and drives him or her crazy before finally diving in to inflict a vicious bite. Late that afternoon there was a brief thunderstorm that drove everybody under the tent. It failed to cool things off though, only made the hot air muggier, like glue, and then the grass was all wet, making some of the women walk around with their long skirts hiked up. For the many who stayed after sundown, there was some relief from the pitiless heat. But soon mosquitoes came out by the billions, replacing the deerflies like shift workers, and more than half the remaining partygoers drifted indoors, with the band playing wanly outside to a handful of people too drunk to feel the bugs bite. Joel knew his party was going to beat Dugan's, hands down. Dugan hadn't even supplied any reefer to his guests!

Running up Catherine Street was like a trip through time, Joel thought, as Stevie Nicks sang about love and growing older. One could see the decades roll by in the architectural styles of the houses from one block to the next—from the 1820s period of his own neoclassical cottage, through the carpenter Gothic in the next block, followed by the Italianate, the mansard, and culminating in the ponderous Queen Anne style. Beyond East Avenue (which had been the city limit until after World War Two), the houses were all banal suburban bunkers. The trees were smaller too out that way. Eventually, Catherine Street ended in a T at Denning Road, where the sprawling new Central High School was located. Cheerleaders were out practicing on one of the playing fields, bouncing up and down in their cute blue and white skirts and sweaters. It was the kind of high school Joel wished he had gone to, instead of the chaotic and disgusting inner-city zoo he attended. Here Joel took a right, then another right, and headed west down Saranac Street, which paralleled Catherine, back toward his house.

Since "Landslide" played, he had listened to "Beast of Burden," by the Rolling Stones, "Rosie," by Joan Armatrading, "Barrytown," by Steely Dan, "Avalon," by Roxy Music, and "Soul Kitchen," by the Doors. On the way home, he listened to "Private Idaho," by the B 52's, "Downbound Train," by Bruce Springsteen, "Jesu, Joy of Man's Desiring," by Johann Sebastian Bach, and "San Diego Serenade," by Tom Waits.

He had spotted quite a few trick-or-treaters along the way, groups of children, some accompanied by mothers, some on their own, and Joel imagined how wonderful it would have been to grow up in the Springs compared to Brooklyn, with its bleak and unending blocks of depressing tenements filled with hopeless people, so many of them gabbling foreigners, its streets brimming with terror for a ten-year-old boy in a Superman costume too afraid to enter any of those buildings and ask for a treat, lest his throat be cut. The memory made him shudder, even though his body was warm from running. The sight of his own beautiful house at the end of the block revived him, the white-painted house with its green shutters, Doric columns in front, and pristine classical lines. He loved the house so dearly. He loved Excelsior Springs, he was so happy to live there, in a clean, pretty town, and he wanted to give the town a gift to show his gratitude.

He was in the process of unlocking the front door when he heard the phone ring inside, and he hurried to answer it, breathless from his exercise.

"Joel? Sandy."

"Just the man I wanted to speak to."

"George tells me you're in some kind of jam."

"Am I ever."

"Is there anything I can do to help out?" Sandy asked.

Glen Toole skulked behind the shelf of calendars in the Running Bear Book Shop, watching the bakery across Grove Street. For days—since he had first spotted her working there as a waitress—Glen had come to the book shop to watch Jennifer Fleming leave the bakery and then followed her around. Each day she had taken a slightly different route after work, but always ended up at the bus stop on Broadway in front of the town hall, where she got on the shuttle to the Greer campus a mile away on the north end of town.

Despite his near-moron intelligence level, Glen Toole possessed as much animal guile as the ferret whose photograph graced the Sierra Club Calendar on the display rack directly to the right of his head. He had followed her for these several days, and he believed (correctly) that he had done so without her knowing. This Halloween afternoon Jennifer emerged from the bakery at precisely two o'clock, wearing a dark green down vest over her pink and white waitress outfit and carrying a canvas tote bag with her books and things. The block to Broadway was a fairly steep hill, and when she was halfway up it, Glen departed the bookstore on her trail.

She stopped first at the Rite-Aid drug store, then at the Sunrise health food store where she bought hypoallergenic cosmetics, then at Adirondack Audio where she bought a three-pack of blank audio cassettes to tape her friends' record albums, and then stopped briefly in the North Country Trust to cash her paycheck. While she was inside, Glen sat brazenly on the cast-iron bench under the bank's twelve-foot-high freestanding sidewalk clock. He enjoyed immensely the knowledge that she was inside. The idea was gradually dawning on him that she was under his control, that she was in the bank *because* he allowed her to go in there. The situation reminded him of a radio-controlled car his brother Hurley once built from a kit. There was the little red car, and then there was the box with the aerial and the joystick that controlled the car. Hurley could make that car go wherever he wanted it to. Jennifer was like the car.

When she came out of the bank, however, Glen's delight evaporated as he realized that she would now cross Broadway and go wait for the Greer bus. A bunch of students was already there waiting for the next shuttle, lolling on the wide town hall steps in the warm afternoon sunlight, and several of them, Glen noted with alarm, were males. Once, he had tried to get on the Greer shuttle just to ride it up to the campus, to see what it was like, and the driver wouldn't let him on because he didn't have a Greer ID card. He was the last one to board the bus so it was already filled with students. Glen claimed that he had lost his ID but the driver didn't believe him. One college boy sitting up front, a rich kid wearing a sneer that made Glen feel like a cockroach, said, "Get off the bus, you townie dickhead," and the whole bus exploded in laughter as Glen indeed got off. He painfully remembered their faces looking down at him from the grimy windows as he stood on the curb and the bus pulled away with a great belch of diesel exhaust. This was several years ago.

To Glen's surprise and elation, however, Jennifer did not cross Broadway to catch the Greer shuttle, as she had the several days previous. Rather, she took a left at High Street and walked toward the west side of town. Glen imagined that his thinking of where he *didn't* want her to go had caused her to not get on the bus. He left his seat on the bench and waited under the clock until she was a hundred paces up the street, and then he followed.

She was such a pretty girl that just thinking about her made his head swim. He imagined that she came from a world that was like the inside of a spun sugar Easter egg he once saw in the K Mart. When you looked in a hole at one end of the egg, you saw a beautiful garden inside. And you could eat the egg. Looking at her golden blond hair from behind, her little fanny wiggling in the pink skirt, she looked good enough to eat, Glen thought. Of course there were lots of pretty girls here in the Springs. That's why he liked it so much in town, instead of out in Locust Grove, where there was nothing but trees and the family always crabbing at him. But most of these pretty girls were snotty bitches, especially the college ones, and they traveled in packs, like bitches, and they never failed to grin among themselves when a pack of them passed him on the street. He knew what they really wanted though, the snotty bitches. They wanted what all bitches wanted. And wouldn't it surprise them to find out that he could give it to them as good as anybody? He could, too.

Jennifer took another right turn at the plumbing supply store on Woodlawn Street. Hanging way back, Glen soon followed. She wasn't like the rest of them, he thought. She always seemed to be alone. She was the kind who went her own way. Maybe she was lonely because she wasn't a bitch like the rest of them. But she wanted the same thing they all wanted, because they were all the same. One block up Woodlawn, he watched her take a left onto Van Wyck Street, a busy thoroughfare of run-down Victorians turned into multifamily apartment houses. He had just made the turn onto Van Wyck himself when he saw her disappear inside the building that housed the Planned Parenthood offices. Glen couldn't read, but he knew that the establishment had something to do with sex because a lot of the bitches at the Mental Health Unit, where he was frequently in residence, were sent down there for medicine that kept them from getting knocked up.

At the sound of the door knocker, Joel hollered for Sandy to come in, and Sandy was a little surprised to find him chopping away at a hunk of cocaine crystal right there in the dining room.

"You've been hard to get a hold of," Joel began, not even looking up at Sandy until, in one of his usual well intentioned attempts at flattery, he added, "A good man is hard to find."

Sandy slid into one of the elegant chairs across the table, his head filled with severe pulsing pain as his tooth now ached with abandon.

"Joel," he began in a quavery voice. "I don't ask for free handouts much—"

Joel felt a tightening on the nape of his neck as he fortified himself for disappointment.

"—but I've got the most unbelievable toothache, and I was wondering if you had any painkillers around here by any chance."

Joel put down his razor blade. He was so grateful that Sandy had not asked him for money that he could have hugged the guy, except he didn't want to give Sandy the impression that he liked to hug guys, and besides, somebody with a toothache doesn't want a hug, he wants relief.

"I've got some Demerol," Joel said.

"What's that?"

"Strong, effective. A synthetic morphine."

"Got anything a little less strong?"

"Darvon compound with codeine."

"Could you let me have some of that?"

"You bet," Joel said, and bustled off to the master

bathroom to get it. While he was gone, Sandy noticed one of his paintings on the wall across the dining room. It was Indian Hill, fall, George's favorite bird hunting spot, painted a year ago, the abandoned farmhouse with the caved-in roof in the foreground, a melancholy place. The frame around the small 12- by 18-inch canvas was gold-leafed and expensive. The painting looked wonderful in it, Sandy thought. Joel soon returned with a couple of gray and red capsules and a tumbler of water.

"Thanks a lot," Sandy said, tossing them back.

"Do you have a regular dentist?"

"Sure. Steve Greenbaum."

"Oh yeah? He's my dentist, too."

"I think I sent you to him."

"That's right, you did," Joel recalled. "He does good work. Maybe you ought to go see him."

"I'm going to try and ride this one out."

"In my experience, toothaches aren't so rideable outable," Joel said. "They just get worse. Pretty soon, abscess set in, and then you've got a terrible, dangerous situation on your hands. Do you know that in centuries gone by people used to die from an abscessed tooth?"

"No."

"They did. It was very common. You ought to go see Greenbaum this afternoon," Joel insisted, adding, "while there's still time."

"While there's still time? I honestly don't think this is going to kill me."

"No, but you said you were going to help me out, right?"

"Yes. I'll help you out."

"With this party."

"That's right. With your party."

"And you can't be having a toothache all goddam day."

"Maybe this stuff will make it go away."

"I think you ought to call up Greenbaum right now."

"Joel, I couldn't even afford it, if I did call," Sandy told him, sensing danger in the money issue, but nonetheless stating the fact.

Joel too recognized the minefield of monetary considerations and hesitated a moment before answering: "You could always tell him to bill you."

"That's true."

"Call him up right now. Use my phone."

"Let me just wait and see how this stuff works."

"Okay," Joel agreed with a sigh. "It's your tooth."

"It's already beginning to work. Really, I feel better."

Joel resumed chopping his cocaine. He didn't offer any to Sandy because he knew that Sandy wouldn't want any. He was one of the few people Joel knew who showed no interest in coke whatsoever. To Joel, Sandy's aversion was both admirable and unfathomable. In fact, except for drinking liquor and smoking a little marijuana at parties, Sandy didn't go in for drugs at all. He once boasted to Joel that he got through the entire decade of the 1970s without taking LSD, as though it was some kind of achievement. And in a weird way, Joel had to agree it was. That Sandy wasn't after his drugs was a primary reason his friendship was so important to Joel.

"Okay," Joel said in a tone of voice that suggested the clearing of an agenda, "this is what I'd like you to do."

"Maybe I better write this down."

"Good idea. There's a pad and pen right on the kitchen counter next to the phone."

Sandy stood up and headed toward the kitchen. In the few moments he was gone, Joel blew a quarter gram up his nose in order to organize his thoughts because what he needed Sandy to do for him was rather complicated. He was sniffling when Sandy returned with the pad.

"By the way," Joel said, as the drug clarified his mind, "have I mentioned how much I appreciate what you're doing for me?"

"I'm glad to help out."

"Have you ever thought of doing any portrait work?"

"There's not much call for it these days," Sandy said. "At least around here."

"But no one's exactly breaking down your door to buy landscapes, either," Joel said, and then, thinking his remark perhaps a bit harsh, added, "I mean, looking at your situation realistically, from a purely business point of view."

"No, you're right," Sandy agreed. "Nobody's breaking down my door to buy landscapes."

"I mean, I like them. I think you're extremely talented. But have you ever thought of doing portraits as a source of income?"

"Not really," Sandy answered, and then reflected a moment. "I did a lot of figure drawing in college. I can do it. I'm not one of these painters who doesn't know how to draw the human form."

"Well, if someone asked you to have his portrait done, would you consider it?"

"Sure, I'd consider it."

Joel nodded as though the answer satisfied him. "All right, then," he said, "this is what I'd like you to do."

Sandy looked expectantly across the table at him.

"I think you better write this down," Joel said and resumed chopping his cocaine. Sandy realized that Joel had suddenly dropped the subject of portrait painting. "You'll have to be over at the casino by four o'clock. First, there's the liquor delivery. . . ." And Joel went on for about ten minutes enumerating in detail all the things that had to be taken care of in his absence: the liquor, the caterers, the florists, the bartenders, the string quartet that was supposed to play in the beginning, the rock band that would follow. Sandy's attention wavered between what Joel was telling him and the pain in his tooth. But he wrote all the important things down.

Finally, Joel got up and vanished into his bedroom, returning shortly with a checkbook and a pen. He began to write out checks to the various companies involved— North Country Liquor Distributors, Bird of Paradise Caterers, Excelsior Florists, the Greer Faculty String Quartette, et cetera. "I'll leave the amounts blank for you to fill in, 'cause I don't know what the exact charges are going to be." He passed the several checks across the table to Sandy. They were signed Richard Dodge and drawn on that same personage's account at the North Country Trust.

"Who the hell is Richard Dodge?" Sandy asked.

"Me, dummy." Joel looked up with a grin on his face. "It's a business account."

"Oh."

"Here are a few more not made out to anybody in particular"— Joel continued signing blank checks—"in case some unforeseen emergency crops up."

"What time are you leaving town?" Sandy asked.

"Three-thirty. I'm going to ride the Beemer down," Joel said, referring to his BMW RS-1000 motorcycle.

"Are you going all the way down to the city?"

"I certainly am." Joel grinned and waggled his eyebrows playfully.

"Whatever for?"

"It's amazing how naive you can be sometimes, but it's one of the reasons I like you."

"Oh," Sandy said, suddenly realizing the purpose of the errand and thinking, *I guess I am naive.*

"It was a last-minute inspiration," Joel explained.

"So, what time do you think you'll get back?"

"Between eight-thirty and nine."

"That soon?"

"On the Beemer—easy."

"Okay then," Sandy said, anxiously standing up and making as though to depart. His tooth was still killing him. "I'll do my best to take care of things while you're gone."

"Hold it a second," Joel said, writing out another check. He scribbled quickly, tore the check out of the book, and handed it across the table. It was made out to Sandy for the sum of $250.

"What's this?" Sandy asked.

"Down payment on a portrait of me," Joel said, smiling expansively, leaning back in his chair with his hands hooked behind his head.

Sandy was authentically stunned.

"But we haven't even discussed it."

"What's to discuss except the final price? You can do it, right?"

"I believe I can."

"A thousand sound okay?"

"Dollars!"

"Not Mexican pesos, my friend. Of course, dollars."

"God, Joel. I don't know what to say."

"You can say, 'okay, it's enough,' or 'no, it's not enough.'"

"It'll do fine."

"Okay, then." Joel extended his hand across the table to shake, and Sandy took it with a feeling of gratitude that, combined with the pain in his tooth, almost brought tears to his eyes.

"I really appreciate this," Sandy told him.

"Excuse me," Joel said, "but it's me who appreciates

what you're doing for me. And what you will do. By the way, have you got a costume for tonight?"

"Not really, Joel. I was going to—"

"There's a perfectly good French cavalry officer's getup at The Little Match Girl. Gwen threw it together for me, but I decided to wear something else instead. You can probably fit into it."

"Okay," Sandy said, blinking, still astonished at this turn of his fortunes.

"And go see Greenbaum today," Joel said, getting up now and leading Sandy to the front door. "I mean it. I know how it is with these dental things. They don't go away. They just get worse until, God forbid, you're in the hospital with half of your goddam head abscessed. Call him!"

"I will," Sandy said and turned toward the door. "And good luck driving down to the city."

"No sweat," Joel said.

"I'll do a great portrait for you."

"I know you will. See you at the casino around nine."

Joel heard the tinny sound of Sandy's Japanese two-stroke engine as he shut the front door and returned to the dining room. There, in an antique gilt-framed oval convex mirror, Joel looked at himself for a moment, sniffled, and thought, *what a guy.*

Glen Toole sat waiting on the steps of the deserted Elks Club building on Van Wyck Street just past Woodlawn. He didn't mind waiting. In fact, he felt good doing it, filled with a new and delightful sense of power, for he knew that the girl, Jennifer Fleming, was in that gray house down the street where the sex doctor was, and Glen believed that he was keeping her in there by the force of his mind. It was like holding her prisoner, but in a fun way, a game, like the kind he used to play with his sister Grace when they were kids. He could let her out any time he wanted—but not just yet. Let her stay in the building and get her medicine.

Glen took out his pocket comb and reshaped his pompadour in the bright sunshine. His pants felt full. The full feeling in his pants seemed to have some connection with his power over the girl. Thinking about how he was able to keep her stuck in that building down the street made him feel good in his pants. He put his comb away, stretched his legs out on the concrete steps and slipped his right hand into his pocket. This way, he could touch what he had in his pants without anybody seeing, for there were plenty of cars passing by on Van Wyck. It felt good to touch himself there. It was fun that the passing motorists had no idea what he was doing. He had only been touching himself a few minutes, feeling better and better, when the girl suddenly emerged from the gray house. Glen felt that he was like the box that controlled the little red car. He had his hand on the joystick, and the girl was the car.

She crossed Van Wyck and walked up Woodlawn. Woodlawn was the street where all the carriage houses were located for the big mansions on North Broadway a block over. Woodlawn, Glen knew, also eventually led to the college. The street dead-ended, and a pretty footbridge crossed a creek into a woodsy part of the campus between the tennis courts and a bunch of other buildings Glen didn't know the purpose of. He was sure that the girl was heading up to the campus via that footbridge. It was a beautiful day, and it was so pretty going up to the campus this way. He followed her at a distance two blocks up Woodlawn before he was seized by an inspiration.

It had something to do with a story that was read to him years ago in grammar school, before they took him out of the regular class and put him in the special class. It was a story about three billy goats and a monster who lived under a bridge. The monster was called a troll and when anyone crossed over his bridge, he ate them.

Glen ran a block east to North Broadway, then ran up the avenue of mansions for two very long blocks and cut west again toward Woodlawn. He was a heavy smoker and his lungs ached when he stopped running, but he felt it was worth it. He glimpsed the girl in her pink dress now a long block back, but made it a point not to gawk at her. Instead, he simply jogged ahead two more blocks to the dead end. There in a grove of paper birch trees was the footbridge. He hurried across it and glanced back once more. She was still way, way down the street. He quickly slipped into the creekbed and hid under the bridge.

There was no water under the bridge. The creek only ran in the springtime and dried up completely by fall. Glen looked up through the tiny spaces between the planks. Down there under the bridge he had never felt so much in his true element. He leaned against the rocks and felt inside his pants again. All he had to do to keep the girl coming toward him was to touch himself. Soon she'd be there. He felt so confident that he took the joystick out of his pants and worked it directly. To have his hand right on the control gave him tremendous pleasure. His brother Hurley had never let him work the joystick on his box— only watch. Now Glen had one of his own that nobody could take away from him, and it occurred to him that if something happened to this girl, he could always find another girl to replace her, to go wherever he wanted her to go and do whatever he wanted her to do. It was not long before he heard Jennifer walking through the dry leaves, *crunch crunch*, that lay in the curb at the dead end. His heart flew into his throat. Moments later, her shoes resounded hollowly on the wooden planks, *clomp clomp,* and he could see her shadow through the slits.

"Who's that on my bridge?" he asked in the troll's voice and seized her ankle. She screamed once, but he managed to pull her through the railing and off the treadway with remarkable speed, and then get his hand over her mouth so she couldn't make any more noise. At last, holding her pinned and squirming against the rocks, he made ready to gobble her up.

In great pain, but nonetheless feeling that an enormous burden had been lifted off him, Sandy dialed his dentist's number from the red telephone in the garret that he could now afford to remain in—and Roy Greenleaf be damned! On the first ring, a recorded message came on. Mariachi music played blandly behind it.

"Hello," a woman's voice said, as Sandy's heart sank. "You have reached the office of Dr. Steve Greenbaum. The doctor will be on vacation until Monday, November third. In the event of an emergency, call Dr. Jack Jorgensen." A number was given. Sandy hung up the phone, temporarily bewildered. The pain soon prompted him to call this Dr. Jorgensen, but by this time he had already forgotten Jorgensen's number, and he had to call Greenbaum's answering machine again to get it. Finally, to his vast relief, a human voice answered at Jorgensen's end. It was a woman. Sandy quickly explained that he was one of Dr. Greenbaum's patients and that he was suffering a terrible toothache that required emergency attention.

The receptionist listened politely and in an apologetic voice said, "I'm awfully sorry, but Dr. Jorgensen has gone for the day."

"Oh no," Sandy moaned. "It's only two-thirty in the afternoon."

"He doesn't see patients after two o'clock on Fridays."

"Then how come you're there?"

"Dr. Ambler is still in the office."

"He is? Can I possibly make an emergency appointment with him?"

"Dr. Ambler is a periodontist."

"He must know how to do the routine stuff though."

"Dr. Ambler does gums. He doesn't do teeth."

"Not at all?"

"I told you, he's a periodontist."

"Well, he must have worked on a few teeth before he branched out, for God's sake—"

"I'm sorry, sir, but he just doesn't anymore."

"Dr. Jorgensen must refer his patients to somebody."

"He refers them to Dr. Greenbaum."

"Great. He's on vacation."

"I'm sorry, sir."

"Are you positive this Ambler won't take an emergency tooth case?"

"It's just not what he does."

"Ask him. Please, just go ahead and ask him."

"I can't do that, sir. He's with a patient. But I assure you that he'd tell you the same thing."

"Do you have any idea what kind of pain I'm in?"

"Of course, I do. Sir, there are at least nine other dentists in Excelsior Springs, and they're all listed alphabetically in the yellow pages of the phone book. In fact, I'll read them right off to you right now."

"Why didn't you say that before?"

"Does it matter, sir?"

"No. Not really. You're right."

"Have you got a pen?"

"Yes."

She proceeded to rattle off several names and numbers. Sandy stopped her after three, realizing, after all, that he too had a copy of the telephone book right there on the table.

"Do you recommend any of these guys over the others?" Sandy asked.

"I'm sure that any of them could handle your case. I'm sorry, but I've got a bunch of other calls here. The console looks like a Christmas tree. Good luck, sir."

She hung up. Sandy immediately dialed the dentist at the top of the list, a Dr. Dale Clark. Once again, his heart sank as the phone rang three times unanswered. But on the fourth ring, someone picked it up. It was a man's voice.

"Hello?"

"Is this Dr. Clark's office?"

"Dale Clark, speaking."

All choked up with gratitude, Sandy outlined his predicament and begged the dentist to give him an emergency appointment.

"Sure. No problem. Come right over," Dr. Clark said and gave an address across town on High Street. Before he hung up, Sandy kissed the telephone.

TEN

Dr. Dale Clark's office was the first floor of a wood frame house near the hospital. The house had been sheathed with the sort of green asphalt shingles that turn the color of pea soup after two decades of exposure to the elements. Here and there the green had flaked off entirely, revealing scrofulous black spots. The elm trees that once shaded it had been cut down years ago, so that only stumps remained in the unkempt strip of grass between the sidewalk and the curb. Altogether, the house made a bleak and forlorn impression on Sandy as he parked his motorcycle on the street.

The pain in his tooth had gotten even worse as he drove across town, until it was so fierce that the sign on Dr. Clark's front steps appeared to be painted in double letters. A smaller hand-lettered card was inserted on the screen door: Ring bell and enter.

The waiting room was empty, and nobody was sitting in the receptionist's area behind a kind of window. Thinking someone would return shortly, Sandy took a seat and began leafing through an old copy of *People* magazine. Muzak lilted from an overhead speaker, giving the impression of business as usual. Despite the pain, Sandy began to read an article about an up-and-coming movie actress whose looks knocked him out. (Off camera, he learned here, she was a "rodeo nut" and had "a personal relationship with Jesus.") Before he could finish the article, the pain broke his concentration. He went over to the window and said, "Hello? Is anyone there?"

"Just a minute," a man's voice replied from the depths of the office, and he recognized it as belonging to Dr. Clark.

Sandy retreated to his seat and rapidly leafed through another issue of *People*, but there was no sign of Dr. Clark. After another five minutes elapsed, Sandy returned to the counter. Though he craned his neck to peer through an inner door, he could see nothing but a blank wall. The receptionist's desk was immaculate. In fact, there was nothing on it but an empty desk blotter, a beige phone, and a note pad bearing a drug company's logo. "Hello in there . . . Dr. Clark?" Sandy appealed again. "It's me, the guy who called a while ago."

"The fellow with the toothache?" the dentist replied distantly.

"That's right."

"I'll be right out."

This time Sandy did not return to his seat but rather pressed his forehead against the wall, while the pain pulsed implacably through his skull.

"Oh, there you are," a sonorous voice said at his left ear. Sandy looked around to see Dr. Clark leaning on the receptionist's desk in his baby-blue work smock. The dentist had a broad smile on his face that was at once reassuring and peculiar, but what unnerved Sandy most was that Clark looked nineteen years old.

"You're the doctor?" Sandy asked.

"I'm the doctor," Clark affirmed with a boyish dip of the head. This head was adorned with a very large nose, which acted as a resonator and gave Clark's voice such a sonorous tone. His face was pitted in spots with acne scars and he wore plastic aviator glasses. He continued to smile as Sandy studied him. "What do you say we have a look at that little devil?" Clark said, then came around the receptionist's cubicle and threw open a door that led down a short hallway.

"Have you been in practice long?" Sandy inquired, following behind.

"All summer," Clark said as they arrived at the examination room.

"You just graduated from dental school this year?"

"Every dentist has to sometime or other," Clark quipped. "For some reason they want you to do it at the beginning of your career rather than in the middle or just before you retire. Please have a seat."

The equipment looked rather old to Sandy, perhaps secondhand. The padded chair, for example, was mended in two places with green fabric tape that didn't quite match the chair's original color. And the instrument console didn't match. It was pink, with a bulbous look that seemed straight out of the 1950s and a plastic insignia that resembled an old Pontiac hood ornament.

Clark continued to smile as he laid various steel probes on the circular work table at his elbow. Sandy relaxed into the softness of the chair, thinking that his day-long misery would soon be at an end.

"Beautiful out today, huh?" Clark remarked jauntily.

"Gorgeous."

"Halloween."

"I know."

"All those parents out there giving sugar to each other's kids." Clark shook his head. "What a dopey society we live in."

"You're telling me."

"Might as well give the kiddies rat poison."

Sandy looked at Clark askance.

"I mean, for all the harm it does them," the dentist explained. He attached a paper bib to a little chain and clipped it around Sandy's neck. Then he switched on the overhead light and adjusted the height of the chair. Finally, he selected an instrument and leaned forward. "Which tooth is the troublemaker?"

"Lower right. One of the molars."

"Okeedoke. Open wide, please."

Clark descended with the probe. To Sandy it looked like a logger's peavey. He cringed in anticipation. He could see his open mouth and terrified eyes reflected in Clark's eyeglasses. Clark inspected the site with an earnest expression on his face. The smile was gone.

"Nice work in here," he observed. "Who's your regular dentist?"

"Steve Greenbaum," Sandy managed to say, even with the probe at his lips.

"He's got a helluva practice. A *helluva* practice. The guy's practically minting money over there."

Clark entered Sandy's mouth with his probe. Sandy heard the screak of steel on enamel. The pain, however, remained steady, pulsing.

"Okay, okay, I think I see the bad guy," Clark said. "Tell me: do you feel this?"

Clark proceeded to insert the tip of the probe in a large cavity in Sandy's second molar. He might as well have used a fireplace poker. Sandy howled and jerked his head away. Clark withdrew the probe.

"Sorry about that. We'll numb it up before I go back in there."

"Please."

"That's a helluva cavity. A good two millimeters. I'm surprised you haven't felt any pain before today." Clark got a steel and glass syringe out of a drawer and filled it with an ampule of Novocain. He approached Sandy with the needle held just out of eyeshot. "Open wide now."

Sandy complied and closed his eyes. He was not particularly fearful of Novocain shots, and he welcomed the cessation of feeling in the tooth. There was a slight pinch as the needle went in. In a few seconds it was over.

"Let's take a couple of pictures in the meantime, huh?"

"Sure."

Clark got out some photo blanks and swung the X-ray machine forward from behind the console. He laid a lead-lined apron over Sandy's torso, set up the film in his mouth, and took two exposures of the tooth in question.

"Relax for a few minutes. I'll go develop these babies."

Sandy nodded and sank back into the seat. The pain in his tooth was slowly but surely ebbing away for the first time in hours. Then he remembered Joel, the check for $250, the portrait commission. He thought of Robin, picturing her in her Burberry trenchcoat, interviewing some farmer about the pumpkin harvest. What kind of a schmuck had he been not to call her? He wanted her back, that was for sure. But what if she wouldn't have him back? The idea made his stomach hurt. He'd have to change, he thought. He'd have to stop taking his frustrations out on her, quit blaming her for being able to take care of herself, give up resenting her sheer, uncomplicated generosity. But what would he have to do to get Robin back?

"Here we go," Clark said, reentering with the two

X-ray shots clipped to a metal frame. He threw the switch on a white glass viewer and laid the pictures on it. "It's as plain as day," he said, slapping his thigh.

"What is?" Sandy asked when Clark failed to explain.

"Okay," the dentist began. "See that dark, round, blob-shaped thing around the distal root?"

"I guess."

"That's an abscess."

"Uh oh."

"Uh oh is right," Clark concurred. "The pulp chamber's fully infected. These pictures are bad news."

"What are you going to do?"

"That's partly up to you. I recommend a root canal. Ever had that?"

"Yes. Once."

"That's what's called for here."

"It's expensive," Sandy said.

"It's not cheap. The other option, of course, is extraction. But I strongly recommend against that. It's cheap, but then you've got no more molar, and in the long run that means nothing but trouble and much more expense. Ultimately, with an extraction, we're talking bridgework. You've got to throw a bridge in there or else the little soldiers on each side of the empty socket cave in. Do you have any idea how much pressure the jaw muscles exert on a tooth in the simple act of chewing?"

"No."

"Think about it. Over the course of a lifetime. We're talking serious stresses. I strongly recommend root canal. I can start it here, clean this guy out, and then Greenbaum can finish up when he gets back from vacation. The whole process takes an average of three appointments. One to—"

"I know."

"Of course." Clark puffed out his cheeks and folded

his arms. "Anyway, that's the whole story. What do you say?"

"Please proceed."

Edmund Black was in the living room of his house with the shades all drawn, listening to one of his new records, eating a meatball submarine sandwich, and reading a *New York Post* story about a Long Island slaying, when the telephone rang.

"City Morgue," he answered the extension at his elbow.

"Is that any way to answer a phone, you goddammed fool," his mother asked at the other end of the line.

"Sorry, Ma. I didn't know it was you."

"I suppose if you knew it was me, you wouldn't answer like a goddamned fool."

"That's right."

"Next time I'll send a telegram in advance, advising you of the exact hour of my call, and then you can answer the phone without being a goddamned fool."

"Okay."

"Are you eating something?"

"Yempphh."

"Would you show me the courtesy of not chewing into the goddamned phone when I'm talking to you."

Edmund swallowed. "Sure, Ma."

"I got a call just a few minutes ago from that Mr. Hankinson at the Chase Manhattan Bank, Edmund."

Edmund nodded his head.

"Edmund, are you listening to me?"

"I hang on your every word, Mother."

"Do you know what he said to me, this Mr. Hankinson?"

"He said, 'Marry me and take me away from all this.'"

179

"I should have known better than to ask."

"He said, 'Shake yo' groove thang.' "

"Shut up your sassy mouth, you goddamned fool. I'll tell you what he said. He said you're fiddling your accounts again."

"Fiddling? What's that supposed to mean?"

"You know exactly what he's talking about. You're kiting checks."

"I don't know why you believe him."

"I suppose I should believe you."

"Your own flesh and blood against some self-interested honkie shylock, some plunderer of widows and orphans? Absolutely."

"I wish I knew what has to happen to you before you take your life seriously."

"I take this accusation *very* seriously, Mother. Kiting checks! Good God! If word gets around, our credit will be no good anywhere. All our purveyors will stop purveying. Our servants will cease to serve. Call our attorneys at once. I intend to sue this—"

"Shut up. There's no sense trying to discuss anything with you, since you refuse to act like an adult. So I'll pretend you're still a child and just tell you how things are. First of all, it is obvious that you have run through your whole year's allowance from the Morgan Guaranty fund. That, I'm sorry to say, is your business. It's your trust fund—except how anybody could fail to live on an income of thirty-eight thousand dollars a year in upstate New York, I'll never know. Especially when that person doesn't do anything but sit around the house all day."

Edmund rolled his eyes and held the receiver six inches away from his ear.

"Are you listening to me, boy?"

"Yes, Mother."

"I have covered those bad checks of yours for the last

time. Now, I want you to tell me what you are going to live on until the first quarter of next year."

"I'll have a porch sale. It's all the rage up here in the north country."

"How many thousands of dollars do you expect to raise that way?"

"Oh, I dunno. I could bake a few things the night before. That usually brings in the yokels for miles around. I could even sell weenies, you know, as sort of a loss leader."

"I don't believe you've given your financial situation a moment's thought."

"Why should I, with you doing it for me?"

"I see how it is. You're simply not capable of being serious. Keep it up, boy, and the courts are going to declare you incompetent. You won't see another dime of your grandaddy's money."

"And who's going to petition the court? You?"

There was an elongated interval of silence on the line.

"I will send you a check for three thousand dollars in the mail this afternoon, Edmund, because I will not have you embarrassing me at the place where I do my banking, and I will not tolerate a rerun of the trouble you caused me at Manufacturer's Hanover four years ago. As of this morning, your Chase Manhattan account is closed, so don't even try that scam again. You ought to be able to live on fifteen hundred dollars a month until the end of the year without any undue suffering. Do you hear me, boy?"

"I hear you," Edmund said, gnashing his teeth.

"When I think of what your grandaddy had to go through to make something of himself, to leave something to those who came after him; and then when I think of you, and what you're doing with yourself—why, it just makes me . . . it makes me—"

"Sick?"

"That's right. It makes me sick."

"Don't be sick, Mother. You'll ruin a perfectly good phone."

"It's not the only thing that makes me sick to my heart today," she said, ignoring his remark. Edmund could hear some snuffling at her end as of tears being shed into a tissue, and then, in a voice close to breaking, his mother said, "Your sister called just a few minutes ago. She's getting married."

"Big deal. It's the third time."

"This time it's different, Edmund."

"They always say that."

"That's not it. This time she's marrying a white boy."

Unseen by his mother, Edmund's jaw dropped at the news. A look of profound bewilderment made pinspots in his eyes.

"Did you hear what I said, Edmund? She's marrying a goddamned white boy."

"So am I," Edmund mumbled.

"What did you say?"

"I said I'm going to marry a white boy, too."

George Wells left his cottage dressed in a suit and tie for the first time in as long as he could remember. It was a tan poplin summer weight suit he had bought ten years ago for the oral defense of his master's thesis. The necktie was rather wide by present-day standards, and its psychedelic paisley pattern was so raucous it appeared to move.

He climbed behind the wheel of his blue pickup, amazed that he was still there at all. Since Greenleaf's visit, a weird giddiness had taken hold within him. The shotgun was back in the closet. George felt like a wrongly convicted prisoner granted a last-minute stay of execution, off on a mission to finally prove his innocence.

He stopped briefly downtown—double parked in front of the Feedlot's pseudo-western saloon facade—and went inside to look for the restaurant's owner, Kenny Burkhart. The other waiters—younger guys in their twenties—were already busy setting up the dining room for the supper shift, wiping down flatware, folding napkins, and scooping butterballs into monkey dishes with an ice cream dipper—chores George had done thousands of times over the years. The smell of rolls baking in the kitchen was deeply comforting.

George found the slim, casually dressed, thirty-nine-year-old owner at the waiters' station near the kitchen door, replacing a heating element in the automatic coffeemaker. Burkhart looked up, noting George's suit and tie.

"I can't work tonight, Kenny. Something's come up."

"What? Harlowe's party?"

"No. It's my dad. I've got to go see him in the hospital."

"Oh, gosh, that's too bad. Is he going to be all right?"

"No," George said, his knees almost buckling. "He's probably going to die."

Burkhart quickly stood up, speechless.

"Anyway, I didn't want you to worry about where I was. You should be okay with three guys and a busboy on. Harlowe's putting out a big spread so it'll probably be quiet here tonight."

"Uh, sure, George. No problem," Burkhart said. "And, uh, good luck."

"Is the lip numb yet?" Dr. Clark asked, as he put a new bit in his high-speed drill.

"Not really," Sandy said, touching himself there.

"How about the tongue?"

"Just a slightly fuzzy feeling."

"What do you say we give it another little shot of jungle juice?" Clark asked with a wry smile.

"Sure. Please."

And so the needle was administered a second time. Overhead, the piped-in Muzak played the same up-tempo rendition of Bob Dylan's "Blowin' in the Wind" that Sandy had heard earlier in the shopping mall. Clark whistled along to it as he studied the X-ray shots. Then, still smiling, he spun around, took up the high-speed drill, and asked Sandy to open wide.

"My lip's really not very numb yet."

"There must be some tingling."

"There's some. But I can still feel it. And the tongue, too."

"Hmm. What do you want me to do?"

"I don't know. You're the dentist."

"I can give you some more juice."

Sandy sighed. The shots didn't hurt much, but they were becoming tiresome, to say the least. "Where does that stuff go, anyway, when you shoot it in there?"

"Oh, it rattles around."

"Rattles around? Where?"

"In the soft tissues. People are just so much mush, you know. Highly organized mush."

"How come this stuff isn't working on me?"

"It'll work eventually, believe me," Clark declared with boyish confidence as he loaded the syringe a third time. "But everybody's different."

"Can you become immune to this stuff?"

"No."

"Then what's the problem?"

"No problem." Clark continued to smile. "You happen to have a wisdom tooth left in there. Most people, it grows in sideways or upside down and they have to get it yanked. So much the better for you. You've still got yours. However, it tends to block access to the mandibular branch of the trigeminal nerve. Nothing to worry about. We'll just load you up till it conks out. Open wide now."

Sandy could not even feel the third needle go in. Soon, his lower lip, chin, and the right side of his tongue began to tingle noticeably.

"Getting there?" Clark asked.

Sandy nodded, his eyes closed.

"Okay, then, let's put this bad boy out of its misery."

Clark hung the suction hook over Sandy's lip and descended with the drill in hand. He seemed all nose and eyeglasses. Sandy felt the drill make contact with the tooth. It whirred musically. He became aware of the smell of burnt bone. Clark now sang along with the Muzak, a lavish orchestral version of Police's tune, "Every Move You Make." He had just completed the first verse when Sandy howled in pain. Clark withdrew the drill.

"How are you doing?" he asked.

"It's killing me."

"You feel this?"

"Yes."

"I don't see how. You've had three injections." Clark practically scolded him.

"I still feel it," Sandy said apologetically.

"How's your lip?"

"Tingly."

"Tingly? Not numb."

"No. It's not numb."

"Jeesh . . . Okay, we'll load you up some more," Clark said, shaking his head. This time he took pains to inject Novocain all around the vicinity of the tooth itself. "Why don't we wait a minute," he said, folding his arms and looking annoyed. "I've never seen a patient like you."

"In what? Four months of practice?"

"Nope. Not even in dental school," he replied, failing to catch the sarcasm. "You're something else. How's the old lip doing?"

"I think its finally starting to get numb."

"Jeez, I would think so. After four injections." Clark glanced at his watch. He hooked the suction tube over Sandy's lip again. "Let's get on with the job, huh?"

Clark proceeded to clean out the pulp chamber. Sandy felt some discomfort during the drilling, but nothing he felt justified in complaining about. When the pulp chamber was free of infected tissue, Clark prepared to negotiate the first of the three root canals. This was done using tiny little surgical reamers, or files. As soon as he inserted one in the canal, Sandy nearly hit the ceiling.

"I can't believe you feel this," Clark remonstrated, his hands on his hips.

"You . . . better . . . believe it," Sandy said, recovering his breath slowly. "Because it hurts like hell."

Clark closed his eyes and nodded in irritation. "I have to give you an intrapulpal injection then."

"A what?"

"A shot directly into the tooth itself."

"Oh, my God."

Clark was already filling the syringe. He squirted some of the solution into the rinse basin. "Come on, open up," he said impatiently.

"You're going to shoot that thing straight down my tooth?"

"If I don't, we're never going to get out of here. Come on. Open."

"I'm afraid of this shot."

"There's nothing to be afraid of. You've already had four others."

"But this one is going to hurt a lot more. I can tell."

"You'll feel a slight pinch. That's all. After that, blotto."

"Don't you have any laughing gas?"

"Don't use it."

"I don't know if I can take this."

"You want me to send you to an endodontist?"

"What's that?"

"This is all they do: root canals."

"I'd never get an appointment this late on a Friday afternoon."

"That's right. You wouldn't. You'd have to wait until Monday. And if I put a temporary in this thing the way it is now, with those diseased roots still in there, you'll have such pain that you'll think your whole head's gonna explode."

"So?"

"It's up to you."

"But obviously I haven't got any choice."

"Your choices are extremely limited."

Sandy closed his eyes and reluctantly opened his mouth. A moment later he felt what seemed like a .38 caliber bullet shoot down the center of his bad tooth and strike some innermost seat of agony never before revealed to exist within the confines of his own body. Clark pulled out the needle and prepared to resume reaming the roots as Sandy lay shuddering and moaning in the chair.

"Believe me," the dentist said. "The worst is over. You couldn't possibly feel it now if I took a ball peen hammer to this tooth. If you do, I'm sending you directly to the Smithsonian Institution as a medical curiosity. Open wide now."

Clark was right. The tooth was finally numb, absolutely dead to sensation. Sandy sank into the cushions as his tense muscles finally relaxed. Clark worked quickly and methodically. He hummed and sang along with the Muzak again. Sandy's thoughts had precipitated into a gray haze like the light on a television screen at four in the morning when all the stations have gone off the air. When the infected nerves were removed, Clark sanitized the vacant canals with a solution of sodium hypochloride. Finally, to prepare the hole for its temporary filling, he reached once more for the drill to burr off the rough edges. He had barely touched the tooth with the drill when Sandy heard him say, "Uh-oh," and opened his eyes to see Clark gingerly hanging the instrument back up.

"Whu . . . ?" Sandy said, his mouth utterly numb and cluttered with the suction hook and cotton wads.

"Just sit tight a moment."

Clark vanished for a moment and returned shortly with an X-ray blank. He pulled all the cotton out of Sandy's mouth, put in the film, and asked him to hold it in place with his forefinger. He took the picture, vanished again, and came back in a while with a dark expression on his youthful face.

"Look!" he said, thrusting the metal film holder at Sandy, who took it and tried to examine the X-ray in the blinding overhead light.

"Whu . . . ?"

"It's broken," Clark said, as though someone had pulled a lowdown trick on him. "The damn thing just cracked in half on us."

"Whu . . . ?"

"The tooth!" Clark angrily snatched the film away from him and brandished it like a lawyer waving a piece of damning evidence in a courtroom. "The tooth!"

"Whu . . . ?"

"The fucking thing is cracked right down the middle," he said, raising his voice almost a full octave. "It can't be fixed now. It has to come out."

"Whu . . . !"

"It has to be extracted."

"Whu di' you do—?"

"Does it matter? Will that make it whole again? Look, it happened. It's history. There's no point arguing about it. The tooth can't stay in there. It's *kaput*. Do you understand? It has got to go."

"But—"

"There's nothing else to discuss. I'm telling you, it has to come out. If I don't take it out now, you're going to have serious problems over the weekend." Clark was already rummaging in his drawer for the necessary implements, and as he found them, he laid them on his little round work shelf. "Come on, open up. Open up, goddamnit!"

Sandy, cringing in the chair, and bewildered, opened his mouth. Clark descended, scowling, with the forceps and snarled as he fought to extract the two halves of the cracked molar. Sandy felt the pressure of his hands, but the extraction was otherwise absolutely painless. When it was over, his head fell back against the cushioned chair with a thud. Clark put some gauze packings into the empty socket. "Leave this cotton stuff in for a half hour or so until the bleeding stops," he said indifferently. "Don't drink any hot liquids." He took the paper bib off Sandy, balled it up, and angrily tossed it into a trash can. "Okay, you can go now."

Sandy just lay there, gazing back in amazement.

"I said you can go now," Clark told him, as though speaking to an imbecile. He turned away to gather up his instruments for the sterilizer.

Sandy slowly climbed out of the chair, feeling dazed and very weak on his feet. It did not occur to him that he hadn't eaten a thing in almost twenty-four hours. He used the arm of the chair to steady himself. The whole side of his head from his ear to his neck was numb. It felt as though he had mud caked on it.

"Oh, by the way. Leave your name and address here before you go," Clark muttered, then proffered him a pen and a notepad.

"Whu fuh?"

"Why, for billing purposes, of course."

"You're guh bill me?"

"Certainly. You think I do this for kicks—"

Sandy slapped the pen and notepad out of Clark's hand. Then, with one of those adrenaline surges that are the privilege of gravely wounded animals, Sandy lunged for the dentist, grabbed him by his blue smock, flung him into the still warm chair, and pinned his slender throat to the cushioned headrest with one hand. With the other, he removed the bloody gauze packings from his mouth and flung them against the wall.

"All the collection agents in the world couldn't get me to pay you a plug nickel for what you did to me," he told the suddenly red-faced dentist in a voice full of phlegm and outrage. "You'll be lucky if I don't sue and put you out of business."

"Just don't hit me," Clark said.

Edmund was still staring at the telephone minutes after his mother hung up on him when it rang.

"What do you want now?"

"I beg your pardon. Mr. Black?"

"Who is this?"

"This is Mrs. Ricketts at the North Country Trust. Is this Edmund S. Black?"

"It may very well be."

"I'm sorry, sir. Are you Mr. Black or aren't you?"

"Let's say in theory I am Mr. Black."

The woman cleared her throat. "Well, Mr. Black. The Chase Manhattan of New York has sent us a notice of insufficient funds on several checks drawn on your account there and deposited here on Tuesday this week."

"So?"

"You've written quite a few checks on your account here since then, Mr. Black."

"So?"

"You have no funds to draw against here."

"So?"

"Well, we'd like you to come down and talk about it. We have our Friday evening hours tonight, Mr. Black. Five o'clock to seven."

"I'm not Mr. Black."

"Pardon me? Did you say that you're *not* Mr. Black?"

"That's right. I'm not Mr. Black."

"But a moment ago you said you *were* Mr. Black."

"I said in theory."

"I'm sorry, sir, but I don't understand."

"I was only pretending to be Mr. Black to find out what you wanted."

"Is this five-three-five zero-six-nine-seven?"

"Yes."

"But you're not Mr. Black?"

"No."

"May I ask who I'm speaking to, sir?"

"Mr. White."

"Does Mr. Black live there?"

"He comes and goes."

"Do you expect him back today?"

"It's hard to predict."

"Are you employed by Mr. Black, sir?"

"What is this, madam? Twenty questions? If you want to know whether I will inform Mr. Black about this call,

191

then you may rest assured that I shall relay the particulars of your allegations down to the last detail. It so happens Mr. Black left town on urgent business this morning. Even as we speak he is halfway around the globe inspecting his cocoa plantations in Pago Pago, where a revolution is under way. I had a cable from him not an hour ago. Damage, he says, was negligible, you'll be glad to hear. They got the last of the pods off the trees and loaded onto the tankers before the insurgents climbed the fences. Tomorrow he jets off to Bora Bora, where a typhoon threatens this year's pearl harvest. There's some concern about the rubber crop in Mindanao as well. Bark beetles they say. He is due back here in headquarters Monday morning. Is there anything else?"

"No. Just ask him to come in and see us on Monday."

"Depend on it, madam. And remember, good things come to those who wait. Carry on."

As soon as he hung up, the front doorbell rang.

"Jesus Christ on Christmas. We're under siege here!" he muttered, as he padded off to answer it.

He opened the door to find two policemen standing on the porch.

"What cunning costumes!" Edmund cried in delight. "Wait right there."

He bustled back into the living room, where the various packages from his foray downtown lay in a heap on the floor, and rummaged through them to find the bags of candy he had bought at the supermarket. Shortly, he returned to the door.

"He must be the one," said the officer with a neat red mustache whose nameplate said Hayden.

"We've received a complaint about you, sir, from a Mrs. Lucy Devore," said the second officer, shorter and dark-haired, whose nameplate said DiMarco.

"Never heard of the slut," Edmund told them jauntily. "Okay now, who wants Snickers and who wants Almond Joy?" he asked, holding out two fistfuls of candy bars.

The officers exchanged unbelieving glances.

"Mrs. Devore alleges that you were abusive to her and her children, sir," Hayden said.

"They weren't children," Edmund countered. "They were visitors from another solar system. And I was nice as could be. Under the circumstances, that is. Did you make those outfits yourselves?"

"You want me to read him his rights, or you do it?" DiMarco asked Hayden.

"You do it," Hayden said.

"Make up your minds," Edmund said. "Snickers or Almond Joy. You can have either one or the other."

"You have the right to remain silent and refuse to answer any questions," said DiMarco, reading from a card inside his hatband. "Anything you say may be used against you in a court of law."

"All right, be a couple of little piggies and have both," Edmund said, thrusting out the candy bars.

"If you desire a lawyer and cannot afford one, one will be provided to you without cost. Do you understand the rights I have explained to you?"

"Come on, take the shit," Edmund said, dumping the miniature candy bars at their feet. "I won't stand here all day like a cigar-store indian."

"Now that I have advised you of your rights are you willing to answer my questions without an attorney?"

"Very well, go fuck yourselves," Edmund said, slamming the door in their faces. The doorbell rang almost immediately and Edmund reopened the door. "You again! What is it this time? Tickets for the PBA picnic? No, thanks."

"Please come with us, sir," Hayden said.

"But I'm not in costume. You'll have to go trick-or-treating without me."

Hayden and DiMarco exchanged another portentous glance. Then each drew his service revolver and took a step away from Edmund.

"You're under arrest, sir," Hayden said.

"Please get into the car." DiMarco motioned with his head at the black and white Ford with the revolving red gumball light idling directly in front of the house. Edmund tried to slam the door on them again. But this time Hayden quickly seized him, spun him around, and got him in a choke hold, the officer using his brawny forearm to throttle Edmund. DiMarco handcuffed Edmund, then hurried downstairs and threw open a door to the cruiser's rear seat. Hayden, meanwhile, dragged Edmund down to the cruiser, flung him inside, and got in behind the wheel.

"Isn't this carrying a joke too far?" Edmund said in a voice somewhat froggy from being choked. "I mean, I've heard of trick-or-treat. But kidnap or treat? Never."

"Keep on talking crazy, buster," DiMarco said.

"I see what it is. Foolish me! You two don't like chocolate. Well, all you had to do was say something. I had a whole bag full of the most adorable little candy pumpkins."

It was less than four blocks to the central police station in the back of the town hall on High Street. Edmund was forcibly marched inside. Hayden and DiMarco emptied his pockets.

"What's this?" asked the desk sergeant, one Brian McGinty, pointing to the three Black Beauty capsules that Joel had given Edmund earlier in the day.

"My heart medicine."

"Have you got a prescription for it?"

"Of course, I do."

"Let's see it."

"I don't carry it on my person, oaf. It's at home."

"Okay. Hayden, DiMarco, take this gentleman back to his place so he can get this here prescription."

"Uh, wait." Edmund pictured the plastic bag of marijuana sitting right out on the coffee table in the living room. "I just remembered. I threw it out."

"Mister," the sergeant said with the faintest trace of a smile on his freckled Celtic face, "you're in a peck of trouble."

ELEVEN

Joel Harlowe would not be thwarted from his heart's desire just because he did not know his beloved last name. Among the many useful items he kept around the house was a copy of the current Greer College directory. What he faced was a simple matter of systematic investigation. All he had to do was comb the listings for girls named Kelly who lived in the Hildebrand dormitory. Greer was a small college to begin with—only 2239 students in all, and about one-fifth of them males—and it was unlikely that there would be more than one Kelly in that particular dorm. And if there *was* more than one, if there were two, five, eight, well then, by golly, he would call them all until he located *his* Kelly.

The process turned out to be somewhat more tedious than he had anticipated. For one thing, naturally, the students were all listed last names first, so Joel couldn't simply run his finger down the lefthand margin until he spotted the enchanted name. Their given names were

therefore not all lined up neatly, and what with the extremely small print, it hurt Joel's eyes to scan the entries.
The directory ran to seventeen double-columned pages in
all. Even more discouraging, he did not encounter a single Kelly until page twelve, and this was a Kelly Quinn
who lived in Beedle. He underlined her name and continued his search, wondering if perhaps Kelly had switched
dorms since the directory was printed. Then, on page
sixteen, he saw the name Seagraves, Kelly, connected by
a string of dots to the word Hildebrand with a four-digit
number adjoining. Though he was certain that this was
the one, he read through to the end of the list for the sake
of absolute thoroughness, but did not come up with another Kelly.

Seagraves. Joel stopped to muse. The name was perfect! It spoke to him of adventure on the bounding main,
of lives heroically lost to the ocean's mysterious depths.
No doubt she was descended from a long line of naval
officers, brave admirals, intrepid Argonauts, captains of
the line. Fiery images of the great sea battles flashed in his
brain: Lake Erie! Hampton Roads! Manila Bay! Midway!
The great watery slogans of war rang in his ears: "Don't
give up the ship!" "Remember the Maine!" "Damn the
torpedos!" He envisioned a sepulchral gallery lined with
the portraits of Kelly's brave ancestors, their dark uniforms
immaculate, their golden epaulets gleaming (here and
there a sleeve pinned up where a volley of grapeshot
carried off a limb), their handsome faces so dauntless, the
eyes far seeing, full of courage, patriotism, rectitude!
Seagraves! It was a great American name!

Joel shuddered as the reverie came to a misty end. To
fortify himself to make what could be the most important
phone call of his life, Joel inhaled two more hits of cocaine from the snorter. His mind clarified instantly while
all doubts and trepidations fled. He dialed the Greer

switchboard and asked for Kelly's extension. The dormitory phone had a queer ring, rather like a buzzer. It buzzed four times. The intervals between the buzzes stretched from a second to what seemed like an hour. On the fifth buzz, someone picked it up.

"Hello."

"Kelly?"

"Nope. This is Betsy."

"Oh. May I speak to Kelly, please."

"She's not here right now."

"Oh? Where is she?"

"I have no idea."

"Do you know when she'll be back?"

"No."

"Do you think she'll be back in the next half hour or so?"

"I really haven't the slightest idea when she'll be back."

"All right. Thank you."

"May I say who called?"

"I'll, uh, try her again in a while."

"Okay. 'Bye."

Joel's disappointment was sharp, but did not last very long. Too many other things crowded his mind. Still wearing his jogging togs, he threw on a hooded sweatshirt, left the house, jumped in the Austin-Healy and made a final swing downtown before his departure for the city. He stopped first at the Merry Rovers Travel Agency on Broadway and booked a Tuesday morning flight for two to Eleuthera in the Bahamas. He had his hair trimmed at Shear Madness, picked up his Robin Hood costume at Gwen Chapman's shop, stopped by the casino in Congress Park (no one was there yet, except the two old ladies from the historical society who ran the museum on the second and third floors), and finally returned to his house on Catherine.

At home, he showered, shaved for the second time that day, and put on the Robin Hood outfit. He had never worn a pair of tights before. He had to admit that they felt rather good. He felt sleek and athletic in them, as though he could bound ten feet over a high jump bar. And they showed his well muscled legs to great advantage. He admired them in the mirror, though he was a little alarmed at the sight of his genitals bulging against the stretchy fabric, and he put on a pair of his regular black under-pants over the tights for modesty's sake. The tunic was loose-fitting and comfortable and would be great for danc-ing in later. Gwen had come up with a pair of deerskin booties which were feather-light and fit perfectly. Finally, there was a simple green mask to which Gwen had glued a few sequins and feathers. Joel wasn't sure about these trimmings. He didn't think Errol Flynn had worn any sequins or feathers in the movie, and he didn't want anyone to think that he was the kind of guy who used a costume party as an excuse for dressing like a flit. God knows, the tights were questionable enough. He'd take the mask along with him, but he'd have to think hard about whether to actually wear the goddam thing or not.

Joel glanced at his watch. It was three-thirty—no more time to waste shilly-shallying in front of the mirror. He disappeared briefly into his vast closet and soon re-emerged with the beautiful leather jumpsuit that he had had custom-made in Lake Placid some years ago. The leather was supple goatskin, dyed a deep cordovan. It was lined with the plushest mouton piling, including a tube collar that came up over his chin when fully zipped and kept out the wind at high speed on his motorcycle. He had worn the suit many times at temperatures below freezing, and it never failed to keep him warm as toast.

The leather had been completely waterproofed as well, with many applications of silicone.

He climbed into the suit before the mirror, wearing the green tights and tunic underneath. The suit closed by way of a zipper that ran from his crotch clear up to his chin. Joel loved to look at himself in the leather jumpsuit, imagining the impression he made on other people. With a full-face helmet under his arm, he appeared somewhat like a heroic astronaut about to embark on a fantastic voyage to new worlds. He glanced at his watch again. Twenty minutes to four, it said. He had to get a move on.

But first, he had to give Kelly another try.

"Hello."

"Has Kelly come back yet?"

"No."

Joel's heart sagged. "Can I leave a message?"

"Sure."

"Tell her . . . tell her that I love her very much and . . . and that I've decided to go to med school."

"You love her very much, and you've decided to go to med school," Kelly's suitemate, Betsy, repeated as though she were writing it down. "Who is this, by the way?"

"Nobody," Joel said. "She'll know who it was."

"Okay. 'Bye."

Joel was wondering if, in fact, she might not know who had left the message, when his telephone rang.

"Yes?"

"Joel?"

"Pop?"

An electrical thrill ran through Joel, buoying his spirits at once.

"Joel, where did you get the money to buy such a thing?" Fred Horowitz asked.

"Are you there?"

"Am I where?"

"At the new condo."

"I'm at my place."

"The old place in Tampa?"

"That's right. In Tampa."

"Why aren't you at the new place?"

"It's not for me, Joel, this fancy new place."

"What do you mean it's not for you? It's for you."

"It's not for me."

"It's yours. I bought it for you."

"Joel, where did you get the kind of money to buy such a place as this? A duplex penthouse! You know, I stopped by the sales office of the complex and asked what are these apartments going for, and the woman in charge—a young girl your age, by the way, very attractive, and very smart, no doubt, to have such an important job—she tells me that this duplex penthouse apartment sells for three hundred ninety thousand dollars, Joel. I almost had a heart attack. This is practically a half a million dollars."

Joel's pride was boundless. It seemed he had waited his whole life just for this moment, and he wanted to savor it, to wring out all the pleasure that it held for him.

"I only wish Mom was there to share it with you," he said.

"Never mind your mother, Joel. Where does a person come up with half a million dollars to pay for such a palace in the sky?"

"Does it have a nice view of the water, Pop?"

"Never mind the view. How does someone pay for such a thing?"

"Don't worry about the payments, Pop. It's taken care of."

"That's what I mean: how?"

"It's all paid for."

"Joel, for Chrissake, where do you get the money to buy such an apartment?"

Joel hesitated a moment. It was beginning to sink in that his father wasn't merely engaging in flattery.

"Where, Joel?" his father demanded in a voice growing somewhat shrill with impatience.

"In business," Joel told him.

"Sure, business. What kind of business?"

"Import-export."

"From import-export you get this kind of money? What is it you import-export? Gold? Diamonds?"

"Does it matter?"

"I want to know. What kind of business is my son in that he can plunk down half a million dollars on an apartment without batting an eyelash."

"It's not half a million, Pop."

"Excuse me. A little over a third of a million. How's that? I want to know, Joel. What?"

"What, what?"

"What kind of business you're in."

"It's diversified," Joel said, losing heart rapidly. "Lots of different things. It doesn't matter anyway, Pop. I've got great news: I've decided to go to medical school."

"To be a doctor?"

"Of course, to be a doctor. What else? To be a lawyer?"

"Now, all of a sudden, you're going to be a doctor?"

"A heart surgeon, Pop. I've made up my mind to go for it."

"Joel, I don't understand. You're twenty-eight years old."

"So?"

"What kind of cockamamie thing is it to go to medical school at your age. Don't you know how long it takes?"

"Four years."

"And another four years training in the hospital after that. By the time you're set up in your own practice, you'll be forty years old, for Chrissake."

"I'll be thirty-six."

"Thirty-six, forty, what the hell's the difference?"

"Pop, you don't understand. I'm already in business. This would be more like a sidelight, a hobby."

"A hobby! Are you out of your mind, Joel? Medicine is not a sidelight. You have to give your all to it."

"I don't mean to suggest that I wouldn't give my all to it—"

"What do you mean, you don't mean? You just said you plan to do it as a hobby. Tell me: am I hearing things? Did you say it or not?"

"I said it. I said it! But believe me, if I became a doctor, I'd give my all to it. Can we just forget that for now, because frankly it's just something in the planning stage. Can we talk about something else? Something I know is very important to you?"

"Sure. What?"

"Pop, I found a terrific girl."

"When?"

"Uh, some time ago."

"What's her name?"

"Kelly."

"What is she? Irish?"

"No, Pop. She's American."

"Is she Jewish at least?"

"No. But she's very beautiful and brilliant and comes from an excellent family background in Connecticut."

"Joel, why a Catholic girl?"

"Who said she's Catholic?"

"With a name like Kelly, what else could she be? And Joel, believe me, Catholic girls bring a husband nothing but misery. They're lousy in bed, and every time you do it, there's another mouth to feed.''

"Pop, she's not Catholic.''

"So what? The Protestants are worse!''

"Pop, for God's sake, this is the late twentieth century.''

"They don't have Jewish girls anymore? Joel, this smart, attractive girl who runs that sales office: *she* was Jewish.''

"You could tell without asking?''

"I asked.''

"I see. Tell me, Pop, why don't *you* marry her?''

"Don't you talk smart to me, Joel. I'm still your father. And your mother should be alive to hear what you just said! I'm sure she's spinning in her grave.''

The picture of his mother spinning around in a casket six feet under suddenly made Joel queasy. He sat on the stool beside the kitchen counter.

"Pop, will you do me a favor?''

"What?''

"Reserve your judgment about Kelly until you meet her?''

"Sure. When can I meet her?''

"Soon.''

"Why don't you bring her down here for a few days?''

"I can't.''

"You can't? Why not? You never come down here to see me. Always to see you I have to schlepp off to some island that gets the same amount of sun as we get here in Tampa, or someplace they don't speak English. What is it with you and Florida?''

"There's nothing with me and Florida, Pop.''

"I think you have a complex about it. In five years since I'm down here, not once have you come to visit me.''

"I just don't like it there, that's all. Besides, flying

first-class can hardly be called schlepping, and as long as I'm willing to spring for the tickets, I don't know why you mind meeting me at some of the world's most beautiful and interesting places. We had a terrific time in Nassau for Hanukkah, didn't we?"

"It was seventh heaven, Joel, but—"

"And Passover in Paris! All the museums and restaurants we went to!"

"It was terrific. I never had such a worthwhile heartburn. But Joel, you know I've got a life down here in Tampa. I've got friends, acquaintances, people I'd like to introduce my son to. Maybe it's—what's the word? —conceited, but I'd like my friends to see what a good-looking, successful son I have. I don't see how you can begrudge your old man that. It's normal, isn't it?"

"I suppose."

"What do you mean, you suppose? Of course, it's normal. It's *normal*!"

"Look, maybe I'll come down."

"When?"

"I don't know. It depends on when Kelly can get away."

"She a working girl, this Kelly?"

"That's right. And I don't know when she's scheduled for a vacation."

"What's her occupation?"

"She . . . she works with boats."

"With boats. What is she, a sailor?"

"That's right. Her father owns one of those sailing ships that cruises off the coast of New England. She works for him."

"Is that where you met her?"

"That's right. This August, on a cruise."

"That's some business to have: to sail a boat for a living."

"It's great, Pop. I think a lot about doing it myself."

"Only you must not see much of her."

"We get together quite often."

"Where?"

"Here. She comes here. Or I go there."

"There? Where's there? The middle of the ocean?"

"No. Newport. You know, Rhode Island."

"I thought you said the family was from Connecticut."

"They are. They just dock the boat in Newport."

"Oh. But they can't run those cruises all year round."

"Of course not."

"Well, she must get some time off in the off-season, Joel. It's getting to be winter already."

"Halloween isn't quite winter, Pop."

"Hey, tomorrow's the first day of November, am I right?"

"Yes."

"You tell me who goes on a pleasure cruise off New England in November."

"They don't sail only up here. When it gets cold, they head down to the Caribbean."

"You mean down this way?"

"Yes. I mean no, actually, way past you. Down to the islands."

"They must stop in Florida."

"Not on the Gulf coast where you are, Pop."

"Well, maybe we could go for a cruise on this boat of hers, down in the islands when they get there."

"Sure," Joel agreed, glancing at his watch, which said ten minutes to four. "Maybe we will. Listen, Pop, I have to get off now. Tell me: When are you going to move into the new place?"

"I don't know, Joel. What do I need two bedrooms and a big dining room for? And on the twentieth floor—*oy yi yoi!*—it makes me dizzy up there."

"You can never have too much space, Pop. And in a few days you'll get used to the view. You'll love it. You'll see. I'll send you a telescope."

"Please, Joel, don't send me a telescope."

"Okay, binoculars. You can watch the boats out on the water. You can watch the girls go by."

"I can watch the girls go by my window here without binoculars. Please, Joel, I like it here in my trailer just fine."

"I can't stand the idea that you live in a trailer."

"Maybe so. But it's not an idea that a person has to live in. A person has to live in a real place. I'd get lost in this penthouse."

"Then you're not going to move in?"

"Joel, I don't want to sound like an ingrate, but it's not for me."

"I see," Joel said, glancing again at his watch. "So what do you plan to do with a half million dollars' worth of real estate and furnishings? Huh, Pop?"

"I don't know, Joel. Maybe you should, uh, put it back on the market."

"You definitely want to sell it, then?"

"It's not for me to sell, Joel."

"Yes, it is. It's yours. You own it, Pop."

"But I don't want it Joel. You sell it."

"I got it for *you*, Pop."

"You sell it, Joel, and put the money back into your business, whatever it is. I'm sure it's already gone up in value since you bought it. Please. By the way, what's all this sniffling I hear. You sound like you have a cold."

"It's nothing, Pop. A slight stuffed nose."

"It's hat and glove weather where you are. Don't play games with your health, son. Believe me, it's the most precious thing a person has in the world."

"I believe you, Pop."

"So, maybe you and this Kelly will come down for Hanukkah this year. What do you say?"

"Sure, Pop. Maybe."

"Just a couple of days. Let the old man show off a little, huh? Then, if you can't stand it, I'll go anywhere in the world with you for the rest of the holiday—except, please, not Russia. And Egypt I can live without, too."

"Okay, Pop. I've got to go now."

"It just isn't for me, Joel, this big place. I like being only two steps away from the ground. Old people fall down a lot, you know?"

"I know, Pop. I really have to go."

"See you around Hanukkah then, son. Bye."

"Bye-bye, Pop."

Joel hung up the phone carefully, as though it might blow up in his face unless handled with the utmost care. There was a hollow feeling in his chest, and his temples throbbed. He filled the chamber of his cocaine snorter and inhaled the drug in one nostril and then the other. Within seconds, the pains in his head and chest ebbed away, and his world view quickly became satisfactory again. His father would come around. Old people were resistant to change. It was a universal law. He'd soon see the benefits of life in a luxury apartment and eat his words.

Joel wrote the word *telescope* on a notepad beside the phone and went down the hall to his bedroom closet. There, he reached inside one of the teakwood cubbyholes where he kept his shoes, and behind a pair of oxblood wingtips, he felt a small hard object. He withdrew the seven-millimeter Bellamorti automatic pistol and checked the clip. It was full of cartridges. He pulled on his steel-toed, calf-length motorcycling boots—they too were reddish-brown and handmade to match the leather suit—and inserted the pistol inside the boot, so he could reach

it with his right hand in the event of an unforeseeable
business problem. From a large magnet screwed underneath the night table beside his bed, Joel pulled a snub-
nosed .32 caliber Smith & Wesson revolver. He spun the
cylinder to make sure it contained five bullets—the sixth
chamber he left empty under the hammer to eliminate the
chance of an accidental discharge—then slipped the hand-
gun into a pocketlike holster on the inside of his cycling
suit, just in front of his left armpit.

In the bathroom, he shook a handful of Black Beauty
biphetamine capsules into his hand, popped one in his
mouth and dropped the rest into a zippered pocket. He
washed the pill down by drinking right out of the faucet.
Moving quickly to the kitchen, he flung open a cabinet
and pulled a king-size box of Cheerios off the shelf. Inside
the box were neat bundles of hundred dollar bills in lots
of fifty, each bundle with a paper tape around it. Joel
removed fifteen bundles from the Cheerios box, and another five from a box of Wheaties beside it. He stuffed the
$100,000 into a plastic trash bag. Finally, he grabbed his
helmet, his insulated cycling gloves, and the leather booties that went with his Robin Hood costume. He decided
to leave the mask behind on the grounds that it was
definitely too effeminate.

His keys lay on the dining room table, and he snatched
them up as he hurried out of the house. He felt like he
was suffocating in the leather cycling suit. Outside, the air
was cool and crystalline, and he felt invigorated as he
strode out to the garage, a modest, separate clapboard
structure built 110 years after the house. He unlocked and
threw open the door. In the rear stood his motorcycle, the
black BMW RS-1000. He tossed the leather booties and
the garbage bag full of money into a sleek fiberglass
storage compartment on the back, put on the shiny black
full-face helmet and tightened the chin strap, climbed

aboard the bike and rolled it out of the garage, which he locked behind him. The big engine came to life at a touch of the electric start. Unlike Sandy's ridiculous clattering Suzuki, the BMW's engine purred. The custom 5.5-gallon touring tank was full, enough for the entire round-trip. He checked a police radar detector, the size of a cigarette pack, clamped on his handlebars. The green light indicated it was in working order. A slim wire with a small jack on the end dangled from the chin of his helmet. The wire was connected to two tiny speakers located inside the helmet. He plugged the jack into a tape player built into the bike's windscreen. A compartment beside it held a selection of cassettes, tapes Joel had recorded himself with music tailored to his precise motoring needs. He took out a tape labeled Road Sounds #1 and slipped it into the player. The tape came on in the middle of a song, Bruce Springsteen powerfully singing the words:

I'm going down, down, down, down
I'm going down, down, down . . .

Joel punched the shift lever down into first gear with the toe of his boot. The transmission answered with its characteristic, solid, reassuring *thunk*. He released the clutch and rolled out onto Catherine Street, headed out of town the back way, where nobody would see him leaving.

George Wells, his mouth dry and head aching, drove out of town on South Broadway. Before World War Two the town limits had opened up to a graceful vista of orchards, farm fields, and woods, but now the roadside was crammed with a clutter of fast-food stands. There were fifteen of these establishments within a half-mile strip, which the Chamber of Commerce, in its first enraptured flushes of avarice and venality, had dubbed Excelsior Springs' Million Dollar Gateway. George wanted to blow it all up.

At a complicated five-way intersection, he bore right onto Route 50, which veered southwest toward Delft. In front of the K Mart Plaza a construction crew was widening the road to four lanes. The jackhammers were deafening, and the air was acrid with the odor of hot asphalt. George rolled up his window and waited for the flagman to wave him by. Amid this frightening, noxious din, George tried to turn his thoughts to the old farm up at Indian Hill.

Birds would be moving in the sunlit scrub, grouse, maybe even some wild turkeys. Mostly, though, it would be quiet—a few diehard crickets chirping in the asters, the rustle of leaves in the oaks around the ruined farmhouse. He could be happy there, George thought. Maybe he should take Greenleaf's money, after all, buy the old place and move up there, away from the Springs and its spreading tentacles of so-called progress. But then there was the matter of Mill Creek. By taking Greenleaf's money for the place on Marcy Street, wasn't he also more or less abetting the destruction of the trout stream?

A horn blared behind him. George straightened up with a start. His head throbbed and his hands left beads of sweat on the plastic steering wheel as the flagman waved him through.

Five miles down Route 50, he entered Ralston Spa, which had enjoyed a brief shimmer of fashion in the 1850s before being totally eclipsed by its grander sister to the north. George recalled that a large percentage of the patients on the psych ward had been residents of Ralston Spa. Thinking about his old job at the hospital suddenly reminded him—with a force that left him momentarily breathless—that his father awaited him in a hospital at the end of the road. He realized now that he had no idea what he might say to his father when he walked into the hospital room. The part of him that had once loved, hated, and battled the old man felt as though it were only now stirring from a long sleep of the dead.

Glen Toole swiveled back and forth on his stool at the lunch counter in the five-and-ten-cent store on the spot that once had been occupied by the lobby of the Republic Hotel, where presidents and the crowned heads of Europe once had trod. No presidents had come to Excelsior Springs since Woodrow Wilson, and the last crowned head to pass through was the nearly penniless Grand Duke Nicolae of Romania, dispossessed by the communists, who traveled the northeastern U.S. as a salesman for the Troy Lavatory Supply Corp. in the 1950s.

The lunch counter at the five-and-ten was a favorite among the ex-patients of the Excelsior Hospital psychiatric ward. In fact, it could practically have been considered an annex of the ward, a clubhouse. They came here from all around town to swap the latest tales of woe and persecution, of food stamps denied, of welfare checks swiped, of medications raised or lowered, of pending court dates for petty crimes. Among the innumerable eateries in town, the food here was far and away the most abysmal. The most complicated item on the menu was a grilled cheese sandwich. Mostly, the call was for coffee, that staple beverage of the unemployable, for whom killing time is a life's work.

"Gonna get me a car," Glen told Skip Pirtle, thirty-five, who held the record for the most separate admissions to the local psych ward (seventeen) without having been labeled chronic and shipped off to the state hospital at Sardis.

"Yeah?" Pirtle replied. "What kind?"

"Sports car. Gimme a cigarette, huh?"

"How you gonna buy a car if you can't buy a pack of butts?"

"You'll see. Come on, lend me a smoke."

Pirtle grudgingly fished a box of Marlboros out of his soiled red-checked wool hunting shirt and flipped it open for Glen. "Whadja, spend your whole check already?"

"Never mind my check. I can make things happen."

"You're crazy, you know that?"

"I can make people do what I want. Look, I just made you give me a cigarette."

Pirtle snatched the cigarette from Glen's mouth and stepped on it. "I s'pose you made me do that."

"Course not. You made yourself do that."

"Well, see?"

"I didn't say I could stop you from doin' something stupid that you want to do. Come on, gimme another cigarette."

"You already had yours."

"I didn't hardly have none of it. You were the one stomped it out. Come on, gimme a smoke."

Pirtle fished out the box again and gave Glen another, saying, "These here cost a dollar a pack."

"I know that."

"You ought to buy your own damn butts."

"Why should I when I can get 'em off you?"

"You're crazy, you know that?"

"I used to be crazy, but I ain't crazy no more," Glen said, taking a deep drag on his cigarette and smiling. "I got powers. I can make people do things. I got a secret."

"Yeah? What's that?"

"I ain't tellin' you. I told you: it's a secret."

Pirtle lit a cigarette. Looking at Glen askance, he wrinkled the single black eyebrow that gave his head the appearance of a cookie jar. "I always knew you were crazy," he said.

TWELVE

The red art deco electric clock above the sink in Sandy's kitchen area said nine minutes to four. He was due at the casino at four, but after his ordeal at the dentist's this Halloween day, he desperately wanted a shower. So he went into the bathroom area and experimentally turned on the hot water. To his surprise and relief, clouds of steam soon billowed up over the jury-rigged shower curtain. He stepped briefly back into the kitchen and poured himself a jelly glass of the cheap straight sherry that he used for cooking Chinese style. It was the only liquor he had. The right side of his face was still completely numb and a goodly amount of the sherry dribbled out the side of his mouth and down his neck. Still, it tasted wonderful. It left a glowing warmth in his empty stomach and was absorbed rapidly into his bloodstream, where it began to soothe away all the manifold horrors of his day.

He left his clothing in a pile on the kitchen floor and,

with his eyeglasses still on, stepped quickly into the shower, where he turned the water up as hot as he could stand it and let it stream down over the top of his head. To be free of pain seemed an ineffable luxury. He sucked some of the water into his mouth and when he spit it out saw that it was tinged pink with blood, reminding him for an angry moment of Dr. Clark—but the enveloping heat briefly lulled his mind back to sweet blankness. Before long, however, a nagging sense of obligation prompted him to turn off the faucets and reach for a towel. He did not want to let Harlowe down.

He had barely stepped out of the tub when his phone rang, and he hurried, dripping, through the kitchen to answer it.

"Hello?"

"Tote that barge, lift that bale . . . ," sang a bass voice at the other end.

"Edmund?"

". . . you gets a little drunk, and you lands in jail."

"Is that you, Edmund?"

"Yes. I'm in jail, Dickie."

There was a series of strange clicks on the line, followed by a dial tone, and then the phone went dead. Sandy diddled the button, but could not get a dial tone back. Only then did he remember the call from the woman at the telephone company that morning, and her threat to cut off his service. He glanced back at the clock. It now said four o'clock. He didn't quite know what to make of Edmund's call, but he assumed it was just some more of the same nonsense that had been going on all day next door. So he put on a fresh pair of jeans, a clean football jersey, his running shoes, and his father's flight jacket, and hurried down the stairs.

"Edmund? Are you there?" he called up to the empty balcony from the driveway, but there was no reply. Though puzzled, he thought no more about it for the time being, pulled his helmet on over his wet hair and motorcycled down to the casino in Union Park.

McCumber's casino, built in 1879 by the former bare knuckles champion and later congressman (d. 1913), was a three-story red sandstone building distinguished by the huge fourteen-foot-high arched windows that afforded a view of Union Park from what had been the spacious main gaming room on the first floor. Now the roulette wheels, dice cages, dealer's shoes, and baize-topped card tables were gone, replaced by the mahogany and horse-hair furniture that had graced the lobby of the Great Federal Hotel, and which the city had picked up at auction in 1955. To the left of the main gaming room was a long narrow barroom, with its original, elaborately carved oak bar, cabinet work, and beveled mirrors. Beyond both the bar and the main gaming room, in a wing of its own, was the grand ballroom. The room was beautifully dominated by a barrel vault ceiling into which were set twelve octagonal stained glass windows designed by the master, Louis C. Tiffany, each representing a different sign of the zodiac. To the right was a raised bandstand, thirty feet wide. On the far side of the ballroom were double doors leading into an equally impressive kitchen, which in its heyday could produce a supper for five hundred patrons.

The liquor truck had just pulled into Union Park and was maneuvering to align its rear with the front entrance of the casino when Sandy arrived. The truck's side was emblazoned with the name North Country Liquor Distributors, Inc. Sandy put his bike up on its kickstand while the truck driver jumped down from the cab. He was a brawny man in his fifties who looked like he still regularly worked out with weights. He carried a clipboard under his arm and a pencil behind his ear.

"You Mister Harlowe?" he asked Sandy.

"Actually, no. But I'm supposed to take delivery of this stuff."

"Okay. Get the door, huh?"

Sandy hurried up the red sandstone steps to the casino's front entrance only to discover that the door was locked. He knocked on it loudly, hoping to attract the attention of the museum ladies on the second and third floors, but a sign in fancy Victorian lettering on the door's etched glass windows stated, Museum Hours: 11:00 A.M.–4:00 P.M. Daily, and nobody answered.

"I'm afraid it's locked," he reported to the delivery man.

"You gotta go get the key from Mr. Jelton at the town hall," the driver explained with his eyes closed (the lids fluttering) as though he had encountered this problem twenty-seven times before.

"Listen, would you mind terribly waiting until I come back with the key?" Sandy asked him.

"Naw, go ahead," the driver said with a sharp shrug that denoted annoyance. "I ain't goin' nowhere."

"Okay, I'll be back in five minutes."

He had just kicked his bike's engine back to life when a truck from the Excelsior Florists pulled through the park's ornate limestone and cast-iron entrance gate, with the truck from the Bird of Paradise Caterers right behind it.

"Oh, my God!" Sandy muttered to himself. To the liquor truck driver he said, "Would you mind terribly telling these other guys that I had to go get the key?"

"No," the liquor truck driver said, crossing his arms belligerently and fluttering his eyelids again. "I don't mind *terribly*."

"Thanks."

Sandy waved at the other two truck drivers, who had no idea who he was, and sped off out of the park up

Broadway toward the town hall. On the way, he forgot
the name of the man who supposedly had the key. Then,
once in the office of the Director of Parks and Recreation,
he was informed by a lady with bright blue hair and yellow
nicotine stains on her fingers that the man who had the
key, Mr. Jelton, had gone home for the day.

"But it's only ten after four."

"He leaves at four."

"But the casino's been rented and paid for," he
pleaded with the blue-haired lady. "There are three delivery trucks with food, liquor, and flowers waiting in front
of it. I've got to get that key, ma'am. Would you please
call this guy at home?"

The blue-haired lady angrily stubbed out her cigarette
and placed the call. She whispered into the phone, eyeing
Sandy suspiciously all the while.

"He'll meet you down there in fifteen minutes with
the key," she said, hanging up the phone and lighting
another cigarette.

"Thanks a million," Sandy said, and rushed back outside. He had started the motorcycle and was about to
hurry back to the casino when the lighted sign above the
door to the police station at the rear of the town hall
caught his eye. Harking back on Edmund's phone call, he
switched off the bike, and cautiously went inside.

"You don't happen to have an Edmund Black here in
the jail, do you?" he inquired rather timidly of an officer
on desk duty, a Sergeant Bloch, who had replaced Sergeant McGinty at four o'clock for the swing shift. Bloch
opened a heavy ledger.

"We got an Edmund White," he told Sandy.

"May I speak to him for a minute, please?"

"I thought you wanted a Black?"

"I must have been confused."

A patrolman so young that he still had a ripping case

218

of acne escorted Sandy down a dreary green corridor through a locked door to a block of four small separate cells. Everything was painted the same mint green, the floor, the radiators, the wire baskets over the bare bulbs, even the iron bars. Edmund was the only prisoner. He lay on the gray blanket that covered his narrow cot with his knees drawn up and his face to the wall.

"There's someone to see you, pal," the officer said, not as unkindly as it may appear.

Edmund glanced over his shoulder. Then, crying, "Dickie!" he fairly flew off the cot and seized the iron bars of his cell.

"What's going on, Edmund?" Sandy asked guardedly, but instead of answering, Edmund only cocked his head at the policeman barely a few steps away. "Uh, officer, would you leave us alone for a moment?" Sandy said.

"Can't," he said. "Rules."

"Never mind him, Edmund. What are you doing here?"

"I knew you'd come, Dickie! And all the way from Nairobi, too!"

"This isn't a movie, Edmund. I only have a couple of minutes."

"But love is forever."

"Do you want to stay in here, or do you want to help me get you out?"

"Oh, I want to leave this wretched place! But Dickie, I've committed a terrible crime, and they've promised to shoot me at dawn."

The officer chuckled.

"Shut up, motherfucker," Edmund told him.

"You're not supposed to talk that way in here," the officer said.

"Uh, why don't I go back out and speak to the

sergeant," Sandy suggested. Moments later, he and the officer were back out at the desk. The sergeant read the charges off the ledger: harassment, resisting arrest, possession of drugs. "What's his bail?" Sandy asked, taking out his wallet with the two crisp fifty dollar bills George had lent him that morning.

"Five hundred," the sergeant said.

"Five hundred! Who sets the bail around here?"

"We do."

"What if I put a hundred down?"

"To get him out, you have to pay the full amount."

"Can I go speak to my friend again?"

"Sure."

Sandy was taken back to the cell.

"I just found out the story from them," he told Edmund, who was on his cot once more, lying on his back with his head near the bars.

"Tell them I refuse the blindfold. I shall die like a man or not at all."

"What on earth is the matter with you today?"

"Just full of the old Halloween spirit, I guess."

"Can't you be serious for thirty seconds."

"I doubt it."

"Try."

Edmund grimaced and made fists of his hands as though straining his abdominal muscles.

"It's no use," he said, giving up.

"Well, your bail's five hundred dollars. What do you want me to do?"

"Why, spring me, of course. You don't want to see me pumped full of lead slugs at dawn, do you? It's bad for the heart."

"Do you want me to go home and get your checkbook?"

"I've got it right here, Dickie," Edmund said, producing it from his back pocket.

"We don't take checks," the officer said flatly.

"Okay, Edmund, write out a check to cash for five hundred dollars, and I'll go get your bail money at five o'clock when they reopen the bank."

"I say, you are a chum."

"But, please. No funny stuff."

"Cross my heart."

A pen was borrowed from the patrolman. Edmund wrote out the check and passed it through the bars. It contained no funny stuff—a clear sign to Sandy that, despite all his shenanigans, Edmund was at least tired of playing Prisoner on Death Row.

"There's nothing I can do until the bank opens. But I'll be back in an hour to get you out of here."

"I shall use the time till then to compose a sonnet on the nature of mortality. Adieu, mon ami."

On the way out, two officers were bringing in Willie Teal, the wino. Though his feet were dragging between them, the diminutive Teal was still conscious, if drunk.

"Hey, chief!" He saluted Sandy in a slurred voice as they passed each other.

"Hello, Willie."

"They say I'm drunk."

"I'd say so, too."

"Well, I am!" Teal agreed brightly. "Getting cold out, chief. Brrr. Winter comin' on. Whoa. Goo' evenin', sergean'. Great to be back in the ole home sweet home."

Sandy returned to the casino just in time to meet Jim Jelton, the man with the keys, who unlocked the front doors. Feeling guilty about making the liquor man twiddle his thumbs for half an hour, Sandy helped him unload the various cartons and bring them inside. When they were done, he checked the contents of the cartons against the invoice while the driver moved his truck out of the way so the florist could back up to the entrance. The liquor delivery included twenty-four bottles of Russian vodka, six Jack Daniel's sourmash whiskey, six Scotch whiskey, six light rum, three dark rum, three tequila, three gin, three cognac, one each light and dark vermouth, one triple sec, one cassis, twenty-four liters California white chardonney, six liters California red sauvignon, and ten cases of Chandon California champagne. The final tally on the bill was $2,275.58. The figure had a certain eye-popping effect on Sandy, but as Joel Harlowe's surrogate, he very quickly acclimated his mind to the size of it, took out the checks that Harlowe had given to him earlier, and filled in the blanks on the one made out to the liquor company. As he handed it to the burly driver, the flower delivery man brushed by with an armload of orange gladiolas.

"Where do you want these?" he asked.

"Just put them down anywhere."

"They're s'posed go in water somewheres."

"Okay. Bring them through the ballroom, and put them in one of the sinks way back in the kitchen."

"You want me to put 'em all back there?"

"All?"

"Yeah. I got a whole truck full."

"Jesus. Well, as many as you can."

As the flower man bustled off, the liquor man stepped forward with the check. "Are you Richard Dodge?"

"No," Sandy replied, momentarily baffled.

"Well, where is he, this Mr. Dodge?" the driver said, handing back the check and pointing to the name in the upper left-hand corner. Only then did Sandy remember who Richard Dodge was.

"Why?"

"Why? 'Cause I wanna talk to him, that's why."

"He's not here," Sandy said.

"Look, this liquor was ordered by a Mr. Harlowe."

"I know, but Mr. Dodge is paying for it."

"I'm sorry. I can't take this check."

"You don't understand. Richard Dodge is the one who's giving this party. Mr. Harlowe works for him."

"Okay. Where's Mr. Harlowe?"

"Well, he's not here right now either."

"When's he showing up?"

"Not for several hours, actually."

"And you work for Mr. Harlowe, I suppose."

"That's right."

"I can't take this check."

He tucked it in the half-zipped opening of Sandy's father's flight jacket and stooped down to lift up one of the champagne cases.

"What are you doing?"

"I'm puttin' this liquor back onna truck."

"Wait. You can't do that."

"Hey, I'm doin' it, buddy."

"No wait. I'll get cash."

"Two grand in cash, huh? Where you gonna get it?"

"The bank opens up again at five o'clock. If you'll just wait here a few minutes, I'll go up and get the money."

"Hey, look, I been here an hour already. I got two more stops to make an' a long drive back to Albany, for Chrissake."

"Please. I swear I'll get the money."

The driver put down the carton. "I'll give you fifteen minutes. After that, *pffffft*, I'm outa here."

"Thanks."

Sandy had just turned toward the door when a gangling youth dressed in a Molson's beer jumpsuit accosted him with a clipboard.

"You Mr. Harlowe?"

"No. But I'm in charge here."

"He's in charge here." The liquor man echoed Sandy snidely and cackled.

"I got four kegs of beer for you."

"Wait with him," Sandy told the lanky kid. "I'll be back in just a few minutes." On the way out he managed to avoid Barbara Lazarus, the chief caterer, by pulling on his motorcycle helmet and pretending not to hear her.

Downtown again, Sandy left his bike in a slot between two parked cars right in front of the bank. A line had formed at the bank's ornate, cast-bronze doors, which were intricately figured with such North Country motifs as pine trees, rugged mountain peaks, leaping stags, and a roaring panther. The line was composed mostly of Greer students bundled against the growing chill in brand-new ski parkas and puffy mountaineering jackets. The shopfronts across Broadway glowed a warm yellow in the creeping twilight. Dead leaves tumbled down the sidewalk on little gusts of wind. Here and there gangs of older children in costume paraded along Broadway, making bellicose noises at the grown-ups they passed. Sandy glanced nervously at his watch, worrying about the liquor man bugging out of the casino.

At precisely five o'clock, a guard in a tan uniform threw open the bronze doors and the Greer kids piled into the bank with Sandy right behind them. Instead of going to a teller's window, he went directly to one of the officer's desks in an area next to the bank's enormous stainless-steel main vault. Here he sought out Mrs. Ricketts, a demure, white-haired woman about fifty-five who had helped him open his own account five years ago and to whom he customarily turned when one of the tellers gave him a hard time about a check. Mrs. Ricketts knew that he was a painter, always asked him how he was doing, and in general treated him very sympathetically. Sandy was not consciously aware of how much Mrs. Ricketts resembled his dead mother.

Explaining that he was extremely pressed for time, and apologizing, Sandy cut short their small talk and got right down to business, producing, first, Edmund's check for $500. Mrs. Ricketts took one look at it and handed it right back saying, "I'm sorry, but Mr. Black hasn't any funds in his account here."

Sandy was stunned. For a few seconds he wondered whether he might try to appeal to Mrs. Ricketts by explaining that he had to get Edmund out of jail. But that seemed untenable for any number of reasons. The check was simply worthless.

"Did he buy a painting from you?" she asked.

"That's right," Sandy replied, his mind still churning.

"What a shame."

"Oh, he's good for it," Sandy assured her, trying to add up a column of whopping figures in his head. He wished he had written down the dollar total of the liquor bill. All he could remember now was that it was something over $2,000. The beer man would probably want a couple of hundred for four kegs. The florist's bill could be as much as $1,000—it was a wild guess. The musicians and the caterer might demand some of their money up front. Joel could always take care of the remainder when he showed up later. But in the meantime there could be many problems as yet unforeseen and requiring cash. And then there was the matter of Edmund's bail. He couldn't just let the poor guy rot in the city lockup. The way he was carrying on, they might even ship him over to the psych ward, and the thought of Edmund having to be stuck with the likes of Glen Toole sealed Sandy's decision to bail him out with Harlowe's money.

He took out one of the blank presigned Richard Dodge

checks and, using one of Mrs. Ricketts' pens, made it out to himself for the sum of $5,000. Mrs. Ricketts flinched when she read the figure.

"Who is this Mr. Dodge?" she asked.

"Check the account," Sandy said, evading her question. "I'm sure the funds are there."

Mrs. Ricketts left her desk to use the computer console. Until she returned, Sandy nervously chewed the inside of his cheek, which was still absolutely numb.

"There are sufficient funds in the account to cover this check," Mrs. Ricketts announced, as she settled back into her chair.

Hugely relieved, Sandy said, "I'd like it in hundred dollar bills, please, except for two hundred in twenties."

"You want cash?"

"That's right."

"I'm afraid I'm going to speak to Mr. Riddle about this," she told him, meaning the president of the bank.

Sandy glanced at his watch. It was ten minutes past five.

"Wait, please!" he said, and very rapidly tried to explain that Richard Dodge was a very important high-society art collector who was throwing an enormous party at the casino tonight—"You must have heard of it; why don't you come?"—and that he had placed Sandy in charge of organizing it, and that he had four minutes to get back to Union Park with the money to pay for the liquor delivery, et cetera, and that his own future was on the line if anything went wrong with Mr. Dodge's party.

"This is highly irregular," Mrs. Ricketts said when he was finished, but he sensed her sympathy.

"You've known me for—what?—five years now, Edna?" he added, taking the small but strategic liberty of using her first name, which could easily be read off the triangular wood and brass nameplate on her desk.

She nodded her head.

"I'm not skipping town or anything. You can trust me. Please, I beg you, get the money."

"All right," she agreed with a sigh and left her desk again to get the cash. Sandy's head pounded as he sank back into his chair's cool, red leather backrest. She returned two minutes later with a white teller's envelope bulging with bills.

"I can't thank you enough," Sandy said, getting up, seizing her shoulders, and kissing her on the cheek. She gasped, then smiled gamely, watching him stuff the envelope in his pocket.

"Aren't you going to count it?"

"I trust you," he told her, then grabbed his helmet to leave.

In the vestibule at the bank's entrance, Sandy nearly collided with Robin Holmes, who was on her way in to deposit her paycheck, which she had been prevented from doing at lunchtime when she was sidetracked by Edmund and his anxiety attack.

"Hello, Sandy," she said in an uncertain tone of voice.

"Hello, Robin," he replied, just as tentatively.

For a long moment he searched her face. Her eyes seemed to dart all over him, as though he were difficult to take in except in fragments.

"I want to talk to you," she said.

"I can't now," he said, glancing once more at his watch (thirteen minutes after five, it said). "I'm sorry. We can talk at Harlowe's party tonight."

He brushed past her and out the door. She wheeled and watched in wrath and wonderment as he mounted the bike and dropped down on the kick start.

"You bastard!" she yelled out the door, though he could not hear her with his helmet on and the engine running. "I wouldn't be caught dead at that goddam party!"

There was a shopping center at the edge of town where George Wells had first hunted woodcock and partridge as a thirteen-year-old boy with his father's 20-gauge side-by-side, which the old man hadn't used since he was a boy himself, which he hadn't known George had borrowed, and for whose unauthorized use he had arranged a thrashing for the boy when George returned from Donnelly's Woods (as the tract was then called) with a fat partridge. George had fecklessly presented the bird to his father for their supper table in boyish triumph. His father gave it to Johnny Hatto, the flunky, to dispose of, and the thrashing was also assigned to that peculiar, egoless, genderless servant who functioned for thirty shadowy years as Lewis Wells's majordomo. The instrument chosen for this thrashing was a braided leather quirt which had belonged to George's mother, an avid horsewoman. Johnny Hatto wordlessly laid on the ten prescribed strokes with cool precision. Later that night his father came to George's room and told the boy that he was welcome to use the shotgun as long as he asked permission beforehand, but also told him not to bring any dead things into the house.

"What'll I do with the birds I get?" George asked.

"Give them to that butcher, Wolzniak, down on Clinton Street in the third ward," his father replied, after giving the matter a few moments' deep thought. The third ward was Polish and poor, made up of ramshackle wooden tenements filled with factory workers who unfailingly voted Democratic, meaning they voted for Mayor Wells. Even a single partridge had been a political consideration, George now marveled as the light turned green.

He never did bring any birds to the Polish butcher. Rather, he brought them to the Toque Blanc restaurant,

Delft's only "foreign" eatery in those days, where the owner, a Hungarian named Franz Janosh, would prepare one or two for George in exchange for the others in his gamebag. It seemed an eminently fair deal to George. A few years later, when he was in high school, Janosh gave him his first job waiting on tables. George loved the feeling of walking out of the place at the end of a Saturday night with twenty-five dollars cash in his pocket. He loved the warm festive atmosphere of the restaurant—compared to the morbid gloom of his father's big house on Genesee Street.

Three years after shooting that first bird and being thrashed for it, George took his revenge on Johnny Hatto. Late on a Christmas eve, the aging errand boy had come up to George's room to deliver an envelope. The envelope contained five $10 bills.

"What's this?" George asked, fingering the money.

"It's your Christmas," Johnny said, and when George appeared not to comprehend he repeated, "It's your Christmas from the boss."

George knew very well what it was. What really upset him was that his father had gone out to some ridiculous lodge dinner, a political affair, that night instead of staying home with George and his brother Davey. And the sight of Johnny Hatto standing there staring at him as though he were some kind of moron filled George with an ire he had never known before. He had been lifting weights with a set of barbells that he bought with his restaurant money, and before he really knew what he was doing, he had seized the comparably less robust Johnny Hatto by the lapels of his funereal dark suit, flung him onto the floor, and pinned him to it by laying a 240-pound barbell across his throat. Johnny Hatto could breathe easily enough, but he could not budge the barbell off his throat to save his life.

"I think I'll leave you here for a while," George told the immobilized factotum and proceeded downstairs where he made himself a peanut butter sandwich and watched twenty minutes of *A Christmas Carol* on television before returning to free Johnny. The oddest thing about the whole incident was that when Johnny Hatto naturally complained to George's father, the mayor practically busted a gut laughing and told the "humorous anecdote" to his many cronies and associates for months afterward.

The outskirts of Delft were markedly shabbier than those of Excelsior Springs. Almost nothing standing had been built after 1963 when the first of the four big factories shut down on a week's notice and the town began its long, downward spiral into bankruptcy.

Past the shopping center and its small surrounding clusters of bungalows—bought by the last generation of factory foremen to believe that the town had a future—Adirondack Street began its steep descent to the river. Here, between the rooftops, George could glimpse the beautiful valley in the clear twilight of this Halloween evening. The sight of the river winding to the west like a silver ribbon powerfully drew him down a side street of large, decaying houses. The street led ultimately to a cemetery perched at the very edge of the bluff above the town.

George parked his truck along the sidewalk, overgrown with weeds, in front of the arched cast-iron entrance that seemed in danger of toppling backward. Dry leaves swirled among the headstones as he surveyed the rows trying to remember where his mother was buried. He hadn't visited her grave since the year he dropped out of Cornell, as though he were ashamed to come around anymore. The cemetery was in no better condition than any other part of the town. Thistles, burdocks, and milkweed grew in prickly clumps where a lawn mower had not been heard in years. George held the lapels of his suit jacket closed against the chill and brushed through the weeds that had overgrown the ancient brick pathways. Beggar-ticks and cockleburs clung to his pant legs. Strangers' names, like meaningless nonsense words, crowded his mind as he read the headstones. Where was she? Had he lost her again?

The sun had just gone down, and a bright orange band was all the daylight that remained beneath the cloudless and incredibly lucent peacock-blue sky. Down the winding river valley, pinpoints of light twinkled in the rooms of faraway farmhouses. As he approached the far corner of the cemetery, the vista became more and more familiar until finally, at twenty feet, he recognized the pink and black granite headstone with the still terrifying inscription on it:

EVELYN BURKE WELLS

1926 – 1955

As he hurried toward it, his shoe caught on a loose brick and he stumbled forward. At precisely the same moment he fell to the ground, something shot past his face with a heart-stopping flutter of wingbeats, and George had no more than a few seconds to watch the silhouette of the partridge fly off into the deepening twilight. Lying in the weeds, his pulse racing, George was sure that the bird had touched him.

THIRTEEN

Albany went by in a blur, the bluish lights of the state university pale against the streaked orange sky. Maybe that's where he'd go to med school, Joel thought, zipping past a southbound potato truck with Quebec license plates at ninety miles per hour while he listened to Warren Zevon sing "I'll Sleep When I'm Dead" on the speakers implanted in his helmet. He might even take some law courses on the side. Nothing too rigorous, just a few extra credits each year. That way, by the time he finished med school he'd be part of the way toward his law degree. If some chiseling bum of a patient tried to bilk him in a malpractice suit, he'd meet the fucker head-on in a court of law. Probably save a lot on malpractice insurance that way, too, not to mention the many benefits tax-wise. Dr. Joel Harlowe, attorney-at-law. He hoped his father would stay healthy until he had his doctor's certificate. Then, if the old man got sick Joel could handle it himself. *My life is in your hands, son,* he could hear his father say. *I know,*

Pop. Don't worry. I've done over a hundred of these transplants already. Piece of cake. It'd be fun delivering his own babies, too. He could do it at home. Of course, they'd need a bigger house than the cottage on Catherine Street. One of those huge Victorian heaps up on North Broadway would be perfect. Kelly could roll out of bed and walk to class. Their bed. Jesus, she was incredible in bed, Joel thought, harking back on those tawny limbs, the caramel and marshmallow breasts. But fantastic as she was, could he remain faithful to one woman for the rest of his life? Realistically, no, Joel admitted to himself. The human animal wasn't designed that way. It wasn't a moral issue; it was biology. A person had to face facts. Every time he turned a corner in the Springs, there was another gorgeous creature, and sooner or later he'd want to get in bed with one of them. Why get married, then? Well, marriage was another matter. Marriage wasn't just fucking. Animals fuck. Bugs fuck, for God's sake. Marriage was an institution, a concept that separated man from the beasts and bugs. (*I should take some philosophy courses, too,* Joel mused.) Vladimir Nabokov (one of his favorite authors) put it something like this: the gap between ape and man is immeasurably greater than the one between amoeba and ape. You could say that again, Vlad. Marriage was having a family, working together toward ideals, building a future so that our children might live in a better world than—

Joel's reverie was interrupted by the orange light blinking on the radar detector clipped to his handlebars. There was a strident beeping sound as well. He rapidly decelerated from 90 miles per hour to 55, the speed limit, and moved over into the right-hand lane between a Chevy station wagon and an old Volkswagen Beetle. Sure enough, a half mile further down the thruway, he spotted the unmarked state police car lurking behind the concrete buttress of an overpass on the median strip. One mile later, Joel cut over into the passing lane, twisted his throttle wide open, and watched his speedometer needle move up steadily past 60, 70, 80, 90, 100, 110, 115 and finally 120 miles per hour. He could have cranked it higher, but he wanted to save a few thrills for later on, so he relaxed the throttle and cruised at an even 100 for a while, streaking past the other cars and trucks as though they were barely moving at all.

He made it from Albany to Woodstock in less time than it took to listen to the flip side of his Road Sounds #1 tape, and he pulled over to the shoulder briefly to find another cassette and otherwise fortify his mind. It was a few minutes past five o'clock. The sun had gone down behind the Catskill Mountains looming directly to the west, and the streaking headlights of cars whizzing by made the world seem harsh, ominous, and unreal. He inhaled two chambers full of cocaine from his snorter, and within seconds the thruway no longer seemed threatening at all, but rather an inviting playland of speed and adventure. He was approximately at the halfway mark of his journey, and the thought that he'd have to drive at least 100 miles per hour the rest of the way in order to meet Roberto on time at LaGuardia airport was something he took as an exciting challenge. He'd always wanted to race motorcycles, but since the terrible accident at Sebring years ago, it wasn't something he'd actively pursued. Now, here was an opportunity to have some real fun.

Joel climbed back aboard the idling cycle. He rummaged around the fairing compartment until he found the tape marked Road Sounds #2 and inserted it in the tape player. Mick Jagger and the Rolling Stones began singing their energetic number "Start Me Up" from the *Tattoo You* album. Joel punched down the shift and let out the clutch, slipping back into the flow of traffic. Once in the passing lane, he went through the gears in six seconds flat and, leaning low into the protective windscreen, leveled off at a cruising speed of 110 miles per hour.

Sandy returned to the casino one minute late, but the liquor man was still there, along with the beer man, the flower man, and something new, a farm truck full of pumpkins. The caterers had simply marched into the kitchen and begun assembling the hot and cold hors d'oeuvres.

The liquor man gave the hairy eyeball to Sandy when he pulled out the huge wad of hundreds and twenties, counted out $2280, and told him to keep the change. The man scrawled "paid" across the bill and walked out of the casino muttering about rich punks. The flower bill was $1120 and the delivery man took a Richard Dodge check without any complaint, as did the beer man for $180. The pumpkin man, a rawboned, hollow-eyed farmer from Shrewsbury, not only demanded cash ($215) but insisted that Sandy help him unload the pumpkins because he had a bad heart. And so the farmer stood in the truck bed rolling the giant squashes to the edge of the tailgate with his foot, while Sandy carried all seventy-eight pumpkins (some two at a time) into the main gaming parlor, where he piled them on the floor beneath the twice-life-size portrait of Paddy McCumber (by J.S. Sargent) that dominated the room.

After that, he lugged the ten cases of champagne and the twenty-four liters of white wine into the walk-in refrigerator in the kitchen. The head caterer, Barbara Lazarus, a cheerful, tall, bosomy woman very imposing in her kitchen whites and chef's hat, and holding a huge steel bowl of herb mayonnaise and a giant whisk, pleasantly informed Sandy that the gladiolas were cluttering up her sinks, and that they had to be put somewhere else if she and her two helpers were to do their jobs. She asked after the absent

Joel Harlowe—apparently a friend—but didn't say any-thing about being paid. So Sandy took the flowers out of the sinks and put them temporarily out on the bare tables in the dining room, thinking he'd find something to stick them in. A quick search of the premises did not turn up anything remotely suitable in the way of vases, so he decided to buy a bunch of plastic trash cans at the super-market. In any case, it was practically quarter to six. Edmund was still languishing in jail, and didn't Joel say something about picking up a costume at Gwen Chap-man's shop?—which might close for the day any minute!

He left the casino again and sped over to the police station, paid Edmund's bail with Joel's money, but did not stick around to greet Edmund when he was released—thinking Edmund might just use Sandy's presence to make another crazy scene and get himself in more trouble. Then it was one block over to Catherine Street and The Little Match Girl shop. Gwen was showing a customer (a Greer student named Liz Coffin) a garish rhinestone neck-lace and matching earrings from a glass-topped display counter filled with junk jewelry. Liz had already selected a thirty-year-old red sequined cocktail dress that looked like it had once belonged to a twenty-dollar hooker.

"Hi," Liz said, batting her eyelashes at Sandy in a theatrical manner.

"Hi," Sandy said back. His right lower lip was still numb and he was able to smile with only half his mouth. "Novocain," he explained, pointing to it.

"What do you think?" Liz asked, holding the earrings to her earlobes. She was the same height as Sandy, and they stood face to face.

"They look lovely on you," he said, a little bewil-dered that she had asked his opinion.

"Okay," she said with a sigh and plunked them

down on the counter. "I'll take them and the necklace, too."

As soon as Liz had lowered the rhinestone earrings, Sandy could not help noticing the earrings that she already had on. Her left earlobe was pierced with three holes. The lowest held a gold earring in the design of a little seashell, just like the one he had found next to his bed first thing this morning. His heart fell into his stomach. In the other two holes she wore a beaded gold hoop and a small diamond stud. Sandy walked around to her right side. Liz watched him circle her, smiling in an eerie, sphinxlike way. Her right earlobe held only one earring, a large pink fluorescent plastic doodad. Her face seemed familiar, but living in a small town, many faces ended up looking familiar.

"Where do I know you from," Liz said, lighting a long, dark brown, filtered cigarette. "I can't help feeling that we know each other."

Sandy couldn't help feeling that she was trying to fuck his mind. On the other hand, he had no specific recollection of being in bed with her the night before. He didn't even remember leaving Ubu Roi or walking home— that's how drunk he had been.

"We've probably just seen each other around," he said.

"Sure," Liz said, with a sardonic little laugh that sent a chill down his spine.

"Uh, Joel Harlowe said there was some kind of costume down here for me." He turned desperately to Gwen, who was tallying a bill of sale for Liz's purchases.

"I made a really gorgeous outfit for him, but he changed his mind about it at the last minute," Gwen said, then turned to Liz. "That'll be sixty-five and a quarter all together."

"Is this the Joel who's having that big party at the old casino?" Liz inquired.

"Uh-huh," Gwen affirmed.

"Are you going?" Liz asked Sandy, paying her bill and picking up the paper bag with her purchases.

"I may drop by," he dissembled.

"Then maybe I'll see you there later," she said with another of her mysterious smiles and, even more alarming to Sandy, touched her fingertips to his cheek in a fey gesture of farewell. "Ciao," she said at the door and blew him a kiss.

"What was that all about?" Gwen asked when she was gone.

"Huh? I don't know. Nothing. College girl. I don't even know her. I'm in a terrible hurry, Gwen," he appealed to her, then explained how Joel had left him in charge of everything.

"All right," she said. "Come into the back with me and try it on."

Five minutes later he emerged from the room where she did her sewing wearing the uniform of an officer in Napoleon's imperial hussars. Though Sandy was two inches taller than Joel, the costume fit well enough. The breeches had been made of an elastic material and laced up the back so he could let the waist out an inch. He and Joel were both a 38-regular in the chest, so the tunic fit, too. The sleeves were a little short, but with the ruffled cuffs sticking out, nobody would notice. Gwen gave him a paper bag for his jeans, football jersey, and his father's flight jacket. There were no pockets in the breeches, and only one small one sewn inside the tunic, where Sandy stuck the wad of hundred dollar bills and the Richard Dodge checks.

"You look wonderful," Gwen said with a sigh at the door. "Don't you wish men still dressed this way?"

Sandy nodded, but his mind was really on the girl with the earrings and whether or not he might have possibly spent the previous night with her. How could someone not remember a thing like that? he wondered.

"The running shoes are a little weird, though," Gwen said, picking a piece of lint off his tunic.

"Huh . . . ?" Sandy said, flinching as though startled out of a daydream.

"It'd look better with riding boots."

"I know."

"Do you have a pair?"

"Of course not."

"Oh, well . . ."

"It's a beautiful costume, Gwen." Sandy hastened to assure her. "I feel privileged to wear it."

"Life would be more fun if men dressed this way all the time," she said with another wistful sigh.

He thanked her again, left the store, and fastened the bag of clothes on the rear rack of his motorcycle under a couple of elastic shock cords. A customer came out of the Black Rose in complete Dracula drag, including fangs, white makeup, and white tie. He adjusted his black cape, walked past Sandy as though he were going home for supper after having one with the guys, and disappeared around the corner on Burgoyne Street. Sandy knew there was one more important thing he had to do before returning to the casino, but he couldn't remember what it was. I'm going senile, he thought. Then it came to him: plastic trash baskets for the flowers. He jumped on the kick start and took off for the supermarket.

Glen Toole sat on the bicycle rack beside the entrance to the Top Shopper supermarket watching people come and go. He was enjoying his newly discovered power over them. He had discovered that he could make them go in the entrance and come out the exit a short while later. It gave him an exciting feeling in his pants to do this. The feeling reminded him of being the troll under the bridge and how he had gobbled that college bitch up. He was on the lookout for another college bitch now. If one came by alone, he would use his powers to make her go into the supermarket, and while she was in there, he would steal in the back seat of her car and hide there, a troll. So far a few had come by, but only in groups, none alone.

Glen was very fond of motorcycles, so naturally he noticed when Sandy pulled into the lot and parked toward the rear next to the store's giant dumpster. Then, as Sandy walked back toward the entrance and took his helmet off, Glen saw who he was: the cocksucker who used to hold him down in the psych ward when the doctor gave him those knockout shots. He hated the cocksucker as much as he hated anybody in the whole town. Who did he think he was, anyway? And what kind of stupid outfit did he have on? The cocksucker looked like a trombone player in a marching band.

Glen used his powers to make Sandy go inside the store, then skulked past the entrance to have a look at that motorcycle. As he came closer, he noticed that there was something bundled on the rack, a paper bag. It was fairly dark over by the dumpster. Glen decided to pee in the cocksucker's gas tank. The idea made him crack up laughing. He stole closer to the bike until he was right beside it. If he stood on his tiptoes, Glen calculated he could pee right into it the way it was leaning over on its kickstand. He opened his fly. But just as he reached for the gas tank cap someone started up their car in the lot and switched on their headlights, catching him in their beams. Glen turned away from the light and hid his face. In a few seconds, the car's headlights swerved off of him. When it was dark again, he reached for the gas tank cap but discovered that it wouldn't unscrew. Looking closer, he saw that it had a keyhole in it. Then another car entered the lot and caught him in its headlights.

By this time, Glen was nervous about hanging around the bike. Instead of peeing in the cocksucker's gas tank, he decided to steal the paper bag that was bundled on the rack. He glanced all around to make sure that nobody was watching, then grabbed the bag out from under the elastic shock cords and ran with it around the back of the supermarket across High Street and then up Woodlawn Avenue.

He didn't stop running until he reached the Bible Pentecost Church of Jesus on the corner of Vermont Street. Deep in the alley alongside the church, he finally opened up the paper bag. At first he was greatly disappointed, finding only the cocksucker's old clothes. But then, in that dim alley, illuminated by the ambient light of a streetlamp, he saw that the package included a leather jacket. It was an old jacket, soft and broken-in, just like his brother Hurley's old baseball mitt that he was never allowed to borrow. It had a smell like spice and looked like something that Indiana Jones, the movie hero, wore in pictures.

Glen took off his own jacket, a green fatigue coat that he got at the Army-Navy store on Broadway for twenty dollars. He was sick of it. He wasn't a buck private anyhow. And it wasn't none too warm neither, he thought further. He dropped it on the ground and tried on the leather one. It felt good. The lining was a quilted, satiny material, and he could already feel it was warmer than that damn army coat. The only problem was the sleeves. They were long on him. They came up over the knuckles of his hands when he hung his arms straight down by his sides. But there was a good part to that. He could scrunch up his hands and keep them warm in there.

Glen started to bundle up the other clothes inside his old army coat when he felt something flat and hard in the blue jeans. He searched them, and lo and behold, it was a wallet, a red nylon one like they sold in the camping shop. His heart thumping, he opened it up and peered inside. There were a couple of bills and a check in it. He looked at the bills, but didn't recognize the portrait of Ulysses S. Grant. It took him another moment to realize that the bills were fifties. He almost shit in his pants. Two fifties! Well, goddamn! He was rich! Here it was, Friday night, he didn't have hardly half a buck in coin to his name, and now all of a sudden he was rich! He must have made that dumb cocksucker leave his wallet right out there begging to be stolen. He had powers!

Glen kept the bills and the check and bundled up the wallet and the rest of the clothes inside his old army coat. He stuffed the coat in a trash can beside the back entrance of the church. Then, feeling warm and powerful and imagining himself the very image of the hero Indiana Jones, Glen headed back downtown to the No-Name Bar, to show Skip Pirtle the new coat he just won off this dumb cocksucker in a poker game and to buy the whole gang a drink.

Sandy had not even noticed Glen Toole sitting on the bicycle rack next to the entrance of the Top Shopper. He was completely preoccupied with trying to recall what had happened after that second brandy in Ubu Roi. He remembered Joel standing off in a corner putting the moves on a Greer girl. George was talking to him about hunting for birds. He vaguely remembered dancing with somebody, or trying to anyway, in the back room with the disco lights and the music roaring like a freight train out of the giant speakers in each corner, and then going out the fire exit to the alley behind the bar to throw up. That's right. He remembered throwing up because he took care to put the package with the sweater in it some distance away, so he wouldn't get anything on it. And then, didn't he go home?

At this hour the supermarket was crammed with shoppers, many of them hill people from the far-flung bosky precincts north of Locust Grove, buying frozen pizzas and other treats with their paychecks from the pulp mills. The men were almost all skinny and tubercular-looking, while their wives were the size of prize heifers, quite a few of them three-hundred-pounders, great waddling brutes with cigarettes plugged into their scowling faces. Sandy wended his way through them to the housewares aisle where he found a selection of plastic garbage pails and picked six round ones, each eighteen inches deep. They came in one color: beige. He was just turning past a two-for-one sale of diet cola when he almost collided with Robin Holmes.

"I guess this is one of the drawbacks of living in a small town," she remarked and then tried to wheel her cart past him.

"Wait," Sandy said, grabbing hold of the cart. "I want you back."

Robin recoiled. "Now you want me back?"

"Yes. I do."

The tendons in her neck stood out, and she reached into the cart for her Mark Cross pigskin briefcase—a gift from her father when she was promoted to her reporter's job at the *Banner*. Sandy merely stood in place, glumly watching the arc of that briefcase as she swung it sideways at his head. He didn't even put his hands up, thinking that somehow she would see it as a sign of contrition and sincerity if he simply took the blow like a good soldier. As a matter of fact, there was a hardcover book in the briefcase (Virginia Woolf's diaries, 1911–

1919) and it rocked his head with considerably more force than he had anticipated. He briefly experienced an internal planetarium show for wheeling stars, the words "you bastard" echoing in his brain. Then she was gone, and there seemed little point in pursuing her or the argument for the time being. The briefcase had made contact with the numb side of his head, but he could taste blood as it flowed from the reopened wound in his gums where Clark had pulled his tooth. Out of morbid curiosity, he dribbled a few drops onto the store's floor, where they made spiky red stars on the linoleum.

"Oooo, yukky!" a child, wearing the mask of some hirsute extraterrestrial beast, exclaimed as its bovine mother wheeled the shopping cart it was riding in past Sandy. His ears ringing, Sandy went through the express line with his six plastic trash buckets, paying with Joel's money. His head was still a little fuzzy out in the parking lot, where he secured the plastic buckets to the motorcycle's rear rack using the elastic shock cords. It wasn't until he got all the way back to the casino that he realized the bag of clothes, including his wallet and his father's leather flight jacket, had been stolen.

Edmund Black hurried home from the police station up High Street and then right onto Serpentine in the evening murk. Dressed in only a thin oxford shirt, he shivered. Gangs of goblins could be seen roving everywhere, trooping up and down the porch steps with their shopping bags of candy loot, darting down the side streets emitting shrieks and catcalls. Festoons of toilet paper adorned the trees and telephone wires in front of Edmund's house, and the same pranksters had squirted shaving lather on the windows of every parked car for two blocks. Now and then a firecracker would go off, something powerful like a cherry bomb. The neighborhood had taken on the air of a war zone. Altogether this upstate Halloween was a far cry from a version Edmund remembered years ago in his apartment building on 67th Street and Park Avenue in New York City.

He, his sister Sappho, and brother Billy had decided to dress up as natives, that is, African tribesmen. They were inspired by the movie *Mighty Joe Young*, about the capture and exploitation of a giant gorilla, which had played on the *Million Dollar Movie* television show all week. Their mother Gladys had gone to an Urban League dinner honoring Eleanor Roosevelt that night, leaving the kids in the care of the maid, Mrs. Urqhart, a British spinster, whose Mayfair accent the children loved to mimic and to whom they paid scant attention. Sappho, who showed artistic promise even at age ten, designed the costumes—grass skirts made of shredded newspapers and matching lion's mane headdresses. Billy made their spears out of broomsticks and curtain rods. Edmund, seven, helped decorate the cardboard shields. Bedaubed and bedizened with fingerpaint, the three Mau Maus, as Billy dubbed them, stole down the fire stairs to the next floor. Their first call was at the apartment of Sergei Kublinsky, the violin virtuoso granted political asylum earlier that year by the Kennedy administration. Madame Kublinsky was the one who answered the door (her husband practiced sixteen hours a day in a soundproof room). Knowing little about the rites of an American Halloween and generally intimidated by the ethnic mishmash that was New York City, her new home in exile, she opened her door to the spectacle of three "pygmies"—as she told the police— brandishing pointed weapons at her and uttering such menacing cries as "Oooga-booga," "Walla-walla," and "B'wana macumba." Understanding that they wanted something and that they wouldn't quit bounding around her foyer until they got it, she offered the contents of her pocketbook, which happened to be over ninety dollars in cash, quite a haul for three kids twelve and under. The police caught up with them about fifteen minutes later on the building's eighth floor. Billy's refusal to surrender Madame Kublinsky's money led to their removal to the 19th Precinct station house a few blocks away, and led also to their mother being summoned from the Roosevelt dinner at the Waldorf-Astoria. In the meantime, there was all sorts of scare talk about reform school from the sneering desk sergeant. Eventually, with her good friend Adlai Stevenson accompanying her uptown in a U.N. limousine, Gladys Black settled the "misunderstanding" and the money was returned. The children were all sent home to bed with Mrs. Urqhart, and Mrs. Black went back to the Waldorf with Ambassador Stevenson in time for the coffee and speeches. Edmund, Sappho, and Billy, now confined to the apartment, concluded their Halloween festivities by bombarding Park Avenue with water balloons. After that year, Billy decided he was too old for Halloween, Edmund remembered sadly.

Except for a single lamp left burning in the living room, Edmund's house was dark. With its weed-filled yard, dangling rain gutters and peeling paint, Edmund was struck as never before by the place's utter failure to meet his expectations. The carefree, romantic, screwball-comedy life of the perpetual house party that he had once projected just hadn't panned out. For the first time in as long as he could remember, the place looked simply depressing to him. He lingered a few minutes beside the rusting cast-iron fence and considered fleeing the house, the town, his life. But it would be another few days before the check from his mother arrived, and until then, his mobility was circumscribed by a severe shortage of funds. Besides, he began to rationalize, of all the endless nights of the long and pointless year—of all the many pointless years!—wasn't Halloween the most befitting to both his house and what he thought of, for lack of a better term, as his peculiar destiny. It was cold out on the street. Edmund's teeth began to chatter. He turned up the cracked marble footpath to the decaying porch and went inside.

Joel Harlowe pulled onto the shoulder of the thruway seven miles shy of the New Jersey border and roughly thirty miles from the Empire State Building. It was 5:30 P.M. and he had just set some kind of two-wheeled speed record for the stretch between Woodstock and Harriman. During that leg of his journey, night had stolen across the Hudson Valley. The moon had not come up yet, but toward the southeast a rosy glow hung above the horizon. Joel knew that the glow came from the billionfold lights of the wondrous city.

He flipped down the kickstand of the idling bike and walked a few paces to and fro along the roadside to stretch his legs, which were stiff from riding in one position. Taking off his gloves, he fished the cocaine snorter out of a pocket in his leather suit and was alarmed to discover that it only contained one more hit of the drug, and a pretty meager hit at that. He was beginning to feel a little out of sorts again, ill at ease, draggy, and it would be another half hour before he would meet his connection, Roberto, in the parking lot at LaGuardia airport. Of course, what was half an hour? Nothing. It wasn't as though he was about to go through some kind of cold turkey horror show withdrawal number in the next half hour. It was just that the most interesting, the most beautiful, the most *demanding* leg of the trip lay ahead in those crowded, curvy, pothole-riddled miles of the Harlem River Drive and then the maze of expressways across the Triborough Bridge in Queens. It would have been more pleasant to *not* run out of the drug just at this juncture, that's all. But he could live with it. No big deal.

Of course, there was the prospect of the about-face, two-hundred-mile return trip upstate to consider.

To steady his nerves, therefore, to quell any further nagging feelings of malaise, to steel himself for the rigors of the road ahead, Joel decided to take two more Black Beauties, swallowing them without water, and broke open a third, which he sniffed straight out of the gelatin capsule. Drawing the bitter powder deep into his sinuses, he felt his brain light up like the electric service grid of a small town during a storm surge. He felt at once an oceanic swelling of confidence and euphoria. The idea came to him that he was inventing the world as it happened, and he had to admit that he was doing a pretty damn good job. Not bad at all.

He climbed back on board his motorcycle, put a tape of George Gershwin tunes in the player, flipped down his face mask, and floated back into traffic. He hadn't gone three miles when he saw the red lights flashing behind him. At first, there were any number of things he couldn't believe in connection with this sudden appearance of the police. He couldn't believe that they were coming after him, for instance. He couldn't believe that his radar detector (absolutely the best money could buy) had failed to pick up these bozos. He couldn't believe that something he was making up as he went along (i.e., the world) would present such an obnoxious complication at a time like this.

Then it occurred to him that he had invented the police precisely to make this part of the trip more exciting. And so, embracing this hypothesis, Joel decided to give them a run for their money. With a simple twist of his throttle, he surged forward at 125 miles per hour, weaving in and out of the other southbound vehicles as though they were gates on some kind of fantastic motorcycle slalom course. It reminded him of the drills they used to practice on the test track at the Ventura Institute. Maybe it had been a mistake to give up auto racing just because of one little crash, Joel thought, as he wove in between a tractor-trailer hauling liquified propane gas and a May-flower moving van—temporarily obscuring the flashing lights of the police in the rearview mirrors on his handle-bars. Maybe he'd have time between medical school and his law courses to enter a few road races next season. This sure was fun.

A mile ahead he saw a line of lighted thruway toll-booths. Under the circumstances, he felt that it would be a waste of time to stop and futz around fishing for a quarter in his pockets. So instead, he swerved sharply to the right—cutting in front of half a dozen decelerating cars and trucks (in one case, causing a Datsun to back-end a Buick)—and rode up the grassy embankment at the end of the row of tollbooths. When he had neatly circumvented this obstacle, he briefly heard the squawk of alarms and the ringing of bells. But by then he had opened his throttle again, and in a little over thirty sec-onds the blaring sirens and bells lay a mile behind him. The police car, too, was a mere flashing red speck of light in his rearview mirror. In another minute, he came to Exit 13-S, the Palisades Parkway, southbound, and he leaned so far over to make the turn up the off-ramp that his footpegs scraped the pavement and sent a roostertail of yellow sparks curling out behind him.

The Palisades Parkway was one of those curvy, vin-tage 1940s roads designed for a top speed of fifty miles per hour. It had hardly any straightaways. Anyhow, this Friday evening most of the traffic was coming the other way, north, out of New York City. Joel fell into a comfort-able rhythm leaning in and out of the endless curves at ninety miles per hour. He soon passed the sign that declared he was entering the state of New Jersey. It was academic by this time, for he had left the New York State Police car far behind, and his radar detector did not pick up anything new from Ridgewood all the way to Fort Lee.

At a few spots along the way, where the parkway ran close to the actual rim of the Palisades, Joel could glimpse the glittering lights of lower Westchester and then the Bronx across the Hudson River, spreading in a luminous web far to the east. To him, the lights seemed like a direct extension of his increasing mental powers. These welling powers, while awesome to behold, were beneficient, for everywhere he turned the light of his mind, good would appear. These reflections had a clear and unmistakable meaning to Joel: his mind would produce works of supreme importance to mankind, specifically through the study of medicine and law. As a doctor, he would discover the key to prolonging human life indefinitely; as a lawyer, he would find a way for mankind to live in peace with its immortal selves. He and Kelly would live and love forever!

Then, the trees came to an end, the apartment towers of Fort Lee suddenly loomed to his right, while to his left the George Washington Bridge arced across the dark river like a gorgeous holiday swag of pure light. He slowed down on the parkway exit, with its tiny turning radius, and followed the arrows to the bridge's approach ramp, stopping to pay the three-dollar toll just like his fellow human beings in the cars around him. The Gershwin tune "Embraceable You" came on through his headphones in a heartbreakingly tender orchestral arrangement that perfectly summarized the exaltation of power and love in twentieth-century urban America. Sitting straight up on the bike so as to see over the side better, he drove up the

ramp to the bridge's road deck until the magnificent panorama of Manhattan Island opened before him, its dazzling diamond lights blazing in tribute to Joel Harlowe's
goodness and genius.

FOURTEEN

George Wells checked in with the charge nurse at the fourth-floor nursing station. She was an older woman in her late fifties. She had not been on duty the two other occasions George had visited the old man since he was hospitalized in August. Meeting the famous patient's son for the first time now, she said admiringly, "Aren't you the very image of the mayor when he was in his prime!" George tried to smile as though she had paid him a great compliment, but the remark couldn't have made him more uncomfortable, and his attempted smile left him feeling, for a moment, like a common politician. Then, in a graver voice, the nurse said, "Why don't you go in and see him?"

Why, indeed? George had to ask himself as he walked down the long corridor to his father's room. Why? Because the doctor had said, that was why.

Someone had taped dime-store cartoon cutouts of jack-o'-lanterns, black cats, and laughing witches along the otherwise bleak sea-green corridor of the long-term care unit. This newer wing of Delft General Hospital had been built in the late 1960s at the very edge of the downtown area doomed to demolition. Mayor Wells, who helped arrange the financing, had enjoyed a healthy cut of the federal funds allocated to pay for the addition. George felt increasingly uneasy as he approached his father's room. He began to sweat, though the hospital temperature was a perfect sixty-nine degrees. There was a fizzy feeling in his head. He wondered for a moment if he was coming down with some illness himself. Then, he stood before the door to room 412. Someone had taped a cartoon figure of Frankenstein's monster on it.

The door was ajar a few inches and George could hear voices within. The voices were low, and he could not make out any words, but to his astonishment, there seemed to be some laughter. He wondered whether he had the wrong room, but a paper tab in a little brass holder on the door had the name Lewis Wells typed on it. George did not understand how his father could be near death and still laugh, let alone talk. He stood outside the door for minutes on end until a nurse started down the far end of the hall with a tray of meds. Then he gently pushed open the door and took two steps into the room.

Johnny Hatto sat in an aluminum and orange Naugahyde armchair to the right of his father's bed. As George entered, Johnny glanced sharply up and moved to the edge of his seat, anxiety draining the blood from his already sallow, thin face. The old errand boy had never looked more like an undertaker. His bony throat—the same throat that George had once pinned in hatred under a barbell to the floor of his room—projected through his frayed, white collar with an inch around to spare, and his dark tie looked greasy. He sat very primly at the edge of his seat, knobby black shoes together, and waxy feminine hands neatly folded in his lap.

"Hiya, Georgie," he said with enough fake friendliness so that George felt a little stab of pain in his stomach. No one else in his whole life ever called him Georgie, not even his father.

"Hello, Johnny," George said. His father said nothing.

Since his father lay nearly supine in bed, George was not able to gain an impression of him until he stepped closer to the bed, and then he could see how the preceding three weeks since his last visit had left the old man a wasted husk. The radiation therapy had made his once leonine silver hair fall out months ago, of course. But his cheeks were noticeably more sunken, and his skin had turned a terrible jaundiced gray-yellow color like beeswax. Altogether, he looked like a hatchling of some enormous species of bird. The only equipment he was hooked up to was a glucose IV and a nasal oxygen tube that hung just under his nostrils.

"Hello, Dad," George heard himself say, but it felt as though someone else, a stranger, was speaking the words.

"Your dad and I go back a long ways, don't we, boss?" Johnny spoke queerly, George thought, as if they all didn't know that.

The old man made a sort of grunting sound.

The room itself was oddly naked of anything personal belonging to Lewis Wells, as though to underscore the temporary nature of its occupancy. There were no flowers either, not even any cards taped to the wall. George wondered if all the old man's political cronies were dead and gone. But he doubted it, since his father, at seventy-two, was not so ancient to have outlived them all. Even Johnny Hatto was several years older than his father. Quite a few of the old gang must have still been around— except that now that he was no longer mayor, Lewis

Wells was no concern to them. The only object in the room not issued by the hospital was a stuffed toy monkey, propped up on the nightstand beside the bed. It had the look of something new but cheap, something purchased, say, in the hospital gift shop. George slowly came to the realization that Johnny must have bought it, and the idea was enormously saddening, especially when his father spoke up for the first time, saying in a small dry voice, "Leave us alone for a while, huh, Johnny?"

"You sure, boss?"

"I'm sure."

"I'll be right outside, you need anything."

Johnny reluctantly departed the room, but George observed that he left the door ajar behind him, so he went over and shut it.

"Sit down. You're making me nervous," his father said.

George sat down in the chair vacated by Johnny. It was still warm, with an old man's warmth.

"Where's Davey?" the old man asked.

"Los Angeles, I suppose," George said. "Do you want me to call him? Ask him to fly home?"

"Why?"

George did not know how to answer this question, since the answer was so painfully obvious. He rephrased his reply. "If you want to see him, I'll call and tell him."

"I don't want to see him," the old man said. "He's no good."

"Don't say that, Dad."

"Why not? It's true. Never was any good. Never amounted to a damn."

George's younger brother Davey was a heroin addict on methadone maintenance who sometimes worked as an assistant sound engineer in Hollywood. Once or twice a year he called George to borrow money. Yet George still felt sufficiently protective of Davey, where their father was concerned, to say, "It's been hard for him, Dad, you know that."

"Hard? That's a good one. It was too easy. He had whatever he needed."

Except a mother, George thought. Not even the memory of her, like George had. But how could he even mention such a thing at a time like this? Besides, the old man wasn't to blame for that. Rather, he knew that the old man blamed Davey for depriving him of his wife. "I know he cares about his father," George said simply.

"Horseshit," the old man muttered. "What are you doing here?"

George was astounded. He felt more and more as though he were a stranger observing this scene between himself and his father. It was every bit as ghastly as he had imagined it would be since the doctor's phone call. "I'm here to see you, Dad. That's all."

"Think I'm licked?"

"No, you're not licked," George lied.

"You're just saying that. You think I'm licked, don't you?"

"What does it matter what I think," George answered in despair and abruptly left his seat. Still, he felt that he could not just walk out. The old man had been nasty and argumentative all his life, at least with his sons. Why should he behave any differently now?

"I'm not licked," the old man said.

George now stood silently before a large plate-glass window to the right of the bed. The window ran from a knee-high radiator to the ceiling and was four feet wide. George felt uneasy standing before it, as though he might somehow pitch headlong out of it. But he could not return to the chair either, and there was nowhere else in the room to go without staring into a wall.

The window overlooked the eight downtown blocks
that had been gutted in the botched urban renewal scheme
that crowned Lewis Wells's political career. George looked
down on the desolate scene, an urban abyss lighted eerie
pinkish-yellow by a grid of brand-new quartz halogen
street lights—the only element of the renewal scheme that
had ever been completed. The eighteen-acre parcel of
land was supposed to contain a new civic center, a hotel,
and an atrium shopping mall, but as the 1970s waned,
and one factory after another closed down, and the population declined by twenty-eight percent, and Delft's utter
bankruptcy as an industrial town became more apparent,
no developer or consortium of investors wanted to touch
the project with a ten-foot pole, and so the blocks remained empty—Lewis Wells's most visible political legacy.

Though he did not consider his childhood in Delft as
particularly happy, George could now remember the old
downtown business district only at its most festive. For
instance: a Christmas eve some years before the barbell
incident with Johnny Hatto. He was in the sixth grade at
the old Ontario Street grammar school. After it let out that
day, he and a bunch of his chums headed downtown, full
of high spirits because it was the beginning of their two-
week vacation. The first good snow of winter had begun
falling around noon, and enough had accumulated to
promise excellent sledding through the holiday. The flakes
were big, like the snow in one of those liquid-filled paper-
weights that you shake to make the snow fly. By the time
they got downtown, it was twilight. The holiday lights
were turned on over the streets, and the store windows
were all aglow with enticing displays of toys and clothes
and sporting goods. Holiday shoppers, overloaded with
shopping bags and parcels, bustled along the sidewalks.
Christmas carols played over loudspeakers outside Ermer's
Department Store, Delft's grandest emporium. Sidewalk

Santas rang their handbells and cheerfully cried, "Ho, ho, ho! Merry Christmas!" as though they actually meant it. Businessmen in hats and overcoats left their buildings on Algonquin Street wearing big smiles after their annual Christmas parties. There were bigger evening crowds than usual in the downtown taverns. The electric streetcars were still running then. George and his friends bombarded several of them with salvos of snowballs before a policeman snuck up on them and grabbed George by the collar of his coat with one huge white-gloved hand and George's classmate Billy McQuillan with the other. The rest of the boys ran around the corner and hid in the alley behind the Mohawk Oyster House. The policeman demanded his and Billy's names. George gave his, and when the cop discovered that he was the son of Mayor Wells, he let both boys free at once *with an apology*. The incident made George appear absolutely charmed among his circle of pals. It was perhaps the only time in his life when he was glad to be the son of Lewis Wells.

Then there were the summer street-dances when George was a little older and discovering girls. The dances were sponsored by the local radio station as a way of keeping teens from drag-racing out on the county highways. On Saturday nights in July and August, the block along the west side of Union Square was roped off, and a small flatbed truck parked at one end with a stack of remote broadcasting equipment and Delft's most popular disc jockey, Larry Phebus, spinning the platters. Larry played "Quarter to Three," by Gary "U.S." Bonds and "Travelin' Man," by Ricky Nelson. George and his friends experimented with cigarettes. A horror movie called *The Fly* with Vincent Price was playing at the Strand Theater just beyond the roped-off dance area. The older, hoodier teens all congregated near the marquee, drinking quarts of beer out of paper bags and doing crude imitations of

Vincent Price for the benefit of their hoody girlfriends. George remembered slow dancing to "Surfer Girl," by the Beach Boys, with his first love, Debbie Dowling, daughter of Clarence Dowling, owner of the Iroquois Paper Company, largest of Delft's four factories. Dowling was also Fulton County Republican Chairman and thus Lewis Wells's mortal enemy. George mainly remembered the feel of Debbie's thirteen-year-old breasts softly pressing against his ribcage and how sweet her mouth tasted when she kissed him later in a quiet corner of the square.

Looking down on the now desolate scene of those happy memories, it seemed to George as if everything good about the way of life here had been eradicated as utterly as the civilization of the Incas. Where did people in Delft go now on Christmas eve? Where did they go to the movies? What did kids do on hot summer nights?

"You haven't amounted to a damn, either," George only half heard his father say as he struggled to escape a floodtide of regret.

He turned away from the window to the old man lying in bed, who was even more of a shocking sight now than when George had first come in, as though his father were not merely a victim of death, but a grinning skull-faced personification of it, a bringer of it, like one of those ghouls on a pale horse in an old etching by Dürer. "What did you say?"

"I said you haven't amounted to a damn," his father repeated in a labored but distinct whisper.

George heard him clearly this time and angrily shoved the chair out of the way. Almost at once the door opened and Johnny Hatto stepped into the room.

"You all right, boss?"

"Get out," George demanded, but the old lackey just stood resolutely in the doorway. George picked up the toy

259

monkey on the bedside table and hurled it at him. Johnny withdrew.

"A goddam waiter, that's what you are," Lewis Wells said, followed by a croak of a laugh. "Pipsqueak."

George sat down at the edge of the narrow bed and looked into his father's gray eyes, so pale surrounded by their jaundiced whites. There seemed almost no substance left to the body under the blankets. The handsome, tireless, six-foot-four leader of men for three decades was reduced to a talking skeleton. Yet there was just enough of him left to hate, and George now leaned forward with his hands clutching the mattress at either side of the old man's skull until he could feel his diseased heat. "You are a despicable wretch," George told him quietly, firmly, and with absolute conviction.

"I was the biggest thing that ever happened to this town," the old man said defiantly.

"You killed this town."

"Let's call it even, then," the old man whispered, and no sooner had the last word left his lips than George saw his chest deflate under the blankets and heard the last breath his father would ever draw rattle out of his throat like dry leaves blowing through a drainpipe.

Joel Harlowe glanced down at the digital clock on his windscreen. It was seven minutes to six o'clock. As he came off the George Washington Bridge ramp and touched the concrete of Manhattan, little waves of ecstasy pulsed through him like an electrical charge. He attributed this to the karmic overflow of the city, theorizing that with his unique mental abilities he was like a lightning rod for all that excess energy.

Feeling so supercharged, therefore, while riding a high performance motorcycle, he decided to make the Triborough Bridge over to Queens in two minutes flat, and easily accomplished it at speeds of better than one hundred miles per hour, though several other startled motorists on the Harlem River Drive battered their cars in his wake. Then on the Triborough, with the east side of Manhattan Island blazing galactically to his right along the dark funnel of the East River, and with the 59th Street Bridge, the United Nations, and the Chrysler Building all swinging brightly into view, along with ten thousand other lighted buildings, Joel was struck by a breathtaking notion: why not come back to Manhattan after concluding his little business deal at LaGuardia and go to the Palm Court of the Plaza Hotel and buy everybody there a drink—before departing once more for his beloved Excelsior Springs two hundred miles back up the thruway. What an idea!

The fantasy grew more elaborate and specific as he came off the Triborough Bridge and began to traverse the limbo lands of Queens. The way he imagined it, he would pull right up to the front entrance of the Plaza Hotel, park the Beemer on the sidewalk, and hand the several doormen each a hundred dollar bill, telling them to keep an eye on the bike for a few minutes. International financiers, socialites, celebrities would gape at the dashing figure in the beautiful brown leather cycling suit. Pulling off his gloves, he would proceed inside the glittering lobby and up the stairs to the Palm Court, where famous movie actresses, rock stars, and literary lions would all look up from their silver plates of foie gras as one, their jaws dropping. Joel would hand the captain a hundred dollar bill just to get his attention, order a drink for everyone in the room and champagne for himself. No! Fuck that. Champagne for everybody. Finally—and this was the juicy part—when the whole room was hosed down with Dom Perignon, he would stand up, tap on his glass with a knife until they all stopped buzzing about his sudden incredible appearance among them and—this was the topper—*he would invite everybody in the room to follow him up the thruway to his Halloween Ball at Excelsior Springs!* Wouldn't that blow their minds back home when he showed up with Robert Redford, Diane Keaton, Dustin Hoffman, Meryl Streep, and God-knows-how-many other stars in a caravan behind him. And if they didn't happen to have their cars parked anywhere in the vicinity of the hotel, let them take taxicabs upstate. Joel would pick up the tab for that, too. It would cost a ton of money, of course, but wasn't he traveling with a ton of money even as this elaborate and superlative idea spun out sweetly in his mind? Didn't he have a hundred-thousand dollars right behind him in the cargo box of his motorcycle, even as he threaded his way in and out of traffic on the Grand Central Parkway in Queens, with Astoria to his left and the blue, red, green, and white lights of LaGuardia airport up ahead?

The digital clock said five minutes after six. Roberto and his partner, a little weasely fucker whose name Joel couldn't remember, ought be there by now. Joel corkscrewed off the LaGuardia exit of the parkway and entered the airport complex proper. With its old-fashioned control tower, art deco terminal, and quaint hangars, LaGuardia looked like a toy airport Joel had once gotten as a Hanukkah present from his beloved father and mother. Had they known something about his destiny? he wondered.

Joel's mouth was dry. He had to content himself with the knowledge that soon he would be sipping champagne at the Plaza. He turned in at the long-term parking lot and stopped for a moment to take a ticket that was spewed like a tongue out of a squat, toadlike machine. A metal gate swung out of the way, permitting him to enter. Slowly, he crept up and down the lanes in first gear searching for Roberto's gray van. Behind him, a plane shot up off a runway, its jet engines roaring, and its beautiful bulk swerving high over the nearby marshes until it too became a little toy in the dark sky. His heart pounded. This was exciting! Moments later, he spotted the van.

There was an empty space between the van and a beige Mercedes Benz parked one slot over. As Joel pulled into the space, he could see the shadowy form of a head in the front passenger window of the van. Joel pulled off his helmet and set it carefully down on the seat of his bike. The front door of the van opened, and a small, wiry man with South American Indian features stepped out. He wore a Japanese baseball jacket, new designer jeans, and expensive cowboy boots. It was Roberto's weasely partner.

"*Hola*." He greeted Joel and then smiled. A gold tooth glinted in the artificial light. Then, another figure appeared soundlessly from behind the rear of the van. He was bulkier, more Spanish than Indian, wearing a Ralph Lauren country knockaround jacket in taupe. Joel recognized the jacket because he owned one just like it, and he decided at once that he would have to get rid of it, maybe give it to Sandy. The bulkier man stepped forward from the shadows with his hand outstretched.

"Jo-el, my friend," he said, using two syllables as though the name derived from a Superman comic book.

Joel took the hand. It jangled with gold jewelry as he shook it. "*Buenas noches,* Roberto."

"Are you ready to do business?"

"Yes."

"*Muy bien.*"

Roberto stood before Joel for a moment as though he were measuring himself—he was two inches taller. Then he tapped on the side door of the van. It rolled open. Inside was a third Colombian, also attired in expensive sportswear. He sat in a space about a yard square surrounded by corrugated cardboard cartons. At a signal from his boss, the third man reached into a carton and pulled out a Cabbage Patch doll. He removed its clear plastic slipcase and twisted its head off. Inside it was another plastic bag filled with white powder.

"Let's have a taste," Joel suggested.

Roberto told his subordinate to open the bag, which he did by slitting the corner with a large folding knife. Roberto took out a gold enameled cigarette case and had the helper dump a little heap on its flat surface. This he passed to Joel while he rolled a hundred dollar bill into a tube. Joel snorted part of the heap into one nostril and the rest into the other.

"Superb," he pronounced seconds later. The whole world suddenly seemed possible to him.

"The best," Roberto said.

"But that's no half-ki."

"Of course not," Roberto said, smiling. "Chino."

The third man fished around in a cardboard box and soon extracted a second doll. It too contained a bag of cocaine. Together, the two bags comprised a half-kilogram. He taped up the corner of the first bag where it had been cut open and placed both bags in a plain paper sack. It had a grease spot on it, as though it had previously contained a sausage sandwich. A plane, this one coming in for a landing, screamed directly over their heads. Roberto held onto the paper sack, waiting. All Joel could think about—his head scintillating—was the way those celebrities would look at him in the Palm Court when he ordered champagne for the house.

"The money, Jo-el."

"Uh, certainly," Joel replied and unzipped his leather cycling suit down to his solar plexus. He rather regretted that he had worn the Smith & Wesson up top and the automatic in his boot because the revolver only held five bullets with the one empty chamber, and if push came to shove, he didn't know whether he could take out all three men with five shots; nor, he considered, would there be any opportunity in the heat of things to even reach for the automatic if events got hectic. This was going to be real cowboy stuff. As for actually having to kill the three, he had no compunctions whatever. They were unregistered aliens. Criminals. Scum.

"Jo-el, the money," Roberto repeated, his smile beginning to dissolve.

"I've got it right here," Joel said, pulling the Smith & Wesson.

Another plane roared off a runway in the near distance.

"Don't be a stupid *chocha*," Roberto said, backing up against the van with his hands up as he saw the gun, but Joel didn't hear him. Nor did he hear the door of the Mercedes open behind him beneath the roar of the jet engines. In fact, Joel did not suspect anything amiss until he felt the hairy forearms of a fourth, unseen Colombian ram his Adam's apple into the back of his throat, resulting in a pain so sharp and intense that the pistol flew out of his hand without a shot. Only then did he suspect that events had suddenly slipped out of his control. And it still somehow never occurred to him that the others might do him any real harm until Roberto retrieved the gun, pushed the muzzle right against Joel's abdomen and emptied the cylinder into him, *pop-pop-pop-pop-pop,* saying only the word *"Maricón."*

Two of the bullets shattered his spinal column and all five perforated some vital organ. Joel slid to the ground against the bike, astonished, as gasoline poured on his head from several holes shot in the tank. Then there seemed to be a crazy rush all around him. A gabble of Spanish. Things opening and closing. Engines starting. The squeal of rubber. Despite this unanticipated turnabout, Joel felt a special kind of excitement welling within him. It was greater than any drug, or combination of drugs, he had ever tried, a feeling that something entirely new and marvelous was about to happen to him.

Sandy could have gone back to the supermarket where his clothes and wallet were stolen, but what would be the point? he wondered. Surely the thief would have absconded by now. There was nothing to do, really, except notify the police—a lot that would accomplish—and try to keep his eyes peeled around town for some creep walking around in his father's flight jacket. He was halfway across the casino's barroom—all the liquor still lying around in cartons—on his way to the kitchen with the six plastic trash buckets, when he remembered that the $250 check from Joel had also been in the wallet. The check represented his November rent, due tomorrow. He would have to get Joel to stop payment on that check and write out a new one. The North Country Trust had regular Saturday hours, 10 A.M. to 2 P.M., so that was cool. He just hoped Joel wouldn't be so hungover tomorrow that he slept all day.

Resuming his path to the kitchen, Sandy glanced at his watch. It said quarter to seven. In less than two hours the partygoers would start flocking in. God knows how many people Joel had invited. Probably half the town. Delicious cooking smells wafted out of the kitchen. The Novocain was finally wearing off. His lower lip only felt a little bit fuzzy, and with his tongue he could feel the space where his tooth had been pulled. It dawned on him that he hadn't eaten a thing all day long.

The kitchen was aswirl with activity. Leading her three Bird of Paradise helpers—young women like herself with earnest, intelligent faces—Barbara Lazarus stood at a center table piping out cheese puffs onto a baking sheet from a pastry bag. One helper was deep-frying shrimp toasts with the fantails sticking up, then laying the cooked ones out on paper towels to drain. Another was whisking a sweet-sour sauce that would soon blanket a chafing dish full of ground-veal balls. The third helper was spooning a pâté spread from a stainless steel bowl into a ceramic terrine shaped like a goose. Every square inch of counter space seemed to be covered with a tray of tempting tidbits: little crabmeat tartlets awaiting the oven, Parmesan cheese straws just out and cooling, stuffed mushrooms, chicken wings in hoisin sauce, platters heaped with raw vegetables and bowls of different dips, rosy slices of smoked salmon arranged on a fish-shaped platter with a pewter head and tail, a four-foot-long board of cheeses, and in a sink, a steaming colander filled with a pink mountain of just-boiled jumbo shrimp. Waiting to be sliced were three Smithfield hams and an equal number of Vermont cob-smoked turkeys. Sandy's stomach felt as if it were turning cartwheels.

"Mind if I taste a few of these?" he asked Barbara.

"Please, try whatever you like," she said, looking up from her pastry bag with a big smile. "By the way, that's quite an outfit."

"Thanks."

"There's something about a man in a uniform."

Dizzy with hunger, Sandy proceeded from counter to counter sampling one delicious morsel after another. He found it something of an unpleasant novelty to have to chew on only one side of his mouth, but the strangeness was more than offset by the absence of pain and the exciting flavors of everything. He had made two full circuits of the kitchen and settled in by the sink to peel himself a few shrimp, when he happened to ask Barbara when the bartenders were supposed to show up.

"I have no idea," she replied.

"Do they show up whenever they feel like it, or what?"

"I really don't know. I don't have anything to do with the bartenders," she told him, shoving one pan of cheese puffs into the oven and pulling out a sheet of baked ones. Sandy merely watched her with a familiar sinking feeling in his gut, a sensation that had become all but second nature to his minute-by-minute functioning this excruciatingly long Halloween day.

"Are you telling me that you don't arrange for the bartenders who are supposed to work this party?"

"That's absolutely what I'm telling you," she said. "We only do the food."

"I'm in big trouble," Sandy said gravely, washing his shrimpy hands and shaking them dry because there were no towels around.

"Didn't Joel arrange for someone?" Barbara asked.

"He must have forgotten about it."

"You are in big trouble," she agreed. "You need at least three people to work that long bar for the number of people coming. I've done scads of weddings and parties here."

"How many people, exactly, did Joel tell you to cook for."

"Four hundred," she said, popping a cheese puff in her own mouth and holding one out for Sandy.

"I am in real big trouble," he said, declining the tidbit.

Nine minutes later he was turning in the front entrance of the Greer campus, looking for some students to hire to mix drinks. Where to look? Where to go? The temperature was plummeting. He nearly froze driving the mile up to the campus with nothing on but the hussar's tunic and a thin cotton shirt, and the thought of some creep running around town wearing his father's flight jacket became doubly galling.

The first place he checked was Griggs Hall, the student snack bar, activity center, and all-purpose hangout, but at seven o'clock on a Friday night the place was all but dead. Only a few solitary grinds or social lepers sat alone over Cokes.

"Does anyone here know how to tend bar by any chance?" Sandy addressed these scattered individuals without much hope. A half dozen faces stared blankly back at him and Sandy withdrew. Growing desperate, he proceeded to enter a dormitory—Beedle Hall—and soon stumbled upon a room crammed with students. It was a TV lounge and about thirty kids, mostly female, were watching *Entertainment Tonight,* a show that broadcast news about the world of show biz. Sandy posed his question about bartending just when a sexy British rock star began expounding on his worldview. Several of the girls turned sharply around and snapped, "Shut up!"

One athletic-looking male, lounging in red Greer sweats with the hood pulled up so that he looked like one of Santa's helpers, said, "I worked at a bar at Lake George this past summer."

"I need someone for tonight. Will you work?"

"How much?"

"Fifty dollars," Sandy said, pulling the figure out of thin air. It was Joel's money anyhow.

The kid wrinkled his nose. "I don't think so," he said.

"Sssshhh!" another girl said.

"A hundred," Sandy offered desperately.

"Gee . . . okay."

"Come to the casino downtown as soon as possible. Wear some decent clothes."

"Okay," the kid said.

"Hey, do you have any buddies who know how to mix drinks, by any chance?" Sandy asked.

"Will you shut up, you asshole!" another girl snarled as the British rock star ventured to disclose his ideas on matrimony.

The boy with the sweatsuit shook his head. Sandy withdrew. A tour of several other dormitory TV lounges produced a freshman who knew how to work a beer tap, and a girl who knew most of the ingredients in drinks but never actually worked behind a bar. They would have to do.

No sooner had he returned to the casino, however, and begun uncrating all the liquor, when it came to him, as in an epiphany, that there were absolutely no mixers, no juices, no sodas, no fruit, no ice, and not even any glasses to serve the drinks in. Pausing a moment to marvel at the number of little things that can go wrong when you decide to throw a big party, Sandy motorcycled back to the Top Shopper, bought several hundred dollars' worth of supplies plus two hundred pounds of bagged ice cubes and every plastic cup in the store. Bringing it all back on his motorcycle was, of course, out of the question, so he called two taxicabs, loaded them up, and dispatched them to the casino. All the while, he couldn't help wondering what would have happened if Harlowe had never asked him to help out. He couldn't imagine Joel running all over town for one stupid thing after another, as he had done since four o'clock in the afternoon. In the face of all this chaos, Sandy thought, Harlowe would have thrown up his hands and begun taking Quaaludes.

He followed the taxicabs back to the casino and began unloading them, lugging the bags of soda, juice, fruit, ice, and plastic cups inside with some help from the cabbies to whom he had promised lavish tips. It was amazing, he thought, the way money solved problems.

For the first time since Joel had left him in charge, Sandy began to feel good about it, to feel that it was actually going to come off and be a wonderful party. In the long run, it was probably better for the party that Joel had left all these last-minute details in somebody else's hands. It was weird, though, how everything always seemed to work out for Harlowe, Sandy thought. Joel Harlowe was an amazingly lucky guy. Sometimes it seemed as if he led a charmed life.

FIFTEEN

Edmund Black propped a small framed mirror against a pile of books on the desk in his bedroom and began smearing white greasepaint on his face. His chest stung from having shaved it minutes earlier, and then having mistakenly applied after-shave. The initial pain had forced him to jam a towel in his mouth to keep from crying out, it hurt so badly.

In the background across the room, a show called *Lifestyles of the Rich and Famous* was playing on a small television beside the disheveled bed. Tonight, the program's British host was leading the viewing audience on a tour through the Tennessee estate of a fabulously successful country-western crooner. The star was just now showing off the private indoor skating rink he'd had put in off the master bedroom for his wife, a former Olympic figure-skating hopeful. "This way she kin git a gold-medal hug from me each and every mornin'," the star explained, grinning so that his eyes made porcine little slits. Edmund pictured the star's direct forebears as a gang of bug-eyed, lynch-mob cretins too ignorant to spell their own names. "The Lord Jesus sure been good to us," the crooner said.

His face completely covered with the white makeup, Edmund began to apply lavender shadow above his eyes, trailing it out to big winglike points at his temples in the manner of a Las Vegas showgirl. The false eyelashes he had purchased in the drug store proved particularly troublesome for a person of his limited experience. By the time he got them glued on, *Lifestyles* had taken its audience halfway around the globe to visit the manor house of an English lady novelist renowned for having produced more books than any individual in the history of literature. Her 358 novels addressed various aspects of the love question. They were all written by means of dictation, which eliminated a lot of nuisance, she said. She received the show's host in her boudoir. The enormous room was decorated in so many different shades of pink that it looked like a gynecologist's nightmare. The novelist, who was said to be in her late eighties, did not look a day over sixty. Edmund was fascinated by her voice, which was as musical as a carillon. He mimicked the novelist, following her remarks line for line while he plucked his eyebrows.

"A gull must know her own heart," the novelist advised aspiring females everywhere.

As Edmund parroted her, his phone rang.

"Oh, hell," he exclaimed, flinging down his tweezers in disgust and crossing the room to answer it. "A gull must know her own heart," he trilled into the phone, holding it carefully so as not muss his makeup.

"There you go, being a goddamned fool all over again."

"Oh, it's you, Mother!"

"I've been calling for hours. Where have you been?"

"Out performing good works among the homeless."

273

"Buying drugs, I bet."

"Succoring the sick, refting the bereft, making the lame leap for joy—"

"Shut up. There is something I think we neglected to get absolutely straight before: this foolishness of your sister's. She is planning some kind of big wedding out there in Chicago. Well, our family will not be participating in this sham. Do I make myself clear?"

"She's participating, and she's part of the family."

"Not anymore. I am disowning her. On Monday I am meeting with my attorneys and with Mr. Smithson of the Morgan Guaranty Trust and I intend to see that she is cut off from your grandaddy's money without a red cent. I will not stand for some ofay gold digger pissing away money that was earned by the honest sweat of the sons and daughters of slaves."

"Let me see if I've got this right, Mother. You want a show of solidarity here? You want to boycott Sappho's wedding? Just like in the old lunch-counter days?"

"That's it in a nutshell, Edmund. I'm proud of you. For the first time in years—it seems like—you begin to show a glimmer of comprehension."

"But then, who will come to my wedding?"

"The day that you get married I will fly in the entire Talapoosa Institute marching band, and that's a promise."

"Better buy one hundred and four airplane tickets, Mother, because I'm about to jump the broomstick myself."

"Uh-huh," she said skeptically. "Who's the lucky girl?"

"Me!"

There was a pause on the line long enough that the first verse of the Talapoosa Institute football fight song could have been sung through it.

"You listen to me, you goddamned fool of a pissant fairy," his mother eventually said, her words fairly crackling through the wire. "None of us is going out to this . . . this *thing* in Chicago. And as for you, boy, you had best get yourself straightened out, too, hear? And fast. Because as soon as I'm done cutting off Sappho, I'll be putting a whole squad of lawyers on your case, so you better think long and hard about how you're going to conduct yourself in front of a judge at your competency hearing. Are you still listening to me, boy?"

"Raptly."

"Well then, what do you have to say for yourself?"

"A gull must know her own heart."

George Wells hadn't set foot in his father's house for more than a year. Like everything else in Delft, Genesee Street looked seedier than he ever remembered it. He had counted five For Sale signs in front of houses on the block over from Adirondack Street alone, and the big Geneva sandstone house next door that had belonged to Leroy Sukeforth, who owned the Strand Theater, was entirely gone, demolished like the theater downtown. A biting wind blew up the hill off the dark Mohawk River, past the silent factories, and George shivered as he fumbled with his keys at the front door.

As soon as he entered the old house and switched on the hall light, he was nearly overwhelmed by a rich combination of scents—tobacco, whiskey, old varnished wood—that brought back a torrent of painful memories. The house stank of politics. George clutched the newel post at the bottom of the front stairway and took several deep breaths trying to steady his nerves.

The front parlor had hardly changed in thirty years. Here was the sofa before the fireplace where the old man liked to sit drinking straight rye, mostly alone, listening to Benny Goodman records. Even in the dim hall light, the upholstery looked tattered and stained. He went upstairs.

275

The first room he came to on the second floor was Johnny Hatto's. George flicked on the light and peered in. It was as neat as a bachelor soldier's quarters, or perhaps the room of a frightened little boy futilely trying to stave off a family disaster by being extra tidy. A pair of worn slippers stood together on a throw rug beside the carefully made bed. Except for framed photographs of Franklin Roosevelt and John F. Kennedy, the dresser top was bare. His curiosity stirred, George looked in the closet. Inside hung two suits, one black, one blue. Beneath them was a pair of highly polished black brogans. That was all.

The next room was Lewis Wells's study, his sanctum sanctorum. George and Davey had been warned as boys to stay out of it, and even now, with the old man gone, George entered warily. Nor, when he slid into the red leather chair behind the huge desk, could he escape the feeling of doing something wicked. Various papers lay in piles upon the desk: deeds, titles, certificates, long legal documents of many pages in fine print. To the right sat a ten-inch-wide amber glass ashtray in a leather holder. The ashtray contained several unfiltered cigarette stubs, perhaps the last his father had ever smoked before he had to go into the hospital on Labor Day. George sat quietly in the chair. The stillness of the house, even of the street beyond, was unnerving. He idly slid open the top center drawer. Inside was a fat manila envelope, its flap unglued. He took it out of the drawer and peered inside. It contained several dark bundles. He switched on the brass desk lamp now and shook out the contents of the envelope. Three bundles of bills tumbled onto the desk blotter. As if he had uncovered something obscene, George quickly drew the window blinds, even though the house next door no longer existed. The money amounted to $2500, all in twenties. He stuffed the bills back into the envelope and began searching the other drawers. It took him half an hour to go through the six desk drawers. In them he found more than a dozen envelopes containing amounts of money ranging from $150 to $5450, all in bills of $50 or smaller. It came to more than $30,000.

Stunned, George left the desk and searched the room for something to put the money in. He found a battered briefcase in the closet. The closet contained several cardboard cartons. The cartons were filled with reams of legal documents dating back to the 1950s. But in one he found a shoebox full of money. He brought this over to the desk and dumped the bills there. It contained $37,450 in $50 bills. He discovered another box of money at the rear of the closet's upper shelf and more envelopes of bundled bills in a four-drawer filing cabinet. Altogether, he came across $114,725 more.

When he was satisfied that he had thoroughly searched the office, he proceeded down the hall to his father's bedroom and went inside. The room was almost as unfamiliar to him as the room of a perfect stranger. He had not been in it for so many years—decades! The last time, a winter night when he couldn't have been more than ten, he had stolen in just to look at the photographs of his mother on his father's dresser. His father came home unexpectedly from some political affair and flew into a rage when he found George in his bedroom. He told his son never to set foot in it again, and George took him literally in the years that followed, always feeling that the room must have harbored some dark and sinister secret. At times, the gruesome notion occurred to him that his father had had his mother stuffed and that he kept her in the closet—an idea directly traceable to a horror movie of the sixties.

He proceeded into the room, even now, with the old man dead, feeling anxious and ashamed about being there. Above the bed hung an oil portrait of his mother, done in an impressionistic style, all pinks and pastel greens and mauve shadows in the background. She had posed in a sundress, and George could practically feel the humidity of that long-ago summer day on the cool young skin of her bare shoulders. Nothing in the portrait prefigured the calamity of childbirth that would kill her a few years later. George could hardly bear to look at it.

He turned instead to search his father's dresser drawers. There was clothing, of course, but no money, and only a miscellany of cuff links and tie clasps in a leather caddy on the top. Some may have been gold. George couldn't tell. He moved on to the closet beside it. Many suits hung here, good suits, from a custom tailor in New York City. There were absolutely no casual clothes, not so much as a sport shirt. At the very rear of the closet stood a squat gray metal safe, a three-foot cube. It was securely locked, the combination unknown to him. George tried to budge it, but it weighed close to five hundred pounds and his weight-lifting days were long behind him. There would be time enough in the weeks ahead to get into it, he thought, and crossed the room to another closet. The door was sticky, but came open with a good yank. Pulling the light cord inside it, he was astounded to discover that it was full of women's clothes, clothes of a bygone era, his mother's clothes.

The discovery that the old man had secretly kept her clothes all these years startled him, as though his childhood fears about the mummy in the closet had come true. His heart thumped loudly in the close confines of the little room. Yet he could not resist the temptation to examine the clothes—they seemed so small; he'd always imagined her much, much larger—and as he held a handful of silk to his face, he ever so faintly detected her scent, or thought he did. His mind reeled backward thirty years. He was little again, a five-year-old boy in a miniature suit and tie. Somebody was lifting him up by the ribcage over a big burnished wood box with brass handles. As he seemingly flew above the box, she came into view, lying in repose in the box's cushioned satin interior, asleep, and yet fully clothed, dressed in a gown as she had been for her sister's wedding, a bouquet of flowers clutched in her unmoving hands.

"Kiss Mommy good-bye," a man's voice said. He honestly didn't know whether it was his father's voice or not. He remembered flying downward toward her face, screaming, then blankness.

In a panic, George rushed from the closet, tripping on a hatbox on his way out and landed face first on the carpet in the bedroom. His shirt felt cold and wet under his arms and all the way down both sides. For over thirty years he had forgotten the particulars of that funeral day, except for the view from the cemetery. And suddenly he sensed in that failure to say good-bye all the composite failures of his life so far, while he felt at the same instant a peculiar and surprising upwelling of pity for the old man who had cherished her clothing along with her memory.

In a little while, he picked himself off the floor, turned off the lights, and left the room, proceeding downstairs with the briefcase full of money. In the front parlor he poured himself a stiff drink of rye whiskey in one of the crystal tumblers stacked on the cherry lowboy that served as a bar. Then he settled into the sofa before the unlit fireplace, reached for a nearby black telephone, and dialed a long distance number.

"Davey?"

"Yes."

"He's dead."

A pause, then a sigh on the other end.

"When?"

"Just a little while ago over at the hospital."

"Were you there?"

"As a matter of fact, yes."

"How did it . . . was it terrible?"

"It was just sad," George said.

"And you just happened to be there?"

"No, the doctor in charge called me up yesterday, told me it was near the end."

"I see. Well, what happens now?"

"He gets buried."

"No, I mean with his . . . his estate."

George hesitated a moment, picturing his brother shooting up a bag of heroin, snorting a line of cocaine, remembering all the different drug rehab programs Davey had been in year after year. "I'll call his lawyer, Bill Pomeroy," he said.

"You sure Bill's still alive? He was an old fart when we were little kids."

"I'm sure someone around here will know who was in charge of Dad's affairs."

"I suppose," Davey agreed. "Have you been home yet?"

"I'm calling from there now."

"Did you poke around any?"

"Sure, I walked through the place. It's sad. The whole town is sad."

"I always had this crazy feeling that when he died there'd be bags full of money stashed in every nook and cranny," Davey said. "When I was about thirteen, I once found three hundred bucks wrapped inside the evening paper on our doorstep. Did I ever mention that to you?"

"No. I don't think so."

"You must have been away at college by then. He never missed it either. Never said a word about it, anyway."

"I found a safe up in his closet."

"Yeah, I forgot about that. What's in it?"

"I have no idea. I'll have to get the combination."

"Right. That's probably where it's all stashed."

"Probably," George agreed.

"He must have had bank accounts and investments, too. I'm sure he was loaded. Better check it out thoroughly."

"Of course. Listen, I don't know that much about how these things work, but I suppose I'll have to arrange a funeral and everything. I can pick you up at the Albany airport."

"I think I'll pass, George. You always got along with him okay. You bury the bastard."

George was stunned to silence—not because his brother refused to fly east for the funeral, but at Davey's naive conception of the way things really had been between George and the old man.

"I mean, I hate to dump it all in your lap, George, but let's face it, he couldn't stand me. And, frankly, I haven't had much use for him either for a long, long time. Not to mention your being there already."

"I understand, Davey."

"I just want what's coming to me."

"Of course."

"So let me know what happens with the lawyers and all."

"All right."

"And poke around the old place. You might turn up a couple of thou. You never know."

"I will."

"By the way, I don't want to sound creepy about it or anything, but did he happen to have any last words? I mean, you were there and all."

"No. He didn't," George said. "He was asleep when I got there, and then a short while later he just slipped away."

"That's too bad. I always figured he'd have some real

zinger ready on his way out. Pretty ironic that he . . . that it happened on Halloween night, though, huh?''

"I guess."

"I mean, of all the nights of the year. But then to me, he was always very much a Halloween sort of father, you know what I mean?"

"I think so."

"Anyway, keep me posted, will you George?"

"Sure, Davey. 'Bye."

George sat with the phone on his lap for a little while, finishing his whiskey and listening to the silence. It was cold in the house though, the furnace was not on, and despite the whiskey, George began to shiver. Eventually, thinking of the warm comfort of his truck and anxious to escape Delft, if only until tomorrow, he got up from the sofa. He had picked up the briefcase containing nearly $185,000 in cash when the front door opened and Johnny Hatto walked in, stooped and halting in a heavy, gray overcoat.

"I seen the light," he said, removing his hat.

"I beg your pardon," George said, thinking for a moment that Johnny was announcing some kind of sudden spiritual conversion.

"I seen the hall light from the street." The old man pointed to the brass and opalescent glass fixture overhead.

"Oh. Of course."

"He's down to the home now," Johnny remarked next, and again George was perplexed.

"Whose home?"

"The funeral home: Boyle and Grimes on Owasco Street."

"Right. The funeral home. Thank you for seeing to it, Johnny."

"The ambulance done it. Mind if I come in?"

"No. Please," George said, thinking how strange it

was for the old guy to have to ask, since he had been living here for decades.

"I could stand a drink."

"Help yourself," George said, putting down the briefcase.

Johnny went to the parlor, poured himself two fingers of rye in a crystal glass, and knocked it back like a shot. Then, in his old man's shuffling gait, he returned to the hall where George remained.

"We went back to the beginning, the boss and me," Johnny said, glancing repeatedly down at the floor and back at George, his thin lips quavering. And then crying out, "He was my whole life!" he fell against George's chest sobbing, his bony shoulders heaving and a gnarled hand clutching George's lapel like a man clutching for a lifebuoy on a dark, storm-tossed sea. "Where'll I go now?" he sobbed.

"You can stay here."

"We went back to '36, me and him. FDR and all." Johnny began to compose himself, holding George by the forearm now to brace himself and dabbing his tears with his coat sleeves. "It was a different world. You should've seen him in them days. He had it. You could tell even then."

"I'm sure he made provisions for you, Johnny."

"You should've seen him against them strikebreakers down to the wire works in '38. Two hundred scabs. Sent 'em all packing back to Utica on the noon train. I seen it. I was there."

"You stay here for now," he told the old errand boy, physically detaching himself from his grasp. "And turn the heat on. There's no need for you to freeze." George reached again for the briefcase. It was quite heavy.

"You find the money?" Johnny asked.

George didn't reply. It astounded him to consider

that Johnny had known about all those bundles and boxes full of cash and hadn't taken it himself. And yet how could he have *not* known about it? George was afraid to know the answer one way or the other.

"That's all right. You keep it," Johnny said, patting him on the arm. "He was savin' it for you."

That Johnny expected him to believe this pathetic lie only amazed George more, as much as it moved him deeply and caused him to regret that Christmas eve so long ago when he hung the barbell across Johnny's neck. He thought of the pitiful toy monkey on the table beside his father's deathbed, and his vision soon blurred as tears pooled in his eyes.

"Let's have a drink to him, Georgie, you and me. What do you say."

"All right."

Johnny shuffled into the parlor, poured two more whiskeys, and brought the glasses back to the hall.

"To the boss, Mayor Lewis Wells!" Johnny held up his glass, his rheumy eyes glistening in the weak light.

"To my dad," George said, clinking glasses.

"And to Delft," the old man said, his voice breaking with grief, "the greatest little city in the Empire State!"

Stuffed into the pink monstrosity of a prom dress, his face painted white and bedizened like a Kabuki mask within the rococo curls of the blond wig, and unsteady on his feet in a pair of spiked heels, Edmund Black descended the impressive front stairway in his large, gloomy house and answered the doorbell. Outside waited Rupert Van Der Wie, aka Cecil Wonton, who flinched when the door was thrown open to reveal what looked like a primal woman-as-devil vision he'd seen while tripping on peyote some years ago.

"Ieeyuh!" Cecil cried, fairly leaping back to the porch rail. Then collecting his wits, he said, "Oh, it's you."

"It's me! It's me!" Edmund trilled, in the breathless falsetto of the English woman novelist. Then, noticing Cecil's costume, which wasn't much of a costume at all in the Halloween sense, Edmund's red-painted bee-stung lips turned down in a broad scowl while he crossed his muscular brown arms in front of his gown's sleeveless bodice. "Look at you, you slob!" he said, casting an opprobrious gaze up and down Cecil's outfit of Topsiders, khaki pants, pink oxford shirt worn over a fuchsia polo shirt (the inner collar standing up), and a brass-buttoned blue blazer, somewhat shiny at the elbows.

"Do you want me to go home and change?" Cecil asked, his face still screwed into a look of horror and his words hanging on the near-freezing air in white puffs.

"No, never mind that. We'll figure out something. Only you'd think that for fifty Yankee dollars a fellow might put himself out just a little. Well, don't just stand out there like a zombie. Come inside."

They repaired to the large living room with its effluvia of magazines, fast-food wrappers, and sparse modern furnishings.

"At least you're on time," Edmund said. "I like that in a man. Drink?"

"A beer would be fine."

"Beer? What do you think this is? A rathskeller? A ballpark?"

"I'll have whatever you're having."

"Vodka martini, straight up. The bottle's in the kitchen. Hungry?"

"I don't know."

"Well, I'm starved. While you're down there making our drinks, call up for a pizza. Anchovies and onions. Got it?"

"I think so."

"Well, don't just stand there like a statue. Move!"

Cecil hurried off to the kitchen. Edmund rolled a joint from the plastic bag lying on the coffee table, wondering where on earth he was going to find a suitable costume for Cecil at this late hour. He had inhaled the first toke of the powerful Hawaiian weed when it came to him. Just then Cecil reentered the living room nervously carrying two large-stemmed martini glasses.

"Ah, refreshments!" Edmund exclaimed, taking one glass and downing its entire contents in a few swallows. "Did you order our pizza?"

"Yes."

"Pepperoni and mushrooms?"

"You said anchovies and onions."

"Ha ha. Just checking. Here," Edmund said, handing him the lighted reefer, "make yourself at home. I'll be back in two shakes of a lamb's tail."

And so saying, Edmund left Cecil Wonton in the living room and went upstairs. His destination was that former second-floor linen closet in which he kept all the T.W. Black memorabilia, including some of his grandfather's earthly effects. As he lit the votive candle and then shut the door behind him, a powerful tide of emotion swept through him. At first, he could not quite recognize the emotion, but then, noticing that the eyes of his grandfather in the Steichen portrait appeared to bore into him like two red-hot augers, he identified it as . . . shame.

He took the framed photograph, and the companion shot of his father, A.L. Black, the poet and dreamer, off the red velveteen surface they rested on and placed them face to face on the floor. Next Edmund removed the velveteen coverlet, revealing an antique trunk. Kneeling now, and holding the candle overhead, he opened the trunk lid. Inside was a miscellany of books, papers, and old clothes. Among these was a bundle wrapped in brittle, eighty-year-old paper, tied with blue ribbon. Attached to the ribbon was a paper tag, and written on it in old-fashioned script (his grandmother's hand), in blue-brown ink, were the words *Suit Worn by T.W. Black on Occasion of his Dinner with Pres. Theo. Roosevelt, Dec. 20, 1903.*

He brought the suit downstairs and told Cecil to try on the jacket. Just then, the doorbell rang. It was the pizza. Edmund paid with a check, tipping the teenaged delivery boy with a bag of miniature Mars bars.

"The sleeves are a little long on me," Cecil said, modeling the black worsted wool suitcoat.

"He was a bigger man than you are," Edmund said, sweeping a lot of miscellaneous clutter off the glass coffee table and placing the pizza box on top. "Come, my good man. Let us break bread together."

"You go ahead. I'm not hungry."

"Sit down!" Edmund insisted fiercely, and Cecil sank to a seat on the sofa. "Now, let me try to sketch the scene for you," Edmund resumed in a calmer tone of voice, handing Cecil a slice of the pie. "A winter's eve, a few nights before Christmas, 1903. My grandaddy is met at the north portico of the White House by a butler in uniform with white gloves. This butler, born in slavery like my grandpa, sneers at him. He shares the belief of the majority of Americans who have even heard of my grandpa that T.W. Black is uppity—dining at Windsor Castle with the Queen of England and all. He has never had to hold open the front door of the White House for a black man before. Even the president of Liberia was spirited inside through a side entrance. T.W.'s hat and overcoat are requested. He rides the newly installed elevator up to the third floor family quarters. There, waiting for him, is Teddy Roosevelt himself, all teeth and eyeglasses."

The doorbell rang. Edmund got up from the sofa, grabbed a handful of candy bars from a heap on the floor, took them to the front door, and flung them out to the shrieking trick-or-treaters as though they were a pack of slavering animals. Somberly, he returned to the sofa, adjusted his wig, and resumed his story.

"The Roosevelt household is in its usual uproar," Edmund said. "The boys are running every which way playing Indians—a detail not lost on T.W. Princess Alice, the president's daughter from his first wife, is having another loud argument with her stepmother about smoking cigarettes in public. Also on hand is the president's old ranching buddy from Dakota, Tom Clapp. They have shot grizzly bears together. The company is all called to table.

" 'Mr. Black,' the president begins, helping himself to several slices of boiled tongue from a silver tray which is being carried around by another old relic of an ex-slave, 'I have listened with great interest to reports of your recent speech at the Montgomery Industrial Exposition. But I am confused. Just what did you mean when you said, "Cast down your bucket where you are"?' Come on. Tell me," Edmund pressed Cecil.

"Are you asking me?" Cecil answered with growing unease.

"That's right. Explain yourself."

"I don't know what you want me to explain?"

"What you said at Montgomery in 1903."

"But I wasn't in Montgomery in 1903. I wasn't even born yet."

"You were born in 1859, and in 1903 at Montgomery, Alabama, you said, 'A ship lost at sea for weeks spied a distant friendly vessel. "Water! Water! We die of thirst!" cried the captain of the first, and a signal came back: "Cast down your bucket where you are." A second time the cry, "Water! Water!" Again the signal: "Cast down your bucket where you are." And a third and fourth signal for water likewise was answered: "Cast down your bucket where you are." The captain of the distressed vessel, at last heeding this cry, cast down his bucket, and behold it came up full of fresh sparkling water! How could such a thing be in the Atlantic Ocean?' Answer me!"

"I don't know," Cecil said. "A miracle?"

"Wrong! They were at the mouth of the Amazon."

"I don't get it."

"Which is exactly what President Roosevelt's ranching buddy, Tom Clapp, says, spearing a parslied potato with his fork as though it were a garfish on the upper Missouri. 'I don't get it, Black,' he says. Notice he omits the *Mister*. 'What's the Amazon got to do with the uplift of your people?' 'One-third of the population of the South is of the Negro race,' my grandpa explains to this trigger-happy Dakota clod. 'Nearly sixteen millions of hands will aid you in pulling the load upward, or they will pull against you downward. We shall contribute one-third the prosperity or we shall prove a veritable body of death—stagnating, depressing, retarding every effort to advance the body politic.' Don't you get it now?" Edmund fairly roared at Cecil, who dropped his cold slice of pizza on the coffee table and in fear made himself very small on the sofa.

"I may have to go soon," he said.

" 'No race can prosper until it learns that there is as much dignity in hoeing a field as in writing a poem,' you told those four thousand honkies at Montgomery. 'The wisest among my race understand that agitation on the question of social equality is the extremest folly,' you said. 'No race that has anything to contribute to the markets of the world is long ostracized.' "

Edmund was standing and screaming at the top of his lungs by this time, while Cecil Wonton cringed against the foam rubber sofa as though to hide, thinking indeed that the great she-devil of his hallucinations had, after some fashion, returned to do him in. "Liar! Liar! Uncle Tom!" Edmund screamed, and would have attacked Cecil except that the telephone rang. He lurched down the hall in his high-heeled shoes to answer it.

"Will you please just fuck off, Mother!" he yelled into the phone.

"She get to you already?"

"Sis?"

"Yes."

"Don't do it," Edmund said, sliding down against the wall to the kitchen floor and beginning to blubber. Back down the hall, the front door could be heard to open and close as Cecil Wonton split, leaving T.W. Black's jacket in a heap on the floor.

"I guess she did get to you."

"Don't marry that white boy," Edmund blubbered into the phone, repeating the phrase over and over until it hardly sounded like words.

"Have you been drinking, Neddie?" she asked, using the nickname that nobody else had used since he was a boy at home.

"Yes," he replied between sobs. "I don't know what to do anymore."

"Come out to Chicago. We can talk about it."

"I won't watch you marry some honkie."

"I wish you could hear yourself."

"I can hear myself fine."

"You sound like a little kid."

"I don't care."

"Did Ma threaten to cut you off again? Is that it?"

"She's gonna take me to court and say I'm crazy. I'm scared, Sis."

"What she says and what she can really do are two different things, Neddie. I learned that a long time ago."

"No. I'm afraid she's right. I *am* losing my mind."

"As long as you're afraid of it happening, you must be okay. It's the ones who think they're perfectly all right that you have to worry about."

"I can't even leave the house any more. I go to pieces."

"For goodness sake, Neddie, you've been hanging around your old college town for almost ten years now—"

"Four of those years I was in school."

"Okay, six years since graduation."

"Five."

"The point is, it's long past the time for you to get out. I bet what you're feeling is just nature's way of telling you to move on."

"But I have no place to go. I can't go back to the city with *her* there."

"That's why I wish you'd come here. Chicago's every bit as big as New York. It's wonderful. And I could get you a job on the magazine. You'd have a ball here."

"Well, I guess you cast down your bucket where you are, didn't you."

"Don't go dragging our grandfather into it." Sappho's voice suddenly grew grave and angry. "He's gotten enough bad-mouthing from people who don't understand a thing about what he accomplished."

"He was a Tom!"

"He lived in a totally different world, and he was a great man in his time and his place."

"In his place! I guess that says it all, doesn't it? He knew his place."

"What about your place, Neddie?"

"I don't have to know my motherfucking place."

"Because you're so hung up and confused about who

the hell you are that you're afraid to leave your place, that haunted house of yours. You're a spook living in a spook house. You're nobody living in noplace. And you've got no right to denigrate someone who bravely went out into the world and made something of himself if you won't venture out—"

She stopped herself suddenly. In the background a faint gabble of conversing strangers could barely be heard on the crowded line.

"Hello? Neddie? Are you still there?"

"I'm here," Edmund said quietly, the tears streaming down his painted face in sooty mascara trails. He slowly pulled the blond wig off and let it fall to the cold tile floor beside him.

"I'm sorry," Sappho said. "I didn't mean to lecture you."

"I'm really scared, Sis."

"I wish you'd come out here."

"I'm afraid I'm going to end up like our father."

"I don't believe in that kind of tragic destiny. His death was a waste. You want to know what I think, Neddie? I think he believed he was making some great romantic poetic gesture. I think the truth is his poetry wasn't much better than ordinary, and he knew it, and the only chance he thought he had to match T.W.'s fame was by throwing himself off the 59th Street Bridge. He read too damned much Hart Crane. And I'll tell you one more thing: he couldn't have been half as concerned about us kids as he was for his literary reputation. I mean, what kind of a person kills himself, leaving three little children without a father? I'm sorry. Here I go lecturing you again."

"I didn't really know him. I was so little when he . . . did it."

"Well, you don't have to follow in his footsteps. Believe me. It's not engraved up there in the stars."

"T.W. must have done a job on his head."

"How do you know our daddy didn't do the job on himself?"

"You seem to think no one has any effect on anybody else."

"Of course, they have an effect. But you don't have to be a slave to it. Look at our mother: possibly the most overbearing, manipulating, tyrannical bitch in the western hemisphere. I've fought with her and hated her for as long as I can remember. But she hasn't done a job on me. I am a happy and successful woman who feels absolutely fine about herself in spite of all the messages from Ma that I should feel like an ugly, incompetent, foolish baby who has no idea how the world works or what to do in it."

"I don't think you can compare Ma's effect on you with T.W. and our father."

"Why not? The point is I'm not blaming anyone or making excuses for what I do with my own life, or what I don't do. And frankly, I get a little impatient when I hear other people do it, black or white. T.W. himself didn't have time for blaming. He was too busy with the practical problems of existence, of building the Institute. He could have spent his whole lifetime blaming Whitey for creating slavery and depriving him of his African heritage and keeping him under his bootheel after slavery and all the rest of that. But he didn't. He just got on with his job. He cast down his bucket and got on with his life." Sappho paused for a moment. "I don't believe the way I'm running my mouth. Can you possibly forgive me? I must sound like the old bitch herself."

"No. You sound like a magazine editor."

"That's reassuring. Oh, Neddie, I wish you'd come out here."

For a long time he didn't reply, though Sappho could hear him sniffling over the wire.

"Okay," he eventually said.

"No kidding?"

"Yes. I will."

"You don't have to come to the wedding. I mean, I'm sure you'll really like Chris a lot once you—"

"I'd like to come to the wedding."

"Would you? Really."

"Yes."

"It'd make me so happy to have someone from the family there. Isn't that disgustingly sentimental?"

"Yes. But I understand."

"And don't worry about the old bitch. You're not any crazier than I am."

"Hey, Sis. Remember that Halloween we got dressed up as Mau Maus?"

"I sure do."

"I was thinking about that today. That old Russian lady who called the cops on us. And Billy. I sure do miss my big brother."

"Me, too."

"But you turned out okay. For a girl."

"Hmmmm. I'll have to think about that one."

"Believe me, it's a compliment."

"Just call me with your flight number, and we'll be there to pick you up at the airport. I'm so thrilled that you're coming. Happy Halloween, Neddie."

"Thanks. Bye."

Though it was chilly on the tile floor, Edmund remained there, quietly trying to imagine a life away from Excelsior Springs. It was difficult after all these years, but he could actually begin to imagine it.

She felt as though she were winging through ice-cold space toward the world. This was certainly the strangest dream that Jennifer Fleming had ever had. The world was a gleaming silver ball far, far away, like a solitary Christmas tree ornament, and she was silently, steadily winging home. It seemed to her that she was returning to it after some terrible adventure, but now all the trouble lay behind her and she was flying home.

She stirred in the ditch under the footbridge and felt the earth beneath her body. She understood that her long flight was at an end and that somehow she had suddenly landed back in the world. The world was cold and lumpy. And yet high above shone that same beautiful silvery ball. She understood that it was the moon. Years ago someone had told her a story about a princess who wanted to hold the moon in her hands. She felt like that princess. But she did not know why she was here, lying outside in the moonlight.

When she tried to swallow, she felt as though someone had jammed a peach pit down her throat, a hard, rough, raggedy lump. It hurt to swallow, and the peach pit just stayed there. Her neck muscles ached. When she tried to move her legs, she discovered the right one was doubled back beneath her. It seemed to take forever to move it. Then a sharp pain crackled through her knee and, for a few moments, took her breath away. Bad as it was, the pain was familiar. She had hurt the same knee before playing a game on a grass field with a curved stick. That time she also remembered looking up at the sky, but it had been blue then.

SIXTEEN

The Greer Faculty String Quartette had taken up their positions just inside the former gaming room so that Joel's guests would be treated to the lovely strains of baroque music as soon as they stepped inside the casino's entrance. They tuned their instruments under some duress because the rock and roll band scheduled to play later on had arrived and was conducting a sound check, replete with shrill high-pitched electronic squeals, glitches, chord bursts, synthesizer arpeggios, random drum thwackings, and a seemingly endless chorus of the incantation "testing one two three."

At the same time, Sandy Stern was trying to determine if the college students he had rounded up to be bartenders really knew anything about mixing drinks.

"Martini?" Sandy quizzed the three.

"I think it has gin in it," said Rick, the athletic boy he had found in the TV lounge.

"Vodka," volunteered Heather, one of the two girls.

"That's a vodka martini," Rick argued back. "A regular martini has gin."

"What else goes in it?" Sandy asked.

"Ice?" Rick answered, obviously unsure.

"And you supposedly worked as a bartender last summer?" Sandy said.

"Well, I bussed tables mostly—but on Labor Day weekend when it was really jammed, I helped out at the bar for a while.

"Great," Sandy said.

"An olive. It has an olive in it," said Deena, the girl he had hired to draw beers.

"Okay, gang," Sandy said with a sigh, holding up one of the two thousand plastic cups he had purchased, "let's start from the beginning. This is the glass where you put the drink."

Wearing a handsome old leather aviator's jacket that he "won off this guy in a poker game," Glen Toole swaggered into the No-Name bar on Burgoyne Street. Of the thirty-odd customers in the place, all were on public assistance of one kind or another. Glen, for instance, drew federal disability payments under the social security program because he was deemed too crazy to find useful employment. So did his friend Skip Pirtle. Skip's sometime girlfriend Lolly Hoad, on the other hand, collected regular welfare. Even the half-dozen outright winos in the place collected public money informally by begging on the street. Tonight, Friday, was "welfare night," meaning the welfare recipients had all gotten their bimonthly checks that day and were now out spending some of it. The disability people, like Skip and Glen, got theirs on the alternate weeks. A blue pall of tobacco smoke filled the place, and country-western music played on the jukebox.

"What kind of poker game would let you into it, who

don't even have enough money to buy cigarettes?'' Skip challenged Glen.

"I was down to the Top Shopper tryin' out my powers and made this old woman drop a twenty right there in front of me on the ground."

"That's stealin'," Lolly said.

"It was finders keepers," Glen disagreed. "That's how I got into the game."

"Oh yeah?" Skip said. "How come you didn't just stay right there and use them powers you got to make everybody else drop money for you."

"When you got powers like I do that's boring," Glen said. "Hey, Mike!" he cried to the bartender and proprietor of the No-Name, Mike Norman, who hated Glen's guts, "get my friend Skip here another beer and make me one of them Tequila Sunrise jobs."

"Hey, what about me?" Lolly said, hurt.

"What about you?"

"Ain't I in on this party, too?"

"Course you are, hon," Skip said.

"What you drinkin'?" Glen asked grudgingly, peering over her somewhat flattened skull at the crowd, as though he were looking for celebrities in it.

"I'm drinkin' beer, but I want one of them Sombreros."

"Okay. You got one, lady," Glen said.

"Hey, thanks!"

After making the drinks, Mike Norman, a slight, nervous man with a birthmark across his face like a splash of tan housepaint, scowled impatiently as he waited for Glen to pay. Glen whipped out a crisp fifty dollar bill, snapped it in front of Skip and Lolly's faces so as to make an impression, and finally handed it across the bar.

"Where'd you get that fifty?" Skip asked.

"There's more where that come from," Glen told him, sipping his Tequila Sunrise through the strawlike swizzle stick because it seemed like the sophisticated thing to do.

"That's not what I ast you," Skip said. "Where'd you get it?"

"That poker game, like I told you three times already. You deaf?"

"I never heard of no game around here what had fifties on the table."

"This was a high-stakes game."

"Then how the hell'd you get in it with twenty dollars?" Skip grinned at the precision of his logic.

"What do you care? Who's buyin' the drinks around here anyways?"

"He's got a point, hon," Lolly said, cutting a concupiscent glance at Glen.

"Hey, who's side are you on?" Skip asked.

"I might just take up poker full time now," Glen said. "Go pro. Hey, gimme a smoke."

"Jesus Christ, you got more'n fifty dollars. You ought to buy me a whole damn carton."

"Maybe I will. But gimme one for now, huh?"

Skip took the pack out of his shirt pocket and shook one up for Glen.

"See," Glen said, taking the cigarette and grinning. "I got them powers. Hey, barkeep! Give us another drink."

Robin Holmes lit a candle on the table in the living room and sat down to a plate of stir-fried shrimp with pea pods on brown rice. She had made the meal herself in the wok, and the apartment was redolent of ginger, garlic, and sesame oil. The third floor apartment had been advertised as a one bedroom, but the so-called bedroom was really little more than an alcove in a dormer. There wasn't even a door between it and the living room, just a curtain rod from which Robin had hung a length of plum-colored velvet.

She thought briefly about turning on her small black-and-white television, but the shows broadcast at this hour on a Friday night were made for children and mental defectives, and she felt that it would reflect poorly on her self-respect to watch one of them. Instead, she put on the classical music station out of Albany. They happened to be playing the most Godawful lugubrious Felix Mendels-sohn, and after it got to her, she tried the Greer College radio station, WGRR, but they were playing the musical themes from horror movies interspersed with a lot of impromptu Halloween blather, and so she finally switched off the radio altogether.

Across the tidy room, with its secondhand sofa and bookshelves of bricks and unpainted pine boards, was a poster of a blown-up *New Yorker* magazine cover. Per-haps, she thought, it was time to try living in the city for a while. Several of the friends she had graduated with had apartments in Manhattan, and she could stay with one of them until she found a place of her own. Living in New York City had been her major life goal as long as she could remember—ever since she was a girl in Wappingers Falls watching the trains full of beautifully dressed men and women commuting on the Hudson River Line. To work for a glamorous magazine—maybe even the hal-lowed *New Yorker* itself!—that was her idea of heaven. And then Sandy came along. And here she was, stuck in her college town, working for what was surely the most rinky-dink newsrag on the east coast, writing about grange suppers.

And yet she had believed in him absolutely, in the essential dignity of what he was trying to do with his life, and she had seen so clearly and vividly the life that they could make together, even if it meant being poor. And

that vision had eclipsed her earlier dreams of the gad-
about life of a literary ingenue in the big city, which
began to seem more like a fantasy out of an old Katherine
Hepburn movie anyway. Indeed, she heard nothing but
horror stories about her college chums who were down
there. Her old roommate, Wendy Wallace, for example,
had to pay $900 a month for a roachy studio apartment
on East 11th Street. You couldn't throw a tennis ball in
any direction on her block without hitting a junkie. And at
the publishing house where Wendy landed a job, she was
an overworked cipher in the textbook division. After two
years of it, Wendy was doing nothing but trying to bag a
husband, a Wall Streeter like her daddy, someone to take
her away from it all. I *am* away from all that, Robin
thought, still gazing at the poster.

She stabbed a stir-fried shrimp with her fork. It was
cold, and this rueful solitude seemed to rob it utterly of
flavor or interest. She pushed the plate forward off the
woven grass placemat and lay her head on the table while
her eyes filled with tears. The prospect of going over to
the casino to talk to Sandy filled her with dread. She
could just picture herself and Sandy in the middle of a
mob of partygoers. She would vomit on the spot, she
thought. She would go wild. She felt like a goddam yo-yo,
to be reeled in and hurled out and reeled in again at this
man's pleasure. It was humiliating.

And yet she couldn't quite conceive of a life elsewhere and without him. She didn't want to think about a
life without him. She wanted the life that she wanted with
him. She wanted him.

After a while Robin got up from her seat at the table,
blew her nose in the paper napkin, and brought the
plateful of stir-fried shrimp into the kitchen to save in a
plastic container. She knew now that one way or another
she would have to go to that damned party at the casino.

She wouldn't lower herself to putting on some stupid costume—as though she were actually going there to be a part of it all. No, she would go in her work clothes, a reporter's notebook jammed in the pocket of her trenchcoat and a camera slung around her neck. She would wear the costume of her occupation and take a few pictures of the goddam soiree for goddam Fred Garrity. And if Sandy happened to be around, then maybe they would have that talk.

Impulsively, she reached for the wall phone next to the refrigerator and dialed Edmund Black's number. She was thrilled to hear the busy signal because it meant that he was still home.

Annie Gaines, dressed in a black body stocking, stood before the full-length mirror on her bathroom door. She had bought the body stocking a couple of years ago to wear to an aerobic dance class that she had since dropped out of. She was surprised how well her figure appeared in it. Naked, she could hardly bear to look at herself. All she would see were her fallen breasts and the slightly pro-truberant belly. But in the body stocking these blemishes were a lot less noticeable, and she did not look half bad, she thought, for a woman pushing fifty.

On the rim of the sink was a glass jelly jar half-filled with white gesso. Holding a copy of *Gray's Anatomy* in her left hand as a reference and a paintbrush in her right, Annie began painting the major bones of the human skel-eton directly onto the black body stocking. She had done self-portraits using a mirror before, but never using herself as the canvas. It was tricky. Altogether it took Annie half an hour to daub in all the bones, including the many ribs, but the result was very satisfactory.

All afternoon and evening, since Sandy's brief and peculiar visit, the determination to go to this Halloween ball at the casino had grown and grown in her, until now, at a quarter after eight in the evening, she was quite excited about it and looking forward to having a good time. It had been ages since she'd been to a good party—or any party for that matter—aside from a few stodgy art show openings where people stood nervously clutching plastic cups of bad wine punch and nibbling cheap crackers. None of her middle-aged faculty friends—the ones that remained—ever threw more than a dinner party for six. And being divorced, being the odd woman out, she was invited to few of those even. She couldn't remember the last time she had been to a really large, lively party.

She washed her hands, rinsed out the paintbrush, and admired her costume in the mirror. It pleased her tremendously. It couldn't have been more in the spirit of the occasion. This was, after all, All Hallows' Eve, the night that the living mocked the dead who mocked the living. In many ways she had never felt so fully alive as she did now in this tranquil period of her life, the awful storms of marriage and child-rearing behind her. And paradoxically, she had never felt less afraid of death.

Annie searched the medicine cabinet for some makeup. She had hardly worn any in the years since she moved out of town to Locust Grove. Outside, a rising night wind caused the branches of a box elder to rattle against the roof of the house. She would have to saw that limb off one of these days, Annie thought. She soon found a cake of blue-gray eye shadow that her daughter Jodie had forgotten after one of her visits home from college. Some mascara was hiding behind a card of cold capsules. Several old lipsticks turned up and an eyebrow pencil, too. Her hair blow-dried and the makeup applied, Annie barely recognized the face in the mirror. She looked—of all ridiculous things—glamorous. Would Sandy even recognize her? For a final touch, she dabbed some Guerlain perfume on her wrists, her ears, and the back of her neck.

Minutes later, she locked the house up and paused a minute outside before getting into her car. With the nearly full moon rising through the swaying treetops and the wind faintly moaning like the dead of the ages, Annie could easily imagine the superstitious terror of some medieval peasant on the Eve of All Hallows. Across the road at a distance, a dim blue light glowed in the Tooles' mobile home. No doubt the family was all gathered around the television, watching the living mock the dead who mocked the living.

George Wells drove his pickup truck north toward Excelsior Springs through the moonstruck countryside with the briefcase containing $185,000 on the seat next to him. Though he had the heat on full blast, he felt that he could not warm up. His fingers were cold on the steering wheel. Since he had left the house in Delft, a strange lump had taken up residence in his throat. A tumult of conflicting thoughts roared through his brain. Though they frightened him, he tried to sort them out.

For instance, could he ever forgive himself for saying what he had said to his father the last moment that the old man was alive in this world? But he had meant every word of it. He just didn't know if it was forgivable under any circumstances to speak so cruelly to anyone at a moment like that, whether they deserved it or not. And then to find his mother's clothes in the closet upstairs! The lump in his throat felt as though it was the size of a hand grenade and about to burst.

He glanced—for perhaps the fiftieth time—at the brief-case beside him on the seat. Where had it all come from, he wondered, this unholy bonanza of cold cash? How many hands had it passed through? How many grubby little fixes did it represent? How many people lost something precious, or suffered somehow, or simply had their lives diminished because of his father's bottomless venality? If any fortune was ill-gotten, certainly this was a classic case. But was it equally evil to sneak off with it? Would it now corrupt him in some way? George wondered. What about giving it back to the people it belonged to? How? Run an ad in the paper asking anyone who ever paid a bribe to Mayor Lewis Wells to come forward at a given date for a refund? Ha!

He hated to admit it, but the truth was he had no intention of disclosing the money's existence to his brother Davey. He would not share it with him. He was sure that Davey would just shoot the money into his veins or blow it up his nose. Then again, maybe that was the most logical way for it to end up—converted from one type of corruption to another. But no, he decided, real life was more than mere symbolism. Besides, there would be some other money for Davey once the estate was settled, probably quite a bit from whatever bank accounts and investments the old man had, and whatever Davey did with his share of that would be his affair. The house itself must be worth at least $70,000, even at Delft's pathetically depressed real estate prices.

As he passed down Main Street of Ralston Spa—the phone wires festooned with strips of toilet paper and masked teenagers skulking past the shopfronts—the truth began to take shape out of the tumult in his head. The truth was that George already had a very specific purpose in mind for all the money. The idea emerged fully formed, as though one part of himself had carefully worked out all the details while another part struggled with the pain of his memories and regrets. And the idea was this: he could use the money to save Mill Creek from Roy Greenleaf and to buy the old farm up at Indian Hill. He suddenly felt like a long lost wayfarer glimpsing the lights of home.

The three girls convened in Kelly's room at the Hildebrand dorm. (Kelly's suitemate, Betsy, had indeed taken off for the Fall Sprawl weekend at the University of Vermont.) A box with one remaining slice of a large pepperoni pizza lay open in the middle of the floor amid a clutter of shoes, clothes, and accessories. Kelly, dressed only in her apricot silk panties, sat at her desk looking into a small, self-illuminated magnifying mirror, applying gold glitter to the skin above her eye sockets. Her hair was temporarily pinned up with a large aqua plastic clip. At her left hand on the desk stood a large V-shaped martini glass, from which she paused every few minutes to sip Russian vodka.

Liz Coffin and Molly Kinlock sat on Kelly's bed engaged in an art project. Liz had picked up some plain fabric masks at a local store called Craftworld, plus a variety of sequins, glitter, and jewellike doodads to decorate the masks, and she and Molly were now gluing the glitz on. Liz was wearing the red-sequined 1950 cocktail dress, rhinestone earrings, and necklace that she had picked up at The Little Match Girl Shop. Molly was wearing a smoke-colored charmeuse gown with string straps that looked hardly more substantial than a nightgown. It was a little something she saw at Bendel's in New York City and charged on her Visa card. It complimented her pale skin very nicely, and without a bra her nipples were clearly outlined against the sheer fabric. An Excelsior Springs souvenir ashtray lay on the bed amid all the scattered baubles, and in it was a joint of marijuana, which the girls took turns puffing on.

"I hope these townies appreciate the pains we're

taking," Liz remarked as she glued on a final fake ruby and placed her mask on the radiator to dry.

"There's always Jeff VonWaggoner's party," Molly said. "I heard a lot of guys say they were going there."

"That is absolutely the last resort as far as I'm concerned," Liz said, now offering the joint to Kelly, and helping herself to a sip of the vodka.

"Well, I say we try this casino bash, and if that turns out to be a dud, we go to Jeff's, and if that's bad, we go to Ubu."

"I'm so sick of the bars in this town," Liz said, crossing her arms and slumping against the wall, "I could scream."

"Here, have some more of this and everything will seem like fun," Kelly said, handing back the joint. She got up from the table and strode across the room to her closet. Liz enviously eyed Kelly's magnificent body, which was tall like hers, but with slimmer hips and large, beautiful breasts. It distressed Liz that her own little breasts did not fill the cups of the cocktail dress. The unequal distribution of mammary tissue in the world was just more proof to Liz that God did not exist. She wanted to write a paper on it.

"How does this look?" Molly asked, holding her mask over her eyes and casting a sexy off-the-shoulder glance at Kelly.

"Smashing," Kelly said, slipping on the black Karl Lagerfeld evening dress that her mother had worn once to a Museum of Modern Art reception. The dress featured a plunging open back.

"*You* look smashing," Molly said.

"Let's get smashed," Liz said, downing the rest of Kelly's vodka.

"I'm pretty stoned right now," Kelly said.

"There better be some good drugs at this party," Liz said.

"I think there'll be a lot," Kelly said.

"Whose car should we take?" Molly asked.

"Not Lizard's," Kelly said. "It's like a toxic waste dump in there."

"The maid keeps forgetting to clean it."

"Mine's drafty," Kelly said, refering to her VW Rabbit convertible. "Let's take Molly's. It's coziest. And clean." Molly drove a BMW. It was a gift from her father on her twentieth birthday. There was an old joke among the Greer faculty that none of them could afford the payments on their students' cars.

After several minutes of stoned confusion, of grabbing this thing and that, the three girls left the dormitory and got into Molly's car in the parking lot outside. Liz sat in the back with her legs up on the seat, lighting a fresh reefer. Kelly stuck a cassette in the dashboard tape player.

Molly giggled. "I must be pretty stoned," she said. "I can't fit the key in."

"Want me to try?" offered Kelly.

"Uh-uh, honey, you're not driving," Liz said to Kelly from the back seat. "Molly's the designated driver. She hasn't been hooking down vodkas like you and me."

"There, I've got it," Molly said.

The engine came to life, purring with precision engineering. With the car running the tape began to play and the passenger compartment filled with the sumptuous contralto of Joan Armatrading.

> *Feeling guilty*
> *Worried*
> *Waking from tormented sleep*
> *This old love has me bound*
> *But the new love*
> *Cuts deep*

"That song makes me so sad," Molly said.

"I hope I'm never that much in love," Kelly said.

"Au contraire," said Liz. "Bring on the heartbreakers."

Greer College had been erected on the site of an old estate known as Woodlawn built by a nineteenth-century timber baron and horse fancier. Many of the drives around campus were carved out of existing carriage roads. Molly pulled out of the Hildebrand parking lot and proceeded down the southeast drive. She had just rounded a corner near the footbridge in the wooded glade that students used as a shortcut to Woodlawn Avenue when she was startled by something weird on the road up ahead. At first she thought it might be some sort of elaborate Halloween gag, someone in costume. It looked like a creature that had crawled from the grave. A ghoul. Kelly screamed. Molly hit the brakes. The BMW fishtailed, then came to an abrupt halt straddling the shoulder and a shallow ditch. Jennifer Fleming, her eyes blackened and her chin covered with dried blood, reached up into the shaft of dusty light and screamed, "Help me!"

The door to Edmund Black's house was open a crack— Cecil Wonton had failed to close it correctly upon his hasty departure. Robin Holmes warily ventured in after ringing the doorbell.

"Edmund?"

"I'll be down in a minute," he replied distantly from upstairs.

She wandered into the living room. A large pizza lay in its box on the coffee table missing only one of its slices, and that slice sat right beside the box uneaten. The pie was cold. She noticed that it was decorated with anchovies, which she disliked intensely. To order a large pizza and then not eat any of it seemed so perfectly typical of

Edmund, and yet its exact significance bewildered her. Then she heard footsteps on the stairs.

Edmund slowly descended the broad stairway in what looked at first to Robin like a tuxedo. But soon she saw that it was not a tuxedo but rather a business suit of antique cut. For one thing, the jacket buttoned rather high. He also had on a high celluloid collar and an old-fashioned puffy gray silk tie. What's more, he seemed so strangely placid in demeanor that she found it rather unsettling. She had expected to find him bouncing off the walls, so to speak, in one of his usual manic moods.

"Are you all right?" she went so far as to inquire.

"I'm fine," he assured her.

"I guess I expected something a little more drastic in the way of a costume," she said. "This is just an old suit."

"It belonged to my grandfather."

"It's . . . it's in beautiful condition."

Edmund smiled. "Thanks. How about yours?" he asked, fingering the lapel of her trenchcoat.

"It's not a costume. I'm a reporter for the *Banner,* and that's what I'm going to this affair as. Edmund, there's something I have to ask you. If I don't, it's just going to bother me all night."

"What?"

"How come you ordered a whole large pizza and didn't eat a single bite of it?"

"It came with anchovies."

"You mean it came that way by mistake?"

"No, I ordered it that way. I loathe them."

"Then why did you order them?"

"Well, I didn't want to make a pig of myself," he said, offering his arm to Robin. "Shall we go to the ball, little missy?"

Robin put her arm through his. "Yes, let's go."

SEVENTEEN

The first guest arrived at 8:27, a girl dressed as an eggplant. Even if Sandy had known her, he would not have recognized her, besides being occupied just then with showing his bartenders how to mix a margarita. The Greer Faculty String Quartette was playing an arrangement of Gluck's stately *Chaconne*. The pumpkins and the orange gladiolas had been distributed all around the ballroom and the gaming parlor. Trays of cheeses and croustades, pâté, pastry morsels, vegetable crudités, dips, and heaps of shrimp were strategically placed on table tops while the heartier aroma of roasting meats wafted through the huge rooms. What with the new paint job and the shampooed rugs, the old casino hadn't looked so lovely since a great-great-granddaughter of Israel Babcock married an Argentine polo player there in 1929.

The eggplant was not lonely for long. A werewolf accompanied by a ballerina arrived at 8:32, followed at once by someone dressed up like the President of the

United States (including plastic pompadour), followed by a witch, a bag lady, Superman (Sandy easily recognized Tim Hosley, who owned a foreign car repair shop), an Arab terrorist complete with grenades and dynamite sticks, a cartoon character known as Gumby who looked like an enormous green rubber eraser, a fright-wigged rock-star with blackened eyes and leather domination garb, Puss 'n Boots (a female), and before much longer a mob of other costumed characters out of legend, off the silver screen, off the pages of literature, direct from the boob tube, and fresh from the grave.

Sandy, who found himself stuck behind the bar mixing drinks, recognized about half of them. There were Tom and Taffy Wright, a couple of professional folksingers who lived up in Shrewsbury, dressed up as the comedians Laurel and Hardy; there was Sally Noyes, a waitress from the Black Rose, covered with feathers like a giant chicken; there was the burly restaurateur Jeff Osborne (his walrus mustache a giveaway) gotten up as the female rock star known for wearing black lace underclothes and fingerless gloves; there was Parke Tracy, ski bum, whose father owned half of Excelsior County, dressed in rags like a wino; there was Tom Dugan, dressed like Elmer McClusky, along with Elmer in a version of the preppy outfit Tom wore each and every day; there was Amy Alexander, the local news anchor from the NBC affiliate in Albany, wearing a rodent costume with a yard-long pink tail (whether rat or mouse it was uncertain); there was Thad Spooner, who owned the little goldmine called Ubu Roi, made up with a lot of blue veins and running sores, like one of the walking undead; there was Whitney Riddle, whose family founded the North Country Trust, and his wife Jane, dressed up as Rocky Balboa and his one-time ring opponent, Mr. T; there was Stan Covington, who did a little marijuana farming on a spread out near Locust Grove, clothed as a hippie; there were Greer profs Bob and Ariel Coombs (English Lit and Women's Studies) dressed as Huckleberry Finn and Joan of Arc; there was Miranda Munsinger, widely regarded as the best-looking attorney-at-law between New York City and Montreal, costumed as Eve in a scant little outfit of green silk leaves sewn onto a bikini; there was Aaron Schram, a sculptor and wild man, painted white and draped in a sheet like a marble statue, with his wife Mary in a three-piece men's suit and a false beard; and there was Billy Rhoden, the bartender at Ogden's, dressed as a rainbow trout. Among these and scores of others who comprised this first wave of arrivals was George Wells, dressed in his poplin suit. Seeing him, Sandy immediately came out from behind the bar.

"Hey, great costume, George," said Lowell Piercy, placing an arm around George's shoulders. Piercy, with George, had been among the hippies who gravitated to the Springs during the Vietnam years. He had evolved into a stockbroker. Tonight he was dressed as a hillbilly. He had never seen George wearing a suit and tie before. "The briefcase is perfect," he added. A moment later, a female in his sights, Piercy departed for the ballroom.

"Did you go down to the hospital?" Sandy asked George, who nodded. "You look like you could use a drink."

"I sure could."

"What?"

"Something strong."

Just then, the rock band started playing in the ballroom. Sandy glanced at his watch. It was nine o'clock. He poured two stiff brandies in a couple of plastic cups. "Follow me," Sandy said, leading him to the large restroom between the bar and the ballroom. It was easier to talk in there. Sandy knocked back half his drink in one gulp, slumped against the wall with its old-fashioned black and white tiles, and closed his eyes for a moment. "You wouldn't believe what it's been like around here today," he said.

"I guess you got a hold of Harlowe, then, huh?"

"Yes. You were right. He's got a good heart. But it's been sheer hell here."

"Is he around now?"

"Not as far as I know. Unless he snuck in dressed as an eggplant. Did you see your dad?"

"Yes."

"How is he doing?"

"He's dead."

Sandy gagged on his brandy for a moment. Some of it went up his nose.

"I wanted to let you know." George changed the subject. "I, uh, found some more cash around the house, in case you need to borrow a few hundred."

"That's awfully nice of you," Sandy said, coughing to clear his throat. "Did he pass away before you got down there?"

"Pardon me?"

"Your dad."

"Oh. No. While I was there."

"Oh, gosh. Did you get a chance to speak to him?"

"Yes."

"It must have been hard."

"It was very difficult," George agreed, and Sandy could tell by the way his friend's mouth quivered that he was still overwhelmed with emotion. "I feel a little out of place actually, coming here to this big party."

"Of course."

"But I just couldn't go home by myself."

"I understand," Sandy said. "After my mother passed away, I went down to this big bar on M Street in George-town. Clyde's. It was a Sunday afternoon. There were about two hundred congressional aides there getting bombed and watching the basketball playoffs on TV. I needed to be around that kind of stupid normality."

George nodded his head. "Remember," he said. "If you still need a loan—"

"Joel commissioned me to paint his portrait."

"See, I told you he'd come through."

"He did. You were right."

"That's great."

"So I guess I'll be all okay for a couple of months, at least. Listen, I don't want to seem morbid or anything, but I have quite a bit of experience making funeral arrangements, in case you need some help that way."

"Thanks," George said.

"Call me tomorrow. Well, I better get back out there. Are you going to be okay?"

"Yes. Thank you," George said, then adding with a fervor that was unusual for him, "Hey, I think I've figured out a way to keep that bastard Greenleaf from wrecking our trout stream."

"But he's already in there with the bulldozers."

"Don't worry. I'm going to get those bulldozers out of there."

"How?"

"I can't go into it here. Trust me."

"Okay," Sandy said, baffled but heartened. "I trust you."

They left the restroom. Another hundred people had arrived in the interim. Among them were three Greer girls bearing the alarming news that one of their fellow coeds had been beaten and raped on the campus by an unknown assailant and that they had just taken her to the hospital emergency room and notified the police. Sandy heard it from Gwen Chapman (who looked lovely as a flapper in a shimmering beaded black dress from her own shop). They were standing between the bar and the gaming room, and as Sandy started to deplore the incident, he turned his head to see Robin Holmes and Edmund Black walking toward the ballroom.

"Hi." Sandy greeted them both warily, thinking of Edmund's daylong craziness and all the blows that Robin had landed on his own head. Edmund, in an old black suit, seemed eerily calm, and Robin was still in her work clothes, a camera slung over her shoulder.

"I'm glad you came," Sandy told her. He awkwardly tried to reach for one of her hands, but she plunged them into the pockets of her trenchcoat and made a face.

"Let me guess who you're supposed to be," Edmund said. "Napoleon in jogging shoes?"

"That's a pretty good guess," Gwen Chapman said. She was working on her third gin and tonic.

Edmund, taking Gwen by the elbow to check out the band, left Sandy and Robin alone.

"Maybe we can find a quiet corner and have a chat," Sandy suggested to Robin, who glared at him for a moment, then acquiesced by closing her eyes and nodding her head.

Just then, Sandy heard one of the bartenders, the boy, crying, "I'm in the weeds! I'm in the weeds!"

"What's that supposed to mean?" Robin asked.

"He's swamped," Sandy said. "I've got to go help them. Harlowe left me in charge."

"Where's Harlowe?"

"He went to New York to buy drugs."

"The night of his big party? That's weird."

"Yeah. But that's Harlowe. Can we talk later, please?"

"Yes," Robin replied. She swung her camera around, popped off the lens cap, and took a close-up of Sandy with the flash on. "Go do your job."

316

Glen Toole tossed back his fifth Tequila Sunrise, and in a bold gesture that left the patrons of the No-Name gasping with gratitude and suspicion, slapped the second of his two stolen $50 bills on the bar and ordered a round for everyone in the house.

"You sure are crazy," Skip Pirtle said with a semi-toothless smile of admiration.

"There's more where that come from," Glen said, lighting another one of Skip's cigarettes. "An' I'm gon' git me some." And so declaring, he hitched up his pants, lurched to the door, waved farewell to the throng now crowding the bar to get their free drinks, and staggered off into the night.

It was cold outside, and he stopped in the harsh glare of a street light to zip up the stolen leather jacket he was wearing. At this hour, Burgoyne Street was full of Halloween revelers, many of them college students and quite a few in costume, making their way between a couple of popular bars on Grove Street and the more numerous joints a block away on Catherine. Hardly one group passed Glen—swaying back and forth in place, a cigarette dangling from his lips, obviously plastered—without making a remark or giggling.

"Smartasses," Glen muttered as a particularly boisterous bunch passed him. "I'll get you smartass bitches. You sonofabitches, too. Fuck yourself. I got powers."

Eventually, he gave up on the jacket's zipper, which was old and tricky to get started, and resumed staggering down Burgoyne. At the corner of Grove Street, he paused in front of the bake shop, tittering as he recalled first seeing the girl there, the girl that he staked out and then led all around town like a remote-controlled toy car, the girl he had gobbled up under the bridge. Now that he knew how to do it, he'd come back soon and get another one.

A jeep with Connecticut license plates, full of more Greer girls who had been drinking, came barreling down Grove Street and blared its horn as it swerved around Glen, cries of "Move, asshole!" left hanging in the chilly air as it continued toward Serpentine.

"Fuck yourself," Glen muttered, and briefly considered casting an evil spell on the vehicle, but his attention was distracted by the lights of the old casino, ablaze in Union Park. Many cars seemed to be parked around it and, cocking his head, he thought he detected the thump and rumble of rock music coming from inside. He staggered over to investigate.

Every now and then, Glen Toole knew, people held parties in the old casino, mostly rich cocksuckers. There had been times during the past few years when Glen lacked a place to live in town and slept in the park. The summer before last, for example, he and Skip all but set up housekeeping here in the Peerless Spring pavilion on the other side of the duck pond. The pavilion was a decaying wooden gazebo, about twelve feet around. The spring itself had stopped spouting years before, its pipes clogged with mineral deposits. The roof of the place was still in fair shape though, and it kept most of the rain out. They had a couple of milk crates for furniture and beat up any kids who nosed around their "hut" looking for trouble.

One of the parties that year especially stuck in his mind. It was during August, the racetrack season, when the town filled up with rich sonofabitches. The woman who threw it, he'd heard, was supposedly the richest old bitch in all of Excelsior Springs. Her husband owned all the trains in America, or something. The other rich cocksuckers who came to her party had to get dressed up in old-fashioned outfits, like the kind they wear on TV in movies about Civil War times. The men all had on fancy suits with flaps hanging down over their ass and top hats, and the bitches all wore big puffy dresses, only real low in front so you could see the top of their bazoombas. Many of them arrived at the party in horse-drawn carriages, and Glen had gone over to pet the horses. A guy driving one of the rigs told him to get lost. He told the driver to fuck himself, and the guy hit him with a whip. He should have beat the crap out of that sonofabitch, Glen thought, but he . . . he forgot why he hadn't. But he sure should have. After that, he had watched the party from one of the big side windows. That was when he saw what really excited him. They had set up gambling tables inside, real beauti-ful ones, with that green fuzzy cloth on top. And in the center was a huge wooden roulette wheel. He couldn't believe the size of it. His brother Hurley had a roulette wheel at home in Locust Grove, but it was just a little plastic thing, hardly as big as a fry pan. This one was the size of a truck tire, and the white ball was as big as a pullet's egg. That and the way those bitches looked in those puffy dresses left an indelible impression on his mind.

It occurred to him now, as he lurched down an asphalt footpath inside the park, that perhaps a similar sort of wingding was going on at the casino this Hallow-een night. He'd go look in the window and find out. If they had the gambling tables out, maybe he'd even go inside and sit down at a poker game. After all, he was ready to turn pro. This was probably his lucky night, the luckiest night of his life. Didn't he have powers? Didn't he make money appear when he wanted it? Didn't he show that whole bunch down at the No-Name? Thinking about it, about the long day's many wonderful events, made him feel good in his pants.

Soon he was standing outside the ballroom wing. A band was definitely playing inside. He could feel the vibrations through the wall, never mind what they were playing. The vibrations made him feel good in his pants. The exhaust fan from the adjoining kitchen was blowing out delicious food smells, too. But the windows on this side of the building were too high to peek into. Holding the leather jacket closed against the chill, Glen loped around the rear of the large old building.

On the other side, where the big gaming room was, were six huge arched windows that went practically from the floor all the way to the ceiling. There were no gambling tables set up, Glen was disappointed to discover, but hundreds of people, including many of the most gorgeous bitches in town, were all dressed up in the most amazing costumes. In particular, Glen soon noticed a woman wearing nothing more than leaves around her titties and personal place. The crack between her titties was deep. They were big ones. It made him so hot in his pants that he unzipped his fly and began to touch himself. Just knowing that he was touching himself and watching her with all those other people around made him feel so good. He had powers, he thought, as his pleasure mounted. It felt so good that he wanted all those people to see his powers, to stand in awe and thrall before him, as he stood before them. And this notion taking hold within him as his pleasure welled, Glen Toole climbed up on the marble windowsill and showed his powers to the assembled throng.

George Wells, exhausted both emotionally and physically, and concerned about toting around a briefcase full of money, had been on his way out of the casino when he spotted Roy Greenleaf standing in the gaming room with a drink in one hand and the head of his bear costume under his other arm. George was startled to see him at the party until he realized that Greenleaf was just the sort of guy who would be one of Joel Harlowe's better customers.

The real estate mogul was chatting with the beautiful young attorney Miranda Munsinger, she of the primeval silk-leafed bikini.

"Roy," George said, moving in to form a triangle between them.

"Why, hello, George." Greenleaf greeted him affably. "Nice costume." He pawed the lapel of George's suit jacket, apparently a little drunk.

"I'm dressed up as a Realtor," George bantered back.

"Touché," Miranda Munsinger said. He'd seen her in the Feedlot.

"We're the back-to-nature gang," Greenleaf said, putting a paw around Miranda's bare shoulder.

George cleared his throat. "I thought you and I might talk for a minute," he said in a tone of voice that contrasted with all the joking. Sensing that it was something private between the two men, the bikini-clad attorney gracefully withdrew, ostensibly to get a another drink.

"You been thinking about my offer?" Greenleaf asked, easily shifting into his business manner.

"Yes."

"Did you cash the check?"

George didn't say. "How badly do you want my ten acres, Roy?"

"A hundred thou really is my top offer, George."

"That's not what I mean, exactly. I have a different kind of deal in mind."

Greenleaf, puzzled yet interested, sipped his drink and looked at George intently.

"You recently bought some property out in Locust Grove, around Mill Creek," George said.

"That's right."

"I'll sell you my place on Seward if you sell me that parcel on the creek," George said.

"A straight swap? No way. That's thirty-eight acres out there," Greenleaf replied.

"How much did you pay for it?"

Greenleaf hedged.

"Come on, Roy. I can easily find out."

"I paid fifty-five thou for it. But you've got to realize I'm in the process of developing it. That land's already worth much more to me than I paid for it."

"You haven't put any houses up though. You haven't even started building a single unit yet."

"No. But I've cleared several sites."

"Let's say I'd cover whatever it cost you to get the bulldozers in there. And out."

"You're really serious about this, aren't you?"

"Absolutely."

"But George, you don't seem to understand that developed, with houses on it, that land is worth half a million to me. I mean, in sheer net."

"If you sold all the houses."

"I wouldn't have started the project if I didn't think I could sell them all eventually."

"Eventually can be a long time," George said. "Look at it this way. If I sell you my ten acres right on the edge of town, you've got a much better chance of selling those solar homes of yours, and quicker, too. You don't know for sure what's going to happen to the economy a year from now. There might be another oil shortage. People may not want to buy a house twelve miles out of town."

"I don't see what's so special about those thirty-eight acres," Greenleaf said. "You can find parcels that size all over Excelsior County."

"This one's got a trout stream on it."

"Another fisherman, huh?"

"Anyway, that's the deal," George said ignoring the remark, which he suspected was directed at Sandy. "I'll give you a fair price for it: let's say a hundred and ten thousand. That's double what you paid for it."

Greenleaf eyed him ruminatively for a moment, then finished his drink.

"The dozers have cost me ten already."

"All right. A hundred and twenty."

"You'd have to take it as is," Greenleaf said, "with the homesites all cleared. I mean, there's nothing that can be done about it at this point. No reclamation job or anything."

"I understand that. The woods will come back on their own."

"A hundred and twenty thou is a hell of a lot for a trout stream," Greenleaf said, grinning and shaking his head.

"Depends on your point of view. Frankly, Roy, if you want my place as bad you say you do, I don't see how you can afford to pass up my offer."

"All right," the developer said, holding out his bear paw again, "you've got yourself a deal, my friend."

George had just clasped the paw when a shriek resounded behind him, followed by another, and then a third. The gabble of conversation stopped abruptly, though the chords of rock and roll still thundered from the adjoining ballroom. All around George and Roy Greenleaf arms flew up and pointed to the window behind them. Framed within, on the other side of the glass, as in diabolical counterpoint to the huge portrait of Paddy McCumber, stood Glen Toole, his eyes rolling back in his head as he appeared to strangle a small pink snake that squirted dismal jets of fluid onto the windowpane before he keeled over backward off the marble sill.

More shrieks erupted, followed by the cries of men: "After him!"

Sandy heard the commotion and leaped over the bar,

joining the stampede to the door. From the casino's front steps he saw a pack of strangely costumed figures led by someone in a furry suit chasing another figure in dark clothes around the right side of the duck pond. Sandy followed at a trot, wondering what the person pursued had done. The person in question was soon tackled by the furry suit on the asphalt footpath a few yards short of the dilapidated old Peerless Spring pavilion. Roy Greenleaf kneeled on the downed figure's shoulders while Jeff Osborne and George Wells each held a leg.

"That's my jacket he's wearing!" Sandy declared before he even realized that the person subdued was Glen Toole.

"Sonofabitches!" Glen hissed. His fly was still open. A police siren could be heard whooping blocks away.

"Turn him over!" Sandy told George and the others. The others seemed baffled. "Flip him onto his stomach!" Sandy insisted, and they complied. He pulled Glen Toole's "Star Wars" wallet out of a rear pocket. In it was the $250 check that Joel Harlowe had made out to him hours before, but the two fifty dollar bills were not there. "Where's my hundred dollars?" Sandy asked him.

"Wasn't any hunnert," Glen muttered into the footpath.

No doubt he'd already spent it, Sandy realized.

"Where's the rest of my stuff?"

"Fuck yourself."

It was like the old days in the psych ward, Sandy thought—except this wasn't the hospital. He seized a handful of Glen's hair and bounced his forehead off the asphalt. "What'd you do with my stuff, asshole?"

"Garbage can behind a church," Glen confessed.

"Where?"

"I dunno. Over to the west side somewheres. Ow! You're hurtin' me."

The flashing lights of two police cars soon sent bright

red beams bouncing off the park's trees, pavilions, and the casino itself, where hundreds of costumed partygoers stood on and around the stairs, clutching themselves against the chill, while others still inside pressed their masked and painted faces up against the large windows.

"Officer, that's my leather jacket he's wearing," Sandy told one of the policemen as they were preparing to handcuff Glen. The officer eyed Sandy suspiciously. "He stole it off the back of my motorcycle earlier tonight," Sandy explained.

"That jacket *does* belong to this man," said Robin Holmes, who stepped forward, simultaneously scribbling notes in a reporter's pad.

"Who are you?"

"I'm his girlfriend," Robin said. The cop looked her up and down disdainfully. "*His* girlfriend"—she quickly moved beside Sandy—"not this one"—she pointed at Glen with her ball point pen—"and I'm a reporter for the *Banner*," she added.

"Okay, take it off, pal," the cop ordered Glen. As he did, Robin snapped several photos of him. His fly was still open, but that could be cropped for the front page. The cop handed the jacket to Sandy, who held it gingerly as though it were a smallpox blanket, wondering how much it would cost to have it dry-cleaned. Then Glen was handcuffed and assisted into the back seat of one of the police cars. Sandy, George, Roy Greenleaf, and Jeff Osborne all had to give their names in the event that their testimony was needed in any proceedings against the suspect.

While the police cars sped away, speculation began circulating as to whether there was some connection between this ghastly display and the rape reported earlier. Meanwhile, Robin told Sandy that she had to go over to the *Banner* office and write about the bizarre incident for the morning edition. It was her professional duty.

"Please come back when you're done."

"I'll come back," she assured him.

"I'll wait for you here."

"All right."

"I can give her a ride," offered George, who had been standing beside them. "I was on my way home anyway."

Sandy watched them follow the police cars toward the park entrance, where George's truck was parked, before he went back inside.

They drove the few blocks across town to the *Banner* building in virtual silence, and then as George pulled up to idle in front of the entrance, Robin said, "I'm embarrassed about coming over to your house this morning."

"No need to be," George said.

"We're going to have a 'big talk' later, Sandy and me," she said, indicating the quotation marks with her index fingers.

"If it doesn't work out, give me a call," George found himself saying, to his considerable surprise and Robin's, too. "I've been crazy about you for years," he added, surprising himself further. It was as though some new circuitry had connected his tongue to his brain and he was able to express his feelings for the first time in his life. This sudden facility intoxicated him. It made him giggle.

"I . . . I had no idea, George," was all that Robin could say, searching his face as though to discover who he was.

"I was afraid to let on," George explained. "Hey, on the other hand, if it does work out with the two of you, that's fine, too. I'll find another girl." He laughed again.

"Are you okay, George?"

"I'm fine," he assured her. "I'm just glad to be here. I'm glad we're all here."

"I'm glad we're here, too," Robin said. She leaned over and kissed him on the cheek before getting out of the truck, marveling as she trudged up the steps to the newsroom at what a long and strange day it had been.

A convivial spirit reigned once again inside the old casino. If anything, the pitch of excitement seemed higher than before the atrocious incident at the window. The various rooms were now filled with the sweet odor of marijuana rather than roasting hams and turkeys. Many bottles of liquor had been consumed. The crush at the bar had barely slackened off, but it looked like the three student bartenders were finally in control of things, though a little tipsy themselves. A lot of the partygoers had moved into the ballroom to dance. Barbara Lazarus's helpers were clearing away the food platters. The only thing that troubled Sandy at this point was what had happened to Harlowe.

It seemed to him that there were really only two possibilities; either Joel had been in an accident on his motorcycle, or he was still surreptitiously lurking here among them in some clever disguise. Sandy got another brandy from the bar and devised a plan to flush Harlowe out. First, he would organize a contest for best costumes, male and female. Then, at the stroke of midnight, there would be a grand unmasking. It was 11:15.

The contest was easy to work out. When the band, called the Throbulators, finished playing "Twist and Shout," Sandy took the microphone, announced the contest, and said there would be two $100 prizes for the winners. Anyone who wanted to enter only had to get onstage and promenade across. Five finalists of each gender would be chosen by audience response. The two winners would be picked by the Throbulators, who were unbiased.

It went very nicely. Nearly everyone took a stroll across the stage with a lot of vamping and camping. The prizes went to Jeff Osborne in black lace underthings and Miranda Munsinger in practically nothing. Sandy presented them each with a crisp hundred dollar bill. Then he announced that the moment had come for everyone still in disguise to remove his or her mask.

The Throbulators' drummer played a roll. All around the large crowded room masks, headgear, wigs, false beards, and rubber noses came off. Sandy scanned the crowd from the stage. Joel was nowhere among them.

"How about a big hand for the guy who made this great bash possible," Sandy said into the microphone. "Joel Harlowe!"

There was an exuberant round of applause replete with cheers and whistles of approval. But when it finally died down, there was still no Harlowe.

"Hey, where is the bastard?" yelled Thad Spooner, obviously crocked.

"I don't know," Sandy said with a nervous laugh and, anxious to escape the spotlight, handed back the microphone to the Throbulators' lead singer, Tyrone T.

The music resumed. Various people came up to Sandy saying what a strange thing it was for Harlowe to throw a huge party and not show up, and he could only agree. But finally it began to dawn on him that Harlowe had planned it that way all along. That was the reason he had taken such pains to leave Sandy in charge of the Halloween ball: because he never had any intention of coming to it in the first place. Well, Sandy thought, this one would certainly go down in the annals of Excelsior Springs' long and strange history.

He settled Barbara Lazarus's catering bill—which came

to $5,305—with the last of the Richard Dodge checks. Barbara, who had known Joel for several years, said it was okay, she knew the check was good.

At two o'clock, the Throbulators finished their last set. Sandy paid them with cash out of the wad he had obtained at the bank earlier. He had over $900 of Joel Harlowe's money left after he paid the bartenders. With the music over, the remaining partygoers straggled out of the casino, many heading over to Ubu Roi to dance some more, others staggering home. The band dismantled their equipment and began to load up their van. Barbara Lazarus and her crew carried pots, pans and chafing dishes out to her truck. Sandy sat quietly watching it all wind down from a seat at a round table in the ballroom. He was dazed with exhaustion, and for a moment he thought the beautiful gray-haired woman standing in front of him in the skeleton suit was an apparition.

"It's me, silly."

"Annie!"

"Yup."

"Mind if I join you?"

"Please," he said, a little pained at her having to even ask.

"Great party," she said.

"It was, wasn't it. Did you have fun, Annie?"

"Did I ever! I haven't danced so much since 1969. But this fellow Harlowe, isn't it odd, him not showing up at his own party?"

"Well," Sandy drawled in weariness. "It is and it isn't. If you know him."

"I hear he's very eccentric."

"He's quite crazy, actually," Sandy told her with a smile.

"By the way, how's your tooth?"

"My tooth? Oh, my tooth! Jesus, it seems like years

329

ago. It's fine. Well, it's not fine, actually it's gone. Oh, Annie, it's such a long, complicated story."

"I'd like to hear it sometime. I have a great medical curiosity," she said, touching one of her breasts as she pointed out the bones painted on her black body stocking.

"You looked great tonight," he told her, wanting to compliment her without leading her on.

"Where's Robin?" she asked

"She'll be along any time now."

"You expect her here, at quarter to three in the morning?"

"Yes."

She made a skeptical face.

"No, really. She had to write about that guy exposing himself at the window for the morning edition of the paper. She's a slow writer. She'll be back." He stated at this with rather more assurance than he really felt at that hour.

Annie sighed and then yawned.

"Come out to the country and see me again one of these days?"

"You know I will, Annie."

She kissed him on the cheek and then he could hear her footsteps clip-clopping across the floor. He was finally alone in the casino. The lights still blazed. His ears rang with silence. He put his head down on his arms on the table just for a moment.

The next thing he knew, someone was gently shaking his shoulder. He woke up with a start and a sour taste in his mouth. It was Robin.

"What time is it?"

"Quarter to four," she said, glancing at her watch.

"Boy, I know you're a slow writer, but—"

"That guy they arrested."

"Yes?"

"They think he's the one who raped the Greer girl."

"Hey, really? No kidding?"

"You sound thrilled," Robin said.

"No"—Sandy tried to deny it, though he continued to speak excitedly—"It's just that I know that guy from the psych ward. He was committed about nine different times when I worked there. I just *knew* sooner or later he'd do something like this. I knew it."

"You *are* thrilled."

"Well, maybe a little."

"Anyway, they took him down to the hospital, and the girl identified him positively as the person who assaulted her. So, I had two separate stories to write plus a sidebar. I'm so tired, I am practically cross-eyed."

"We never had our talk."

"I know. It's too late tonight."

"All I wanted to tell you was that I love you," Sandy said. "I've been a jerk lately. But I can stop being a jerk. Really, I can. And I thought maybe we could, uh, start making some plans to move in together."

Startled by his declaration, Robin slid into a seat beside Sandy and reached for his hand on the table.

"I've been a jerk, too," she said.

"No, I was definitely the bigger jerk."

"Okay, if you insist."

"Can you forgive me?"

"Yes."

"Do you think maybe we have a future together?"

"Yes," she said.

"I'm not a very good provider."

"I know."

"But I'll get some stupid job, I don't know, washing dishes if I have to, whatever's necessary to keep on going."

She reached up and brushed the hair out of his eyes.

"I believe in you," she said.

"Thanks. That means a lot to me."

"Want to go home?"

"Yes."

"Okay. Let's go home."

Sandy turned off as many of the lights as he could find switches for, when he suddenly remembered that all the champagne was still sitting in the refrigerator. He'd never brought it out. "I don't believe it," he said. "Harlowe's going to have a fit about this."

"He can come and pick it all up in the morning."

"Let's grab a bottle. Whaddaya say?"

Robin grinned, suggesting she didn't object to the idea.

Sandy ran back to the kitchen and soon returned with the champagne. He opened it right away, the cork shooting fifty feet across the huge empty room. "Mmmm," he said, drinking straight from the bottle. "That's not half bad." Robin tried some, but the foam went up her nose. They resumed switching off lights until they were at the front door. Sandy fiddled with the dead bolt on the big double doors so that they would lock behind them.

"Hey, who's going to clean up this place?" Robin said.

"I really don't know," Sandy replied. "That's Harlowe's department."

EIGHTEEN

Sandy climbed on his motorcycle and was about to
pump the kickstart when Robin said, "Let's walk back."

"It's only a few blocks."

"That's what I mean. You can pick it up tomorrow."

"Okay."

He pulled the key, and they started out of the park
toward Grove Street. The moon was so bright that the
trees cast shadows on the yellowing grass. Drunken hooting
carried down Burgoyne Street from the bars over on Catherine. It was so chilly they could see their breath, but
Sandy still would not put on his father's flight jacket,
befouled as it was by Glen Toole. He drew Robin close.

"Edmund may be leaving town," Robin said as they
left the park.

"Really? Did he tell you that?"

"Yup. He's going to his sister's wedding in Chicago,
and he might stay out there for a while."

"Doing what?"

"His sister works for *Business World* magazine as a senior editor out there. He says she's got a job for him."

"It's hard to imagine Edmund in a job."

"I know what you mean."

"Especially the way he's been acting lately."

"I think this town outlived its usefulness for him a long time ago and he's been having a real hard time letting go. But he acted so normal tonight, it was almost weird. I was amazed."

"Do you ever wonder whether this town has outlived its usefulness for you?" Sandy asked her as they turned up the hill on Grove Street toward Serpentine.

"I thought about it a lot tonight, as a matter of fact."

"Well?"

Robin sighed. "I sometimes regret not giving the big city a try. But I don't believe it's possible to live a civilized life in New York without an absurd amount of money. My friends are all miserable down there."

"But are you happy here in the Springs?"

"Yes," she said after a moment's hesitation. "That doesn't mean I necessarily want to spend the rest of my life here. But it's a very tolerable place to live."

For a block they didn't say anything. Then they turned left onto Serpentine.

"I'd like to live out of town on a place in the country for a while, though," Robin eventually said. "My whole life, even back in Wappingers Falls, I've always lived right *in* town. I want to have a garden."

"Maybe we can look around for a place to—"

A block ahead, Sandy saw three figures on the Nethersoles' front porch. All were wearing dark clothes, but between the streetlight and the moon shining so brightly overhead, they were quite visible. Sandy quickened his step.

"Hold these," he whispered, handing the open champagne bottle and his father's jacket to Robin. He broke into a trot. One of the three figures wore a cape. As he closed in on them, he saw the caped figure seize the Nethersoles' jack-o'-lantern off the porch floor beside the door. Sandy started sprinting. The caped figure hoisted the pumpkin over his head. "Hey, you!" Sandy called to him.

"Come on, Mike! Do it!" one of the other figures said.

"Put it down!" Sandy said, but the caped figure heaved it out into the center of Serpentine Street where the big gourd shattered with a hollow-sounding *thwock*. His companions were already clambering down the porch stairs, hooting with glee. The one with the cape followed a few seconds behind them. Sandy took off after him.

The first two split off in separate directions. Sandy followed the third, the one wearing the cape, up Catherine Street. Years of regular jogging paid off as he kept pace with the figure for two blocks, closed in on him on the third, and tackled him on the sidewalk in front of Joel Harlowe's cottage. He grappled with the figure briefly, but soon overpowered him and sat on his chest. The boy he had tackled was perhaps fifteen years old. It was a little hard to tell because he wore green and black camouflage makeup all over his face.

"What'd you do it for?" Sandy demanded.

"I don't know," the boy said.

"You ought to know why you do things. You're a person, not a dumb animal."

"I'm sorry. Please."

"What's your name?"

"Joe."

"Bullshit. I heard one of your pals call you Mike. What's your last name?" Sandy grabbed two fistfuls of the boy's black sweater and jerked his torso up so they were face to face. "Tell me."

"DiMarco," the boy said sullenly.

"Don't ever smash anyone's pumpkin again," Sandy said, shaking him roughly. "You don't know what kind of heartache people go through in their lives when they put a pumpkin out on their doorstep. Understand?"

"Sure," the boy said, even though he had virtually no idea what Sandy was talking about. "I'm sorry. Really."

Eventually Sandy got up off the boy.

"Go home."

"Okay."

"Well? Move!"

The boy got on his feet and started hurrying up Catherine Street, turning to look back over his shoulder twice. Trembling from both his anger and the cold, Sandy jogged the several blocks back to Serpentine, where Robin waited anxiously on the corner. He told her what had happened and, picking up pieces of the pumpkin, explained about Champion getting run over earlier in the day.

"Poor thing," said Robin, who was well acquainted with the old dog.

"We'd better go to my place," Sandy said, holding all the slimy pumpkin pieces. "I haven't fed Clementine all day."

"All right."

Upstairs, however, there was no sign of the cat. Sandy thought it highly unusual, for she almost always met him at the third-floor landing with her tail up in the air. Robin immediately went to the bathroom area behind the folding screen. Sandy noticed that it was warm in the garret. Roy Greenleaf had actually turned the heat back on. He was about to go back downstairs and whistle for the cat when he heard something rustling at the far end of the studio. He switched on a floor lamp and crept down to the far end of the room past his easel.

"Clementine?" He heard loud purring. Soon he discovered the source of it. In a cardboard carton of rags behind the big wooden flat file where he kept all his sketches, Clementine lay on her side with six newborn kittens squirming in a row beside her. He stooped down in amazement. Robin said something from the other end of the garret, but he couldn't understand her.

"What?"

"I *hoped* I'd left this earring over here," she repeated, emerging from behind the folding screen. "I've only got three matching pairs—"

"Come here. Quickly!"

She hurried down the long room.

"I'm a father," Sandy said proudly.

"God, I didn't even know she was pregnant," Robin marveled. "They don't even look like cats. Where are their ears?"

"They don't unfold for a couple of weeks," he explained. "She must be hungry." He went to the kitchen area, filled Clementine's bowl with canned food, and brought it back to her. Smelling the mackerel, she climbed out of the carton and hungrily began to eat. Sandy stroked her back while Robin picked up one of the kittens, which peeped rather like a bird.

"Look, its eyes are closed."

"They don't open for a week or so either."

"You're so funny looking," Robin said to it, cupping the tortoiseshell-colored kitten in one hand and then putting it back with its brothers and sisters. Then, with a groan, she got up, went over to the sleeping area, kicked off her shoes, and sank to her knees on the mattress. She unbuttoned her blouse, pulled her skirt off, flung them aside, and crawled under the covers. Sandy soon joined her.

"Do you know anyone who might like a kitten?" he asked.

"No," she replied as though it were a ridiculous question.

"Maybe you could ask around the office."

"Come here," she said.

He put his arms around her and drew her close to himself.

"You're so warm," he said, intoxicated with the familiar smell of her hair. "God, what a day."

"Hush now."

She opened up to him like a flower. When they were finished making love, she fell asleep almost at once. Though Sandy closed his eyes, his head was full of light and the white roar of silence. Soon he became aware of being hungry, but not just hungry, ravenous. Besides the hors d'ouevres he'd grabbed in the casino kitchen before the party had even started, he hadn't eaten a thing in almost two days. He slid his arm out from behind Robin's head and carefully left the bed. His bathrobe lay draped on the arm of a chair. He tiptoed to the chair, then wrapped himself in the robe to keep warm.

There was barely anything to eat on the shelves besides dried beans, which took hours to cook. In the refrigerator there were only four eggs, age unknown, a rubbery head of bok choy, and a half a jar of red currant jelly. There wasn't even any butter. Using salad oil, he fried himself a four-egg omelette and filled it with currant jelly. Robin slept soundly through the entire procedure.

Then, sitting down at the table, he began to eat the omelette. It was the most delicious omelette he had ever eaten, as far as he could recall. The currant jelly melted and became thick red syrup. He ate quickly at first, but it was a very large omelette, and midway through, he began to slow down.

On the kitchen table, along with the red telephone, his daypack, the jar of pens and pencils, his eyeglasses, and other odds and ends, was the pile of that day's mail. He put on his glasses and shuffled through the envelopes. Among the bills and junk mail was a buff-colored envelope with the words Beacon Gallery, 193 Newberry Street, Boston, Massachusetts, in the upper left-hand corner. At first he regarded it with mere curiosity. Then, the name awakened something in him and he rushed to tear it open.

"Dear Mr. Stern," the letter began. "Sorry to take so long getting back to you, but we are just now organizing a group show to commence shortly after the new year. The theme of the show is "Seeing the Land" and from your slides, received June 25th, we feel that some of your work would fit in very nicely, say two or three paintings. I have returned your slides parcel post under separate cover. We look forward to hearing from you in order to make arrangements."

The letter was signed by Nadine L. McNamee. She was totally unknown to him, and he barely even remembered sending some of his slides to the gallery last June. But the name suddenly acquired a charm and importance comparable only to those of loved ones. Nadine L. McNamee. He read the name over and over, then reread the body of the letter again several times to make sure that he had got it right. Indeed, there was no mistaking its meaning. He was being invited to hang his paintings in a major Boston art gallery.

He was about to shake Robin awake and read her the splendid letter, but he sensed that rousing her from the fastness of sleep would somehow detract from the glory of it all; the good news could wait until morning. Instead, he slowly savored the last of his omelette, read the short letter propped up against the phone several times more, pictured the plushly carpeted Beacon Gallery, and tried to imagine several possible faces for Nadine L. McNamee. He decided that she was a severe-looking brunette who wore turtleneck sweaters and a lot of clunky jewelry—but he adored her nonetheless.

Long after he had finished his omelette, he was still not sleepy. At quarter to six, gray November light began filling the big, arched windows of the garret. While Robin slept, he traversed the long room to his workplace, the letter tucked in the pocket of his bathrobe. It would be nice to include this painting of Mill Creek in the show, he thought, examining the canvas. The water still wasn't quite right, though. He'd have to go back there, maybe even later today, and have a good look at it, really see it, try to fathom what gave it the look of life.

He picked up a brush and opened a jar of the beeswax and linseed oil medium he cooked up in regular batches, based on a formula attributed to Rembrandt. He mixed a little burnt umber with Hooker's green on his palette and with a few sure strokes painted the reflection of a shadow of a rock beneath a clay bank covered with hoary old roots. It felt wonderful to hold the brush again, even at this insane hour of the day, with the world just now turning toward morning.

— Parce que dans les villes, on ne les voit plus.

Le vent lacérait sa voix.

C'était une voix lente.

— En ville, c'est à cause des lampadaires, il a précisé.

Il avait gardé son paquet de cigarettes dans sa main. Il le tournait et le retournait, geste machinal. Sa présence rendait plus étouffante encore l'arrivée imminente de la tempête.

— Mais c'est rare, hein ?

— Qu'est-ce qui est rare ?

Il a hésité quelques secondes, et il a passé son pouce sur sa lèvre. Je l'ai regardé, lui, son visage, ses yeux.

Ce geste qu'il venait de faire.

C'est tout de suite après que j'ai entendu siffler. J'ai eu le temps de me reculer. L'ombre qui m'a giflée était rouge. J'ai senti quelque chose mordre ma joue. C'était de la tôle, une plaque large comme deux mains. Elle a volé sur une dizaine de mètres et puis le vent l'a plaquée contre le sol. Il l'a entraînée plus loin. J'ai entendu crisser le gravier. On aurait dit des dents sur du sable.

J'ai passé ma main. J'avais du sang sur les doigts.

— Qu'est-ce qui est rare ? je me suis entendue demander pour la deuxième fois, le regard toujours collé à la tôle.

Il a allumé sa cigarette.

— Les étoiles, il a répondu.

Il a répété cela, C'est rare les étoiles dans les ciels en ville…

Et puis il m'a montré ma joue, Il faut aller vous soigner.

Dans ma chambre, après, les deux mains collées à la vitre, j'ai vu mon visage, la marque rouge que la tôle avait laissée.

La boursouflure était chaude. On peut mourir d'être griffé par les tôles qui se décrochent.

Les tôles, la rouille.